D0442014

NO LONGER
PROPERTY OF PPLD

MYSTERY   PIKES PEAK LIBRARY DISTRICT
SMIT   COLORADO SPRINGS CO 80901 – 1579
            Breaking point.

190061507

BREAKING POINT

Also by Frank Smith

The Chief Inspector Paget Mysteries

ACTS OF VENGEANCE

THREAD OF EVIDENCE

CANDLES FOR THE DEAD

STONE DEAD

FATAL FLAW

Other Novels

DRAGON'S BREATH

THE TRAITOR MASK

DEFECTORS ARE DEAD MEN

CORPSE IN HANDCUFFS

SOUND THE SILENT TRUMPETS

BREAKING POINT

A DCI Neil Paget Mystery

Frank Smith

This first world edition published 2008
in Great Britain and the USA by
SEVERN HOUSE PUBLISHERS LTD of
9–15 High Street, Sutton, Surrey SM1 1DF.

Copyright © 2008 by Frank Smith.

All rights reserved.
The moral right of the author has been asserted.

British Library Cataloguing in Publication Data

Smith, Frank, 1927-
  Breaking point
  1. Paget, Neil (Fictitious character) - Fiction 2. Police -
  England - Fiction 3. Missing persons - Investigation -
  Fiction 4. Journalists - Crimes against - Fiction
  5. Detective and mystery stories
  I. Title
  813.5'4[F]

  ISBN-13: 978-0-7278-6621-9   (cased)

Except where actual historical events and characters are being
described for the storyline of this novel, all situations in this
publication are fictitious and any resemblance to living persons
is purely coincidental.

All Severn House titles are printed on acid-free paper.

Typeset by Palimpsest Book Production Ltd.,
Grangemouth, Stirlingshire, Scotland.
Printed and bound in Great Britain by
MPG Books Ltd., Bodmin, Cornwall.

Prologue

Headlights probed the sky as a car came over the hill. The watcher raised his head to follow it with his eyes, willing it to turn into the lane that would bring it close to where he lay as it made its way up to the farmhouse. He held his breath, prepared to drop out of sight the moment the lights turned his way.

He swore softly and sank back into the ditch as the car swept past and continued on. It was a road that saw little traffic, and that was the way it had been ever since he had crept into position; just the occasional car taking a short cut across country, or more likely one of the local farmers returning home. Whatever the reason, every one of them had gone by the open gate at the bottom of the hill without so much as slowing down, let alone turning in.

Neither had there been any sign of activity in the old stone farmhouse at the top of the hill. There wasn't even a light in the place, and he was beginning to wonder if there was anyone in the house at all. And he wondered once again if his informant had got it wrong.

Unless, of course, it was some sort of elaborate hoax his informant was playing on him. But he failed to see the point if it was. The man had been very convincing, even if he had been well into his cups at the time. Informant. He liked that word; liked the sound of it. It had a professional ring to it, and if there was one thing he wanted to be, it was professional.

He peered at his Timex by the light of the torch cupped in his hand. Twenty to twelve! Almost four hours since he'd arrived, and not a damned thing to show for it, other than sore muscles, an aching back, and a conviction that he would end up with double pneumonia. To stay any longer would be stupid, he told himself, and yet . . .

He groaned softly. It would be just his luck to leave, then find out later that he'd been too impatient. If his informant had been telling the truth, these people would have to be extremely cautious, even if it was only a dry run, so they might well wait until after midnight. He couldn't possibly get any colder, so he might as well stick it out. Until one o'clock, he promised himself. If nothing happened by then, he would pack it in.

He settled back in the shallow ditch and pulled the ground-sheet around him. It did little to protect him from the cold, but just the act of wrapping it around himself gave the illusion of warmth.

He lost count of the number of times he had checked his watch, but by twelve thirty he'd had enough. Not a single car had gone by during the last half hour. He heaved himself up on one elbow and peered at his watch again to make sure of the time. Twelve thirty-one. Never mind hanging on till one o'clock; he was packing it in now before he froze to death.

He reached for the knapsack and patted the ground around him to make sure he was leaving nothing behind. He staggered to his feet. His legs were numb, his feet like blocks of ice, and it took several minutes of massage and clumping around on the grass before he could really feel them.

He glanced toward the farmhouse before stepping away from the shelter of the hedge and into the lane. Was that a flicker of light behind one of the windows? The house itself was barely visible against a skyline of broken cloud and the fading light of a waning moon, but just for an instant . . .

He stood there, motionless, staring intently into the dark until his eyeballs hurt. Nothing! Imagination, he decided as he set off down the lane. Anyway, who could possibly see him in his dark clothing at that distance? Cold and wet and tired as he was, and with nothing to show for it, there didn't seem to be any point in keeping to cover on his way back to where he'd left the van. He'd come by way of the fields, keeping close to the hedges and low stone walls to avoid detection, but he didn't fancy the idea of stumbling across the fields in the dark. Too many hazards, and the last thing he needed now was to fall over a sheep, or stick his foot in a rabbit hole and break his leg.

So, he might as well walk right down the middle of the lane, because the sooner he could get home and get a good hot drink down him, the better. He'd love a hot bath, but there was no way the others would let him get away with that in the middle of the night.

He was almost down to the gate when headlights came over the hill once more. He ducked low and sought the cover of the hedge. Probably another farmer returning home after an evening in town, but best not take any chances.

The sound of the engine grew stronger, and he realized it wasn't a car but something heavier. A lorry, perhaps? Odd, though. You seldom saw a lorry on this little back road during the day, let alone in the middle of the night. It slowed. He heard the shift of gears. The headlights began to swing in his direction, and he caught a glimpse of a long, box-like van in the light reflected off the hedge and open gate.

It was turning in!

He flung himself into the ditch and covered his face with his arms, listening as the driver stopped, reversed, then swung wide to clear the gatepost. The glare of lights swept over him. The driver changed gears again, and the headlights suddenly went out as the van started up the hill. He waited until it was safely past his hiding place before raising his head to watch as the van continued on with only side and tail lights showing; watched until it turned into the yard and was lost to sight behind the house.

He scrambled to his feet, brushing himself off as he ran back up the hill. He stayed on the grass, keeping close to the hedge, pausing only when he came level with the house. The lane leading to the yard at the back of the house was gravelled, and with the blank wall of the house on one side and a shoulder-high wall on the other, there would be nowhere to hide if someone should come round the corner. He drew a deep breath. He couldn't stop now. He'd come this far, waited this long . . .

Crouching low, he crept along the side of the house. The night air was cold, but he was sweating. His clothes were sticking to him and he could hear the pulse of every heartbeat in his ears. He paused to steady his breathing, listening for any sign of danger before moving on. Nothing. Not so much as a whisper. He moved on, telling himself that whoever had been in the van must be in the house by now.

He had almost reached the corner when he heard voices; two men speaking quietly. He couldn't make out what they were saying, but they sounded much too close for comfort. If they came around the corner . . .

Slowly, testing each footstep, he began to edge backward, eyes glued to the corner, ready to turn and run at the first sign of movement.

Suddenly, a shaft of light spilled out from behind the house. He held his breath, too scared to move. The light flickered, flared and died.

The night closed around him and he breathed again. A lighter! He realized now he'd heard the rasp of flint on the still night air, and the faintest of clicks as the light went out.

He let out a long, slow breath and continued to edge backward, testing every step. Sound carried on the cold night air, and one false step could be his undoing.

Perhaps he could get around the other side of the house. It would mean working his way across the front of the place, probably on his belly to avoid the windows, but it might be worth . . .

A light from behind swept over him, and suddenly the wall on the far side of the lane was starkly visible. He dropped to the ground, pressing himself against the wall of the house. He'd been so intent on the dangers ahead of him that he'd been oblivious to the sound of vehicles on the road below.

And not just one! There were *three* of them! Cars, vans or whatever they were, advancing up the hill – and he'd be trapped if he didn't shift himself.

The headlights of the leading vehicle went out, and he remembered the way the first van had doused its lights once it was off the road. Bent almost double, he scuttled across the lane to fling himself at the wall, clawing, scrambling, heedless of the skin being stripped from his fingers as he pulled himself over the top and dropped to the ground on the other side.

He lay there panting in what felt like a tangle of weeds, listening to the sound of the engines as they went by. Two close together, then the third a few seconds later. He risked a quick look over the wall as the last one disappeared around the corner. An SUV of some sort.

He looked back toward the road. Black as pitch. No more

cars coming up the hill, but that didn't mean there couldn't be more.

It was while he was sitting there with his back against the wall, trying to decide what to do, that he realized the vehicles hadn't stopped in the farmyard at the back of the house, but were continuing on. He could still hear their engines. Fading, but he could still hear them.

So where were they going? There was nothing behind the house except a steep-sided valley. The sounds grew fainter until there was no sound at all.

Shielding the dim light from the torch with his hands, he surveyed the way ahead. It seemed he had landed in an old sheep pen, abandoned now by the look of the coarse grass and waist-high weeds. The ground was uneven and he had to steady himself by holding on to the wall as he worked his way along. He came to a wooden gate. Poked his head up for a quick look.

He could see the outline of the house as well as the outbuildings on the other side of the yard, but the cobblestoned area between them was empty No sign of the van that had preceded the cars; no cars, no people, no light in any of the windows, nothing!

Puzzled but emboldened, he decided to climb over the gate. If it hadn't been opened for a while, chances were the hinges would make a noise, and while there didn't *appear* to be anyone about, a creaking gate might well bring a swift response.

He moved cautiously along the edge of the old stone barns, ready to scuttle for cover at the first sign of life from the house. He came to a gap between the last two buildings, and saw how the vehicles had managed to disappear. A track, almost as wide as the lane leading up to the house, led from the far side of the yard down the hill to disappear into the darkness of the valley below.

His informant had said nothing about this. He'd been on the point of telling him more when he'd stopped in the middle of a sentence, slopped the drinks as he pushed the table aside, and announced that he had to go to the loo.

Not exactly surprising, considering how much the little man had had to drink – except he had never returned. Strange, very strange, because, apart from anything else, it wasn't like the man to leave a full pint of ale *and* a whisky behind.

The watcher went over the scene again in his mind. His informant had been talking in low tones about his work here, when, suddenly, he'd stopped, put both hands on the table and pushed himself to his feet.

'Got to go,' he'd mumbled. Then, as if to reassure his companion, said, 'just going to the loo. Back in a minute.' He'd lurched off down the tiny hallway and never returned.

Nor was the man to be found in his caravan the following day or the day after that. At least he hadn't responded to the pounding on his door. But the manager of the caravan site had said not to worry. 'He goes off for days at a time. Sometimes it's work; sometimes it's the drink. Try the local nick. He's probably in there drying out.'

He hadn't tried the local nick. He'd decided it didn't matter. He had most of what he wanted anyway.

But standing out here now, peering into the darkness, he felt like kicking himself. Clearly, the man had been scared stiff, and he should have recognized that and tried harder to find him.

He sucked in his breath. Too late now for second thoughts; he had a decision to make. If he started down the track and someone came along from either direction, he'd be spotted for sure. There would be nowhere to hide. On the other hand, if he was to make tonight's foray worthwhile, what choice did he have?

He hitched the knapsack higher on his shoulders and stepped away from the shadow of the building.

He heard a sound; the scrape of a boot against stone. He swung round, arm raised to defend himself. A light flashed in his eyes . . .

He didn't see what hit him; didn't feel the blow that pitched him into a darkness deeper than the night itself.

One

'Morning, boss. Good to see you back,' Detective Sergeant John Tregalles said cheerily as he entered the office bearing two mugs of coffee. 'Looks like DI Travis left everything shipshape for you,' he continued, nodding in the direction of the almost empty in tray. He set one of the brimming mugs in front of Paget, took a sip of his own as he moved back toward the door. 'Can't stop. Got to be in court later on this morning. Shoplifting. Petty stuff, but I've probably spent more time on the paperwork than this kid will serve – that is if he doesn't get off altogether because his mum smacked him when he was two. How was the course? Nice change, was it? Straight hours. Nine to five. Bit of a holiday?'

Paget shot a hard glance at the sergeant. He was in no mood for jokes, not this morning. But there was nothing in the sergeant's manner or expression to indicate that he was being flippant. He swallowed the sharp retort that had risen to his lips, but before he could form a more reasonable response, the sergeant glanced at his watch and said, 'Got to run.' He raised his mug in mock salute. 'Coffee's on me this morning. Sort of welcome back. Brewed specially for you in the canteen.' And then he was gone.

Paget picked up the steaming mug and sat back in his chair. Nice change? Bit of a holiday? Hardly. Seconded to Training with less than forty-eight hours' notice, and even less for preparation time, he'd had to step in to run a course on race relations and sensitivity, when he'd only just finished the course himself. There hadn't been much sensitivity in the way they'd handled that!

'They're short-staffed,' Superintendent Alcott had said as if that explained everything.

'And we're not?' he'd shot back. 'God knows we're barely keeping up with things as it is. Why can't they use some of their own people? There were two instructors on the course I took, so why can't they use them?'

'Because,' Alcott explained, 'it's been decided that in order to demonstrate how important this course is, and how seriously it is to be taken by everyone, they are going to start at the top and work their way down. The next four courses will be attended by senior officers only: some of our own, some from West Mercia, and there'll be some from Dyfed-Powys as well. Which means that the instructor has to be a senior officer. So, to put it bluntly, Paget, you've had the course; you are a trained instructor, so I'm afraid you're it.'

Alcott leaned forward and adopted a conciliatory tone. 'I wasn't aware of it at the time, but I've now been told that the course you were on was a shakedown course, a trial run if you like, and you, along with several others, were being evaluated. And you,' he continued as he sat back and pulled a cigarette from the packet on the desk, 'came out on top. And the fact that you've had previous experience in Training clinched it. Sorry, Paget, but there it is. I don't like it any more than you do, but I haven't been given any choice.'

A flicker of annoyance and disapproval crossed Paget's face as the superintendent lit the cigarette and blew smoke into the air. Alcott saw the look and ignored it. It would take a lot more than that to convince him to give up his cigarettes, no matter what the regulations. Neither was the superintendent going to give ground on this course assignment, so there was nothing to be gained by arguing.

'So, when do I start?' he asked.

'First thing Monday morning,' Alcott said, avoiding Paget's eyes as he pushed a thin folder across the desk. 'Course schedules are in there.'

'*This* Monday? And you're telling me at four o'clock on Friday afternoon?'

The superintendent had at least had the grace to look uncomfortable as he said, 'I know it's short notice, Paget, but you'll have the weekend, and I'll have DI Travis keep an eye on things while you're away.'

Travis had kept an eye on things all right, thought Paget sourly, but that was about all he'd done. The DI had left a note on his desk, and a batch of marked folders in the file cabinet, with only the briefest of explanations before taking off last Friday night to spend three weeks' leave in Spain. If Paget hadn't suspected that something like that might happen, and come in on Saturday, he would have been snowed under this morning.

'Just going in to check,' he'd told Grace, although he would have much preferred to spend the time with her after being away in Worcester five days out of seven every week for the past month. 'Be back in time for lunch.' Instead he'd wound up spending most of the weekend at work clearing the backlog and bringing himself up-to-date.

Paget sniffed at the coffee, then set it aside. Tregalles had lied. As he'd suspected, this foul-tasting brew had come straight from the machine down the hall, and it smelt more like tar than coffee.

The phone rang. 'Good morning, Chief Inspector,' Alcott's secretary, Fiona, said crisply when he answered. 'Welcome back, sir. Superintendent Alcott asked me to call and say he would like to see you in his office as soon as possible.'

Paget glanced at the long list of notes he'd made of things he should look into, and sighed. Alcott always wanted everything 'as soon as possible'. 'Look, Fiona,' he said, 'I've got a lot of catching up to do. Unless it's *really* important, tell him I'd like to put off whatever it is until after lunch.'

'I can tell him if you wish,' Fiona said, lowering her voice, 'but I believe it has something to do with a call Mr Alcott received from Chief Superintendent Brock a few minutes ago. His actual words to me were, "Get Paget up here on the double", sir, so I rather doubt if he will consider the time negotiable.'

He groaned inwardly. It would hardly be good news if Morgan Brock was involved. 'In that case,' he said with an audible sigh of resignation, 'you can tell Mr Alcott I'm on my way. And thanks for the warning, Fiona.'

'I have the month-end reports for February,' Fiona said as she entered Superintendent Thomas Alcott's office and dropped them in his in tray. 'They have to be in today, so if you could sign them as soon as possible, I'll make sure they're sent over to New Street this morning. And Mr Paget is on his way up.'

'Good, but don't leave them there,' Alcott told her. 'I don't have time to deal with them right now. I have to get this business with Paget done straightaway, and then I have a meeting at ten. You deal with them, Fiona. You know what to look for. Just mark any questionable ones, and I'll look at them when I get back.'

'Just as long as you don't expect me to forge your signature on them as well,' the matronly woman said tartly as she picked up the reports again. She and the superintendent had been together a long time, and it was on occasions such as this that Alcott sometimes wondered which one of them was really in charge.

'Morning, Fiona. Morning, sir.' Paget stood to one side to let the secretary pass as he entered the office. He was a tall man, broad-shouldered, lean-faced – although not as lean as it had once been, thought Alcott. He hadn't realized until recently how much the DCI had changed in the last two or three months. He certainly looked a hell of a lot better than he had after his encounter with Mary Carr. Even the scar was fading, although part of it was still visible above the collar. But more importantly, his temperament had changed as well; he was more relaxed, less intense. But that, Alcott decided, probably had more to do with Grace Lovett and the DCI's new lifestyle than anything else.

Alcott waved Paget to a seat, then leaned back in his own chair and locked his fingers behind his head. 'Courses go all right, did they?' he asked, then answered his own question. 'I have the report from Training here. They were impressed. They say the critiques were most favourable, so congratulations. Reflects well on all of us over here.'

Paget had a horrible feeling that this was leading up to another secondment to Training. 'Thank you, sir, but if you are even *thinking* about sending me back there . . .'

'No, no, no. Absolutely not!' Alcott assured him. 'No, you did a commendable job over there, but that's the end of it, so you have no need to worry on that score.'

Despite the assurance, warning bells continued to ring in the back of Paget's mind as he said, 'So what, exactly, did you wish to see me about, sir?'

'Ah!' Alcott pursed his lips and frowned as if to emphasize the importance of what he was about to say. 'I had a call from

Mr Brock this morning, regarding a young man by the name of Mark Newman, who seems to have gone missing. Newman was last seen on Thursday morning when he went off to work in his van – he does odd jobs, window cleaning, a bit of carpentry and such – and he hasn't been seen since. Normally, no one would have thought much about it, but when he failed to turn up for his own twenty-first birthday party on Friday night at the local pub, his friends became worried about him.'

'So why are you telling *me* this?' Paget asked. 'From what you've said so far, this barely qualifies for a Missing Person report. You say this chap is an itinerant worker. He has a van, so he probably goes wherever there's work to be had, and he's been held up somewhere. He's young, possibly met a girl, decided to stay on wherever he happens to be, and didn't give a thought to letting his friends know.'

'You may well be right,' Alcott conceded, 'but whether you are or not, Mr Brock has asked us to look into it. He's arranged for you to meet with a young woman by the name of Emma Baker in Whitcott Lacey at three this afternoon. She's a mature student at the Whitcott Agricultural College there. She has all the details.'

'*He's* arranged . . .?' Paget shook his head in disgust. 'Does he really think we're that short of work that we have time to go running off to talk to some girl who goes all a'twitter when her boyfriend doesn't turn up? I'm trying to catch up after being away for a month, and I have cases sitting there that—'

'Believe me, I'm well aware of the situation, thank you, Paget,' Alcott broke in sharply, 'and so is Mr Brock; I made sure of that. But this is not a request. It comes directly from the chief constable. It seems that this young woman, Emma Baker, is Sir Robert's niece, and she spoke to her uncle because she didn't think she was being taken seriously by Missing Persons.'

'When did she report him missing?'

'Saturday morning.'

Paget stared at Alcott. '*Two days?*' he said. 'And she goes running to her uncle? Does she have any evidence that would indicate Newman is in trouble?'

'None, other than the fact that he missed his own birthday party, and Baker insists that he would have phoned or got in touch with her somehow if he was held up somewhere.'

'So why doesn't the chief constable talk to Missing Persons instead of dumping it in our lap?' Paget growled.

'Look,' said Alcott wearily, 'you're not going to win this one, Paget. I've been through all this with Brock, so let's get on with it, shall we? You *will* go out there this afternoon and you *will* meet with Emma Baker. Just go out there and show the flag, so to speak. Take Tregalles with you, listen to what the girl has to say, make the right noises, then let Tregalles pick it up from there. This lad will probably turn up by the end of the week, anyway.'

He pushed a single sheet of paper across the desk. 'As I said, she's a student at the Whitcott Agricultural College, but she's leaving there early today to meet you at the house she shares with several others, including this chap, Newman. It's called Wisteria Cottage. Shouldn't be too hard to find in a village of that size.'

Two

Wisteria Cottage was not exactly Paget's idea of a cottage, but rather a very solid-looking two-storied house, with its mellow stonework almost hidden by thick, leafless vines that looked to be as old as the cottage itself. No doubt they would look much more attractive when they were covered in blossoms later in the year, but on a cold and cloudy day in early March, they looked like thick skeletal limbs clinging to the stones.

Emma Baker must have been watching for them, because she opened the door before they had a chance to knock. She was a tall, slim, fresh-faced young woman with auburn hair and hazel eyes. Older than Paget had imagined; mid-to-late twenties, perhaps? It was hard to tell. She was wearing a faded old cardigan over a sweatshirt and jeans, heavy woollen socks and Birkenstock sandals.

'Detective Chief Inspector Paget?' she said with surprise in her voice, and grimaced guiltily. 'I had no idea . . . I mean I hoped Uncle Bob would take me seriously, but I didn't expect him to send someone like you.' She saw his puzzled look. 'I remember you from the pictures in the paper a few months ago, when you were attacked by that woman,' she explained. 'I'm Emma. Please come in.'

She led them down a narrow hallway to a large kitchen at the back of the house, and like the hall, it had a flagstone floor. 'We could use the front room,' she told them, 'but this is the only truly warm room in the whole place.' She directed them to take a seat at a long wooden table in front of an old-fashioned Aga cooker, then went on to explain that the house had been made over into flats.

'At least, that's what they call them. They're really nothing more than bedrooms, and not very big ones at that. Shared bathroom facilities, of course, which can be a bit of a pain, but it's affordable – just, and we can walk to the college.

'There are four of us living here,' she continued. 'Tom Foxworthy is the oldest; he's studying farm management. Sylvia Tyler is the youngest; she's into animal husbandry, and I'm here to study organic farming. Mark is the only one who isn't attending the college.'

'And the last time you saw him yourself was Thursday morning?' said Paget as they opened their coats and sat down on hard wooden chairs. 'We've read the report you filed with Missing Persons, and as I understand it, Mr Newman's work does take him off to different locations, so I can't help wondering why you are so concerned about his absence after such a short time. You say you spoke to him as recently as Thursday, yet you filed the report on Saturday morning. Would you like to tell us why? Isn't it possible that he decided to stay on somewhere, perhaps because there was work for him there, and it wasn't convenient to return?'

Emma Baker spread her hands and shook her head slowly. Paget could almost see her mentally digging in her heels.

'That's almost exactly what Uncle Bob said when I spoke to him last night, but you're both wrong. I know Mark; he wouldn't do that. I'll admit he's still just a kid in some ways, but he would have let one of us know. All he had to do was give us a quick call. He has a mobile phone. He knew about the party we had planned for Friday night, and he was looking forward to it. Besides, I'm sure he was up to something. I've no idea what it was, but he's been acting strangely lately. He was excited about something. He kept dropping hints of a sort, but nothing specific, if you know what I mean. And then there's the fact that my camera is missing, and I'm sure he took it.'

Paget glanced at Tregalles. Emma Baker didn't strike him as someone who would panic easily. 'I think you had better start at the beginning,' he told her. 'Give us some background on Mark Newman, who he is, his job, how long you've known him, and most of all why you are so convinced that something may have happened to him.'

Emma's dark eyes held Paget's own for a long moment, as if trying to assess whether he was merely humouring her. She nodded slowly, and the tension seemed to drain from her face. 'I'll put the kettle on,' she said as she rose to her feet. 'The water's hot. It will only take a few minutes to bring to the boil.'

Mark Newman, she told them a few minutes later when they each had a steaming mug of tea in front of them, had come to live at Wisteria Cottage about three months ago. He had come into the local pub one evening after doing a job in the village and asked if anyone knew of a cheap place he could rent for a few months, because he knew he could find enough work in the area to keep him there for a while.

'I work part-time behind the bar of the Red Lion to help pay for my tuition and my room here,' Emma explained, 'and he couldn't have come in at a better time, because Tania, one of the original four of us, had just packed it in and gone back home after failing one of her exams And that had left us in a bind. You see, the rent here remains the same whether all the rooms are rented or not, so with one person gone, it meant the three of us had to make up the difference. So, Mark was something of a godsend.'

'What, exactly, does he do for a living?' Tregalles asked. He had his notebook out.

'Almost anything that pays,' Emma told him. 'He cleans windows, he's quite good at painting, and not a bad carpenter. He'll paint your house, clean out your attic, take rubbish to the tip, or walk your dog if there's a bit of money to be made. He's a willing worker, and he's not doing badly. His aim, of course, is to get enough money to take his next year of journalism. He took one year on a scholarship, but he ran out of money, so he decided to work for a year and make enough to continue his studies.'

'Has he ever been gone for two or three days before?' asked Paget.

'Oh yes, but he's always let one of us know if he expects to be away for any length of time. He's very good that way. We live pretty frugally here, and it's important that we know who is going to be here for dinner.'

'But he didn't say anything this time?'

'No. But even if he didn't know ahead of time, he could have phoned to let us know how long he expected to be away. Which is why I'm worried that something has happened to him.'

'Does he have any other friends or relatives? A girlfriend, perhaps, who might know where he's gone?' Paget asked.

'Not that I'm aware of. As far as relatives are concerned,

the only ones I've ever heard him speak of are his parents. They live somewhere on the south coast – Portsmouth or Plymouth, I think – but he doesn't get along with them, so I'm sure he hasn't gone there. And I spent much of the weekend phoning all the hospitals in something like a thirty-mile radius of here, without result.'

'Is there anyone we can talk to who would know more about who his parents are and where they live?'

'No one around here, I'm sure,' said Emma. 'I have asked the others, but they don't know any more than I do. All I can tell you is that Mark didn't get on with them. He once said that his father wanted him to go into the family restaurant business, but when he refused and said he was going in for journalism, they had a big fight about it, and his father more or less threw him out, so I don't think he's gone home.'

'Even so, if we don't hear from him soon, I think we had better try to contact them,' Paget told her. 'There may be something in his room that will tell us where they live. But before we go there, I'd like to go back to what you said earlier about his acting strangely and being excited about something. Can you be more specific?'

Emma frowned. 'I'll try,' she said, 'and I'll tell you what I think, but I don't know if it will make as much sense to you as it does to me. You see, I'm almost sure it has something to do with Mickey Doyle, and some story or other he was telling Mark last Saturday night in the pub. Not this *last* Saturday,' she amended, 'but a week ago Saturday. They had their heads together like a couple of conspirators for the longest time, and Mark kept buying Mickey drinks, which isn't like him at all. He's pretty tight with his money – he has to be because he's going to need every penny if he is to get back into university in September – so he must have expected to get something out of it. I suspect he believed he was on to a story.'

She noticed the quizzical raising of Paget's eyebrows. 'As I told you,' she said, 'Mark was taking journalism, and he desperately wanted to get a job with one of the local papers in order to gain some practical experience. Apparently, someone there told him that if he could come back with a good, top-notch story, they'd consider taking him on. Mark was always going on about it and I can't help wondering if that was what he was going after last week. It might also account for his wanting to borrow my camera.'

'Which you believe he stole,' said Paget.

Emma wrinkled her nose. 'I don't think he *stole* it – at least I doubt if he thought of it as stealing. But I think he took it, just the same, and probably hoped to return it before I realized it was missing. I know he was disappointed when I told him I couldn't lend it to him, but I thought he understood. You see, the camera doesn't belong to me. It belongs to my sister, and it is quite an expensive one. She loaned it to me for a project we are doing at the college, so, as I explained to Mark, it wasn't mine to lend. He said he understood, and said he would try to find one somewhere else, but I think he must have waited until I left for class, then sneaked into my room and taken it.'

'This is a digital camera, is it?' Tregalles asked.

'No. It's a 35mm SLR. An Olympus. I don't know how much it's worth, exactly, but I know my sister paid quite a lot for it three or four years ago, and I'm almost as worried about what I'm going to tell her as I am about Mark.'

'When did you realize the camera was missing?'

'Thursday afternoon when I came home from class. I might not have realized it was missing right away if we hadn't been talking about it that morning, but I noticed it was gone as soon as I opened the door of the closet. It normally hangs on a peg in there. Mark – at least I'm assuming it was Mark – had pulled the clothes over to one side to cover the peg, and that's what drew my attention to it.'

'So Mark was still here when you left that morning?' Tregalles said. 'What time would that be, Miss Baker?'

'I prefer Emma, if you don't mind, Sergeant,' she said. 'And I'd say it would have been about ten to eight. Classes begin at eight, but I remember I was a few minutes late that morning, mainly because of stopping to talk to Mark.'

'Is anything else missing?' asked Paget.

'Not that I'm aware of.'

'Did he say why he wanted the camera?'

'To tell you the truth, he was wittering on while I was trying to get ready for class, and I wasn't paying as much attention as I suppose I should have, but I do recall him saying something about making someone sit up and take notice. As I said, I was running late, and he was holding me up, so I more or less shut him out. Perhaps if I'd paid more attention to what he was saying we wouldn't be having this conversation now . . .'

Emma fell silent for a moment frowning into the distance. 'There was something . . .' she began hesitantly, then snapped her fingers. 'I'd forgotten it until now, but Mark asked me if I had any high-speed film, and if I knew where he could get infrared film.'

'Which suggests night photography,' said Paget thoughtfully. 'Does that make any sense to you? Had he spoken of anything like that before?'

'No.'

'Assuming there is something to your idea that this chap, Doyle, put Mark on to a story, where can we find him?'

Emma shook her head. 'I've tried that route already,' she said. 'I went round on Saturday to ask Mickey if he had any idea where Mark might have gone, but he wasn't home. Lou Cutter, the man who owns the caravan park where Mickey lives, said he hadn't seen Mickey recently. He assumed he was away on a job somewhere – or on one of his benders. Mickey's a joiner by trade,' she explained. 'He works for himself. I'm told he does beautiful work, doing up the inside of old houses and that sort of thing, and people are always after him. Mr Cutter told me that Mickey would have a thriving little business if he could stay away from the drink, but every so often he'll disappear for a week or two, then end up spending the night in custody on a drunk and disorderly charge.'

Tregalles flipped back a page in his notebook. 'Let me see if I have this right,' he said. 'Are you saying that Doyle may be missing as well?'

'No – at least I hadn't thought about it in that way,' Emma said slowly, 'but now that I do think about it, Mickey hasn't been in the Red Lion all week, and I remember Mark asking me a couple of times if Mickey had been in.'

'Perhaps you could give me Mickey Doyle's address,' Tregalles said, and wrote it down as Paget pushed back his chair and stood up.

'Is the door to Mark's room locked?' he asked Emma. 'We'd like to have a look at it.'

She shook her head. 'We've never had to lock our doors here,' she told him. 'I'll take you up.'

Mark Newman's room was at the back of the house. A small window overlooked an orchard surrounded by a wooden fence, beyond which the ground rose steeply to hillside pastures dotted with sheep. The grass between the fruit trees was long – it was still a bit early for cutting – but the trees had been pruned recently, as evidenced by the limbs and branches stacked in neat piles against the fence.

'We look after it,' Emma told Paget when he asked about it. 'It's part of the deal. Our landlady knocks five pounds a month off our rent if we keep it up.'

'How very generous of her,' Paget observed drily.

Emma shrugged. 'Five quid is five quid when you live as close to the line as we do,' she told him, 'and we are agricultural students after all.'

The carpet was old and worn almost through in places, but the floral wallpaper looked fresh and clean, as did the sheets and coverlet on the narrow, made-up bed with an extra blanket folded neatly at the foot. There was an old-fashioned night table beside the bed, with a thick wedge of cardboard under one of its spindled legs to keep it level, and next to it was a chest of drawers. It was old and almost black with age, in stark contrast to a plain, light-coloured wardrobe on the opposite wall.

'The old one fell apart while Tania was here,' Emma explained when she saw Paget eyeing it, 'so our landlady got that one from Ikea. It came in a package and we put it together ourselves. It doesn't exactly go with the room, but it does the job.'

Mark Newman didn't have many clothes, nor did he appear to have much in the way of other possessions, which was just as well, thought Paget, considering the limited storage space. An armchair with a light above it sat in the corner by the window. The chair looked comfortable and well-used, and a pile of paperbacks, most of them science fiction, judging by their titles, lay in a jumbled heap beside it.

A makeshift table, consisting of a narrow sheet of plywood on two wooden trestles had been set up beneath the window, and beside it was a folding metal chair. A small portable radio sat at one end of the table, and next to it was a printer.

Beside the printer was a shallow cardboard box, which, according to the label, had once contained A4 paper. It was empty now, as was the printer tray when Tregalles pulled it out to check. At the other end of the table was another, smaller cardboard box containing a jumble of pencils and pens bearing company names, a wooden ruler, paper clips, elastic bands, a stapler and a pad of sticky notes. On the floor beneath the table was a single-drawer metal filing cabinet that looked as if it might have come from army surplus.

Emma was frowning as she stood looking down at the desk. 'Someone's been in here,' she said. 'This isn't how it was when I came in on Friday morning. There were papers here.' She pressed the eject button on a Dictaphone that was lying there. The deck was empty. 'And his tapes have gone. He had a whole pile of them. They were there beside the radio.'

'And you're quite sure they were here on Friday?' Paget said.

'Positive. I don't make a practice of going into someone else's room when they're not there,' she explained. 'None of us do. But when Mark didn't come down for breakfast, I thought he'd overslept, so I knocked several times, and when he didn't answer, I thought I'd better wake him because I knew he was supposed to be working that day. So I came in, and when I found his bed hadn't been slept in, I looked around for a note. There wasn't one on his door, which is where he would normally leave one if there had been some unexpected change of plan. I wasn't in here long, but I know there were papers and tapes here on the table.'

'Is it possible that Mark came back while you and the others were out of the house on Friday?'

'It's *possible,*' she said with doubt in her voice, 'but, again, he would have left a note, especially knowing what we had planned for his birthday at the pub.'

'What about the others who live here?' Tregalles asked. 'Would they have any reason to come in here or remove anything?'

'No.' Emma shook her head emphatically. 'But even if they did, why would they take the papers? They were mostly old bills and stuff like that. Oh, yes, and there was one of those stenographers' notebooks with the spiral-wire top.'

'There's a printer but no computer,' Tregalles observed. 'Does he have one?'

'He has a laptop,' Emma told him. 'It was here on Friday.' She groaned softly as she glanced around the room as if hoping it would appear. 'There is something very definitely wrong, here,' she said grimly. 'I was worried about Mark before, but now I'm *really* worried. I don't like the look of this at all.'

Before Paget could reply, Tregalles, who was now squatting down beside the table, said, 'Did you happen to notice if there was anything in the waste-paper bin on Friday? Because there's nothing in it now. Not a scrap.'

'Sorry, I don't remember,' Emma said distractedly. 'As I said, I was only in here for a couple of minutes. Mark may have emptied it before he left.'

'Emptied it where?' Paget asked.

'In the recycling bag, if it was just paper. If he did, it should still be there. It isn't due to be picked up until next week.'

'And where is it kept?'

'In the front hall behind where we hang our coats. You can come down and take a look if you like.'

But Paget was watching the sergeant as Tregalles took out a pair of latex gloves and pulled them on before tugging gently on the handle of the filing cabinet. 'Do you happen to know if Mark kept this drawer locked?' he asked Emma.

She frowned in concentration. 'I believe he did,' she said slowly. 'Not that there was very much in it when I saw it open. He keeps records of his jobs in there, copies of invoices, receipts for petrol, meals and things like that relating to his work. I helped him sort through some of it last month when he was doing his income tax. He probably has the key with him.'

'Don't need it,' Tregalles told her as the drawer slid open. He looked up at Paget. 'It's been jimmied,' he said. 'See the scratch marks?'

Paget took a closer look. 'And it's empty,' he said.

'Clean as a whistle,' Tregalles agreed.

Emma drew in her breath. 'Perhaps Mark did come back . . .' she began, then shook her head. 'But he wouldn't need to break into his own filing drawer, would he? He would have his own keys. Which could mean that someone else has been in the house while we were out.' A shiver ran through her. 'And I don't like to even *think* about that,' she ended.

'Have you seen any other signs that might suggest a

break-in?' Paget asked. 'Any indication that the front or back doors have been forced?'

Emma shook her head. 'No, and we do make sure the doors are locked when we go out.'

'Have you been in this room since last Friday morning?'

'Not inside, no. I stuck my head in on Saturday to make sure Mark hadn't returned during the night, before reporting him missing to the police. But I didn't come in.'

'I'll check the doors before we leave,' Tregalles said. He rose to his feet and circled the room, pulling out drawers and looking inside. 'Doesn't look as if there are any papers here,' he announced. 'In fact, there's not a scrap of paper anywhere.'

'I think we'd better seal the room and get it searched properly,' Paget said. 'And I think we should have a chat with the others who live here to see if they can shed any light on this.' He turned to Emma. 'Do you know what time they will be home?'

She looked at her watch. 'They finish at four, so they should be here soon,' she told him. She was about to leave the room when a thought struck her. 'There's something else missing as well,' she said. 'I suppose Mark could have taken it with him, but I don't know why he would. It's what he calls his journal. It's quite a thick book, and he uses it to jot down ideas for stories; articles for magazines and things like that. I know he has submitted some in the past, in fact he received a cheque for an article last month. It wasn't a large amount, but he was chuffed enough about it to stand us all a round of drinks.'

While they waited for the other two students to arrive, Tregalles checked the contents of the recycling bin bag, but found nothing that appeared to have come from Mark Newman's room. Meanwhile, at Paget's request, Emma found a picture of Newman, taken, as she told them ruefully, with the camera that was now missing.

'That's Mark, the tall one in the middle,' she said. 'That's Tom on the right, and the other one of course is Sylvia. And that's Mark's van.' The picture had been taken outside Wisteria Cottage. There was a skiff of snow on the ground, and Emma told them she had taken it less than a month before.

Paget studied the picture. Mark Newman was tall and gangly. He wore a woollen hat, an open, paint-spattered khaki anorak,

dark-blue shirt, faded jeans and heavy boots. He stood wood-
enly between the other two, his body language suggesting that
he was impatient to be away. The back door of his van was
open, and the ladder propped against it only served to
strengthen the impression that he had been interrupted while
either loading or unloading the van, and wasn't too pleased
about it.

Tom Foxworthy was a smaller, dark-haired man, lean-faced,
with deep-set eyes narrowed against the slanting sunlight. His
brow was furrowed, and he stared into the camera with a fixed
intensity as if having his picture taken was a serious business.
He was wearing a dark-blue zipped-up anorak with the hood
thrown back, brown corduroy trousers and heavy brogues. His
hands were thrust deep into his pockets, and he looked cold.

The girl on the other side of Newman was wearing grubby
overalls and knee-high wellingtons. She was a big girl, a bit
on the plump side, but nicely proportioned just the same.
There was colour in her cheeks, and she wore a headscarf that
couldn't quite contain a mass of fair, unruly hair. She was
grinning, eyes sparkling with what looked like mischief as
she looked up at Newman.

'I think that's the only decent one I have of Mark,' Emma
told him. 'He hated having his picture taken, but I managed
to get him to stop long enough for that one. I was trying to
finish the roll before getting it developed.'

'Do you mind if I borrow it?' Paget asked. It was a good
picture of both Newman and his van, and Paget was beginning to get the feeling that he might need it. 'If I could have
the negative as well, I'll have prints made up and get the ori-
ginals back to you in a couple of days.'

'Please take it,' she said. 'In fact you can take the envelope. The negative's inside. I'll get it for you before you leave.
But to be honest, I hope you don't need it, because that could
mean I'm right, and something has happened to Mark. And I
don't want to be right in this case, Chief Inspector. But thank
you for taking me seriously.'

Tom Foxworthy was the first to arrive. He entered by the
front door, hung up his coat, and came into the kitchen
rubbing his hands. 'God, but that wind is cold,' he said as
he came through the door, then stopped when he saw there
were visitors.

Emma made the introductions. Foxworthy looked surprised.
'Police?' he said, frowning. 'Do you really think all this is
necessary, Emma? I mean Mark's only been gone a few days.
I told you, he's either got a job that's taking up all his time,
or he's shacked up with some girl, and probably the battery
in his phone is dead.'

'Someone has been in his room since he left,' said Emma
quietly. 'Some of his things have gone.'

Foxworthy's frown deepened. 'Gone?' he repeated. 'What
sort of things?'

'It appears that Mr Newman's laptop and some paper have
been taken from his room,' Paget told him. 'And before we start
looking elsewhere, I would like to be sure that no one here had
any reason to remove them.'

Foxworthy bristled. 'I don't think I like what you're
suggesting,' he snapped. 'If you think that I . . .'

'I don't think anything at the moment, Mr Foxworthy,' Paget
said heavily, 'and it's a simple enough question: did you have
any reason for removing papers from Mr Newman's room, or
do you know anything that might help us?'

'I most certainly did not remove any papers! And I
resent—'

'Oh, for heaven's sake get off your high horse, Tom,' Emma
cut in sharply. 'The fact is the drawer of his filing cabinet has
been pried open, his laptop's gone, and all of his invoices and
other papers are missing and so is Mark, so the sooner the
chief inspector knows where *not* to look, the sooner he can
start looking elsewhere.'

Foxworthy shrugged a grudging concession, but he wasn't
going to let it go entirely. 'Maybe there was a good reason
for his disappearance,' he said darkly. 'Maybe he cleared out
the drawer himself.' His voice rose to counter the objection
he could see coming. 'He could have forgotten or lost the key,
couldn't he? After all, what do we really know about him?
Nothing, except what he told us, and that wasn't much.'

'What, exactly, are you suggesting?' Paget asked softly. 'Is
there something you wish to tell us about Mr Newman?'

Foxworthy shrugged again and shook his head. 'No, but
I'm just saying, that's all. We don't, do we?'

'Any more than I know about you or you know about me
before we came here,' said Emma coldly. 'Now, why don't

you go up and get washed. I'll be getting dinner on soon – it's my turn tonight.' She turned to Paget as Foxworthy left the room. 'I have to be at the pub by six,' she explained, 'so if it's all right with you, I'll get started on the spuds.'

A door banged at the rear of the house, and a shrill voice, shouted, 'I'm home. God, it's been a shitty day! Hope you've got the kettle on, Emma.'

'Sylvia has arrived,' Emma said with a grin. 'She'll be in as soon as she peels off her working clothes.' She plugged the electric kettle in again.

Sylvia Tyler literally burst through the door. 'Pigs!' she said 'I don't think I ever want to see another bloody pig aga . . . Oooh, sorry, Emma,' she said apologetically, 'I didn't know you had company.' She turned to leave.

Emma said, 'No, don't go, Syl. This is Detective Chief Inspector Paget, and Sergeant Tregalles, and they'd like a word with you.'

'Coppers? Oh, shit! And here am I going on about pigs!' She made a face and giggled. 'Not what you'd call best first impressions, is it, Emma?' She eyed the two detectives warily. 'Not something *I've* done, is it?' she enquired nervously. 'I mean, you're all standing there looking at me as if . . .'

'Oh, do shut up, Syl,' Emma said. 'It's about Mark. He's still missing, and we've been looking at his room. Have you had any occasion to go in there lately?'

'I should be so lucky,' the girl sighed. 'But he's never so much as suggested it, and it's not because I haven't given him enough hints.' She rolled her eyes at Paget. 'He's gorgeous,' she breathed, 'but he's never – you know . . .'

Paget repeated the question he had put to Foxworthy, concluding with, 'So, if you have any idea who might have taken them, we'd like you to tell us.'

The girl shook her head. 'As I said, I've never been in Mark's room.' Frowning, she looked at Emma and said, 'Why would anyone want stuff like that, anyway? Except the laptop. Not that they'd get much for it; it's pretty old.'

'I've no idea, Syl. But if none of us know anything about it, and Mark hasn't been back since Friday morning, then someone must have broken in while we were out.'

'Oh!' Sylvia Tyler's eyes grew round, and she seemed to shrink away from them as she sucked in her breath and grimaced guiltily. 'I forgot,' she said in a tiny voice. 'Sorry, Emma, but it completely slipped my mind. The lock's broken on the back door. I wondered how it had happened at the time, and I meant to ask the other day.'

'Oh, Syl . . .' Emma simply shook her head.

'When did you first notice it was broken, Miss Tyler?' asked Paget.

Sylvia thought. 'Friday. Friday afternoon when I came back from class. I was late getting in, and I had a date, so I was in a bit of a hurry.' She made a helpless gesture. 'To tell you the truth, I didn't think much of it. It had been sticking a bit, and I thought maybe Mark was working on it. He does that sort of thing around here,' she explained. 'I really did mean to mention it, Emma, and I'm truly sorry.' She was struck by a sudden thought. 'Maybe they're the ones who took your camera, and it wasn't Mark at all?'

Emma shook her head. 'No. It was gone when I came home on Thursday afternoon,' she said.

'Mind if I go, now?' Sylvia asked Paget. 'I need a bath. I left my overalls in the back entrance, but I know I stink a bit.'

'Of course, and thank you, Miss Tyler.' Paget turned to Emma as the girl left the room. 'Could we take a look at the back door?'

'Straight down the hall to your left,' she told him, 'but I won't come with you if you don't mind, because if I don't get dinner started now, I'm going to be late for work.'

Three

'Tregalles and Molly Forsythe are on their way to Whitcott
Lacey, and Charlie is sending a man along as well,' Paget
said, referring to SOCO's Inspector Charlie Dobbs. It was
eight twenty and he was in Alcott's office. 'Tregalles will try
to track down this fellow, Doyle, while Molly talks to the
neighbours. She'll be asking if they've seen anything suspicious going on around Wisteria Cottage in the last few days,
and to pick up any gossip about the people who live there.
Charlie's man will cover the cottage itself.

'Emma Baker volunteered to stay home today in case we
need her. She is convinced that Newman's disappearance has
something to do with what Doyle told him in the pub, but
that was more than a week ago, and she could be completely
wrong. However, whether she's right or wrong, it looks as if
someone did break in through the back door and removed
every scrap of paper from Newman's room. The way I see it,
they were looking for some sort of written record, but didn't
want to spend much time there, so they took everything,
including the laptop.'

'Record of what?'

'I'm afraid your guess is as good as mine,' Paget told him.

Alcott snorted. 'How the hell can you *not* notice that
someone's broken into your house?' he said. 'I find that hard
to believe.'

'It *was* noticed by Sylvia Tyler,' Paget reminded him. 'But
she's the only one who uses the back door on a regular basis.
Her boots are often muddy after she's been mucking about with
the animals, so she takes them off there. The trouble is, she
forgot to mention it to anyone on Friday. She says it was because
she had a date for dinner, and she was in a hurry to wash and

change. No one went in or out that way during the weekend, and you would have to be using the door to notice the damage. Tyler admits she noticed it again when she was on her way out yesterday morning, but says she wasn't particularly worried about it because she still thought it was something Mark had been working on before he disappeared. She was running late, which is a habit of hers, I gather, and everyone else had gone, so she pulled the door to and left it. She said she didn't think it would do any harm to leave it, because, as she put it, there was nothing in the house worth stealing anyway.

'Unfortunately, she was wrong,' Paget continued, 'but Newman's room was the only one targeted. There's no evidence they were in anyone else's room, and that worries me. Because, if Newman didn't clear the place out himself – which I think is highly unlikely – then someone else did, and they knew exactly where to go and what to take.

'I'm having a picture of Newman and a description of his van circulated. The picture only shows part of the side of the van, but Foxworthy was able to tell us it's a D reg Toyota, with a ladder rack and ladders on top, which shouldn't be too hard to spot if it's on the road at all.

'As for Emma Baker's camera, she feels pretty sure that Newman took it before he left on Thursday. She spoke to her sister to get the make, model and serial number, and a description is being circulated in case someone tries to flog it over the counter, but I doubt if we'll ever see Newman's laptop again.'

Alcott leaned back in his chair, rocking gently. 'So the chief constable's niece was right to be concerned,' he said softly, as much to himself as to Paget. 'What do *you* think has happened to Newman?'

'I have no idea. All we know so far is what we've been told, which is that he was excited about something. Emma told us that, and the others confirmed it, but whatever it was he kept it to himself. It's an assumption on Emma's part that he was after a story, and that Doyle knows something about it, but we won't know if that is true or false until we find Doyle.

'Having said that, my gut feeling is that Newman could be in serious trouble. It looks to me as if someone searched his room to find out if he had left anything there that would point to where he's gone and why. And if that's the case, he may have stumbled on to something he couldn't handle.'

Alcott nodded. 'Right,' he said with a dismissive wave of the hand. 'Make sure that Tregalles keeps us both informed of any developments, and make sure he understands that the chief constable is taking a personal interest in the case.'

The church clock was striking nine as they crossed the bridge and entered the village of Whitcott Lacey. Detective Constable Molly Forsythe glanced at her watch, then peered up at the church tower.

'That clock is *still* ten minutes slow,' she told Tregalles, who was driving. 'The hands show the right time; they say ten past; it's the chimes that are out of sync. I used to come here fishing with my dad when I was just a kid, and the chimes were ten minutes behind the hands then,' she explained. 'You'd think they'd have corrected it by now, wouldn't you? It's funny, but I'd almost forgotten about this place until you mentioned it this morning. We used to come here quite often in the summer.'

'They're probably so used to it by now that it would throw the whole village out of whack if they changed it,' Tregalles told her. 'Besides, it's the sort of thing that makes the village different. Gives the Cotswold tourists something to talk about when they get home.' He slowed to make his way past an awkwardly parked car in the narrow street. 'I didn't know you fished,' he said.

'I don't,' she told him, 'and I didn't then, not really. I used to sit on the bank and dangle a dead worm on a hook in the water while Dad waded out into mid-stream to fly-fish. I never caught anything, of course, except the odd tiddler or stickleback with a net, but neither did he most of the time. I don't think he really cared whether he caught anything or not; he just liked to be out here, and so did I. And the best part was we always had egg salad sandwiches for lunch.'

There was a wistful quality to the words, and Molly's dark eyes were sombre as she surveyed the street ahead.

Tregalles refrained from comment, remembering just in time that Molly's father had died quite recently. Apparently a healthy man in his middle fifties, he'd collapsed in the street one Saturday afternoon while out shopping, and died in the ambulance on the way to hospital. Aneurysm, they'd said, the sergeant recalled.

Wisteria Cottage was at the far end of the village, and a small white van was parked in front of it. 'Looks like SOCO's here ahead of us,' Tregalles said as he pulled in beside it and they both got out. He led the way up the flagstone path to the house. 'I'll introduce you to Emma Baker, and then I'm off to see if I can find this bloke, Doyle. Have a chat with Emma before you see what the neighbours have to say. See if she's remembered anything that might help since we talked to her yesterday. And find out, if you can, if she and Newman had something going. She might be a bit more forthcoming with you than she would be with us.'

'Is there any reason to believe there was anything going on between them?'

Tregalles shrugged. 'Not really, but you never know, do you?' he said. 'A young lad like Newman, a bit wet behind the ears, and an older woman. Could be she fancied him.'

'Older woman?' Molly stared at him. 'What does that make me, then? I thought you said she was in her late twenties?'

Tregalles shrugged. 'Well, it's all relative, isn't it?' he said. 'I mean, he'd hardly been gone any time at all before she reported him missing. Maybe she came on too strong; he got scared and took off, and she's using us to find him. Like I said, you never know, do you?'

Before Molly could reply, he lifted the heavy door-knocker and let it drop against the iron striker plate.

Cutter's Caravan Court had been there a long time, as had many of the caravans by the look of them. It was located at the base of what had once been a gravel pit sliced out of the hillside about a quarter of a mile from the village. It was hot in the summer and cold in the winter, but it had water and electricity, and compared to the escalating price of houses in the area, it was a cheap place to live.

There were fourteen caravans in all, some big, some small, and all of them looked as if they were there for the long term. It was a clean site, the space between caravans was generous, and some even had raised garden beds beside them. The soil must have been brought in, Tregalles decided, because even dandelions would be hard pressed to push their way through the natural base of hard-packed gravel.

It wasn't exactly gardening weather, but one man was out there digging in his small plot. Tregalles stopped the car and rolled the window down. 'You're pushing it a bit, aren't you?'

he said. 'I'd have thought it would be too early for planting around here.'

The man stuck the fork in the ground and came over to the car. He was tall and lean, with barely an ounce of spare flesh on him, and well into his seventies by the look of him. 'Facing south,' he said laconically. He flicked his head toward the hill behind him. 'All gravel, that is,' he went on. 'Holds the heat. I'll have my peas in by the end of the week.' He took a flat tin from his pocket, opened it and extracted a hand-rolled cigarette. 'So, take the wrong turn down the road, did you?' he asked as he flicked open a lighter.

Tregalles shook his head. 'I'm looking for someone,' he said. 'Fellow by the name of Mickey Doyle. I understand he lives here.'

The old man eyed him narrowly through a curl of smoke. 'In trouble, is he?' he asked.

'Not as far as I know. Why? Is he often in trouble?'

The man pushed out his lower lip and appeared to be giving the question some thought before answering. 'Not often, no,' he said at last. 'Just the odd time when he's had a bit too much to drink.' He paused to pull a piece of loose tobacco from his lip. 'But then, you probably know that better than me, you being a copper. What's he done this time?'

Tregalles chuckled. 'Is it that obvious?' he asked wryly.

'Afraid so.' The man grinned. 'But then, it takes one to know one. I used to be one myself. Thames Valley. Long time ago. Been retired for more than twenty years.' He stuck out his hand. 'Goodale's the name; Frank Goodale.'

Tregalles grasped the outstretched hand as he introduced himself. Goodale's grip was firm. 'So what do you want with Doyle?' the old man asked. 'Not that you'll find him at home. He's probably off on a job somewhere. Come to think of it, I haven't seen him around for a week or more. But you could ask Mary Turnbull – she's Mickey's next-door neighbour, and she looks after his cat whenever he's away. Number eleven over there.' He pointed. 'Doyle's is number twelve.'

Tregalles thanked him, but before moving off, asked him what sort of man Doyle was.

'He's a good man at his trade, I'll say that for him, and he's the sort who will always give you a hand if you need it. But it's the drink that gets him into trouble. He'll go along for

weeks, sometimes months, having a quiet pint down at the Red
Lion, and then all of a sudden he goes on a bender, and he's
gone for days. He usually lands up in the nick, dries out, pays
his fine, and comes back broke. I don't know how many times
Cutter has threatened to chuck him out because he hasn't paid
his rent on time. Cutter is the owner-manager here, not that he
does much managing; the only time we see him is when it's
time for the rent. But Mickey always manages to slide in under
the wire, somehow, and things go on as they were before.'

Goodale plucked the butt of his cigarette from where it
clung to his lip and pinched it out between thumb and forefinger before dropping it on the ground. He put his foot on
it, and glanced up at the sky. 'Enjoyed talking to you,' he said
as he began to edge away, 'but they were forecasting rain this
morning, and I'd like to get the garden dug before that happens.
Go over there and talk to Mary. If anyone knows where Doyle
is, she will, and you'll probably get a cup of tea out of it.'
He winked. 'Or more,' he said, 'if she happens to fancy you.
She's a widow, and she likes 'em young, does Mary.'

Molly Forsythe stood at the end of the main village street,
not quite sure what to do next. She had spent more than half
the morning talking to people, yet she had absolutely nothing
to show for it. The trouble was, with Wisteria Cottage being
on its own half acre at the very end of the village, there weren't
many houses in the immediate vicinity, so it was hardly
surprising that no one had seen or heard anything that might
be considered suspicious.

But they loved to talk, and Molly had found it very hard
to get away without giving offence. She'd had three cups of
tea, the last one so hot and strong that she felt her mouth
would never be the same again. She craved something cool –
anything to put the fire out. Purposefully, she set off down
the narrow street bordered on both sides by an unbroken line
of houses and small shops. It had been many years since she'd
been in Whitcott Lacey, but if memory served, there used to
be a café about halfway down the street. They sold ice cream
in the summer, and she and her father used to stop in there
before leaving for home. She hoped it was still there.

It was. Same old sign above the door: *Breakfast, Lunches,
Teas* and in faded lettering along the bottom, *Ice cream*.

Molly mounted the worn steps and went inside to the warm and welcoming smell of fresh baking. It was like going back in time. The wooden floor was just as scrubbed and uneven as she remembered it; the long counter looked exactly the same; even the heavy cast-iron tables – the ones that wobbled and slopped your tea if you weren't careful – hadn't changed.

Five tables, but only two were occupied, both by women shoppers. Coats open, handbags hanging from the back of their chairs, shopping bags on the floor beside them or on a vacant chair, and tea and scones in front of them.

'Yes, love, what can I do for you?' The woman behind the counter was short and very, very fat, but she had a warm and friendly smile. 'Tea or coffee is it? Scones are fresh made. Came out of the oven less than half an hour ago.' She raised her voice. 'All right, are they, ladies?'

There was a murmur of approval and nodding of heads.

'They do smell good,' Molly agreed, 'and I'll have one, but –' she hesitated – 'I'd like something cold as well. I suppose it's too early in the year for you to have ice cream?'

'Sorry, love, we don't do that till May. But if it's cold you want, I could do you iced tea.'

'That would be lovely,' Molly told her. 'Shall I pay you now or . . .?'

The woman shook her head. 'You might decide to take something home for your tea,' she said, and chuckled. 'No, it's all right, love, pay me when you leave.'

Molly sat down at one of the empty tables and set her bag on it. It wobbled dangerously. She tried to turn it, but it was far too heavy and wouldn't budge on the wooden floor.

'That's a bad one, that is,' one of the woman called to her, indicating the table. 'Anyway, there's no need for you to sit over there all by yourself. Come and sit here.' She moved a shopping bag off a chair. 'There's room.'

Molly hesitated. She had the feeling that everyone there knew who she was, or at least *what* she was, and they saw a golden opportunity to find out what was going on in their tight little community. On the other hand, perhaps she could learn something herself.

'That's very kind of you,' she said, picking up her handbag and moving to join them.

'Joyce Chandler, Ivy Sloane,' the woman said, introducing

herself and her friend. She was a tall, angular woman with deep-set eyes and a friendly smile. Grey hair, fiftyish, Molly guessed, and reasonably well off if her clothes were anything to go by. Her friend, Ivy, was a smaller woman, probably about the same age, but she looked younger with her dyed blonde hair and plumper face. 'And you are . . .?' Joyce Chandler enquired pleasantly.

'Molly Forsythe.' Molly placed her handbag on the floor between her feet. It wasn't because she didn't trust the people she was with, but rather force of habit.

'Visiting, are you?' enquired Ivy innocently.

Before Molly could reply, Joyce Chandler chuckled and put a hand on Molly's arm. 'No need to answer that,' she said. 'You can't keep secrets here. We all know who you are.' Her glance included everyone in the room. 'At least, we know that you're a policewoman, and we know that something is going on at Wisteria Cottage, and we're all simply dying to know what's happened there.'

Everyone at the next table had stopped talking.

Molly smiled ruefully. Even now she was still amazed at how fast news could spread through a village such as this. She'd only been in the place a couple of hours, but it seemed the word was out from one end of the village to the other. But then, it only took one telephone call to get things started.

Her thoughts were interrupted by the arrival of her tea and scone.

'We are curious,' Joyce Chandler prompted gently, as Molly concentrated on cutting the scone in half and applying a liberal amount of butter.

'Perhaps we can "help you with your enquiries"?' said someone at the next table, lowering her voice to emphasize the words of the phrase so often used by the police, and everybody laughed.

Why not? thought Molly as she sipped the ice-cold tea. The situation was unusual, but it might be an opportunity to gain some local knowledge.

'Perhaps you can,' she said as she set the tall glass mug aside. 'Do any of you know the people in Wisteria Cottage?'

Four

Mary Turnbull was eighty-seven, and she managed to work that into the conversation within seconds of inviting Tregalles inside. 'And call me Mary,' she told him when he'd asked if she was Mrs Turnbull. 'Everybody does.' She was a big woman, and she moved with difficulty, leaning heavily on a stick for support. 'It's the osteoparalysis,' she told him, mispronouncing the name of the complaint. She wheezed when she talked. 'It's the cat,' she explained, 'I'm allergic, but what can you do, eh?'

Get rid of the bloody cat was one solution that came to mind, but Tregalles refrained from voicing the thought.

'Well, don't just stand there; come in and close the door,' she said impatiently. 'This old caravan is draughty enough without leaving the door wide open. It's the rheumatics, you see. I have to stay out of draughts. You'll be wanting a cup of tea, I expect, being a policeman. They all do, don't they – on television I mean. Do you know any of them on the tele?'

'Not personally, no,' he said as closed the door behind him and surveyed the cramped interior of the caravan. With Mary Turnbull filling the narrow aisle between stove, sink and cupboards, and with almost every available surface piled high with books, papers, rumpled bedclothes and several bin bags filled with God knows what, he didn't see how it was possible for him to 'come in'.

The woman heaved one of the bin bags toward the back of the caravan, which partially cleared the way, then edged sideways to settle into a seat facing a narrow table still bearing the remains of her breakfast. A ginger cat appeared as if from nowhere and jumped up on the seat beside her. Mary stroked it as it put its front paws up on the table. 'Looking for your treat, are you?' she said in a little girl voice. She put her finger in her mouth then popped it into the open sugar bowl and offered it to the cat. 'There's a good puss,' she murmured as the cat licked her finger clean, then settled down beside her.

'She's a good puss,' she wheezed as she stroked the cat. 'This is Willow,' she told Tregalles. She began to chuckle, but had to stop to catch her breath. 'Pussy Willow,' she panted. 'It's Mickey's little joke. Willow's his cat, but I think she prefers it here.'

Tregalles wasn't surprised; the cat knew when it was on to a good thing.

'Well, sit yourself down, then,' she said. 'There's plenty of room for a little 'un. But be a love and put the kettle on before you do. I could do with another cup of tea myself.'

Directed by 'Call me Mary', Tregalles filled the kettle, set it on the propane burner, then slid into the seat facing her across the table. He made a show of looking at his watch and frowning. 'I'm afraid I'm a bit pressed for time,' he said regretfully – he wasn't, but after seeing the condition of the mugs beside the sink, there was no way he was going to be drinking tea, especially not with sugar in it – 'so I'll get right to it, if you don't mind, Mary. As I said, I'm looking for Mr Doyle, and I'm told you might be able to tell me where I can find him.'

'Is he in trouble again?' It seemed to be an automatic question when Doyle's name was mentioned. 'He's not a bad boy, you know,' Mary continued. 'He made those shelves for me.' She pointed to a set of three small shelves above the sink. 'Never charged me. He knows I'm on the supplement, and I keep an eye on things when he's away. And then there's puss.' She stroked the cat, who was purring softly.

Tregalles shook his head. 'He's not in any trouble as far as I know,' he assured her. 'But I do need to talk to him. I'm trying to find a friend of his, and I'm hoping he can help me.'

'Ah, well, that's all right, then, but I don't think you'll be seeing him for a while. He's gone to Ireland, at least that's what his friends said when they came to pick him up.'

'When was this?'

Mary thought. 'Last Friday,' she said. 'Yes, that's right, it was Friday. Early in the morning, it was. They were so anxious to get going, they forgot all about puss. I had to go over and see to her after they'd gone.'

'You say a friend came to pick up Mr Doyle; have you seen this friend before?'

Mary shook her head. 'Two of them, there were, in a car,' she said. 'I heard them drive in. It must have been before seven; it was still dark, and I hadn't been up long. Can't sleep in like I used to.' Mary lowered her voice to a hoarse whisper. 'It's the bladder,' she confided. 'And once you're up you might just as well stay up, mightn't you? Anyway, I heard this car, then a banging on Mickey's door. It went quiet for a bit, but then I heard Mickey shouting something, so I went out to see what was going on.'

'And what was going on, Mary?'

The kettle let out a piercing whistle. 'Be a love and make the tea,' she said, ignoring Tregalles's question. 'Puss is having her nap, and I don't want to disturb her.'

Dutifully, Tregalles slid out of the seat and made the tea, but when Mary told him to bring the pot and two mugs to the table, he only brought one. 'I'm afraid I can't,' he told her sorrowfully as he sat down again. 'Mouth's still sore from having a tooth out, and I'm not supposed to drink anything hot.'

'Shame,' she said. 'I remember what it was like when I had my tonsils out. I was just a girl, of course. Back then they took your tonsils out for any old reason, but you never hear of it now, do you? Talk about a sore mouth – I remember what it was like trying to—'

'I'm sorry, Mary,' Tregalles broke in, looking at his watch again, 'but I really am pressed for time. You were going to tell me about these men. You said you went out to see what all the noise was about . . .?'

'That's right. Like I told you, I'd only just got up, so it took me a few minutes to get my coat and slippers on, so they were leaving by the time I got outside. I heard Mickey arguing about something, and I called out to him to ask where he was going, but the man behind him sort of pushed Mickey into the back before he had a chance to answer, and it was him who told me that Mickey was off to Ireland to visit some-body. I didn't quite catch it, because he was in ever such a hurry. Said Mickey's alarm never went off, and he wasn't ready when they came to pick him up to take him to the station, so it was a good thing they'd come a bit early, or he'd have missed his train. Then he got in the back with Mickey, and they drove off.'

She paused for breath, wheezing heavily now. 'Just like
Mickey, that was,' she continued. 'In such a hurry to be off
he forgot all about puss, here, *and* he left his door open. I suppose he knew I'd look after her and lock up, but he might've
told me. Mind you, it must have come up sudden like, because
he never mentioned going away at all last time I talked to him,
let alone to Ireland. It all happened so fast I didn't even have
time to find out when he'd be back.'

'You say one man got in the back with Mickey. Did you
see the other one? The driver?'

'Not really. The lights were in my eyes. I saw the door open
on the driver's side, but I couldn't really see who got in.'

'Has anything like this happened before?'

'No, never.' Mary curled a hand around the cat and pulled
her closer. 'I think someone must be ill or died for Mickey
to rush off like that. Maybe his mother, although he never
talked about his family – come to that he's never talked about
Ireland as long as I've known him.'

'So you didn't actually get a good look at his friends at
all?'

Mary shook her head. 'It was all such a rush, and it was
dark and with the lights shining like they were, it was hard
to see anything properly.'

'What about the car? Can you tell me anything about it?
Make, colour, number plate? Two doors, four doors, old, new
– anything at all?'

'It had four doors, but that's all I can tell you.' Mary
turned suspicious eyes on Tregalles. 'What's this all about,
anyway?' she demanded. 'Why are you asking all these
questions? I thought you said you just wanted to talk to
Mickey about a friend of his.'

'I do,' Tregalles said soberly, 'because a friend, or at least
an acquaintance of his, left home without telling anyone, and
I was hoping that Mickey Doyle could help me find him. But
now, from what you've told me, I'm wondering if Mickey
hasn't done the same.'

'I don't think Mickey Doyle has gone to Ireland,' Tregalles
said. 'In fact I suspect he may not have gone anywhere will-
ingly. Mrs Turnbull said she went over to Doyle's caravan
straightaway, and found the door open, the bed unmade,

drawers pulled out, and clothes on the floor. And when I took a look myself, it was just like Newman's place; there wasn't a scrap of paper to be found.

'Mary said she tidied up a bit – and it *was* only a bit – but she says she didn't take anything out of there, apart from the cat, of course. She said there was no note, and she's heard nothing from Doyle since that morning.

'She couldn't describe the men or the car because the headlights were pointed in her direction, so all she could see were outlines and shadowy figures, and no one else I spoke to in the caravan court remembers seeing or hearing anything unusual that Friday morning. Or if they did they're not saying. Some of them were out when I called, but I'll try to get to the rest tomorrow.

'Mary said one of the men told her they'd come to take Mickey to the train, but I checked the local timetable and there's nothing going either way around that time in the morning. Oh, yes, just one more thing: Doyle's van was parked behind the trailer. It was unlocked and all his tools were inside.'

They were in Paget's office: Tregalles, Molly Forsythe and Geoff Kirkpatrick from SOCO.

'I've sealed the caravan and the van,' the sergeant continued, 'and Geoff will be going through both tomorrow. We've cleared it with Charlie Dobbs. I couldn't find a picture of Doyle, but I have a fairly good description, and I think we should get it out along with Newman's.'

'Agreed,' said Paget. 'And since it appears to be developing into something more than a Missing Persons case, I think it's time to bring DS Ormside in on this, so have him circulate Doyle's description. And just in case there is some truth to the story that Doyle has gone to Ireland, I would think these so-called friends of his would be more likely to drive him to Shrewsbury, where there are at least half a dozen trains a day to Holyhead and the ferry. So let's find out if Doyle *does* have friends or relatives over there. Anything else?'

'That's it, boss,' the sergeant told him as he gathered his papers together and stood up. 'I'll go down and talk to Ormside now.'

'Right.' Paget turned to Molly as Tregalles left the room. 'And what did you find out?' he began, but was interrupted by a low buzzing sound coming from her handbag. She raised an enquiring eyebrow in Paget's direction, and he nodded. Molly took out the phone and answered it. She began to move toward the door to take the call outside the office, then stopped.

'Right away,' she said, and closed the phone. 'It's a message from a Mrs Chandler, a woman I met in the village, today,' she told Paget. 'She would like me to ring her as soon as possible. Do you mind, sir? It could be important.'

'Go ahead,' he told her, turning his attention to Kirkpatrick. 'And what did you find?' he asked as Molly left the office.

'Not much,' the man said, 'but it was hard to know exactly what to look for.' Kirkpatrick was a small, soft-spoken man, who had been on Charlie's team for a decade or more, and he was known to be painstakingly thorough. 'At the cottage, I found what I presume to be Newman's prints everywhere in the room, and I found Emma Baker's prints pretty much where she said I'd find them, including on the do-it-yourself Ikea wardrobe, which she said she'd helped put together. I also found prints belonging to Foxworthy all over the worktable in front of the window, and one or two from Sylvia Tyler. I got there early in order to get everyone's prints for comparison,' he explained. 'Foxworthy was the only one who objected, saying he didn't see why he should give them, because he'd never been inside Newman's room. But he finally let me take them.'

'That's what he told us yesterday,' Paget said. 'And so did Sylvia. Have you had a chance to speak to them, or were they still away at the college when you left?'

'Fortunately, they both came home for lunch,' said Kirkpatrick, 'so I spoke to them then. Foxworthy's a touchy sod, isn't he? Swore up and down that he'd never been in Newman's room until Emma Baker reminded him that he'd helped Newman carry the plywood up the stairs when Newman was setting up the table. He said he was never more than two or three steps inside the room and left as soon as he set the plywood top down. And that made sense, because the only other prints I found of his were a couple on the door jamb.'

'And what did young Sylvia have to say for herself?'

Kirkpatrick chuckled. 'I'm afraid I embarrassed her,' he said. 'It took a bit of coaxing, but she finally admitted that she had a bit of a crush on Newman, and she'd slipped into his room a couple of times, as she put it, "to look round and sort of pretend that he was there with her".'

'Did you believe her?'

Kirkpatrick shrugged. 'It sounded just soppy enough to be true,' he said. 'I've got a fifteen-year-old at home who's a bit like that since she discovered boys. And my impression of Miss Tyler is that she's not all that mature.'

Paget nodded. That had been his impression as well.

'There were a variety of prints I couldn't identify on some of the older furniture and on the door and window sill, but my guess is they belong to previous tenants. There were none where I would have expected them to be if whoever removed the papers and the laptop hadn't worn gloves. Something like driving gloves, I suspect, because I found one very small piece of thread caught on the rough edge of the plywood table, and I think when we take a closer look at it, we'll find it's the sort used for stitching gloves like that.'

Paget grimaced. 'It's not much to go on, though, is it?' he said.

'There was one other thing,' Kirkpatrick said. 'I found similar threads on the back door beside the lock. The only other prints on the door belonged to Sylvia Tyler, and when I checked her gloves, they were nowhere near the same.'

Molly appeared in the doorway. 'I called Mrs Chandler back,' she told Paget, 'and it turns out that she is the doctor's wife in Lyddingham. Apparently she comes in to Whitcott to meet her friend for coffee, which is why I found her there this morning. Anyway, when she told her husband that I had been asking if anyone had seen any activity around Wisteria Cottage last week, he said he remembered driving past there Friday morning and seeing two men get out of a car and go through the gate. I asked Mrs Chandler if he recognized them or could describe them, but she says they had their backs to him, and he only glanced at them as he drove by.'

'What time was that?' asked Paget.

'He thinks it would be about half past nine.'

'And classes start at eight, so everyone is out of the house on weekdays by that time,' said Paget. 'It fits. Does he remember anything about the car?'

'He says not, sir, but I've made arrangements to meet him

tomorrow to see if I can jog his memory. I plan on taking the
car book with me to see if that will help.'

'Good! Anything else?'

'I'm afraid not, sir. No one I spoke to today had anything
bad to say about the students in Wisteria Cottage, or the
students at the college in general. There are a lot of them
boarding in the area, and the villagers like that because they
do well out of them. And with the Red Lion being the only
pub in the village, just about everyone knows Emma Baker.
Some of them said they knew Mark Newman because he'd
done some work for them, but no one seemed to know anything
about him.'

Paget nodded. 'What time are you seeing this doctor,
tomorrow?'

'Two o'clock. He's busy in the morning.'

'Right, in that case, perhaps it would be a good idea to go
early and have lunch at the Red Lion and see what information you can pick up about Doyle and Newman. And if
that doesn't bring any results, perhaps you'd better go back
later and try the evening crowd. Any problem with that,
Constable?'

'Sounds good to me, sir,' said Molly, grinning. 'Best assignment I've had for months.'

Five

'Quite a number of my patients come from Whitcott Lacey,' Dr Chandler said in answer to Molly's question. 'I know the place well, and I'm quite familiar with Wisteria Cottage. In fact the owner is a friend of mine.'

The doctor worked from home, a rambling, three-storey red-brick house set well back from the road. A large white sign directed patients to the surgery door around the side of the house, but Joyce Chandler had told Molly to come to the front door, and it was she who answered it when Molly rang the bell.

'Nice to see you again, Molly,' she said as she led the way down a wide hallway. 'Gordon's in his study. Tea will be ready in a few minutes; I'll bring it in.'

Now, seated in a comfortable chair, with tea and biscuits close to hand, Molly faced the doctor across his desk. It was hard to determine his age. His face was deeply lined, and his hair was almost white, but he had kindly eyes, and there was a vitality about him that made him seem younger than he probably was. Early sixties, Molly guessed.

'Your wife said on the phone that you were on your way back here when you passed the cottage last Friday morning, Doctor. Can you tell me what time that was? As close as possible.'

Chandler pursed his lips and steepled his fingers beneath his chin. 'On my way back to the *hospital*,' he corrected gently. 'I checked my appointments diary last night, and as near as I can tell, it would be about nine thirty, so I telephoned the hospital and asked them to check their log, and they said I signed in at ten minutes to ten, which would be about right.'

'Tell me what you saw as you passed the cottage.'

Chandler went on to repeat what his wife had said on the phone the day before, concluding with: 'It was just a passing glance, you understand. It meant nothing at the time. It wasn't until Joyce told me that you were asking questions about Wisteria Cottage that I remembered it at all.'

'You say you only saw the back of the men. Can you tell me what they were wearing?'

Chandler tilted back in his chair and looked at the ceiling. 'One of them, the bigger one of the two, was wearing a heavy jacket, black or could have been navy, but that's all I could see. The rest of him was hidden by the car.'

'Was his head covered or bare?'

The doctor frowned in concentration. 'Couldn't see much because of his collar,' he said, 'but he didn't have anything on his head. As I said, he had his back to me.'

'Long or short hair?' Molly persisted. 'Dark or fair?'

Chandler shook his head. 'I couldn't tell whether it was long or short, because the collar of his jacket hid most of the back of his head. I *think* his hair was fair, but it could have been grey. As I said, I only caught a glimpse.'

'You say he was bigger than the other man. In what sense, Doctor? Taller? Heavier?'

The doctor thought for a moment. 'Certainly taller, and quite a bit heavier, I'd say.'

'And the other man; what can you tell me about him?'

'Again, not much, I'm afraid. He wore a lighter-coloured jacket, a sort of faded blue, and the hood hid his head completely. And, like the other chap, his lower half was hidden by the car.'

'What can you tell me about the car?'

Chandler grimaced and spread his hands in a gesture of apology. 'I'm afraid I can't be of much help to you there, either,' he said. 'My *impression* is that it was an older car; a bit larger than most you see on the roads today. Light-coloured, possibly grey. I don't think it was white.' He closed his eyes, brow furrowed in concentration as he tried to picture the scene.

'I think they had only just arrived, because I remember seeing the second man – the smaller one of the two – having to push his way along between the side of the car and the hedge. But this other car was coming toward me, so my attention was on it more than the one at the side of the –'

He stopped abruptly. 'I'd forgotten about that until now,' he said slowly. 'Funny how that happens, isn't it? I suppose that was why I paid so little attention to the two men. The road is quite narrow there, and with the car parked at the side of the road, there wasn't much room to pass. I remember Fred was looking anxious about his new car as he went by; not that there was any real danger of a collision, but then Fred is the nervous type.'

'Fred?' Molly repeated. She had been about to take a drink of tea, but now she set her cup aside and flipped to another page in the notebook in her lap. 'Are you saying you know the man in the other car?'

'Oh, yes. Sorry, I should have said, shouldn't I? Fred Dawlish is a patient of mine. He lives in Whitcott. Lived there all his life; retired a few months ago. Come to think of it, he may have seen those two men. I'll give you his address if you like.'

Beyond the market square at the top end of the high street in Lyddingham was the green. It was a long, narrow stretch of grass, at the far end of which was the cenotaph surrounded by flower beds filled with the jutting spears of daffodil leaves. In three, perhaps four weeks from now, they would be up and in full flower, but for now, at least, having tested the cold March air, they were on hold.

Molly found a parking space between two cars and pulled in. She'd made notes while talking to Dr Chandler, but she wanted to think about them and jot down any thoughts she'd had at the time. The two men the doctor had described *could* be the same two men who had spirited Mickey Doyle away earlier that morning, but the descriptions of the men and the car were so vague as to be almost useless. Neither Mrs Turnbull nor Dr Chandler could remember the colour of the car – Chandler thought it might have been grey, but he wasn't sure – and Mrs Turnbull wouldn't even venture a guess according to Tregalles.

'You said it was a big car, Doctor,' she'd pressed in an attempt to come away with something in the way of a description.

'Not *big*, exactly,' Chandler said. 'I mean, it wasn't like some of these American cars you see on the road, but it did seem bigger than my Rover, for example. Mind you, it may have just *seemed* bigger because it stuck out in the road, and my only interest in it was to avoid it as I went by.'

Molly had spent the next twenty minutes or so showing him pictures of cars, but he'd finally pushed the book away and sat back in his chair. 'I'm sorry,' he told her, 'but I would only be guessing at this point. It all happened so fast.'

Molly leaned her head against the headrest and sighed. She was no further ahead than she had been before talking to the doctor. And she had done no better at the Red Lion, where she'd stopped for lunch before her appointment with Dr Chandler. Several people said they knew who Newman was, but they knew nothing about him, but almost all of them knew Mickey Doyle. 'Does good work when he's sober,' the barman told her, and the others agreed. 'But he's just as likely to take off in the middle of a job as not,' another man said, 'so you can't rely on him.'

'Best come back tonight,' the barman advised. 'Talk to Jack – he runs this place – or Emma. They might know.'

Molly closed her notebook and started the car. She felt as if she had been going round in circles and getting nowhere. Perhaps Dawlish, the man the doctor had mentioned, would remember something. On the other hand, she thought glumly, if Dawlish had been as worried about scraping his new car as the doctor seemed to think, she'd be very surprised if he'd paid any attention at all to what was happening on the side of the road.

Tregalles was faring no better. He had spent a fruitless and frustrating morning. While Geoff Kirkpatrick searched and dusted the caravan for prints, the sergeant had gone from door to door to ask if anyone had seen the car and the two men who had come to pick up Doyle, but no one had. Nor did they show much interest in the fact that Doyle was missing. The man was often away on a job for a week or more at a time, and the general consensus once again was, if he wasn't away on a job, he was probably either lying in a gutter somewhere, or drying out in a police cell.

That had been the first choice of Lou Cutter, the owner-manager of Cutter's Caravan Court, who lived on site. 'He'll spend a few days in gaol, then come staggering back here, broke and begging me to give him time to pay his rent,' he told Tregalles. 'The little bugger's already more than a week behind as it is, and you can tell him that from me when you find him.'

'We think something may have happened to him,' Tregalles told him. 'Now, you live here at the entrance to the court. Are you absolutely sure you didn't see or hear anyone drive in and out of here last Friday morning? Probably around seven?'

Cutter shook his head. 'If I did, I wouldn't have thought anything about it,' he said. 'As you found out this morning, not everybody in here is retired, and some of them leave for work around that time. Sorry, Sergeant, but I can't help you.'

Neither did things get any better when Tregalles went back to Doyle's caravan to see how Kirkpatrick was getting on.

'Trouble is, I don't really know what I'm looking for in all this jumble,' Geoff said. 'Nor can I find anything that would give me a clue to where he might have gone, and I certainly haven't found anything that connects him to Ireland.'

'What about a workbook? Jobs he was working on? Could he have tucked that away somewhere? Maybe in his van?'

Geoff shook his head. 'I've been through everything,' he assured Tregalles, 'and if there ever was one, it's gone as well.'

Tregalles had intended to meet Molly in the Red Lion at lunchtime, but when it became clear that there was nothing to be gained by staying on, he rang her on her mobile phone to tell her that he and Geoff were on their way back to town. 'How about you?' he asked. 'Any luck?'

'Not so far, but I've only just arrived at the pub, so perhaps I'll do better here. I'll let you know later.'

But when Molly rang him later in the afternoon, it was to tell him that she, too, had little to show for her day out. 'Dr Chandler tried, but he wasn't much help,' she told him. 'He did give me the name of another man who was also passing the cottage at the same time that morning, a man by the name of Dawlish. But when I went to see Dawlish at his house in Whitcott Lacey, there was no one home, and a neighbour told me that he and his wife left for Lowestoft last Sunday to visit their daughter, and they're not due back until the weekend.

'I contacted Emma Baker at the college, and she suggested coming back to the Red Lion about eight this evening, when all the regulars will be in, so I'll come back then. Meanwhile, I'm coming in now; I have more than enough work on my desk to keep me busy for the next hour or two.'

Tregalles sat back in his chair, fingers linked behind his head. Eight o'clock at the Red Lion. Not a bad idea at that, he thought. Perhaps he should go along with Molly. Two could ask more questions than one.

*　*　*

What little sun there had been throughout the day had disappeared behind the hills, and a blustery wind tugged at Paget's coat as he made his way to his car. Another nasty night by the look of it, he thought, and the sooner he was home, the better. He glanced at the time as he drove out of the yard. Almost six! He'd meant to leave earlier, but it seemed there was always just one more thing to be done before he could tear himself away.

How very different things were now, he thought as he drove out of the yard. Before Grace Lovett had come into his life, he'd spent many of his evenings at work simply to avoid returning to an empty house. But now, with Grace there to welcome him, it was a completely different story.

If Grace was there to welcome him. It was a sobering thought, and one he did not welcome, but it refused to go away.

Grace had been working late a lot these past few weeks. Her job as a SOCO analyst was a demanding one, as was his own, but it was happening far too often for his liking, especially as he wasn't convinced that she was fully recovered from her encounter with Mary Carr a few short months ago. She'd made light of it, insisting that she was fine, but *something* wasn't right, and if not that, what was it?

'I think I should have a word with Charlie,' he'd said at breakfast one morning. 'I know you're short-handed, and he depends on you for analysis, but I think he's forgotten just how bad that experience was for you at New Year. I'm sure SOCO could get along without you if you took some time off.'

But Grace had demurred. 'It won't be for long,' she assured him. 'And Charlie has been more than understanding. Besides, I feel perfectly fine. The psychologist pronounced me fit for work, and I don't want it to look as if you're asking for special treatment for me.'

'And the dreams?' he said. 'You know you've not been sleeping well.'

An impish smile crossed Grace's face. 'And whose fault is that?' she teased. 'Not that I'm complaining.'

He hadn't been able to stop himself from smiling in return, even though he knew that Grace had deliberately turned the conversation. God, he loved that woman, but he still found it hard to believe that she was in love with him. And looking back, he simply couldn't understand how he could have been so blind for so long. So much wasted time. But at least they were together now, and he couldn't be happier – except for the nagging thought that *something* was worrying Grace. He couldn't put his finger on it, but there were times when he would catch a glimpse of a haunted look in her lovely eyes – gone instantly the moment he asked her what was wrong.

'Just a bit tired, that's all,' she'd say, and start talking about something else.

'I think the sooner you get rid of that flat in Friar's Walk, the better,' he'd said one evening. Even now, the very thought of what had happened there sent shivers down his spine, and it must surely do the same for Grace.

'Except there's a stiff penalty for breaking the lease,' she reminded him.

'Better that and be rid of it than paying rent for another six months on a flat you're not using,' he'd countered. But Grace had seemed reluctant to talk about it, and he'd dropped the subject, afraid of stirring up the very memories he so desperately wished she could banish from her mind.

What he couldn't banish from his own mind was the fear that Grace's reluctance to get rid of the flat was prompted by her desire to keep her options open. He was as sure as anyone could be that she loved him, but perhaps the transition had been too sudden after leaving hospital, and she needed time to get used to it. Perhaps she was afraid that living together would deprive her of the independence she'd enjoyed for so many years.

He hoped Grace wouldn't be late again tonight.

But there was no car in the driveway when he arrived. Disappointed, he climbed the steps to the front door, where he paused for a couple of minutes to look down the empty road before going inside.

He shed his coat and tie, washed, and began to prepare for dinner. They'd agreed, after several false starts, that he would stick to such basic things as peeling spuds, preparing vegetables, and setting the table, but Grace would do the cooking, and they would share the washing up.

He'd been in for half an hour when he heard her car. Not

too late, tonight, he thought, but when, after three or four minutes, Grace hadn't come in, he went into the front room to look out of the window.

The car was there and Grace was in it, head back against the headrest, eyes closed, hands still on the wheel. He watched her for a moment. Tired, he told himself. She was simply tired after a hard day's work. He'd done the same himself after driving home. And yet he couldn't shake the feeling that there was more to it than that.

Grace opened her eyes and looked up at the window. It was as if she knew he'd be there. She smiled and waved, then got out of the car and ran lightly up the steps.

'Sorry I'm late, darling,' she called as she opened the door. She shrugged out of her coat and tossed it on the oak settle beside the grandfather clock in the hall. 'Miss me?' she asked as he came to meet her and put his arms around her.

'I miss you whenever you're not with me,' he told her.

'Flatterer,' she said, and kissed him, 'but I like it.' She leaned back to look at him, hands still clasped behind his neck, and suddenly there were tears in her eyes. 'Oh, Neil, I love you so much,' she whispered, and pulled him to her so fiercely that he gasped for breath. He held her close; she was trembling.

'Grace . . .' he began hesitantly, but before he could phrase the question, she pulled back, then kissed him again. 'You must be ravenous,' she said, 'and here I am keeping you from your dinner. What *are* we having for dinner, anyway?'

'Your call,' he said as she slipped away, 'but it had better be something that goes with potatoes, carrots and cauliflower. Roast beef would be nice.'

'Dreamer,' she called back as she ran up the stairs to change. 'How about grilled veal chops and a cream sauce for the cauliflower?'

'Sounds good to me,' he called after her. He followed her with his eyes until she disappeared, then slowly made his way toward the kitchen. Grace was right, he *had* been hungry, but now, in these last few seconds, he seemed to have lost his appetite.

Six

There could be little doubt that most people in the pub that night knew who they were when Molly and Tregalles walked in. The hum of conversation died as they made their way to the bar, and stopped altogether when Emma said, 'Back again, then, Sergeant,' loud enough for those close by to hear. 'Any news, yet?'

'Nothing so far, I'm afraid,' he told her, 'which is why we're here now. Any chance of giving us a few minutes of your time?'

Emma shook her head. 'Afraid not for a while,' she said. 'As you can see, we're pretty busy. Perhaps a bit later? Meanwhile, what are you having? We have Banks Mild, Banks Bitter, Draught Bass or Caffreys.'

'I'll have a Banks Mild,' he said. 'And make it a pint. We could be here for a while.'

Emma drew the pint and set it on the bar. She smiled as she looked at Molly. 'You're driving, I take it,' she said. 'What's it to be? Orange juice?'

'No way,' said Molly, feigning indignation. 'We're on expenses tonight, so I think I'll go wild and treat myself to a shandy.' She sighed. 'But you're right, Emma, I am driving, so make it a half.'

'There you are, then, and don't go mad with it,' said Emma as she set the drink in front of Molly. 'I'll try to join you later when things have settled down a bit. Meanwhile, you might like to have a word with that woman over there.' She indicated a small, middle-aged, rather dowdy-looking woman sitting by herself on a seat in the corner, toying with a glass of wine. 'Her name is Olive Kershaw, and that's her husband playing darts – the little roly-poly one. Olive was here that Saturday night, sitting right next to Mark and Mickey Doyle. She might be able to help you.'

The Red Lion was a small pub in a small village, but it was doing a good business, and Tregalles and Molly had to carry their drinks carefully as they edged their way to the corner.

'Mind if we sit here?' Molly asked pleasantly, 'or are you saving this seat for someone?' She indicated a man's jacket hanging on the back of one of the chairs.

'Oh, no. No, please sit down,' the woman told her. She pulled the jacket from the chair and folded it carefully before setting it on the seat beside her. 'It's my husband's,' she explained. 'He's playing darts, and the way they're playing tonight, he'll be there for a good while yet.'

Molly sat down next to Mrs Kershaw, while Tregalles took a seat facing the two of them across the table.

'You're the detective, aren't you?' the woman said when they were seated, and it was only then that Molly realized that Mrs Kershaw had been one of the women in the tea shop.

'That's right,' Molly agreed. 'And I remember you from yesterday, Mrs . . .?'

The woman smiled guiltily. 'Olive Kershaw,' she said. 'I wondered afterwards what you must have thought of us, pushing ourselves forward like that. It really was very rude of us. A proper bunch of old busybodies.'

'Not at all,' Molly said. 'It's only natural that you would be interested.'

Mrs Kershaw fiddled with her glass. 'I'm sorry,' she said, 'but I didn't quite catch your name yesterday. Too much chatter going on. Detective . . .?'

'Forsythe, but Molly will do for now, Mrs Kershaw. And I'd like you to meet my sergeant, Detective Sergeant Tregalles.'

'Oh, dear.' Olive Kershaw looked apprehensive as she nodded in Tregalles's direction. 'I suppose that means you're still looking for that young man from Wisteria Cottage, then? He did our windows not a month back. Nice lad he was. Has there been any news?'

'I'm afraid not,' Molly told her. 'We've been told that a man by the name of Mickey Doyle might be able to help us, but he seems to have disappeared as well. Emma' – Molly nodded in the direction of the bar – 'tells us that you were here the last time the two of them were seen together, which was a week ago last Saturday, and we wondered if you might have overheard anything that would give us a lead to where they might have gone.'

Olive Kershaw patted the seat beside her. 'Sat right next to me, the lad was,' she said proudly. 'Closer to me than you are now. Packed, it was. But then, it's always crowded on a Saturday. There's hardly room to breathe in here. To tell the truth I'd just as soon stay home, but it's the darts. Stan is on the team, and he doesn't like coming alone, so I come along for company.' She made a face and shrugged as she picked up her glass. 'Company until we get here,' she added ruefully, 'but I won't see him again until closing time.' Olive Kershaw swirled the wine in her glass then drank it down.

Tregalles spoke for the first time. 'Let me get you another,' he said, picking up the empty glass. 'Port, was it?'

'Just tell Emma it's for me,' the woman said. 'She knows. And thank you very much, Sergeant.'

'That's the trouble with these small pubs, isn't it?' said Molly sympathetically as Tregalles headed for the bar. 'You get packed in like sardines, and even if you don't want to hear what your neighbour is saying, you can't help it, can you? But in this case, with so little to go on, we're looking for help, so if you *did* happen to hear anything that might be helpful, we'd appreciate it, Mrs Kershaw.'

'It's Olive, my dear, and I'd love to help, but I really didn't hear very much at all, they had their heads together so close. I do know this much, though: young Mark was pouring the beer down Mickey as fast as he could drink it, so I did wonder. I mean Mark is saving up to go back to university – at least that's what he told Stan – and he'll usually make a pint last most of the night, so I was a bit surprised to see him throwing his money about like that, especially on someone like Mickey. To tell you the truth, I was a bit put out with him, because he must have known that once Mickey gets started, he's more likely than not to go off and drink himself silly.'

Molly's hopes were fading fast, but she persisted. 'Are you saying that Mark was encouraging Mickey to talk? Do you know what it was they were talking about?'

Tregalles appeared with a glass of wine in one hand and a fresh pint in the other. He shot a questioning glance at Molly, and she answered with an almost imperceptible shake of the head. He handed the glass to Olive Kershaw and sat down.

'Cheers,' he said as he raised his glass, and was rewarded with a smile as Olive sipped her wine. He looked from one to the other. 'Any luck?' he asked.

'Olive tells me that Mark Newman was sitting where I'm sitting now, but it was quite noisy in here that night, so it would be very hard to hear anything.' She looked at her watch and sighed as she picked up her drink. 'So I suppose we'll just have to see if we can find someone else, who—'

'Oh, but I did hear *some* of it,' the woman said quickly. She'd been enjoying this unexpected attention, and was already preparing in her mind what she would tell the 'girls' about how the police had come to her for information, so she didn't want them to leave.

'I know Mickey was talking about some job he'd been on,' she continued, 'and young Mark kept asking him questions.'

'What sort of questions, Olive?'

The woman frowned in concentration. 'I remember him saying, "When, Mickey? Give me a time. Give me a day" – or was it date? I can't be sure about that. I know he was excited, and he said something about it making a great story. He took out a notebook and started to write something down, but Mickey got ever so upset when he did that, and told Mark to put that –' Olive Kershaw shifted uncomfortably in her seat – 'well let's just say he used some pretty colourful language when he told Mark to put the book away. He said, "I *told* you, nothing in writing."' Olive Kershaw nodded meaningfully as she said, 'It took Mark quite some time to get Mickey simmered down and talking again after that, and I had trouble hearing what either of them said after that.

'Not that I was listening deliberately,' Olive hastened to add. 'Even if I had been, I couldn't have heard much anyway with Mickey talking so low. Mark was between me and Mickey, and even he had to lean very close to hear what Mickey was saying.'

Olive picked up her drink, then abruptly set it aside. 'There was something about farms,' she said slowly. 'I didn't hear what Mickey said, but I remember Mark saying something like, "you mean there are other farms involved?" And Mickey said something like, "they're not all farms," but I didn't hear what he said after that, because he lowered his voice again.'

The woman picked up her drink again. 'Sorry I can't be of

more help,' she said, 'but it was standing room only, and you could hardly hear yourself think in here, let alone hear what anyone else had to say.'

Molly could imagine Olive Kershaw sitting there by herself, with little to do but drink and watch and listen to what was going on around her while her husband spent the evening playing darts. And probably straining to hear what sounded like an interesting conversation right next to her.

'Do you recall if anyone was sitting on the other side of Mickey Doyle?' she asked. 'Someone who might have over-heard what he was saying?'

'No one was. It's like now. I was sitting here, Mark was next to me, and Mickey was in the corner there by the door. There were people standing in front of us, you know, chat-ting in groups like they are now, but I don't think they would have been able to hear what was going on between Mickey and Mark Newman. The two of them kept their heads down like they were planning a robbery or something – not that they were, of course,' she added hastily, 'but you know what I mean, and I could see that Mickey was on edge. Then, just like that, he was gone.'

'Gone?' Molly echoed. 'Do you mean he left before Mark Newman did?'

Olive nodded. 'Quite startled Mark, it did, the way Mickey jumped up. Startled me as well, come to that. Almost took the table with him. Slopped the beer and whisky all over the table. Proper mess, it was.' Olive Kershaw leaned forward and lowered her voice. 'Taken a bit short, I shouldn't wonder, after all that beer,' she confided. 'Left it a bit too long. Said he was going to the loo, but he never came back.'

Molly and Tregalles picked up on the same thing at the same time, but it was Tregalles who asked the question. 'Whisky?' he said. 'I thought they were just drinking beer, and Mark was buying?'

'Oh, he was,' Olive said. 'It was this friend of Mickey's who brought the whisky.'

'When was that, exactly?'

'Just before Mickey left in such a hurry. This man came over to the table and set the whisky down in front of Mickey.'

'And you say he was a friend of Mickey's? Do you know the man?'

Olive shook her head. 'Don't think I've ever seen him before. He wasn't local, but he must have been a friend of Mickey's, because he said something like, "I thought you might be getting a bit dry after doing all that talking, Mickey, so have a drink on me."'

'Can you describe this man?'

Olive Kershaw pursed her lips and looked off into the distance. 'No, I can't, not really,' she said slowly. 'Too many people in the way.'

'Was he tall, short, fat, thin, old, young . . .?'

'Youngish, I should think, but like I said, I only saw his face side-on, so to speak, and I'm not very good at telling ages. He wasn't all that tall. About like that man over there by the bar in the brown jacket. Not that I'm saying he looked like him, of course, but he'd be about the same size – a bit thinner, maybe, but it's hard to tell when they're wearing a mac, isn't it?' The woman frowned. 'I'm trying to think what colour his hair was, but I can't bring it to mind. It *could* have been dark, but I wouldn't want you to hold me to that. I do remember that he had more hair than the man he came in with – the man in the suit.'

Molly and Tregalles exchanged glances. 'You haven't mentioned him before,' Tregalles said gently. 'But you say they came in together. Can you describe him?'

'Oh, yes. It was the suit, you see. He was wearing a suit under his mac. I remember that because you don't often see that nowadays in a pub. Grey, it was – the suit, I mean, not the mac. And he had bushy eyebrows. I remember thinking it seemed a bit odd when he didn't have much hair.'

'An older man, then?'

'Fiftyish or thereabouts. Had a bit of a tummy on him. And a round sort of face.' Olive put her hands to her face and cupped her own thin cheeks to demonstrate. 'I'd know *him* again.'

'Could we come back to the younger man, Olive?' Molly said quickly. Getting information out of Olive Kershaw was proving to be harder than she'd thought it would be, and she could see that Tregalles was beginning to lose patience. 'I'd like you to think hard, Olive. Are you quite sure you didn't see his face when he brought Mickey the whisky? I mean he must have been standing very close to you if Mickey was sitting over there.'

'Oh, he was, but he was sort of side on to me, and he had to push his way through the ones who were standing next to the table. And I didn't like to look up and show interest, if you know what I mean.'

'But you heard him speak,' Tregalles put in, 'and you told us earlier that he wasn't a local man. Do you mean he wasn't from Whitcott Lacey, or the area generally?'

'I mean he wasn't from round here at all,' Olive told him. 'He spoke very nicely, mind; quiet like, but foreign. You can always tell, can't you, no matter how they try to put it on?'

Tregalles stifled a sigh of irritation, and reminded himself that Olive Kershaw was doing her best. 'Can you tell me how he was dressed?' he said.

'Like I said, he had a mac on,' Olive told him. 'All I could see were his trousers. And his shoes. I couldn't help noticing his shoes. Very dainty, they were. Glossy black and pointed like a dancer's. They were foreign, too, I expect. You won't see many of them around here, I'll be bound.'

'Did he say anything else?'

'No. Just set the glass down and left.'

'This other man – the one he came in with; what can you tell me about him?'

'Nothing. I never saw him again.'

'You mean he left?' Tregalles's impatience was beginning to show.

Olive Kershaw bridled. 'I mean I never saw him again,' she said deliberately. 'He could have left or he could have been at the bar, but like I said, the place was so full I couldn't see past the people around this table. Besides, I didn't know then that you'd be asking me all these questions about him, did I?'

'Sorry,' Tregalles apologized. 'I don't mean to badger you, Mrs Kershaw, but it is important that we find out as much as we can. Tell me, did Mickey say anything when the man brought the drink over?'

Olive shook her head again. 'Never said a word. Not even a thank you, come to think of it.'

'And the man just walked away?'

'That's right.'

'So, what did Mickey do then?'

'He just sort of stared after the man, then jumped up and said he had to go to the loo.'

'And he never came back? What about Mark? What did he do?'

'Went over to the bar and got a cloth to mop the table, then sat down to wait for Mickey. He kept looking at the time, then went off to look for him – at least I suppose that's where he went. Then he came back again and started asking people at the bar if they'd seen Mickey, and finally went through to the lounge. I never saw him again after that.'

Neither Emma nor her boss, Jack Tanner, could remember serving a whisky to a foreigner, nor did they remember the older man Olive Kershaw had described. 'We go through a fair bit of whisky in a night, especially on Fridays and Saturdays,' Tanner told them. 'It's all we can do to keep up with the orders, so we're not paying much attention to who's ordering, unless we know them, of course. Trouble is, you see,' he continued as he collected glasses, 'the Red Lion's got a bit of a reputation for "atmosphere, conviviality, and good grub".' He laughed. 'At least that's what it says in the adverts in the local paper, so we're always seeing new people. Sorry.'

They were halfway back to Broadminster before Tregalles roused himself from a gloomy silence. 'What we need to know,' he said, 'is who Mickey Doyle was working for.'

'And who the man was who brought him the whisky,' Molly said. 'They could be one and the same, and it sounded to me as if he was warning Doyle to keep his mouth shut. Which would account for Doyle's sudden urge to leave.'

Molly flashed her lights at an oncoming car with its high beams on. The lights dipped.

'It also suggests that he and Doyle were engaged in something illegal,' she continued, 'or at the very least, something he didn't want talked about in a pub, especially to a budding reporter. So Mickey leaves the pub in a hurry, and no one seems to have seen much of him from that point on, with the possible exception of his closest neighbour. Newman is said to have been excited about something after talking to Doyle, then he disappears on Thursday, and Doyle is whisked off early Friday morning by two men who claim he is off to Ireland. Bit more than coincidence, wouldn't you say?

'So, yes, I think you are right,' she went on without waiting for an answer, 'we have to find out who Doyle was working for, and once we know that, we may have the answers to both disappearances.'

Molly glanced across at Tregalles. He hadn't heard a word she'd said. Head down, chin on his chest, the sergeant was fast asleep.

Seven

Thursday, March 13

Coffee mug in hand, Tregalles sat hunched forward in his chair in Paget's office. '*Someone* out there in Whitcott Lacey has to know what's going on,' he said after telling Paget about the conversation he and Molly had had with Olive Kershaw the night before.

'The way I see it, Newman was looking for a story that would get him a job on one of the local papers, and I think he found it with Doyle. We talked to some of the regulars in the pub before we left, and they all agreed that Doyle rarely volunteered anything when he was sober, but it was quite a different story when he'd had a few too many drinks, and I think Newman took advantage of that. But someone must have realized what was going on, and warned Doyle off, because, according to Olive Kershaw, he took off like a scared rabbit after the bloke nobody seems to know or remember brought him a drink and had a few words with him.

'So, Newman disappears the following Thursday, and two men come for Doyle first thing Friday morning, and neither Doyle nor Newman have been seen or heard from since. Then Wisteria Cottage is broken into and Newman's room is cleaned out – possibly by the same two who came for Doyle.'

The sergeant drew in a long breath and let it out again. 'I don't know what's going on out there,' he said slowly, 'but I have the feeling that somebody is going to a lot of trouble to keep it that way.'

Paget nodded. 'I think you're right,' he said, 'and if that is the case, then it doesn't look good for either Newman or Doyle.' He glanced at the time, hesitated, then shook his head.

'I'd like to go out there with you this morning, but I have to be in New Street in half an hour. It's budget time again, and since everyone is clamouring for a bigger share of the pie, I can't afford *not* to be there. Unfortunately, I will probably be tied up for a good part of the time during the next couple of weeks, so you will have to take the lead on this, Tregalles. And the sooner you and Forsythe get back out there and start putting a bit of pressure on Doyle's neighbours in the caravan park, and anyone else who admits to knowing him, the better.'

Tregalles rose to his feet. 'On my way,' he said as he made for the door. 'All right if I call your mobile if necessary while you're in your meetings over there?'

'Feel free,' Paget told him as he stood up and began stuffing folders in his briefcase. 'But do try to make it good news. Mr Brock doesn't like any other kind.'

Paget felt completely drained by the time the meeting broke up at five o'clock. He wasn't fond of meetings at the best of times, but a meeting chaired by Chief Superintendent Morgan Brock was something else again. With his accounting background, Morgan Brock reduced everything to numbers, ratios and percentages, all backed up by graphs and pie charts that virtually ignored the human factor and the complex nature of the job.

'You're not exactly endearing yourself to the man,' Alcott had warned him yet again at lunchtime. 'His mind is made up and you're not going to shift him, so let it be. We'll just have to find a way to work within the parameters he sets.'

But Paget always felt he had to try, and he had managed – finally – to wring one concession out of the chief superintendent. Brock had grudgingly accepted Paget's argument that a total ban on overtime could, under certain circumstances, lead to unwelcome criticism from the public and the press.

It was the press that did it, of course. If there was one thing Brock did *not* like more than loosening the purse strings, it was bad publicity.

Paget was tempted to go straight home, but with the prospect of several more days of meetings ahead of him, he decided to go back to the office and clear as much of the paperwork on his desk as possible before calling it a day.

There were a number of messages awaiting him when he returned to Charter Lane. He shuffled them into some sort of order and dealt with them swiftly, but the one he didn't recognize he left till last.

Vincent Perelli? He couldn't think of anyone he knew by that name, but apparently the man had said the matter was urgent, and had asked that Paget return his call asap.

He punched in the number and settled back in his chair. The phone at the other end was picked up on the first ring. 'Perelli,' a man's voice said cryptically.

As soon as Paget identified himself, the man broke in with an effusive, 'Ah, Mr Paget, thank you so much for returning my call so promptly. I am so sorry to trouble you at your work, but it is very important that I talk with you about Miss Lovett.'

Grace? What did she have to do with someone by the name of Perelli?

Of course! The penny dropped. Perelli was the owner of Grace's flat. He'd only met the man once, and then only briefly. Short neck, chest like a barrel, tightly curled grey hair. 'What about Miss Lovett?' he asked cautiously.

'It's about the lease on the flat,' the man said. 'You see—'

'Shouldn't you be talking to Miss Lovett about that?' Paget cut in sharply.

'But I have, Mr Paget. Several times, but it is no good. She will not listen to me, and it is a good deal, believe me, sir.'

Paget was tempted to tell Perelli that he didn't want to get involved in what he regarded as strictly Grace's business, but he was intrigued. 'What, exactly are you talking about, Mr Perelli?'

'The lease on the flat. I have tried to tell her she would never get such an offer from anyone else. I am prepared to pay her a reasonable price if she will let it go, but she says no. I ask her if she intends to move back, and she tells me no, but she still won't let me have it back. I don't understand. But I thought if I spoke to you, perhaps you would be good enough to try to persuade her . . .?'

Paget sensed a hopeful shrug at the other end of the line.

'Let me be sure I understand this,' he said. 'Are you saying you have offered to *pay* Miss Lovett to break the lease and return the flat to you?'

'Yes, yes, of course that is what I am saying, and I assure you, she will never get another offer like this.'

'I see.' He didn't exactly, but he was beginning to. Under the terms of the existing lease, there was a penalty that would have to be paid by Grace if she wished to terminate the lease ahead of time. Now Perelli was offering to pay *her* to break it.

But the thought that pushed everything else into the background, and sent a chill into the very marrow of his bones, was that Grace had never said a word about it to him.

'I take it you have someone who wants the flat and is prepared to pay a higher rent than Miss Lovett is paying?' he said.

'That is true, Mr Paget. That is true, but if Miss Lovett will no longer be living there, I do not understand why she will not let me have it back. I have offered her good money. If you would just talk to her, please, Mr Paget, I would be most grateful.'

'When did you last speak to her yourself?'

'Yesterday, last week, the week before, but she keep saying, "Not now, Mr Perelli. Not now." So I say, "When, Miss Lovett?" but she just shakes her head, and gives no reason. She won't tell me why. So, I ask for your help, sir. She will listen to you.'

'What makes you think she will listen to me?' asked Paget neutrally. 'This matter is really none of my affair, and I'm not at all sure that I should become involved. What Miss Lovett does is her own business.'

'But your business as well, now that she is living with you in your house. Is that not so, Mr Paget?'

'I think you are taking a great deal for granted, Mr Perelli,' he said stiffly, 'and I'm afraid I cannot help you. You and Miss Lovett will have to work this out between you. I don't want anything to do with it. Sorry, but that's the way it is, Mr Perelli.'

Paget hung up the phone, sat back in his chair and closed his eyes. What *was* going on? he wondered. Why was Grace being so stubborn about letting the flat go? She certainly wasn't keeping it for the fond memories it held, not after what had happened to her there. So why wouldn't she let it go, especially when Perelli wanted it so badly that he was willing to pay her to break the lease? And he couldn't believe that she was holding out for a better offer. That wasn't like Grace at all.

Once again the fear of losing her took hold. It seemed clear to him now that Grace was clinging to the flat as a means of escape if things didn't work out between them. She said she loved him, and he believed her, but perhaps she was not quite as sure as he was about a long-term commitment. His first impulse was to tell her about Perelli's call, to ask Grace point-blank why she didn't want to let the flat go. But caution raised its head, and he realized he wasn't yet prepared to take the risk. He hoped and prayed that she would stay. If he had his way they would spend the rest of their life together – but as long as there might be some doubt in Grace's mind about their future together, he was not going to be the one to bring it out into the open.

Grace got home more or less on time that evening. More or less because neither of them could ever be sure when they would finish work each day, so they considered themselves to be 'on time' if they arrived home within an hour of each other. Arriving some fifteen minutes after him, Grace kissed him briefly, then stepped back to hold him at arm's length and eye him critically. 'You look tired,' she said. 'You said this morning you weren't looking forward to a day with Mr Brock. Did you make any headway at all?'

'About that much,' he said, holding thumb and forefinger about a millimetre apart.

'And you're hungry,' she said. 'So, enough of this dilly-dallying; I'll start dinner right away.'

'Better still, why don't we go down to the village and have dinner at the White Hart? It isn't the fanciest place around, but the food's good. I took a chance on your not being late tonight and booked.'

Grace hugged him. 'Oh, you lovely man,' she said. 'I'm starving myself, so just give me time to tidy myself up . . .'

'You have twenty minutes,' Paget called after her as she made for the stairs.

Paget turned away as Grace ran up the stairs, his thoughts in turmoil. The way she had greeted him, her concern for his well-being, the way she would come into his arms each time she came home told him more than words that she really did love him. But still hovering like an ominous cloud in the back of his mind was the call he'd had that afternoon from Vincent Perelli.

*   *   *

The small dining room was full, and the lively background chatter coming through from the bar gave the place something of a festive air. 'I like this place,' Grace said as they settled in their seats. 'And the nicest part about it is there's no washing up to do afterwards. We should do this more often.'

'Which reminds me,' said Paget, 'Tregalles was telling me that the Red Lion at Whitcott Lacey serves very good food. Both he and Molly say it's just like stepping back in time. Tregalles is even talking about taking Audrey out there for a meal, so if that turns out well, perhaps we could take a run out there one evening.'

'Sounds great,' Grace told him, but mentally made a note to phone the pub and check their bill of fare before agreeing to go out there for dinner. Tregalles might well be right about the food, but on the other hand, his idea of a good meal was a hot meat pie or a Gloucester sausage and chips.

A young waitress appeared at Paget's elbow, and they ordered drinks. 'The usual sherry?' Paget asked Grace. She thought for a moment, then shook her head. 'I think I'll have a lager for a change,' she said.

He nodded to the waitress. 'And I'll have a whisky,' he said.

'Water on the side?' she enquired.

'Please.'

'Whisky? It *must* have been a hard day,' Grace observed when the girl had gone.

'It was,' he admitted. 'And we have more of the same tomorrow, I'm afraid.'

Grace smiled sympathetically as she picked up the menu. 'Try to forget about Mr Brock,' she said soothingly. 'Don't let him spoil your dinner.'

He picked up his own menu and pretended to study it, but his thoughts had nothing to do with Brock. Difficult as the man was, at least Paget knew what the issues were when dealing with the chief superintendent. But Grace was another matter. He had booked a table here tonight because he'd thought that once they'd had dinner and were relaxing over drinks, he might broach the subject of the flat; perhaps even mention Perelli's call this afternoon.

But looking at her now, head bent, hair gleaming softly beneath the lights, his courage failed him. What if his fears were true, and Grace *was* keeping her options open? What if he forced her into telling him that she wasn't sure that she could stay? He didn't want to lose her. What if . . .?

'Oh, look, Neil,' she said, breaking into his thoughts. 'The special for tonight is lasagne. You like Italian, so why don't you have that? I wouldn't mind some of that myself, but I don't want anything too heavy, so perhaps I'd better have the chicken.'

Italian. Perelli! He took a deep breath.

'Neil . . .?' Grace raised an enquiring eyebrow.

'Chicken,' he said, then added hastily, 'I think you're right; lasagne would be a bit heavy, so I'll have the chicken as well.'

Grace reached over and patted his hand. 'Good choice,' she said approvingly.

And appropriate, given his state of mind, he thought as he set the menu aside.

Eight

Friday, March 14

Paget went in early the following morning to try to get some work done before going over to New Street, but Tregalles was there ahead of him. 'Not that I've got a hell of a lot to report,' he admitted, 'but I can give you what we have so far.'

He sat down to face Paget across the desk as the chief inspector settled into his own chair.

'Mary Turnbull seems to be about the only one Doyle talked to in the caravan park,' the sergeant said, 'but even she couldn't tell me much about the man himself. I spoke to her again yesterday, and she said Doyle often talked about his work and the people he was working for, but she couldn't tell me anything about what he'd been working on recently. She did think it a bit strange, because he was going off to work early each morning and coming home late at night, and he seemed to be quite excited about it, but he wouldn't tell her anything about it. The only thing he did say was that the money was good – *very* good, she said – so she thought the reason he was keeping shtum about the job was because it was something he was doing for someone on the sly, and he didn't want anyone to get wind of it.'

'Did she say how long he'd been on this job?' Paget asked.

'About a couple of weeks. But she gained the impression that he thought it might turn into something bigger, so she was surprised when he suddenly stopped going to work last week. In fact she said he hardly left his caravan the last few days he was there.

'Which might be because of the incident in the pub when he was seen to be talking to Newman,' Tregalles concluded. 'It was a warning he took seriously – seriously enough to lie low for a while.'

'But not low enough, apparently,' said Paget. 'But why didn't this woman tell you all this before?'

'Just never occurred to her that it had any bearing, I suppose.'

'Anything else?' asked Paget as he began sorting through the papers on his desk.

'All but two of the caravan owners have been covered, as well as most of the people in the village, but no one could tell us anything. It seems that Doyle worked strictly for cash. He would never take a cheque; he had no use for cash cards or credit cards, or anything that might leave a paper trail. In fact, even Revenue & Customs have no record of him, which means he's never paid income tax, at least not under the name of Doyle. Forsythe is out again this morning to talk to some of the people he's worked for in the past, and I'm going back out later as well, but I doubt if we'll do any better than we did yesterday.'

'And nothing new on Newman, I take it?'

'We tracked down his parents and Ormside talked to Newman's father. Not that he was a fat lot of help, because Len said he didn't seem to care one way or the other whether his son was missing or not.'

There had been nothing in Mark Newman's room to give them a clue to where his parents lived, but, knowing the boy's birth date, and assuming Emma Baker was right about his parents living in either Plymouth or Portsmouth, Ormside had tracked them down in Plymouth, and spoken to Newman's father on the phone.

'He said he hadn't seen his son for more than a year,' Tregalles continued, 'nor had he heard from him. Seems Newman senior wanted his son to follow him in the family restaurant business, but Mark wasn't having any. He was determined to be a journalist, so they parted company. Len said the man sounded pretty bitter, but he did finally agree to call us if he heard from Mark.

'Emma Baker has been watching the post in case anything comes addressed to Newman, but there's been nothing so far. She's also talked to everyone she can think of herself, but she's had no better luck than we've had.'

'Anything from the university?' Emma Baker had told Paget that Newman had been planning to go back to university in September. 'Derby, I think,' she'd said. 'At least that's where he took his first year, so I assume he would be going back there again.'

Again, Tregalles shook his head. 'One of Len's people is working on it,' he said. 'And just in case there is any truth to what one of the men told Mary about Doyle going off to Ireland, Len has people checking on the trains and the ferries, but they've had no luck so far. Can't say I'm surprised; I think the answer lies closer to home.

'So,' he said with a sigh of resignation as he got to his feet, 'I'll go back out there, and let you know if there is anything to report.' He paused at the door. 'Anyway, apart from all that, how's the inquisition going in New Street? Getting anywhere with our beloved leader, are you? More men? Shorter work week? Longer holidays, maybe?'

'Get out of here before I send you over in my place,' Paget growled. 'And show a little respect. It's *Chief Superintendent* Brock to you, Sergeant.'

Tregalles shrugged an apology. 'Sorry, boss,' he said humbly, 'but I thought I *was* showing a little respect – as little as . . . OK, OK, I'm gone,' he said as he made for the door.

Friday afternoon, school was over and they had the whole weekend before them. They weren't supposed to be there, of course, but nine and eleven-year-old boys have always been inclined to go where they were not supposed to be. To be fair to Jimmy Greenwood and his best mate, Sean Calloway, they were well aware of the dangers – if not of the terrain itself, at least of the amount of trouble they'd be in if they were found out – and both exercised considerable caution in their descent down the crumbling sides of the old quarry to the water's edge.

'See,' said Jimmy, pointing to a half-submerged oil drum and several broken boards. 'Told you. Somebody's been down and smashed our raft. Dunno what happened to the other barrel. Must have sunk, and that one doesn't look as if it's going to be much good either.'

Sean, the elder of the two, squatted down beside the water and scooped up a handful of stones. 'Dunno how,' he said thoughtfully as he threw a stone at the remaining oil drum. 'It would take a lot to bust 'em up like that. Could've been that mob from the Flats, I s'pose,' he said, referring to a gang of young thugs who made occasional raids into Sean and Jimmy's territory to steal bikes or kick out the spokes of those that were locked and chained. He threw two more stones and was rewarded with a satisfying clang as he scored a direct hit with the last one. 'Can't think who else would do it, can you?'

But Jimmy didn't respond. He'd been looking at something on the side of the quarry at some distance from where they stood. 'It was a landslide,' he declared. 'Look, the side's caved in over there. Look at the size of those stones! Boulders, more like. That's what did it. Wish we'd been here to see it.' The thought prompted him to look up nervously at the route they would have to travel to get back up to the top of the quarry.

'Not much we can do down here, anyway,' he said, trying to conceal his fear from Sean. After all, if it could happen once it could happen again. 'Might as well go back up.'

Sean stayed behind to throw a few more stones before following his friend to the top. 'Come on, then, let's take a closer look,' he said, wiping his hands on his trousers.

The two boys trotted along the edge to the place where they could see the grass had been torn away, leaving a long jagged scar in the side of the quarry.

'Better not get too close,' Jimmy warned. 'It might still be loose.'

But Sean was bent over studying something on the ground. 'I reckon a car's gone over here,' he said soberly as he straightened up. 'There's tyre marks and they go right over the edge.'

He moved closer to the edge and peered down. 'Look!' he said excitedly, 'you can see it!'

Jimmy moved forward cautiously. 'I don't see anything,' he said, moving back.

'You're not going to see anything from there, you twit,' Sean said disdainfully. He grabbed his friend's arm and dragged him forward. 'There! See it under the water? And it's not a car, it's a van. Bet it made a hell of a splash! Wish we'd seen it go in.'

'Yeah!' Jimmy breathed as he began to pull back to safer ground.

'Bet somebody's in it,' Sean said. 'They'd be drowned by now, though, I expect. Wonder how they got in?' The gate at the end of the road leading to the quarry had been padlocked for years. 'Let's have a look.'

The older boy set off across the field toward the gate, while his friend followed at a slower pace. Jimmy Greenwood didn't like the way things were going. Unlike his friend, who seemed to be taking it all in his stride, he kept thinking about the consequences of their find.

'Been busted,' Sean said, rattling the padlock. 'Busted and put back again, so you know what that means, don't you?'

Jimmy shook his head.

'It means,' said Sean with exaggerated patience, 'that they closed the gate so no one would know they'd been through. Suicide. That's what it is. Suicide, and I bet there's more than one down there as well. I'm going back for another look.'

'We'll have to tell the police.'

'Oh, yeah? And then what?' Sean scoffed. 'How're you going to explain that to your dad, eh? Don't be daft. We can't *tell* anyone, because we're not supposed to be here in the first place, are we?'

Paget was kneeling beside the filing cabinet when Charlie Dobbs appeared in the doorway of his office.

'Say a prayer for me while you're down there,' Charlie said jocularly. 'We could both use some extra help from what I hear.'

Paget stood up and locked the filing cabinet and dropped the keys in his pocket. 'Couldn't close the drawer,' he said by way of explanation. 'One of the wheels was off the rail. Hardly surprising, considering the amount of stuff packed in there. Anyway, what are you doing over here, Charlie?'

'Alcott wanted to talk about the February stats. To tell you the truth, I was expecting another lecture on how much we've been charging him for our services, but as it turned out, he was quite happy for a change, because the amount of over-time we've charged him in the last couple of months is down by twenty-two percent.'

Paget frowned. 'That's a surprise,' he said. 'I thought you must be swamped, considering the amount of overtime Grace has been working lately.'

'Grace?' Paget's head was down as he cleared his desk and locked the drawers, so he missed the look of surprise on Charlie's face.

'That's right,' he said, straightening up. 'As a matter of

fact, I'm a bit worried about her, Charlie. I think she could do with some time off. I know you depend on her a lot, and she never complains, but couldn't you ease up on her just a bit?'

Charlie's mind was racing. Things had been fairly quiet lately, and Grace hadn't worked more than three or four hours overtime in the past couple of months. So what was Paget talking about? More to the point, what was Grace up to? Whatever it was, he didn't want to say anything until he'd had a chance to talk to her.

'You're probably right,' he said. 'I must admit I do depend on her a great deal, but I'll see what I can do.'

'Appreciate it, Charlie,' Paget told him, 'but please don't tell her I said anything to you. She'd never forgive me.'

Charlie gave a grunt that could mean anything as he looked at his watch. 'Got to go,' he said. 'Talk to you later, Neil.'

Paget's step was lighter as he left the building. He felt better now that he had spoken to the inspector. It was so easy to keep loading the work onto someone you could depend on – he'd been guilty of that himself more than once – and it just needed someone to remind you that there were other resources you could call on. And now that he had drawn it to Charlie's attention, he felt sure that the inspector would do the right thing, and Grace would never know that he had intervened on her behalf.

If it hadn't been for Grace's insistence that he take some time off, Paget would have spent the entire weekend at work, partly to get rid of the mounting pile of paper on his desk, and partly to try come up with some facts and figures of his own that just *might* persuade Morgan Brock to reconsider his position on some of the things he was proposing.

'I understand the need to work some extra hours,' Grace said when he arrived home after spending all day Saturday at the office, 'but enough is enough. You need to give yourself a break. You need to get out in the fresh air and get some exercise. Why don't we do a walk together tomorrow? The weather forecast is good, so why don't we start with one of the shorter walks on the Long Mynd? The scenery is fantastic, and you'll feel the better for it on Monday. You've always said how much you used to enjoy hill walking, yet you've not

so much as put on your boots since I've known you. I understand why, but surely now, Neil . . .?'

Grace was right. He and Jill used to go out whenever they
could get time off together, but he'd been out only once since
she died, and walking the hills alone just hadn't been the
same. He'd put his boots and all-weather gear away and hadn't
looked at them since. But now, with the prospect of Grace at
his side, he found the idea appealing.

'I'm pretty rusty,' he said hesitantly, 'and I know I'm not
in the shape I used to be, so you'll have to bear with me.'

'Just don't expect me to piggyback you off the Long Mynd,'
Grace said, and laughed. 'Anyway, you'll be fine. It's an easy
walk.'

Sunday turned out to be one of those rare sunny days just
made for walking, and with the wind in his face and the sun
on his back Paget wondered why he'd avoided it for so long.

They drove to Church Stretton, then up a winding track
that took them to Shooting Box car park, where they left the
car to begin their trek across the Long Mynd. There had been
almost no wind in the valley, but they were met by a brisk,
exhilarating cross-wind once they reached the top and began
the trek southward along the spine of the Mynd. The air was
fresh and bracing, and Paget found himself savouring it like
wine.

Ahead of them, as they began the long descent toward
Asterton, they could see the colourful V-shaped wings of hang-
gliders wheeling and circling lazily like eagles searching for
their prey.

They paused to rest and watch. 'I love to see them,' Grace
said, shading her eyes against the sun, 'but I don't fancy
hanging out there with nothing under my feet. But I wouldn't
mind going up in a proper glider. They take off from the
gliding club over there, and I've often been tempted to give
it a try. It must be a wonderful feeling to fly like a bird with
just the sound of the wind beneath your wings. Yes,' she said
determinedly as they set off again, 'I'm going to do that one
of these days – when I get up the courage, of course,' she
added with a chuckle as she tucked her arm under his.

By the time they'd made their way down the steep slope
to Asterton, Paget was ready for his lunch, but Grace insisted
on pushing on to Wentnor. 'We always stop there,' she told

him. 'It's a sort of tradition, and they've never let us down yet.' Grace belonged to a group called the Border Patrol, thus named because most of their walks took them along the Welsh Marches bordering Shropshire and Wales.

By the time they reached the village, Paget was more than happy to see the welcoming sign of the sixteenth-century inn – not so much for the food and a drink, although he was certainly ready for them, but for a chance to rest. 'I'm utterly ashamed of myself,' he confessed as he sank into his seat. 'And to think I used to be able to do twenty miles in a day without any trouble at all. How far did you say this was?'

'Eight miles, perhaps a little longer.'

'And this is only the halfway point? Oh, Lord,' he groaned. 'I am in poor shape, but I must admit I am enjoying it. The views are magnificent.'

'And I thought you weren't paying attention,' Grace said. 'You were so quiet up there. You were thinking about work, weren't you?'

'Afraid so,' he confessed. 'I have a bad feeling about Mark Newman's disappearance, and I keep wondering if we're missing something out there in Whitcott Lacey. I don't know what's going on out there, but I think Newman and Doyle got themselves mixed up in something that could prove fatal – if it hasn't already.'

He shrugged apologetically. 'Sorry, love, but I *am* enjoying the walk and I'm glad you bullied me into coming.'

'That'll be the day when I can bully you into anything,' Grace laughed. 'Anyway, that's enough shop talk. There's nothing you can do about it out here, so let's just enjoy the day. And I'm starving, so let's order lunch before the place fills up.'

Nine

Monday, March 17

Paget was still thinking about their day out while driving to work on Monday morning. He'd enjoyed the pub lunch and he'd enjoyed the return journey more than he'd thought he would. His legs ached from the unaccustomed climbing, but it was as if his whole body had been re-energized, and even another go-round with Brock seemed less daunting this morning.

Tregalles was getting out of his car as Paget drove in, and they entered the building together. Molly Forsythe was at her desk, and Len Ormside didn't look as if he'd ever gone home.

Paget looked at the whiteboards. 'I see all the call-back names are scratched off,' he said to Molly. 'Any luck?'

'Afraid not, sir. I think I must have talked to half the people in the village, including Fred Dawlish, the man who was passing Dr Chandler in his car as they went by Wisteria Cottage. He remembers Chandler, and he remembers seeing another car at the side of the road, but he says he was too busy trying to avoid a collision to notice anything about it, and he doesn't remember seeing any men at all.'

'And I suppose,' said Paget, turning to Ormside, 'no one has seen Newman's van, since there's no mention of it on the board?'

'Not a whisper,' the sergeant told him. 'And nothing on Doyle, either.'

Paget eyed the boards bleakly. 'If that van is on the road, it should have been spotted by now,' he said. 'So, since we have virtually nothing to go on in Newman's case, the only thing we can do is concentrate on Doyle. Have we searched our own records and those of the surrounding areas for the times he's been brought in after one of his drunken binges? There may be something in there that would give us a clue about his background.'

'Already done, sir,' Molly told him, 'and there was nothing. It's always the same pattern: he's picked up and brought in after drinking himself into a stupor, spends one and some-times two nights in the cells, pays his fine and leaves. He's never given anyone any trouble, and apart from his drinking, he's got a clean record.

'I also checked with the DVLA in Swansea, but the infor-mation they have is rubbish. It's all false, so it would appear that Doyle has managed to live and work here for years under false pretences. In fact,' she concluded, 'I'm not even sure that the man's name is Doyle.'

Jimmy Greenwood had hardly slept at all over the weekend. He couldn't get the image of the people in the van at the bottom of the quarry out of his mind. And when he had managed to fall asleep, he'd dreamt about them.

He hadn't actually *seen* anyone down there himself, but Sean had – at least he *said* he had when he'd gone back for a second look over the edge, and he'd sounded pretty serious.

'There's two of 'em down there,' he'd said with conviction. 'Lovers, probably. Happens all the time. They jump off cliffs holding hands and smash themselves to pieces on the rocks, then the pieces are swept out to sea and they're never seen again.'

'Why do they do that?'

'I dunno, do I? Maybe their parents won't let them get married 'cause they're too young or something, so they jump so they can be together forever.'

'Sounds a bit daft to me,' Jimmy said. 'Why don't they wait till they're older? Besides, they couldn't jump off holding hands when they were in a van. And it wasn't a cliff, it's a quarry, and the bits can't get washed out to sea in a quarry.'

'That's because we're not close to the sea and there aren't any cliffs round here, you twit. And they aren't going to drive all the way to Barmouth or somewhere like that, are they? Not when they've made up their minds. I mean once they make up their minds to do it, they wouldn't want to hang about, would they? Anyway, I know there's two of 'em down there because I could see their hair waving about in the water inside the van, and their eyes are all bugged out 'cause of the pressure.'

'I didn't see any hair waving about,' Jimmy said as they

left the field. 'Besides, men's hair doesn't wave about. It's too short.'

Sean snorted. 'You didn't see it because you didn't get close enough, did you? If you don't believe me, we can go back and you can take a closer look like I did. I'll hang on to you while you look over the edge.'

He made as if to turn back, but Jimmy said, 'No, no, I believe you. It was just the bit about the hair, that's all.'

'My brother's got long hair,' Sean pointed out, 'so's old Tadpole at school.' Old Tadpole was Mr Tadman, their maths teacher.

'Can't see him driving over the edge of the quarry with a *girl*,' Jimmy said scornfully. 'He's too old for a start, and I can't see a girl fancying Tadpole either?'

Mr Tadman was all of thirty-five.

'We're not talking about Tadpole, though, are we?' Sean said with exaggerated patience. 'We're talking about those two lovers in the van, and he could have long hair couldn't he? Well, he did,' he corrected himself hastily, 'or it wouldn't have been floating about, would it? Look at Samson in the Bible. He had long hair.'

'But what's-her-name cut it off, didn't she? And he didn't drive off the top of a quarry.'

'He could've in a chariot,' Sean shot back. He kicked a stone and watched it lift and fly over the hedge. 'Just think,' he said, 'by the time somebody else finds them, they could be skeletons, still sitting there with their seat belts on, holding hands.'

'What about the horses?'

'What horses?'

'The ones pulling the chariot. Bet they wouldn't jump off a cliff.'

'They would if somebody was whipping them like they did in them days. Anyway, we're not talking about what they did then, are we?' Sean said and changed the subject.

Jimmy didn't *really* think that Sean had seen hair waving about. How could he when all he'd been able to see was the outline of the van, and then only dimly through several feet of water? And he was quite sure Sean hadn't seen any faces, but the images remained, and they were even stronger when he went to bed on Saturday night. Which was why he took his torch to bed with him and switched it on under the covers.

He'd gone to sleep eventually, but when he woke in the middle of the night, the torch had gone out. He tried the switch several times, but the batteries were dead. He pulled the covers over his head, but the images were still there, skeletons with hair waving about and eyes bugged out because of the pressure.

He had to go to Sunday school that morning, but he shot round to Sean's house as soon as lunch was over.

'You didn't *really* see anyone down there, did you, Sean?' he said when they were alone.

'Did, too,' Sean said stoutly. 'Well, I didn't actually *see* their eyes bugging out, but that's what happens under water. It's like when you dive, except they didn't come up.'

'But if it's because of the pressure,' Jimmy said slowly, 'why would their eyes bug out? Wouldn't it make their eyes bug *in*?'

'Don't you know anything?' Sean asked irritably. 'The water gets up their noses, doesn't it? And in their mouths and that's what makes them bug out. I read it in a book.'

'We've got to tell someone,' Jimmy said. 'I mean somebody will be looking for them and wondering what's happened to them.'

'Can't though, can we? And you'd better not, either, unless you want a good hiding from your dad for being at the quarry.'

'We could ring the police and not say who we are.'

But Sean was adamant. His own father wouldn't hesitate to use his belt if he found out that his son had disobeyed him, and he wasn't prepared to chance it.

But after one more sleepless night, the thought of those two dead people beneath the water was more than Jimmy could bear. He didn't care what Sean said; someone had to be told. He had to pass a phone box on his way to school, so he would pop in there and disguise his voice. He'd seen them do it on TV. He'd use a handkerchief over the mouthpiece, except he didn't have a handkerchief, but probably a Kleenex would do just as well.

He practiced lowering his voice as he walked to school. 'This is a man calling,' he said gruffly. 'I want to report –' what was it Sean had called it? Oh, yes, he remembered now – 'I want to report a suicide pack.'

He froze as a heavy hand dropped on his shoulder. 'Talking to yourself, Greenwood?' Mr Tadman asked good-naturedly.

'That's not a good sign, especially first thing on a Monday morning.' He glanced at his watch. 'Better hurry along if you don't want to be late.'

There was a strong breeze funnelling through the valley, and as Tadman strode ahead and Jimmy trotted along behind, the boy couldn't take his eyes off the teacher's hair. It was streaming out behind him in the wind – for all the world as if it were floating in water.

'I'm telling you, that's the name of the place, Tregalles! It's where Doyle was born.'

'Oh, yeah? And my name is Muggins, I suppose,' Tregalles snorted. 'Oh, no, Len, I'm not falling for that one. I suppose you'll be telling me next it's just a short hop over the mountain from Ballykissangel. Right? Sorry, Len, but even you have to admit Ballybunion is a just a little bit far-fetched.'

Jenny Morris, one of the civilian clerks in the office, who had just brought Ormside a sheaf of faxes, said, 'There's a golf course there. You'd know that if you played golf, Sergeant. It's something like one of the top ten in the world.'

'Oh, yes? So you're in on this as well, are you?' Tregalles scoffed. 'Ballybunion!'

'It's in County Kerry,' Jenny said as she dropped the faxes in Ormside's in tray. 'You can look it up on the map if you don't believe me.' She smiled winningly at the sergeant and walked away.

'All right, Len, what's all this about? So you've got something on Doyle, but stop messing me about and let's have it. You say they think they've traced an uncle. Where is he really?'

'All right, don't believe me then,' he said, 'but I'm telling you, he's in a nursing home in Ballybunion in County Kerry. His name is Brendan O'Hanlon, which was Doyle's mother's maiden name, but he's not exactly with it most of the time, if you know what I mean. The local police, the Garda, say that Doyle did come from there, but his mother and father died years ago, and there are no other relatives living in the area. And if Doyle is on their patch, they have no knowledge of it.'

'Any chance that they've got the wrong O'Hanlon?'

'No. In one of his more lucid moments, O'Hanlon produced several Christmas cards sent to him over the years by Doyle from his caravan site address, so they have the right one. The Garda are sending copies through so we can compare the handwriting with that of Doyle – assuming we can find enough to compare it with.'

'Well, I'll believe that,' Tregalles conceded, 'but I'll give you odds there's no such place as Ballybunion.'

'You're on,' said Ormside, and reached for his wallet.

Tregalles eyed him suspiciously, then shook his head. 'Forget it,' he said. 'This is a set-up, isn't it? You and Jenny. So maybe there is such a place and you wanted me *not* to believe it so you could make money on a bet.'

Ormside sighed heavily. 'Didn't they teach you *anything* in school where you come from?' he asked. 'Tell you what, Tregalles: go and take a look on a map for Ballybunion. Start with Ireland. It's that big island to the left of England.'

'I was about to call you,' Ormside said when Paget looked in before leaving for the day. 'They've found Newman's van; it's at the bottom of an abandoned quarry under about five feet of water. An anonymous call came in to Control at 16.10 from a pay phone. They thought it was some kid having them on at first, but when he said there were two dead people in it, they dispatched a car. They spotted the van, but they couldn't tell from above if there was anyone inside or not. One of the uniforms volunteered to go down to see if there was anyone inside, but it turned out to be empty.

'They can't get a diver or a crew to winch it up until later tonight at the earliest, so they've cordoned off the area, put a guard on it and left it till morning. They reckon they can have the van up by about nine if all goes well. I imagine you'll want Tregalles out there when they bring it up?'

'I do, but I'd like to see this for myself, so give me the location and tell him I'll meet him there first thing tomorrow morning.'

Ormside frowned. 'I thought you were over at New Street for most of the week,' he said. 'Finished early, did you?'

Something like a grin tugged at the corners of Paget's mouth as he said, 'It seems the chief constable scheduled Mr Brock for the race relations and sensitivity course,' he said, 'so he won't be available for the rest of the week.'

Ten

P aget and Tregalles arrived just in time to see several scenes of crime officers going over the ground leading to the edge of the quarry directly above the submerged van.

'Not that we expect to find very much,' one of the men confided. 'Too many people have trampled the ground, but we may have better luck with the van.'

Two divers were already in the water, attaching cables, and a short time later the van was winched up to hang motionless over the water for several minutes while the water drained out of it before it was pulled on to tarpaulins spread out on the ground. Men in white overalls and gum boots converged on it, examining the exterior thoroughly before proceeding further.

There was remarkably little damage to the vehicle. The windscreen was gone, as was the glass in one headlight, and the driver's door wouldn't close properly, but other than a few scratches and dents on the bodywork, it was relatively undamaged. The number plates were missing, but there was no doubt that it was Newman's van. Tregalles had brought along the picture Emma Baker had loaned them, and it matched in every detail.

'Did you see any ladders and a roof rack?' Paget asked one of the divers. 'They probably came off when the van hit the water.' He showed the man the picture.

The diver shook his head. 'Nothing like that down there,' he said, 'and being metal, they won't have floated away, will they? Besides, we've searched the length and breadth of the pool looking for the driver and there's nothing down there except for the odd bit of rubbish people have tossed in there from time to time. But we will be bringing up everything we find in the immediate vicinity just in case.'

More water spilled out of the van when the back doors were opened. The interior was a jumble of water-soaked tools, electrical cords, rags, a jacket, odd lengths of wood, brushes, tins of paint and the remnants of wallpaper rolls. One of the paint tins was open, and the oil-based paint had congealed in a glistening sheen on top of the water to cover everything in what looked like green slime.

'But no body,' Tregalles observed quietly, 'so at least we can still hope that Newman is alive.'

Charlie had been thinking about it all morning, but there was nothing for it but to ask Grace straight out. The last thing he wanted to do was become involved in the private lives of his staff, but something was seriously wrong here, and he had to find out what was going on for his own peace of mind.

He'd noticed that Grace hadn't been quite herself, lately. Nothing he could put his finger on, exactly, but it seemed to him that she was more withdrawn, even distant at times, and that wasn't like her at all. Even some of her co-workers had noticed it too, in fact he'd heard one of them making a joke of it, suggesting that it might have something to do with the fact that she was now living with Paget, and wasn't getting a full night's rest. Charlie himself had asked her if she was all right on a couple of occasions, but she'd always assured him that she was fine.

He had to admit that he did tend to put more work her way simply because he knew it would be dealt with expeditiously, but he hadn't asked her to work overtime for weeks. Yet Paget had spoken as if it were a regular thing.

Charlie could see Grace's cubicle from where he sat in his own office. He saw her look up at the clock, then stand up and stretch. Lunchtime. He watched as she picked up her coat and her handbag and started for the door.

Perhaps it was best left alone. There might be a very simple, logical explanation for whatever was going on. On the other hand, if he didn't do it now, the mystery would continue and he'd be left wondering. Besides, now was as good a time as any because the office would be deserted for at least half an hour before the others returned to their desks.

Charlie almost let her go, but as she passed his door, he found his voice and called out, 'Grace! Can you spare a minute before you go to lunch? Do you mind?'

She stopped and stood there in the doorway, a faintly questioning look in her eyes as she shook her head. 'No, I don't mind, Charlie,' she said. 'What's the problem?'

'Of course it's possible that Newman drove the van into the quarry himself, but I doubt it,' Paget told Alcott later that day. 'But my gut tells me that someone else drove it over the edge, and if that is the case, I'm afraid I don't hold out much hope of finding Newman alive. The van's been taken in for further examination, but with everything covered in paint and water, I doubt if they will have much luck with it.

'As for Doyle, we've traced what appears to be his only living relative in Ireland, but there is no indication that Doyle himself is over there. And that's all we have at the moment, but I'll let you know the minute we have anything more.'

'That will be the day when you see Ormside crack a smile,' Tregalles was fond of saying of the dour sergeant, but when Paget came down from Alcott's office, Ormside was looking positively cheerful.

'Looks like things are finally beginning to move,' he told Paget. 'Trader Sam in Tenborough had a man come in this morning to try to sell him Emma Baker's camera. Fortunately for us, Sam had his wits about him, because when he recognized the camera from the description we circulated last week, he told the chap he was pretty sure it was worth a lot of money, but he would like his partner to see it before making an offer. He said his partner knew more about cameras than he did, but he wouldn't be in until after lunch. So he told the man to come back about two this afternoon, when he said he was sure he would have some good news for him. In fact, Sam doesn't have a partner, but he persuaded the punter to leave the camera with him, and gave him a receipt for it, so the man is bound to be back.'

'Any chance that it was Newman himself?'

'Not unless he's disguised himself as a middle-aged man who's going bald. They have him on the shop's surveillance tape. The man gave his name as Bernard Green when Sam made out the receipt, and I have someone checking that out now.'

Paget felt a surge of relief. Finding the van was one thing, but it was unlikely to be of much help in finding out what had happened to Newman. Now, at least, they would have someone to question. He glanced at the clock. 'Get a couple of men over there as soon as you can in case this man comes back early,' he said, 'and tell them to make sure they don't do anything to make him suspicious before they grab him and bring him and the camera back here. This is the first real break we've had, so let's not blow it.'

'Not to worry,' Ormside told him, 'they're already on their way, and they know what will happen to them if they let this chap slip through their fingers.'

Bernie Green squirmed in his seat as he watched Tregalles set the tape recorder in motion. He sat facing Paget across the table, hands in front of him, fingers laced tightly together. They were big hands with large knuckles that stood out like rows of white pebbles beneath the skin; the hands of a manual worker. His clothes, too, were those of a worker: thick woollen shirt, open at the neck to reveal the top of a grubby-looking vest, well-worn jeans and sturdy boots. His shoulders were narrow, his body lean and muscular except for a noticeable gut that bulged over his belt. His face had a thin, pinched look about it, and his receding hairline made it look even longer and narrower than it really was. A self-styled independent building jobber, he described what he did as 'a bit of this and a bit of that, if you know what I mean'. He was forty-one.

He claimed to have bought the camera around ten days ago from a man he'd never seen before in a pub called the Black Swan in Tenborough. He said he'd felt sorry for the man, who told him he was having to sell his photographic equipment, because he'd lost his job, his wife was ill, and he needed the money. Green said he'd offered the man thirty pounds for it, and finally bought the camera for forty.

'I used to do a bit of photography myself,' he explained, 'so I knew it was worth more than forty quid anyway.'

'By about ten times as much,' Paget observed. 'Weren't you surprised that he was willing to sell it for so little?'

'Yeah, well, like I said, he was down on his luck.'

'And I suppose it never occurred to you that the camera might be stolen?'

'Honest to God, if I'd known that, I swear I'd've never

touched it,' Green said earnestly. 'I mean, he seemed so genuine it never occurred to me. He told me he'd been laid off work and his wife needed an operation, but she couldn't get in for another six months or more, so he was trying to raise enough money to go private. He really sounded desperate.' Green shook his head and looked sad. 'And I believed him,' he said with a sigh. 'I s'pose it's more fool me for being soft-hearted, and I'll have to say goodbye to my forty quid as well.'

'You can say goodbye to hell of a lot more than forty quid if you're lying to us,' Tregalles told him.

'You live here in Broadminster,' said Paget, 'so what were you doing in a pub in Tenborough?'

'Ah, well, I'd had a bit of work over there, and it was getting a bit late, like, so I stopped in for a drink and bite before coming back home.'

'If you thought you were dealing in legitimate goods, why did you go over to Tenborough to try to sell it?' asked Paget. 'More work over there, was it?'

'Yeah, well, I did just happen to be over that way, so I thought I'd pop in. I'd heard Trader Sam pays better prices than anyone here.'

'And you just happened to have the camera with you, I suppose?' Paget didn't wait for an answer. 'However, be that as it may, let's assume for the moment that there was such a man in the Black Swan. What reason did he give for not offering the camera to a reputable dealer?'

Bernie sniffed and rubbed the back of his hand across his nose. 'He said he'd tried, but they said they weren't interested in film cameras, not with digital being all the thing now, and they wouldn't give him anything for it.'

'And you believed that as well?' Paget scoffed. 'The lens on this camera alone is worth two or three hundred quid at least. And if, as you say, you were into photography at one time, you would have known that, and so would any dealer. You knew very well that you were buying stolen goods – *if* you bought it at all.'

Bernie was trying to look calm, but he couldn't stop sweating. 'I don't know what you're talking about,' he said stubbornly. 'I told you, I bought it fair and square from this bloke, because I thought I was doing him a favour.'

Tregalles snorted. 'Doing *him* a favour?' he echoed. 'Forty quid for a camera that's got to be worth ten times that much? Doing yourself a favour, more like. What else did you buy off him?'

'Nothing. Honest to God. It was just the camera.'

'So we won't find any more stolen goods at your house when we search it, right?'

Green looked startled. 'You can't do that!' he yelped. 'You've got no right!'

'Believe me, Mr Green, we have every right,' Paget told him. 'In fact, your house is being searched as we speak, so I suggest that you start telling us the truth, because I don't believe a word you've said. I don't think you bought this camera in a pub; I don't think you bought it at all. I think you took it from a man who disappeared a couple of weeks ago, a man who is most likely dead, which means that you are in a lot of trouble, Mr Green. In fact, you could be facing a charge of murder. At the very least you will be charged with receiving stolen goods, so we will need your fingerprints.'

But Green was shaking his head violently. 'I don't know anything about all that,' he said hoarsely. 'Honest to God, I'm telling you the truth! I bought this camera off a bloke in the Black Swan, and if I knew who he was, I'd tell you. But I can't because I've never seen him before. What else can I say?'

'You could try the truth,' Tregalles told him, 'because what you've told us is a load of cobblers, and we don't believe a word of it. You are either very stupid, or you think we are. So what it comes down to is this: *if* you bought the camera from this mysterious stranger in the pub, you would have to be pretty stupid to not know it was stolen. On the other hand, if you did *not* buy the camera from a man in a pub, then you stole it yourself from the man who is missing, and you know what happened to him, so I say we hold you as prime suspect. No matter how you look at it, Bernie, you have a lot of explaining to do.'

Green looked to Paget for help, but the chief inspector's face might have been cast in stone. Green's shoulders slumped and he spread his hands in a gesture of resignation. 'All right,' he said wearily, 'so maybe I did *sort* of suspect the camera was stolen, but I could see the bloody thing was worth hundreds, and all he was asking was fifty quid. I mean, it was too tempting to pass up. But it's not as if I *knew* it was stolen is it? I mean it's not the same, is it?'

Tregalles looked at Paget and just shook his head. 'Go on then,' he told Bernie, 'let's assume that there actually was a man in the pub. We want to know when you bought the camera off him, and we want a description of this mysterious man. And if it turns out you're wasting our time and giving us false information, we will have you for obstruction as well, so make sure you get it right first time, because you won't get a second chance. Understand?'

The man swallowed hard and nodded. 'I think it was last Saturday week,' he began hesitantly, but Tregalles stopped him there. 'I don't want to hear what you *think* it was, Bernie; I want to know *exactly* when it was, so stop mucking about and get it straight.'

'Yeah, well, it was a week ago Saturday; I remember now. But I don't know what I can tell you about what he looked like. I mean he was pretty ordinary. A bit taller than me; sort of average-looking. I don't know what else to say. Honest to God, I don't.'

Paget scooped up the plastic bag containing the camera, and stood up. 'We're wasting our time here,' he told Tregalles. 'Perhaps his memory will improve in the peace and quiet of the cells.' He looked at the clock. 'This interview is terminated at 16.22.'

Five thirty, and Paget was on the point of leaving for the day when Tregalles came into his office. 'Green's been lying his head off,' he said. 'They found two ladders and a roof rack in the yard where he stores stuff next to the house. The ladders and roof rack appear to match those in the picture Emma Baker gave us, but we'll soon know for sure, because I spoke to Emma and she told us what to look for.

'And for a man who says he makes his living by doing a bit of this and a bit of that, he's got a lot of expensive gear in the house. Flat screen TV, computer and a laptop for the wife; sound surround, that sort of thing.'

'By "that sort of thing" I presume you mean the sort that falls off the back of a lorry?'

Tregalles nodded. 'They're checking serial numbers on everything,' he said. 'They reckon it's stuff that's been nicked at some time or other, so even if he didn't nick it himself, he's been doing a bit of quiet fencing and trading on the side. His wife isn't saying anything.'

'Are we quite sure he doesn't have form?'

Tregalles shook his head. 'Not under the name of Green at any rate, but we'll see what happens when they run his prints. He probably does the odd bit of business in the pubs, but he didn't come by those ladders or the roof racks from some bloke flogging them in the Black Swan.'

'On the other hand,' said Paget, 'the very fact that some of Newman's equipment has been found in Green's yard could mean there is evidence there that will tell us what happened to Newman. I want the house and yard sealed off, guarded through the night, and a full-scale search of both first thing tomorrow morning. And just in case Mrs Green is involved, I want her out of there tonight. And let's make sure that Green finds out what's happening; it may just shake him up a bit.'

Paget sat back and thought for a moment. 'Better get someone over to the Black Swan as well,' he said, 'and check out the story Green told us. Now that we know about the ladders and roof rack, his story about buying the camera there doesn't hold up. But it may be that he meets his contacts there to arrange delivery or payment for stolen goods, so have his picture shown around to see if anyone remembers him and anyone he may have met there.'

'Right,' Tregalles said as he stood up to leave, then stopped at the door. 'Emma Baker reckons she can identify the roof racks,' he said. 'She says Newman painted them recently with Rustoleum metal paint, and the leftover paint is still there at the cottage. She says Newman scratched his initials on some of his tools, but she's not sure if he did on the ladders.

'Anyway, I've arranged for the paint to be picked up first thing in the morning in case Forensic needs to do a comparison with the paint on the roof racks, and Emma is prepared to come in as well if we think she can help.' The sergeant grimaced. 'I didn't really want to call her,' he confessed, 'because I knew it wouldn't take her long to realize that now that his stuff has started to turn up, the chances of finding Newman alive are pretty slim. And I was right. She picked up on it straight away. I think that's why she offered to help.'

'Perhaps she can,' said Paget slowly. 'It might save us from overlooking something that she would recognize as belonging to Newman if she could be there during the search of Green's premises. Do you think she'd do it?'

Tregalles nodded. 'I'm sure she would,' he said. 'In fact, I think she'd be only too happy to be part of it and help us out. I'll have a word and let you know.'

Grace made sure she left town on time that evening. Charlie had been sympathetic, but clearly disappointed that she wasn't prepared to confide in him, and he'd made it clear that he was not prepared to lie for her or say she had been working overtime when that was not the case.

'And I wouldn't ask you to,' Grace told him. 'I have never told Neil that I was working overtime; never used you for an excuse, and I'm not asking you to back me up in any way. I have to admit that I have allowed Neil to *think* I've been working overtime, and I feel guilty about that, but I have to sort this out in my own way, and I need time.'

'What if he asks me point-blank about your working overtime?' he said. 'I covered for you yesterday because I wanted to find out what it was all about, but I'm sorry, Grace, I won't do it again if he asks.'

'I know,' Grace said quietly, 'and I don't expect you to. But as I said, Charlie, I just need time to resolve this in my own way, that's all.'

Charlie sighed. 'Neil's no fool, you know,' he said. 'How long do you think you can keep this up, Grace? He's bound to become suspicious at some point. Wouldn't it be better to tell him whatever it is you're into? The man loves you, Grace; I'm sure he would understand and help you if you would only give him the chance.'

How long *could* she keep it up? she wondered now as she made her way home. As Charlie had said, Neil was no fool, and there had been times when she'd caught him looking at her in a way that made her wonder if he wasn't already suspicious about the number of times she'd been late coming home.

And then there were Neil's probes about her flat in Friar's Walk. Why didn't she give it up? Why keep it now that she had moved in with him? Thank God he didn't know about Perelli's offer or he would *really* be wondering what she was up to. She hated keeping him in the dark, but she was convinced it was for the best.

Two months. That was how long it had been going on, and she couldn't see an end to it. The situation was becoming desperate; *she* was becoming desperate. If only she could get a full night's *sleep!* Thank God Neil didn't know how many hours she'd lain awake or roamed the house while he slept.

She crossed the bridge and the house came into view. Good, Neil's car wasn't there. She had time to wash and tidy up – and try to calm herself before he arrived.

Eleven

Ormside had a message for him from the night duty custody officer when Paget arrived the following morning. 'Looks like Bernie Green's memory has improved after a night in the cells,' he said, 'and he wants to talk to you. Shall we have him in? He's not due to be arraigned until eleven.'

Paget shook his head. 'Tell him we're busy for the moment. Let him stew a bit longer.'

And they were busy, which was fine with Paget after days of wondering if they would ever get a break. The team had been dispatched to search Green's house and yard, and Molly Forsythe was on her way to pick up Emma Baker and the remains of the paint she said had been used on the roof rack.

Forensic came back with the information that many of the prints found on the camera were blurred or indistinct, but those made by Green and Trader Sam were plain enough. There were also prints inside the camera, two of which belonged to Green; a partial that might belong to Emma Baker, and two other partials, as yet unidentified. It was thought that one might belong to Newman, but there was not enough of it to make a positive match.

'It could belong to Emma's sister, since it was her camera,' Paget pointed out, 'so let's get someone out there to take her prints for comparison.'

At nine o'clock Paget told Ormside to have Green taken into an interview room, then went up to Alcott's office to spend the next half hour or so going over the morning's influx of paper with Alcott's secretary, Fiona. Alcott was over in New Street, sitting in for Brock while he was away on the course, so Paget was sitting in for him – at least in theory. In fact it was business as usual, with Fiona doing ninety percent of the work. Efficient as ever, the secretary had everything sorted, together with explanatory notes where necessary, and ready for him to sign or deal with.

'About time, too!' Green burst out when Paget and Tregalles finally entered the interview room. The man looked as if he hadn't slept at all; his eyes were bloodshot, the flesh around them was dark, and his hands refused to stay still. 'I've been asking to talk to you since six o'clock this morning, but I might as well have been talking to the bloody wall for all the notice they took down there.'

'We do have other things to do, Mr Green,' said Paget mildly as he and Tregalles took their seats. He nodded for Tregalles to start the tapes. 'So what is it you wanted to tell us? Thought a bit more about this man who sold you the camera, have you?'

Green pursed his lips. 'Yeah, well, I've been thinking about that,' he said, 'and I might have got a couple of things wrong, if you know what I mean. See, I got confused yesterday when your lot jumped me in the camera shop, then brought me in here and started firing questions at me. I got a bit muddled.'

'Are you saying you wish to change your story?'

'Yeah, well, a bit here and there.'

'Like the bit about the ladders in your yard, for example? The ones with your prints all over them? And the roof rack? Must have been a bit difficult getting those home from the Black Swan.'

'Along with the body,' Tregalles put in. 'Where did you bury it, Bernie? Save us digging up the whole yard if you tell us. What *did* you do with Newman's body?'

Green's eyes grew wide and his hands made pushing motions as if they could somehow ward off the allegation. 'Honest to God, I don't know anything about a body,' he said hoarsely. 'I mean, I might have taken the camera, but he told me I could have the ladders and racks for storing . . .' He broke off and took a deep, deep breath as he sank back in his seat and looked up at the ceiling.

'Storing what?' snapped Tregalles. 'Newman's body? Is that it, Bernie? Someone drove into your yard and said, "Don't mind if I drop this body off for a day or two, do you, Bernie?" Deliver it in a white van, did he, Bernie? With roof rack and ladders?'

Colour darkened Green's face. 'It wasn't *like* that,' he breathed, 'and I told you, I don't know anything about a body; it was the van, and he told me I could have the rack and ladders because he knew I could use them in my work. He wanted it out of sight because it might be recognized and remembered with the ladders on.'

'You said you *might* have taken the camera,' said Paget softly. 'Is it *might* or *did*, Mr Green?'

'All right, so I *did* take the camera, but that's all I took,' Green burst out. 'I wish I'd never laid eyes on the bloody thing. But what was I supposed to do, eh? I mean, the van was just sitting there the whole day. I just wanted to see what was inside, that's all. He said they were going to get rid of it where nobody would ever find it, but I knew there was some sort of gear inside because I heard it banging about when they drove in over the kerb. I thought they were going to take it to the crusher, and I couldn't see stuff going to waste if it was any good, so I worked the lock and got it open. I didn't dare take much in case they knew what was there and had a look inside before they got rid of the van. But when I unrolled this piece of rag and found the camera, I couldn't pass that up. I mean, it would have been a crime to put that in the crusher, so I got a stone about the same size and wrapped it in the rag and put it back.'

'And the film?' Tregalles said sharply. 'What did you do with the film, Bernie?'

'There wasn't any film.' Bernie saw the look of scepticism on both their faces. 'Honest to God! I'm telling the truth,' he said desperately. 'There wasn't any film.'

'You keep saying *he* told you this and that, but you also mentioned *they*. How many were there?' asked Paget.

Bernie clasped his hands in front of him and concentrated his gaze on them. 'Two,' he said so quietly that Tregalles had to ask him to repeat the word for the tape.

'Let's have their names, then. Assuming they really exist, of course.'

'Oh, they exist all right! But I only know one, and I wish I'd never met him, because it's his fault I'm here now. But I never had a choice, did I? Not with the wife who's always banging on about her poor brother, and how he almost went to gaol for something he didn't do, and it's not his fault if he's down on his luck and all he needs is a bit of a helping hand. But I'm telling you, the bastard's rotten through and through, but she can't see it. *Won't* see it, more like.

'Yeah, that's right,' he said, meeting Paget's gaze for the first time. 'He's my brother-in-law; the wife's brother, Gerry.'

'Full name and address,' Tregalles said.

'Gerry Fletcher, and he'll bloody kill me if he ever finds out I shopped him. So if you could sort of keep it quiet about where you got his name . . .?'

'Address,' Tregalles said.

Bernie gave a sigh of resignation. 'He lives over Lyddingham way,' he said. 'About halfway between Lyddingham and Whitcott Lacey. It's a conversion. Used to be a pub, but they turned it into two cottages, and his is the nearest one to Whitcott. They're out there all by themselves. You can't miss them. The pub's name is still over the door. It's called the Mason's Arms'

'I know where that is,' Tregalles said. 'What does he do for a living – other than kill people and nick their vans?'

Green ignored the jibe. 'Last I heard he was working for some removals business. Used to be a long-distance driver for one of them inter-continental firms. Been all over in his day, France, Germany, Italy and the like, but he packed that in sometime last year. Said it was too hard on his back, all that driving them big vans, so he's working local now.' He snapped his fingers. 'RGS, that's the one! RGS Removals and Storage. Came in a year or so back. Built that big storage place out Whitcott Lacey way. A big barn of a place out there all by itself. Locals didn't like it; they reckoned it would look ugly. Spoil the look of the country-side, they said – not that it isn't spoiled already with some of the crap they're putting up these days – and fought it tooth and nail. But it went through, of course, and it doesn't look all that bad, sitting back there behind those trees. You can hardly see it from the road.'

'Married? Single?' Tregalles asked.

'Gerry? Single – well, more or less. I think he might be living with some bird called Rose. Least he was. Don't know her last name.'

'What does she do?'

'Dunno if she does anything. I only ever saw her the once. Ran into her and Gerry while we were out shopping a couple of months back. He never actually said they were living together, but they had a lot of stuff in their trolley. Shirley – that's the wife – reckons they are.'

'You said Fletcher *almost* went to gaol once. What was that for?'

'Something to do with Customs. Never did know exactly. Gerry always said it was a case of mistaken identity, but I reckon there must have been something to it, because it was about that time when he started to complain about his back and said he couldn't take the long hauls any more.'

'Let's get back to the night you hid the van in your yard. What, exactly, did Fletcher tell you?'

'He didn't *tell* me much at all,' said Bernie, 'but he was pretty scared. He said he had to get the van off the streets before daylight, because he'd be in deep shit if he was caught driving it.'

'So you must have known that whatever it was he was involved in, it had to be something serious; something criminal, and yet you made no attempt to report it.'

'Yeah, well, like I said, he's Shirley's brother.'

'You mentioned a second man. What can you tell us about him?'

Bernie shook his head. 'Nothing,' he said. 'He stayed in the car out on the street both times.' He saw Paget's eyebrows go up. 'Honest to God, I'm telling you the truth. See, he followed Gerry in a car, and he stayed in it while Gerry drove the van in, then Gerry got in the car and they left. Same thing happened that night when they came back for the van. He stayed in the car, then pulled out and followed Gerry when he drove off in the van.'

'When did all this take place?'

'Week ago Friday. Like I said, Gerry came banging on the door about half six Friday morning just as we were getting up, and said he had to find a place to hide the van. I told him to bugger off and find somewhere else to hide it, but he kept on about how he could go to gaol, then Shirl got in on the act, so I gave in when he promised he'd have it out of there as soon as it was dark Friday night. Even then the bastard lied. Didn't turn up till close to midnight, but at least the van was out of there and I was glad to see the back of it and him.'

'You said the second man stayed in the car, but you must be able to describe the car at least,' said Paget.

'It was dark. It was just a car, and to tell the truth I didn't hang about watching it go.' His voice turned to pleading. 'Look, I'm doing the best I can, for Christ's sake! I don't know what kind of car it was. And to tell you the truth, I didn't *want* to know.'

'Right,' said Paget as he looked at the time. 'We still have half an hour before we have to get you to court, so we might as well make sure we've got everything right. Let's start with Gerry Fletcher arriving at your house on the morning of Friday, March the seventh. What time did you say that was, Mr Green?'

Returning from lunch, Ormside found Tregalles studying a large-scale map of the area around Whitcott Lacey and Lyddingham. 'Still looking for Ballybunion, are you?' he asked innocently. 'You won't find it on that map, Tregalles; I told you it was in Ireland.'

'You know where you can put your Ballybunion, don't you?' Tregalles muttered, still scanning the map. Then: 'I'm trying to remember exactly where this RGS Removals and Storage is out there. I'm sure I've seen it, but I can't remember if it's on this side of Whitcott Lacey or the other.'

'You could always phone and ask.'

'I could, but if I'm going out there to pick up Gerry Fletcher, I'd rather not talk to them beforehand.'

'Then ask Emma Baker.'

Tregalles frowned. 'What's she got to do with it?'

Ormside rolled his eyes. 'Call yourself a detective?' he sniffed. 'Emma Baker serves behind the bar in the most popular pub in the area, right? She might even know Fletcher. Chances are he drinks there, and I'm sure she can tell you exactly where RGS is. Give Molly a shout at Green's place and see if Baker is still with her.'

'Yes, she's here,' Molly said when Tregalles asked the question. 'I'll put her on.'

'Have you ever seen a man by the name of Fletcher in the Red Lion?' Tregalles asked Emma. 'Gerry Fletcher?'

'Fletcher?' she said slowly. 'Yes, I think I know who you mean. Fortyish, whey-faced, grubby-looking, fair hair, pony-tail, ring in his ear – is that him? Comes in quite regularly.'

The description Bernie Green had given them was not quite so unflattering, but the ponytail struck a chord. 'Sounds like him,' Tregalles said. 'Did you ever see him with Mark Newman?'

'No, and I can't see Mark having anything to do with him. Why?' There was a catch in her voice as she said, 'Have you found something, Sergeant? Please tell me if you have.'

'I wish I could,' he told her, 'but we are following a lead. And while you're here, can you tell me where RGS Removals is?'

'It's on the Lyddingham road – well, a bit off it behind some trees, actually, but you can just see it from the road, and there's a sign. About two, maybe two-and-a-half miles up the road from Whitcott. Come to think of it, this man Fletcher might work there, because he's been in several times with a man named McCoy, who works there. He's also been in with another man; Roy something-or-other I think his name is. Does Fletcher have something to do with Mark's disappearance?'

'We think he may be able to help us,' Tregalles said, avoiding a direct answer. 'And thanks for your help, Emma. Have you had any luck over there?'

'Afraid not. They haven't found anything of Mark's other than the ladders and the roof rack. Still,' she said hopefully, 'that could be a good sign, couldn't it, Sergeant?'

What she was really saying was that they hadn't found Mark Newman's body, which was a plus in her eyes. 'Could be,' he said as lightly as he could manage. 'Would you put Molly back on?'

'Are you coming in?' he asked when Molly came on the line.

'Might as well,' she said. 'They've turned everything inside out; even had the sniffer dog in, but they found nothing. I only heard one side of your conversation with Emma, but it sounds as if you have something.'

'Could be the break we've been waiting for,' he told her. 'But I have to go now. Talk to Len when you come in. He'll fill you in.'

Tregalles took with him a young constable by the name of Lyons. His first name was Francis, but the only one who ever called him that was his mother, because he had been nicknamed Leo since his first day at school. He was tall and thin, a fresh-faced youngster with pale skin and red hair. He didn't look strong enough to compete in marathons, but that was what he did whenever he had the chance.

Tregalles drove into the RGS compound and parked in a space reserved for customers. Business appeared to be brisk as he and Lyons got out and made their way inside the cavernous building.

There were three loading bays with direct access to the warehouse and a storage area for containers. A fourth bay, separated from the others by a floor-to-ceiling breeze block wall, looked more like a garage, complete with pit, compressor, hydraulic hoist and a bench full of tools.

'Can't stop,' a worker told him when the sergeant caught his attention. 'Mid-month removals. Been going like blue-arsed flies since the weekend,' he called over his shoulder as he continued on his way.

'I'm looking for the manager. A Mr Skinner?' Tregalles called after him.

'Office,' the man said, jerking a thumb upward to a row of windows overlooking the loading bays. 'Last one at the end of the corridor. Stairs are over there,' he added, pointing.

Tregalles and Lyons followed directions and discovered a set of wooden stairs leading up to a corridor that ran the full width of the building. There were windows on both sides of the corridor, one side looking into the offices where heads were bent over desks strewn with paper, while the windows on the other side of the corridor looked down on a narrow strip of gravel punctuated by potholes and weeds between the back of the building and a chain-link fence.

The door to the office at the end of the corridor was closed, but Tregalles could see two men inside. The man seated behind the desk was big. He wasn't young by any means, but he looked as if he could shift a grand piano all by himself. Shoulders the width of the proverbial barn door, thick neck, bald head, round, shiny face, and a stomach that made it difficult for him to sit close to his desk.

The man who faced him across the desk could be anywhere from forty to fifty. Lean, lined face, hair turning grey, he sat hunched over in his chair, a cigarette smouldering between his fingers.

As Tregalles raised his hand to knock, the man behind the desk looked up and caught his eye. He said something to the man facing him, who got up and came to the door. 'If you're looking to make a booking,' he said, 'they can take care of you in the office at the other end of the corridor.' He began to close the door, but Tregalles held it open and displayed his warrant card.

'Detective Sergeant Tregalles and DC Lyons,' he said, loud enough for the man behind the desk to hear. 'We're looking for Mr Skinner.'

'Detectives?' The big man frowned as he lumbered to his feet and came out from behind the desk. 'Roy Skinner,' he boomed, extending his hand in greeting as Tregalles and Lyons entered the office. His hand engulfed that of the sergeant, who wondered if his fingers would ever come apart again when he finally withdrew them from the big man's grasp. 'And this is Jack McCoy, my foreman.' The second man merely nodded, for which Tregalles, hand still stinging, was grateful. 'Detective Sergeant – what was the name again?'

'Tregalles. And Detective Constable Lyons.'

'Right.' He stood there for a moment in the middle of the room as if trying to decide whether to return to his seat and invite them to sit down, or ask what they wanted first. He chose the latter and looked concerned as he asked, 'What's this all about, then, Sergeant?' he asked. 'Not an accident, I hope?'

'No, nothing like that,' Tregalles assured him, 'but we would like to ask you about one of your people.'

Skinner eyed Tregalles suspiciously. 'What's his name, then, and what's he supposed to have done?' he demanded as he walked back to his desk and sat down. McCoy had already returned to his seat, and it was almost as an afterthought that Skinner waved Tregalles to the only remaining chair. Lyons was ignored completely.

'His name is Gerry Fletcher, and we'd like to talk to him. Is he here?'

Skinner cast a quizzical glance at McCoy and said, 'Is he, Jack?' Then: 'Jack looks after the day-to-day running of the place,' he explained, 'so everyone, other than the office staff, reports to him. Is Gerry about, Jack?'

McCoy eyed Tregalles narrowly as he took another drag on

his cigarette before butting it. 'He's doing a few errands in town,' he said. 'What do you want him for?'

'Do you know when he'll be back?'

'Not for a while, I shouldn't think. He's got quite a bit to do, so he may not come back here when he's finished. He may go straight home.'

'When you say he's in town, which town do you mean? Broadminster?'

'That's right. You probably passed him on your way here.'

'Can you tell me what he's driving?'

'Just hold on a minute,' Skinner broke in. 'Before we go any further, I'd like to know why you want to talk to one of my employees. It must be something dodgy if they sent out two detectives to talk to him, so I want to know what's going on. What's he supposed to have been up to, then?'

'Sorry, Mr Skinner, but I'm afraid I'm not at liberty to discuss that at the moment. All I can tell you is that we believe he may be able to help us with our enquiries into an incident that probably has nothing to do with his employment here. And while we're on the subject, what is his position here?'

Skinner cocked an eye in McCoy's direction, who shrugged and said, 'Driver, loader, you name it. Bit of a mechanic as well. People who work for us have to do anything and everything; it's that sort of job.'

'I must say I was surprised at the size of the place and the activity downstairs,' Tregalles said. 'It seems almost too big for the area.'

'That's the argument people used when they were trying to stop us from coming in here,' Skinner said, 'but it's not. You see, we're a distribution point for the local area, and we combine several functions. You'll see all sorts of big-name container carriers off-loading here. Some of them will bring in as many as four furniture containers at a time. They off-load here for local distribution, and by local I mean anything within roughly a forty-mile radius. We use smaller carriers to take the individual containers on to their destination, or we store them here, depending on what the customer's instructions are. Of course, we do a lot of local moves as well.'

'And you've been here how long now?'

'Two years, give or take.'

'And how long has Fletcher been with you?'

It was McCoy who answered. 'Four or five months, something like that. Used to be a long-distance driver for one of our affiliates, but it got a bit too much for him; away from home a lot, and those long runs can take a lot out of you over time, so they asked if we would take him on. I think he grew up around here, Tenbury Wells or somewhere near there.'

'Ever had any trouble with him?'

McCoy butted his cigarette. 'Like what?' he asked.

'In any way. Would you call him a reliable worker?'

'He wouldn't be here if he wasn't,' Skinner growled. 'Slackers don't last long round here.'

'Mr McCoy . . .?'

The foreman shook his head. 'He does his work like everyone else. As Mr Skinner said, if you don't pull your weight around here, you don't stay long.'

'What do you know about him off the job? Do you socialize at all?'

'Socialize?' McCoy chuckled softly. 'We see enough of each other at work. Our boys work all hours, day and night sometimes, and when they do go home they hope to hell they aren't called out again to do a rush job. A few of us might go down the pub the odd time on a Friday or Saturday night, but even that doesn't happened very often.'

'Right,' Tregalles said. 'But I still need to know what sort of vehicle Fletcher is driving. And the registration.'

McCoy looked to Skinner for direction. 'You don't just want to *talk* to Fletcher, do you?' Skinner said. 'You're going to arrest him, aren't you? Why else would you want to know what he's driving? You're going to have him picked up, aren't you, Sergeant?'

Tregalles's expression gave nothing away. 'As I said in the beginning, Mr Skinner, we need to talk to Mr Fletcher, but that is all I can tell you at the moment.'

Skinner stared hard at Tregalles for a long moment, then shrugged. 'Might as well give it to him, Jack,' he growled. 'The sooner we get this thing sorted, the better. But what I want to know is, will we be a man short tomorrow?'

'It's entirely possible,' Tregalles said. 'In fact, I'd say it's more than likely.'

Twelve

'That's right, a Mazda pickup, red, or at least it used to be. I'm told it's pretty badly faded now.' Speaking on his mobile phone after leaving the RGS compound, Tregalles gave the description and registration to Ormside, along with a list of the places Fletcher was visiting.

'But time's getting on, and his foreman seems to think he'll be going straight home when he's finished, so that's where Lyons and I are going now.'

'Any reason to believe they will try to warn Fletcher?' Ormside asked.

'They might try to contact him to ask what he's been up to, but I have no reason to believe the company is involved in any way. In fact, their main concern seemed to be whether or not he would be in to work tomorrow. Anyway, we'd better be getting on, so I'll keep you posted, Len.'

'Looks like we're in luck,' said Lyons a few minutes later as they came within sight of the roadside cottages. There was an open space in front of the two cottages, and a small red truck with rusted bodywork was drawn up with its bumper almost touching the rough stone of the cottage on the left.

'Pull in behind the truck and block it off,' Tregalles ordered, 'then let's go and see what Fletcher has to say for himself.' A curtain twitched behind a tiny front window, but neither detective saw it as they got out of the car. 'Better take the back in case he tries to do a runner,' Tregalles said as he put his hand on the bonnet of the truck. It was still warm, so it hadn't been there long.

They'd done a good job of converting the old pub into two separate cottages. In fact, if it hadn't been for the name of the pub over one of the doors, it would have been almost impossible to tell which was the original entrance. Built of local stone, the cottages sat at the foot of a steep hill, which, like most of the others in the area, was dotted with sheep. An idyllic setting if it hadn't been for the steady stream of traffic passing within twenty yards of the two front doors.

The sergeant moved to the front door and knocked, then knocked again, harder, sharper.

'All right, all right, I'm coming,' a plaintive voice called out. The doorknob rattled and a slim, attractive woman of indeterminate age opened the door. She had long, chestnut-coloured hair, pale, almost translucent skin, and soft brown eyes that narrowed suspiciously when Tregalles held up his warrant card and introduced himself.

'I'd like to talk to Mr Fletcher,' he said, preparing to step inside. 'And you are . . .?'

'None of your business who I am,' she said coldly, barring his way. 'And he's out.'

'Is he?' Tregalles said, feigning surprise. 'In that case, would you mind telling me what the Mazda is doing here with its engine still warm? We know that's what he was driving.'

'Don't know anything about that,' she said tartly, 'but he's out and I don't know when he'll be back.' She tried to close the door, but Tregalles held it open.

'In that case, I'll come in and wait,' he told her, and thrust the door back so hard that the woman was forced to step back. He took a folded paper from his pocket and held it up. 'I have a warrant for his arrest, which entitles me to search these premises. So please stand aside, unless you wish to be arrested yourself for obstruction.'

Tregalles closed the door and locked it, pocketing the key before pushing past the woman to move swiftly through the cottage, pausing only long enough to check each room to make sure that Fletcher wasn't there. It wasn't hard; the rooms were small and there was virtually nowhere he could hide. Tregalles opened the back door and told Lyons to come inside and check upstairs. The stairs were narrow, the ceilings low, and Lyons had to bend almost double to avoid hitting his head as he went up.

'Now,' Tregalles said, 'you must be Rose. Rose what? Let's have your last name.'

'Ryan,' she said grudgingly as Lyons came down the stairs shaking his head. 'Look under the bed, did you?' she taunted. 'I told you he isn't here.'

'But he *was* here,' Tregalles said. 'Do you have another car?'

'Chance would be a fine thing,' she snorted. 'Does it look as if we're made of money?'

Lyons was shifting uncomfortably from one foot to another.

'There's a shed out back,' he said hesitantly. 'I didn't have a chance to check it before you . . .'

The words trailed off because Tregalles was no longer listening. He'd seen the look on Rose's face at the mention of the shed. He moved swiftly to the back door and out into a small garden overgrown with weeds. Lyons followed, jostling with Rose as she tried to get to the door before him.

'Gerry, go!' she screamed as Tregalles reached the shed. The door of the shed was locked, but even as he stood back to kick it in, he heard the unmistakably cough of an engine being started, and he knew exactly what it was. Lyons ran past him, heading for the back gate. Tregalles slammed his foot against the door. A crack appeared in the wood beside the door, but it refused to give completely. The sound inside the shed rose to screaming pitch as Tregalles slammed his shoulder against the door and stumbled through.

The stench of fumes engulfed him and stung his eyes as he watched the motorbike shoot through the wide-open double door at the back of the shed. Lyons, coming around the outside, lunged at the rider, but Fletcher's fist caught the constable on the side of the face, and Lyons crashed to the ground.

Tregalles ran to help him up. The lad would have a thumping great bruise to show for his efforts, he thought glumly, but that wasn't going to count for much with Paget when he had to explain how Fletcher had managed to escape.

Bike and rider were by now close to the top of the hill, and it looked to the sergeant as if Fletcher had his hand raised as he crested the rise. With two fingers extended, no doubt, he thought angrily. Tregalles looked back toward the house. Rose Ryan was standing at the door, waving madly, and the expression on her face was one of pure triumph.

Paget was reviewing the events of the day with Ormside when the call came through from Tregalles. The sergeant took the call. He listened for a moment, then said, 'He's here now, so you had better tell him yourself.' He handed the phone to Paget, then sat down again.

There were things to be done; a manhunt to be set in motion, and neither he nor Paget would be leaving early tonight.

The clock on the church tower at the end of the village was striking the half hour as Grace made the turn toward home. She winced at the sound, not so much because of the dull, flat notes of the ancient chimes, but because it reminded her she was late once again. There wasn't much point in trying to make up the time now, but still she felt she had to hurry as she went down the hill and up the other side to the house.

She almost clipped the post as she swung into the driveway and hit the brakes within inches of the garage door. She turned the engine off, dropped the keys into her handbag, and it was only then she realized that Neil's car wasn't there, and there were no lights on in the house.

Grace took a deep breath and put a hand to her chest as if to quell the turmoil within. She sat like that with her eyes closed for several minutes, willing herself to be calm. The sound of a car climbing the hill broke into her thoughts, and she wondered if it was Neil. The car went by and she let out a sigh of relief as she got out and entered the house.

The light on the answering machine was blinking. She pressed the button and listened to the message.

'Sorry, Grace, but I'm afraid we're going to be tied up here for a while. We've had a break on the Newman case, but . . . Well, let's just say there are complications. Tell you about it when I get home. I tried to get you on your mobile but it was switched off. I think it's time you changed the battery. Don't bother about a meal; I'll grab something to eat in town, so expect me when you see me. I should be home by ten or so. Love you, Grace. Bye for now.'

Grace sank into a chair and closed her eyes. Thank God for small mercies. She'd been wondering ever since she left town how she was going to explain to Neil why she was late again. She'd managed to avoid lying to him in the past, and she'd promised Charlie that she wouldn't blame her absence on overtime, but if Neil should decide to ask a direct question, she didn't know what she would say.

The truth? Oh, no. Right or wrong, she'd decided that wasn't an option. She glanced at the calendar on the wall, She'd hoped to have everything cleared away long before now, but the situation was getting worse. In fact, tonight had been a disaster. And Perelli, who was a decent man, and had always treated her well, had been almost threatening when he'd rung her at work a couple of days ago. She put her hands to her head; she felt as if the walls were closing in around her, suffocating her.

If only she could sleep . . .

Thirteen

It was an uncharacteristically subdued DS Tregalles who entered Paget's office the following morning. He'd handed in his typed report, together with that of DC Lyons, late last night, and Paget had taken them home with him. Now, as he sat down to face the chief inspector across the desk, Tregalles braced himself for what was to come.

Paget set the report aside and leaned back in his chair. 'There are discrepancies between your version of events and the version Lyons gave me,' he said. 'I take it you've read his report, Sergeant?'

'I have, sir.' It wasn't often Tregalles called Paget 'sir'. Usually it was the less formal 'boss', but he didn't want to take any chances this morning. 'It really wasn't his fault that the shed was overlooked,' he hurried on. 'It was mine. Seeing the truck outside, I assumed that Fletcher was inside, and I told Lyons to watch the back door in case Fletcher tried to make a run for it when I went in the front. Lyons did exactly as he was told. It was only after we failed to find Fletcher in the house that there was any reference made to a shed.'

'But Lyons was at the back of the house, and it should have occurred to him that the shed could be a hiding place, and yet he failed to mention it until later. He's quite clear about that in his report. Do you disagree with that, Sergeant?'

'No, sir, but it was still down to me, wasn't it? I mean I was in charge, and I knew the lad was green; I should have given him better instructions. And he did identify the bike Fletcher was riding as a Harley 1200 Sportster. Seems cars and bikes are a bit of a hobby of his.'

But Paget wasn't about to be sidetracked. 'Better instructions such as . . .?' he asked.

Tregalles shrugged. 'I should have thought about outbuildings, at least,' he said.

'And so should he,' Paget said firmly. 'He may be green,
but he saw the shed, yet failed to mention it when you opened
the back door.'

'Because I told him to check upstairs,' Tregalles countered.
'It was only after we were sure Fletcher wasn't in the house
that Lyons mentioned the shed, and I can't really fault him
for that, sir.'

'But I can,' said Paget sharply. 'Otherwise, how is he going
to learn? He failed to inform you immediately about the shed,
and we are now engaged in a very costly manhunt for someone
who may well be involved in a kidnapping or murder or both.
At least Lyons recognizes that in his report, which is something in his favour, I suppose, but he will be disciplined,
Sergeant.'

'He did try to stop him, and got a black eye for his trouble,'
Tregalles reminded Paget.

But Paget wasn't to be moved. 'I have taken that into consider-
ation,' he said, 'but the fact is Fletcher still got away, didn't
he?' His tone softened as he said, 'I'm recommending the loss
of two days' pay and a note on his record, which will be
reviewed in six months. If his record is good at that time, the
note will be expunged. Any objections?'

Tregalles shook his head. In fact he was relieved. If that
and the bollocking Tregalles had given Lyons the night before
didn't do the trick there was no hope for the man. But in truth,
anyone could have made the same mistake, and Tregalles
mentally crossed his fingers as he asked, 'What about me,
sir?'

Paget eyed the sergeant thoughtfully. 'We all make
mistakes,' he said, 'and I don't think there is anything I can
do that will make you feel any worse about this than you do
already, so consider yourself reprimanded, and let that be an
end to it.'

Tregalles let out a long breath, then frowned. 'Not that
I'm not grateful,' he said, 'but what about Lyons? I mean if
I'm—'

'The reason I'm taking action against Lyons,' Paget cut in,
'is to make sure he understands early on in his career that he
has to be alert at all times, and how costly a mistake such as

he made can be. Not just in time and money, but to the community at large, because we may well have a killer on the loose due to his negligence. Now, we've spent enough time on this already, so send Lyons in on your way out.'

'I spoke to Mr Skinner, the manager of RGS Removals,' Ormside said in answer to Paget's query later that morning, 'and he assured me he would let us know if Fletcher returned there or if they heard from him – not that Fletcher's likely to under the circumstances, but you never know. But we do have one bit of good news – well, more or less. Forensic found what we assume to be Fletcher's prints all over the van they pulled out of the quarry the other day. At least they match those we took from the steering wheel of the Mazda and from his personal things at the cottage.'

Paget frowned. 'How did they manage that?'

'I asked the same question,' Ormside said, 'and they told me that the van is old and coated with oil and grime, and with the water being cold, some of the prints were still readable. And because a lot of the tools were wrapped up and more or less protected, they were able to lift prints from those as well. There are some they can't identify, but they've isolated Newman's, and Green's – seems like Bernie had a look at just about everything in the van while he was at it.'

'Which gives us a solid link between Fletcher and Newman's van, and that means we won't have to rely solely on Green's testimony that his brother-in-law was involved, if or when it comes to court. Anything else?'

'Yes, there is,' Ormside told him. 'They've identified prints belonging to a Nicholas Slater, an Australian. Started out as a wrestler, then went on to do stunt work for film and television; been all over the world, but no one will touch him since he got into a fight and almost killed one of the crew during a shoot. He has a history of fighting, and he did time for that assault. Released three years ago, and there's been nothing on him since. Last known address is Moorfield Road, Coventry, but that was two years ago, so there's no telling where he might be now.' Ormside handed Paget a faxed copy of the man's form sheet, together with a picture of a heavy-set man with blond hair.

'Could be one of the men the doctor saw getting out of a

car outside Wisteria Cottage,' Paget observed. 'Pull half-a-dozen photographs of people of similar build, and do the same with Fletcher's picture, and have them shown to the doctor in Lyddingham. And ask Emma Baker if she has seen Slater before, possibly in the company of Fletcher.

'It's probably a waste of time,' he continued, 'but get on to Coventry and ask them to check out that address. I doubt if Slater still lives there, but you never know your luck. And make sure you tell them that, whatever they find, we don't want him alerted.'

Tregalles spent much of the rest of the day working with the team searching Fletcher's cottage for anything that might suggest where the man had gone, but they came up empty handed. Rose Ryan was questioned at length, but insisted that, as far as she was concerned, Fletcher worked for RGS, and he wasn't involved in anything beyond that. She said she'd never heard of Newman or Doyle; she knew nothing about a van, and she had no idea where Fletcher might be now.

But one thing Tregalles discovered while going through bills and papers was that Fletcher owned a mobile phone, and mobile phones could be traced. He hadn't said anything to alert Rose, but he had taken note of the number and passed the information on. If Fletcher used his phone, or even switched it on, the area he was in could be identified. It might not tell them exactly where he was, but it would certainly narrow the field.

Bernie Green was questioned again, and he, too, claimed he had no idea where Fletcher might be. 'I mean it isn't as if we're close or anything. He may be my brother-in-law, but I can't help that, can I? It's not as if we're mates? Besides, he never tells me anything when I do see him, so, sorry, but I can't help you.'

The Red Lion in Whitcott Lacey was packed. Emma Baker had been rushed off her feet all evening, and she would be glad when it was over. 'Same again, love,' a small man in a tweed cap said, pushing his empty glass across the counter. 'Banks Bitter,' he elaborated as she raised a questioning eyebrow. 'And an Artist's Special for the wife.'

Emma nodded. She pulled the pint, then set about mixing the cocktail. Whisky, lemon juice, sherry and grenadine. She did it mechanically, her thoughts taken up with trying to remember where she had seen the man in the far corner before. He was talking to Roy Skinner. She didn't think they had come in together, but they were chatting away as if they knew each other quite well.

Was he the same man who was there the night Mickey Doyle had taken off in such a hurry? Emma wished she could be sure. He certainly wasn't the man in the suit whom Olive Kershaw had described to the detectives, and yet the thought persisted that there was a connection. Someone had ordered a whisky and taken it over to Doyle. Could it be the man in the corner?

But even if he was the same man, she told herself as she took Tweedy Cap's money and rang it into the till, there was no reason to believe that there was any connection between him and the events that followed. She saw so many different people in the pub every evening that they became blurred in her memory, but if there was even the slightest chance that she was right, it would be worth following up.

She tried not to look at the man, but her eyes were drawn to him again and again. Impossible to judge his age with any degree of accuracy; he could have been anywhere from thirty to forty. Lean, compact body, clean, well-defined features, dark hair that could do with a trim, but it looked good on him all the same. Casually but neatly dressed, clean-shaven, and a smooth, almost olive-coloured skin that made Emma wonder if there could be some Italian or possibly Greek blood there. He was a very good-looking man, attractive and quietly spoken, and yet there was something disturbing about him – a feeling she couldn't quite define.

Emma sighed. She was probably being silly, she told herself, but silly or not, she couldn't let it rest. She *had* to find out more about him. And if nothing came of it, at least she'd know she'd tried to help the police in their search for Mark. Emma made up her mind. Like most non-locals, the man had probably come by car. So, if she nipped out the back door when he left, she could take down the make and registration of his car, and pass the information to Molly Forsythe. Molly would know what to do. She'd find out who the man was.

Fourteen

Tregalles attended the morning briefing, but his thoughts were on the conversation he'd had with Audrey the night before.

'There's nothing to be gained by worrying yourself silly over what happened, now is there?' Audrey had said as they got ready for bed. 'I told you Mr Paget would understand. And you said yourself that he took it very well.

'I mean it could have happened to anybody, couldn't it? You said yourself that the Lyons boy is green as grass, and you can't be expected to think of everything, now can you? And Mr Paget recognized that. The lad lost a bit of pay, which will sharpen him up a bit, and you said yourself that you didn't get so much as a slap on the wrist, so stop stewing over it.'

'But I'm still responsible for what happened,' Tregalles insisted as he slid into bed. 'I know it and Paget knows it, and while it might not appear on my record, it will always be there in the back of his mind.'

'Now you *are* talking rubbish!' his wife told him. 'I'm sure as far as Mr Paget is concerned, it's all over and done with, so stop getting your knickers in a knot and forget it. I'm sure he has.'

But Tregalles wasn't so sure. He kept remembering what Paget had said about Lyons being responsible for causing a costly manhunt and possibly putting anyone who tried to stop him at risk. Paget hadn't come right out with it – he didn't have to, because Tregalles was all too well aware that he was equally responsible, and it had taken him a long time to get to sleep.

'You still with us, Sergeant?' asked Paget sharply.

Tregalles could feel the colour rising in his face as he said,

'Sorry, boss. I . . . aahh was just wondering if there is any way we can get Fletcher to use his mobile without him becoming suspicious.'

'Too risky,' Paget said dismissively. He turned to Ormside. 'Did we get anything on this man Slater?'

'Emma Baker said she recognized him from the picture Forsythe showed her yesterday. She said he used to come in every so often with Fletcher, but she hasn't seen him lately. Forsythe also checked with Dr Chandler, but he said again that that he never saw the faces of the men outside Wisteria Cottage.

'But speaking of Emma Baker,' the sergeant continued, 'Forsythe had a call from her first thing this morning to tell her about a man who came into the Red Lion last night. She says she isn't completely sure, but she *thinks* he might have been there the night Mickey Doyle took off in such a hurry. Anyway, she took down the number of the car he was driving, and asked Forsythe to check it out.' The sergeant shook his grizzled head. 'Got to give her top marks for trying,' he conceded, 'but personally I think she's clutching at straws.'

Paget nodded. 'I suspect you're right,' he said. 'On the other hand, we have so little to go on, we can't afford to overlook anything, so have it checked out anyway.'

'I'll do my best,' Ormside told him, 'but things are stretched pretty thin right now. I've got two people off sick; four people tied up on the rash of car thefts we've had this month, and two more on surveillance at the school on Broadview road, where it's been reported that a man in a van has been asking children to help him find a lost dog.'

He was about to go on, but Paget cut him off with a wave of his hand. Ormside wasn't one to complain about his work-load unless there was a very good reason, so the chief inspector didn't need to be convinced. 'Tregalles is free,' he said. 'He can fill in for you at least until we get some sort of break in the Newman case.'

He looked at his watch, his mind already on other things. 'Now, I must be off,' he said as he began to move away. 'I'll be either in Mr Alcott's office or over at New Street. More meetings,' he added with a grimace, 'but you can get me on my mobile if there's anything to report.'

*   *   *

Ormside scribbled a note on the scratch pad in front of him, then put the phone down and called across to Tregalles, who had just got off the phone himself.

'Gerry Fletcher switched his phone on and made a call,' he said, 'so now we know the area he was in when he made it. Funny thing, though, he didn't call home or his work as you might expect; he called some farmer who lives out in the hills between the Lyddingham and Ludlow roads.'

'Where was he calling from?'

'Great Malvern area, so he didn't go very far from home. The police there have been alerted to watch for him.'

'I don't suppose we know if he's stationary or on the move?'

'We won't know that until he switches on and makes another call,' Ormside pointed out, 'but it would be interesting to know why he called that number. It belongs to an Evan Roper.'

Tregalles shoved his chair back and stood up. 'Do we have an address for the farm?' he asked.

'Sort of, but let's take a look at the map.' Ormside led the way to a pull-down large scale map of the local area and pointed to a brown patch on the edge of Clun Forest. 'I'd say it has to be on one of those roads there,' he said, tracing one of them with his finger. 'Shouldn't be all that hard to find. Simplest thing would be to go out there and ask the locals.'

Tregalles eyed the map thoughtfully. 'Look, Len,' he said earnestly, 'do me a favour and hold off on telling Paget about this, will you? Just for an hour or so. Give me a chance to go out there and find out who Gerry Fletcher called, and why.'

Ormside shook his head. 'He isn't going to like it if he finds out,' he said. 'You heard him say he wanted to be kept informed if anything happened.'

'But he didn't say it had to be right away, did he?' Tregalles countered. 'If I can get out there and get a line on Fletcher, it might sort of offset the balls up I made of letting him get away in the first place. Just an hour or so, Len. I'll keep in touch.'

'Well . . .' It was clear the sergeant wasn't keen on the idea, but on the other hand, Tregalles did deserve a chance to redeem himself. 'Go on, then,' he said, 'but keep me informed every step of the way. And if Paget should call in I'll have to tell him.'

'Fair enough,' Tregalles said as he grabbed his coat. 'Let's hope Alcott keeps him tied up for the rest of the morning.'

Fifteen

'Mrs Roper?'

The thin, sharp-featured woman eyed Tregalles suspiciously 'That's right,' she said, 'and whatever it is, we don't want any.' She would have closed the door if Tregalles hadn't prevented it.

'Detective Sergeant Tregalles,' he said, displaying his warrant card. 'Is your husband at home?'

The woman peered closely at the card through steel-rimmed glasses before answering. 'He's somewhere about,' she conceded. 'What do you want him for?'

'Just want to ask him a few questions, that's all. And, since you're here, I'd like to ask you a few questions as well. May I come in?'

'Place is a mess,' she said cryptically. 'We've had the workers in, and I'm busy. So tell me what you want to know and let me get on.'

'I'm looking for a man named Fletcher,' he said. 'Gerry Fletcher. Do you know him?'

Lips compressed, the woman nodded. 'I know him, well enough,' she said. 'Why?'

'Do you know where he is?'

'No, I don't any more than I know where he was over the weekend. He promised he'd be here first thing Saturday morning, but he never turned up. Next thing I hear the police want to talk to him, but they didn't say what for on the wireless. So what do you want him for?'

'We think he may have information about a missing person,' Tregalles told her. 'And the reason I am here is because we understand that Fletcher rang this number earlier today. Did you take the call?'

'No.'

'What about your husband? Did he take a call from Fletcher?'

The woman shrugged. 'Might have done while I was out collecting the eggs,' she said, 'but he didn't say.'

'So you know nothing about the call?'

'No.'

'Where can I find Mr Roper?'

'He'll be out the back. You can go round if you like.' Without waiting for a reply, she closed the door and Tregalles heard the key turn in the lock.

The yard behind the house was empty, but Tregalles heard the rattle of a bucket coming from inside one of the old stone buildings at the far end of the yard. He was about to walk toward the sound, but stopped to take in the view of the valley behind the farm.

The ground dropped away sharply to the valley bottom where a line of trees followed the course of a meandering stream. The grass was fresh and green, and sheep, many of them accompanied by playful lambs, were grazing their way across the hillside on the far side of the valley. The air was warm and clear beneath a cloudless sky, and the sun lay over the scene like a golden blanket. Tregalles was a city boy at heart, but even he was impressed with the magnificent scene.

Off to his left a narrow but well-travelled track snaked its way down the side of the hill to the valley floor where it ended at a long, low barn nestled in the trees. Some distance from the barn was a tractor, silent and still as if abandoned at the end of the last row of newly-turned furrows. There was no sign of a driver. Tregalles glanced at his watch. Even tractor drivers must stop for elevenses these days he decided.

'What do you want?' a voice asked suspiciously.

Tregalles turned to see a stocky, grey-haired man with a bucket in his hand, standing in the doorway of one of the buildings. The sergeant pulled out his warrant card and introduced himself.

'You must be Mr Roper,' he said. 'Your wife said you might be back here.'

'Did she, now? Didn't look like you were looking for anybody to me,' he said. 'What do you want?'

The man's belligerent tone annoyed Tregalles, but he was determined not to get off on the wrong foot. 'I was admiring the view,' he said. 'You're a very lucky man; it's like a little world of its own tucked away back here. It's beautiful.'

'For those as has time to stop and look at it, maybe,' said Roper dourly. He set the bucket down and took out a packet of cigarettes. He lit one and blew a stream of smoke in Tregalles's direction. 'Like I said, what do you want?'

'Gerry Fletcher. He rang you early on this morning.'

Roper, facing into the sun, squinted against it. 'So what if he did?'

'Why did he ring you? And more to the point, why didn't you let us know that he called you? You must have known we wanted to talk to him. Your wife said you heard it on the radio, and it's been in the papers.'

'None of my business,' Roper said with a shrug. 'He wanted money, and when I told him he wasn't having any of mine, he hung up.'

'Why would he think you'd give him money? How well do you know him?'

Roper drew on his cigarette. 'He's done some work for me from time to time,' he said.

'Is that all?'

'Don't know what you mean.'

'I mean you must know more about him than that. How long have you known him?'

'Couple of months.'

'So how did he come to work for you?'

'Met him in the pub one night,' Roper said. 'We got to talking, and I happened to mention that some of my machines are getting on a bit and they keep breaking down, and he offered to come out and take a look at them. Said he was good at that sort of thing. Didn't believe him at first, but turned out he knew what he was doing. Trouble is, you can't rely on him. He was supposed to come up here on the weekend to do some painting in the house, but he didn't come. Didn't phone, either, so when he rang this morning and said he needed money, I told him I've got no money to spare, and even if I had I wouldn't be giving it to someone who's in trouble with the police. He said it was all a big mistake, but I told him, mistake or not, I didn't want any part of it.'

'Did he say where he was calling from?'

'No.'

'Did he tell you anything that might help us find him?'

Roper shook his head. 'I've told you all I know,' he said.

'Is there *anything* you can tell me about his personal life?' Tregalles asked desperately.

Again, the farmer shook his head. 'Never asked and he never said.' He dropped the cigarette on the stones and ground it out beneath his heel, then picked up the bucket and walked straight toward Tregalles. If the sergeant hadn't stepped aside to let the man pass, he felt sure that Roper would have walked right over him.

Tregalles was surprised to find Paget there with Ormside when he returned to Charter Lane. Surprised and just a little bit apprehensive, because it was clear by the expression on both men's faces that something was amiss, and he was afraid it might have something to do with him.

'Len tells me you've been out to see the farmer Fletcher rang this morning,' Paget said as Tregalles joined them. 'What's his relationship with Fletcher?' The expression on Paget's face was grave, but he didn't sound angry or put out.

'Don't know if there is one to speak of,' Tregalles told him. 'It seems Fletcher has been doing some work for him, fixing up some old machinery, and he was trying to persuade Roper to advance him some money. But Roper turned him down and hung up on him.'

'Fletcher didn't say where he was?'

'Roper says not. He's a surly bugger, but I have no reason to doubt the man.'

Paget gave a non-committal grunt. 'Be that as it may,' he said, 'there's been another development since you left. A fisherman found a body in the Severn down near Highley. Apparently it's been in the water for some time. And from the description and the clothing, it could be Doyle, so it's even more important now that we find Fletcher, because he's the only lead we have to whatever is going on here.'

'You think he killed Doyle?' Tregalles asked.

'If he didn't he probably knows who did,' said Paget, 'and if that *is* the case, then whoever is behind all this won't want him talking to the police, so the sooner we find him the better. Have we had anything back from Great Malvern?'

Ormside shook his head. 'I alerted them as soon as we found out that Fletcher was in their area, but I've heard nothing since.'

'Keep checking with them anyway, and make sure they understand how important it is that we find this man.'

He turned his attention to Tregalles. 'I want you to attend the autopsy on this body they pulled from the river,' he said. 'Starkie wanted to delay it until Monday, but when I told him how important it was for us to find out if it is Mickey Doyle, he agreed to do it first thing tomorrow morning. Seven o'clock sharp, so make sure you get there on time, Tregalles. You know how he hates tardiness.'

Tregalles was not a happy man as he drove home that evening. It had been some time since he'd been an observer at an autopsy, but the one thing he remembered vividly was the smell. Just the thought of having to stand there and watch someone cut up a body that had been in the water for a couple of weeks was more than enough to start his stomach churning. And he couldn't help wondering if this, too, was some sort of punishment for allowing Fletcher to escape.

Eleven o'clock. Bernie Green waited for the chimes to finish before winding the clock on the mantelpiece and following his wife upstairs to bed. He was halfway up the stairs when he heard a tapping sound coming from somewhere at the back of the house. He went back down the hall and paused beside the open kitchen door. There it was again, louder now, insistent.

Someone was knocking on the back door. It had to be Hector Burgess, his next-door neighbour. He was the only one who came round to the back door, usually to borrow something, or to ask if Bernie had seen Wallace, his cat. Muttering under his breath, Bernie strode through the kitchen to the back door and flung it open.

'Do you know what time it is, Hec–?' he began, then changed it to: 'Bloody hell!' as Gerry Fletcher pushed his way inside and slammed the door behind him.

'Got nowhere else to go,' Gerry said breathlessly. 'I need the key to the yard, Bernie. Got to get the bike off the road.'

But Bernie was shaking his head. 'Oh, no,' he said. 'You're not barging in here like that. I'm in enough trouble as it is because of you. I'm out on bail, for Christ's sake! They could sling me back in gaol if they find you here. Oh, no. On your way, Gerry.' He reached over to open the back door, but suddenly found himself slammed against the wall with Gerry's forearm across his throat.

'So what have you been had for, then?' Gerry asked suspiciously. 'They catch up with you for fencing stolen goods, did they?'

'For trying to sell that camera I got from that van you brought in here,' gasped Bernie hoarsely. He saw the narrowing of Gerry's eyes, and knew he'd made a bad mistake.

'So *that's* how they got on to me,' Fletcher snarled. 'You bastard! I wondered, but I never thought it was you.' He rammed his forearm tighter against his brother-in-law's neck. 'You shopped me, Bernie? What did they promise you for that?'

'I didn't mean to. Honest to God, I didn't mean to, Gerry. They kept on and on at me. They were talking about *murder*, Gerry. Some bloke called Newman who's disappeared. You know what they're like, Gerry. Honest to God, I mean, what could I do?'

'You could've kept your bloody mouth shut for a start,' Gerry sneered as he lowered his arm. 'And for your information, I didn't have nothing to do with that. But you made a deal for yourself, didn't you, Bernie? You'd like to see me in gaol, wouldn't you? Well let me tell you something, Bernie, if I go down I'll make sure you go down with me. I'll swear that you were involved up to your neck. I'll tell them all about the stuff that goes in and out of your yard, and I'll tell them you and me have been partners for years. How would you like that, Bernie? Eh? Now give me the bloody keys. Like I said, I've got to get the bike off the road.'

Bernie fished the keys out of his pocket and Fletcher snatched them from his hand. 'Now don't go locking the door on me while I'm gone,' he warned, 'because I'm going to be staying here for a while. And don't try ringing the filth while I'm out, either, because like I said, if I go down, I'll take you with me.' He opened the door, then paused. 'Oh, yeah, and make yourself useful while I put the bike away; put the kettle on, or better still, get me a beer and find me something to eat. I haven't had a thing since lunchtime, and I'm bloody starving.'

Sixteen

G race stood there in the dark, willing herself to stop shaking so she could close the bedroom door quietly. She took a deep breath and used both hands to draw it shut, then made her way down the stairs and into the kitchen. She closed the door and switched the light on, then stood there for a moment to catch her breath. Her heart was pounding; she could feel it thumping in her chest; hear the pulsing rush of blood inside her head with every beat. Her nightgown felt like a second skin clinging to a body soaked in sweat, one minute hot, the next ice cold.

Grace wrapped her dressing gown around herself, then filled a glass with water and gulped it down. She refilled the glass, then sat down at the table and leaned her head back against the wall. She closed her eyes, waiting for the pounding in her chest to subside.

It was no good. She couldn't go on like this. There had to be another way, she told herself, because what she had been doing wasn't working. Perhaps you *should* tell Neil, the voice of reason said persuasively. Perhaps . . .

No! she told herself firmly. This was something she had to do herself, and she'd long ago decided that Neil was not to know. But how? Her mind began to drift . . . The glimmering of an idea began to form. Perhaps there *was* a way. If only she had the courage! Grace closed her eyes, concentrating hard . . .

It was dark beneath the water, dark and cold and such a long way to the surface and the light. She was trying desperately not to panic, but her arms refused to move; her hands were numb, and her fingers wouldn't work, and she couldn't hold her breath much longer. She kicked out hard and felt a sudden stab of pain . . .

Grace gasped for breath as she opened her eyes. Slumped over, head buried in her arms on the kitchen table, her neck was stiff and her shin was throbbing with pain. She lifted her head to look at the clock, blinking against the light as the nightmare faded.

Ten minutes past *six*? Could that be the *time*?

Grace bent to rub her leg. She must have banged it against the table leg when she'd kicked out in her dream, and it was tender to the touch.

She flopped back in her chair. Thank God it was Saturday. Grace didn't set the alarm on the weekends because that was the only time she and Neil could sleep in. The only time *Neil* could sleep in, she corrected herself; she hadn't had a decent night's sleep for weeks, although she would never admit that to Neil.

Still, she'd better get back to bed in case he woke up and wondered where she was.

Grace was partway up the stairs when she remembered. The alarm *was* set! Set for six thirty! Neil had set it himself, saying he couldn't afford to take the whole weekend off when there was so much to do. Tregalles would be attending the autopsy of the man they thought might be Doyle, and Sergeant Ormside would be in the office as well. 'Sorry, Grace,' he'd said, 'but there really is a lot to do, and I feel I should be there.'

She opened the bedroom door carefully, then slipped into bed. Neil didn't so much as stir as she pulled the covers over herself and snuggled down beside him.

Oh, to be able to sleep like that! she thought jealously as she lay there tense and rigid, waiting for the alarm to ring.

'There you are, love,' said Shirley Green as she slid a plateful of eggs, bacon, sausages and a large slice of fried bread in front of Gerry Fletcher. 'You get that down you and things won't look half so bad as they did last night. I don't know what Bernie was thinking about when he said you couldn't stay. Of course you can stay, can't he, Bernie? It will all sort itself out given time. You'll see.'

'The police want to talk to him about a *murder*, for God's sake!' Bernie protested from the other side of the table. 'That isn't the sort of thing that gets sorted, Shirl, so the sooner he's out of here the better for all of us. We could both go to gaol if he's found here.'

'That's not what they said on the telly. They said they believed he could help them with their enquiries. I watched it three times, Bernie, and that's what they said. I thought they could have used a better picture, though. Did you see it, Gerald?'

Fletcher spoke through a mouthful of egg and sausage. 'No, I bloody didn't,' he growled, 'and I've told you time and time again, Shirl, I don't like to be called Gerald. I never have liked it from the time I was a kid. It's Gerry!'

'You'll get the hiccups if you talk with your mouth full,' his sister told him. She set a plate in front of her husband, who looked at it and said, 'What the hell is this, Shirl?'

'What's it look like? It's scrambled eggs, that's what it is, Bernie. There's three eggs in that lot, and there's toast.'

'So where's the bacon and sausages?'

'Where do you think? If I'd known Gerald – Gerry – was coming, I'd've gone to the shops yesterday, but I didn't know, did I? You said yourself, last night, that he hadn't had much to eat all day yesterday, so I reckon he deserves it. Besides, he's my brother and a guest in this house.'

'For God's sake, woman, he's not a guest in anybody's house; he's a bloody fugitive from the law, and what you're doing is called aiding and abetting, and you can go to gaol for that, so the sooner he's out of the house the better.'

Fletcher emptied his mouth and jabbed a fork in Bernie's direction. 'Neither one of us would be in trouble if you'd kept your thieving hands off that camera and kept your gob shut,' he said. 'It's because of you I'm on the run, so you owe me, Bernie.'

Bernie scowled as he poked at his scrambled eggs. 'You can't stay here anyway,' he said stubbornly. 'The police have been round looking for you once already, and they'll be back. They'll expect you to come here.'

'Then you'll just have to make sure they don't find me, won't you, Bernie? So shut up and let me get on with my breakfast before it goes cold.' He shoved his mug across the table toward his sister. 'Tea's cold as well,' he complained. 'Put the kettle on, Shirl, and make another pot. And make sure it comes to the boil this time.'

* * *

Tregalles drove with the windows wide open, but even that did little to get rid of the smell. It was in his clothes, his hair, his mouth, his nose, and it wasn't going to go away until he'd showered, scrubbed and cleaned his teeth and changed. He hated autopsies, and he could never understand how anyone could ever get used to it, let alone make a career out of it.

This one had been particularly bad. His spirits had risen when Starkie remarked that the body was in fairly good condition, considering how long it had been in the water. 'Water's cold this time of year,' he said. 'Slows things down quite a bit.'

But the sergeant's hopes soon faded. The skin was like slime, peeling off at the touch, and Tregalles had come close to losing his breakfast as the pathologist began to cut and probe. He could sympathize with the poor fisherman who'd first hooked the body in the river. They said he'd been taken to hospital suffering from shock. Tregalles wondered if the man would ever go fishing again.

'Age would be about right for your man, and he didn't fall into the river accidentally,' Starkie said as he unravelled nylon rope from around the hands, feet and waist. 'And I doubt very much if he drowned. Forensic will be taking a closer look at it, but it looks to me as if there was a weight attached to the end of this rope, and it came loose. No telling how far he drifted after that. As to how he died, I wouldn't be too surprised to find that this broken neck had something to do with it.

'Prints are out of the question, of course. Teeth haven't been attended to in years, by the look of them, but if he ever did go to a dentist, they shouldn't have any trouble identifying him.' Starkie had gone on to say that two of the man's fingers had been broken at some time in the past, and his right leg was half an inch shorter than the left due to a poorly set break below the knee.

'Probably done about eight to ten years ago,' he said, 'and whoever did it should be shot. I hope to God it wasn't done in this hospital.'

But it was Starkie's next words that had caused Tregalles's heart to sink. The casual tone was gone as the pathologist said, 'I think you should take a closer look at this, Tregalles. Unless I'm very much mistaken, this man was tortured before someone broke his neck and finished him off.'

Tortured! The last thing Tregalles wanted to do was move closer, but Starkie had insisted. 'This man was burned,' he told the sergeant. 'Right through to the bone. It looks to me as if someone used a blowtorch on him. There, see? Scorch marks on the bones.' Starkie straightened up and took off his glasses to face Tregalles across the table.

'I've seen bodies that were charred to the bone after being in a fire,' he said tightly, 'but this . . .' He paused to draw a deep breath before going on, 'this was deliberate, and it's enough to make me wonder if we made the right decision when we abolished capital punishment.'

The pathologist looked grim as he put his glasses on again and bent once more to his task. 'Whoever did this,' he said softly, 'has no feeling and no conscience, so be warned, Tregalles. I don't know what this case is all about, but I *can* tell you that you are dealing with a very sick individual, and the sooner you can put him away, the better it will be for all concerned.'

Who were these people and what were they up to that they'd felt it necessary to go to such lengths? Tregalles wondered as he left the hospital. And if Doyle had been tortured, had Newman encountered the same fate? Tregalles had never met Mickey Doyle, but he'd built up a picture of the man in his mind, and he couldn't repress a shudder when he thought of what had happened to him.

Assuming, of course, that it *was* Mickey Doyle lying there on the metal slab.

As Starkie had said, proving whether or not the body was that of Doyle shouldn't be hard if the man had ever been to a dentist in recent years, but it might be quicker to talk to Doyle's elderly neighbour and cat-sitter, Mary Turnbull.

Tregalles picked up the phone and thumbed in his home number. He normally avoided making calls when he was on the move, but he was willing to make an exception this time. This was an emergency.

'Put the coffee on, will you, love?' he said when Audrey answered. 'I'm on my way home right now, and I'm going to need it. And I hope you haven't got any ladies in for elevenses, because I'm going to be bollock-naked when I come through that kitchen door and go upstairs for a shower.'

*   *   *

It was two o'clock in the afternoon by the time Tregalles arrived back at the office 'So, how did you get on with Mrs Turnbull?' Ormside asked as Tregalles poured himself his fifth cup of coffee of the day. 'Is the man they pulled out of the river Mickey Doyle?'

Tregalles nodded. 'When I asked her if she knew if Doyle had broken any bones in the past, she knew right away that we'd found a body. Poor old dear started to cry. I think she was really fond of him. Anyway, she told me about how he limped because of the way his leg had been set so poorly years ago, and she told me exactly how and when he'd broken his fingers, so I don't think there's any doubt that it's Doyle.

'I've been on to the local water authority to see if they can give us any idea of where the body might have gone in,' Ormside said, 'but I'm not holding my breath. They say they'll give it a try, but they don't hold out much hope. The river is high at this time of year, and it's running fast, so there's no telling how far the body drifted down river after the weights came off.'

Tregalles sipped his coffee. He couldn't get the picture of the body in the mortuary out of his mind. 'Anything on Fletcher?' he asked. 'Any more phone calls?'

'Not a peep since that one yesterday morning. And he hasn't called his wife or Bernie Green, at least not directly. But that doesn't mean to say he hasn't been in touch in some other way.'

Tregalles looked at his watch. 'I think I'll call round on Bernie again before I go home,' he said. 'You never know, he might let something slip. I see Lyons is here today as well. What's he doing?'

Ormside grunted. 'Trying to show us how keen he is, I expect,' he said. 'I told him he wouldn't be paid, but he said he knew that. Why?'

Tregalles shrugged. 'Thought I might take him with me. Show there's no hard feelings. He's not a bad lad; just needs a bit of ginger up his arse to keep him on his toes, that's all. So, unless you need him . . .?'

Ormside shook his head. 'Better than having him moping around here,' he said with feeling, 'so he's all yours.'

*   *   *

Bernie Green opened the door to the length of the safety chain, and peered through the narrow opening. 'I might have known it was you,' he grumbled, 'and you can leave off leaning on the bell for a start. What do you want?'

'Catch you in the middle of something, did we, Bernie?' Tregalles asked. 'Took you long enough to come to the door. I was thinking something might have happened to you and we might have to break in.'

'I was in the bog if you must know,' said Bernie. 'So what *do* you want?'

'Doing a bit of tidying up, then, were you, Bernie? What were you hiding this time? New camera to replace the one we took off you, was it? Mind if we come in?'

'Yes I do mind. And my brief told me I don't have to talk to you without him present, so you can sod off.'

'Just wanted to know if you've heard from your brother-in-law, Bernie. Have you?'

'No I haven't.' Bernie began to close the door but Tregalles's foot was in the way. 'Mind if we have a look round the yard, then?' he asked.

'Yes I do bloody mind! I told you, I'm not talking to you and you can't come in here or in my yard without a warrant, so get your foot out of the door.' For all his bluster, Tregalles could see that the man was nervous to the point where he was sweating, and he wondered why. But Bernie was right. He couldn't force the issue without a warrant.

Tregalles sighed heavily. 'I'd hate to see you and your wife go down as accessories to murder,' he said. 'Are you really prepared to spend the next few years in prison for protecting a killer?'

'I told you I don't know anything about that,' Bernie said. 'Just because he shifted the bloke's van doesn't mean he killed him.'

'Oh, not that one, Bernie,' Tregalles said. 'This is another one. Didn't Gerry mention it? Must have slipped his mind. Mickey Doyle is the name. Somebody – probably Gerry – broke Doyle's neck before dropping him in the river with weights on. Just happens that Doyle was seen talking to Newman not long before they both disappeared, and we suspect that Newman might have gone the same way. Just hasn't come up yet, but he will. Oh, yes, and we have Gerry's prints, as well as those of his mate, on the van we pulled out of the quarry where he dumped it.'

Tregalles turned to indicate Lyons. 'See that black eye?' he said. 'Your brother-in-law did that, Bernie, so he's also wanted for assaulting a policeman and evading arrest. You might keep that in mind if Gerry should happen to get in touch. You will let us know if that happens, won't you? I'll leave you my card. You might need it sooner than you think.'

Seventeen

Upstairs, standing to one side of the window in the front bedroom, Gerry Fletcher eased the curtain aside just enough to watch the two detectives go to their car. But they didn't get in immediately. Instead, they walked along to the entrance to the yard next door to the house, and one of them – the tall skinny one with the bruise on his face where he'd hit him – hoisted himself up to look over the wooden gate. He hung there for a moment, then dropped back and shook his head.

Looking for the bike, Gerry surmised. It was hidden well enough, but not if they came back with a warrant and really searched the place. He watched as the two men returned to the car and drove away, and was about to turn away when something familiar caught his eye. He squeezed his eyes shut and looked again.

There was no mistake.

He moved swiftly to the head of the stairs. 'Bernie!' he yelled. 'I need your binoculars.'

Bernie appeared at the bottom of the stairs. 'Never mind binoculars,' he grated. 'I want you out of here before they come back with a warrant.'

Fletcher almost leapt down the stairs to push Bernie aside. 'Shirley?' he bellowed. 'I need binoculars. Where the hell are they?'

Shirley appeared from the kitchen. 'What do you want them—' she began, but was cut off by her brother.

'For Christ's sake, just get the bloody binoculars, Shirl. When I say I need them, I don't mean next bloody week; I mean I need them now!'

'No need to go on like that,' said Shirley placidly. 'You only have to ask. Now, where are they, Bernie? You had them last.'

'Never mind the sodding binoculars,' Bernie yelped. 'He's
wanted for *murder*, for Christ's sake, and I don't want him
in my house!'

'I remember now, they're in the sideboard,' Shirley said.
'Ah, yes, here they are, Gerald.'

'For Christ's sake, woman,' Bernie bellowed, 'didn't you
hear what I said? He's wanted for *murder*! That was the police
at the door.'

'And you believed them?' his wife said derisively. 'They
were just winding you up, hoping you'd let them in. But you
know as well as I do that Gerry could never *kill* anyone. Now,
could you, Gerry?' she said turning to her brother.

''Course I couldn't, Shirl,' he snorted. 'Now, just give me
the bloody binoculars and shut up the both of you.'

Back upstairs, Fletcher adjusted the binoculars, parted the
curtains just enough to allow him to see clearly, then stepped
back to avoid being seen himself as he focussed on a car some
distance away on the other side of the street. It was an older car
and a familiar one, and someone was sitting in the driver's seat.
There was too much light on the windscreen to make out who
was behind the wheel, but only one man drove a car like that.

He sat down on the bed. How the hell did they find out
that he was here? How could they possibly know?

The answer, he told himself, was they *didn't* know. At least
they didn't know he was inside or they would have probably
kicked the door in and come for him by now. They were
watching the house because they knew it was one of the few
places he *could* go. And they'd have someone watching Rose
as well in case he was stupid enough to go back there. Rose
could take care of herself, but he hoped it wasn't Luka who
was watching her. Gerry couldn't suppress a shiver as he
thought of the cold-eyed man who rarely spoke, but you only
had to look at him to know you wouldn't want to cross him.
Luka gave him the creeps. He was probably the one who'd
done for Doyle. Breaking a man's neck and dropping him in
the river sounded like Luka's style, but he couldn't have done
it alone. Someone must have helped him; probably Slater.

Thank God he'd had the sense to run yesterday. He'd been
stupid to call the farm; even more stupid to think that they
would help him, but he hadn't realized that until it was almost
too late.

He'd been surprised, even pleased, when Roper had put Slater on. 'I've been helping the old man, here, by doing a bit of ploughing for him,' Slater told him, 'but I'll come and pick you up. Just tell me where you are. And don't worry, Gerry, we'll take care of you.'

Yeah, right! Those words had a whole different meaning now.

He'd remained where he'd told Slater he would be for the first half hour or so, but decided to cross the street to stand beneath an awning when it started to rain. There, he pretended to be interested in the stamps and coins displayed in the window rather than in the reflected image of the street.

He remembered how thankful he'd felt when he saw the van pull in on the other side of the street, and watched Slater get out.

He hadn't sensed any danger as he left the shelter of the awning and stood at the kerb waiting to cross. He saw a gap in the traffic and was about to step off when he saw movement in the van. Someone was in the back; someone who had poked their head over the back of the driver's seat to take a quick look up and down the street. All Fletcher had seen was the back of the head, but it was enough to send a chill down his spine.

Luka!

Sitting there now on the side of the bed, Gerry remembered the fear that had gripped him when it had finally dawned on him that he had become a liability, and they'd sent Luka to take care of him.

Fighting the urge to run, he'd put his head down and joined the steady stream of shoppers and walked away. He'd kept walking until he was well away from the area, finally taking shelter in a small shop in Albert Road. It was a poky old place, selling wools and linens and the like, but it was surely one of the last places they would think of to look for him.

He'd told the shop assistant that his wife had said she would meet him there. There was no one else in the shop, so he'd spent half an hour there before saying his wife must have been held up, and he'd better go out and look for her.

He'd made his way to where he'd left the bike in a narrow service lane behind a row of shops in Church Street. He was thankful he'd had the forethought to throw the plastic tarp over the bike before leaving it, not just because it had kept the rain off, but because both Slater and Luka would have recognized it instantly and waited for him to appear.

Even so, he'd spent close to twenty minutes huddled in a doorway, watching the street and the alley before he'd managed to get up the courage to go for it.

He'd avoided the main roads leaving the town, skirting Worcester and continuing on north until he got to Bridgnorth, where he'd turned west. The tank was barely a quarter full, he had no money, and the last place he wanted to be was Broadminster, but he was tired and he was hungry, and he had no choice. If he could get to his sister's house, she'd let him stay there to rest up for a couple of days, and she'd lend him money. Bernie would object, but he knew how to get around Shirley, so to hell with Bernie.

But now the bastards were out there, waiting, watching the house, and he had to get away. He was tempted to take another look, but decided not to; Slater might be watching with binoculars as well.

Bernie was waiting for him when he came down the stairs. 'You might fool your sister,' he said coldly, 'but you're wanted for murder. That's what they said, and I know they weren't bluffing. Who is this Doyle? They said his neck was broken and he'd been dumped in the river.'

'Don't know what they're talking about.' Gerry's eyes shifted to one side, and Bernie knew he was lying.

'But you do know about Newman, don't you, Gerry? Because that was his van you brought here. His van they found your fingerprints on.'

'You going to believe everything they tell you?' Gerry flared. 'There's no way they can have my prints on there, not after . . .' He cut his own words off and shook his head. 'There's no way!' he repeated.

'I should call the police and tell them you're—' Bernie began, but the words were cut off when Gerry grabbed him by the throat and squeezed – hard!

'You make that call, mate, and it will be the last call you ever make,' he hissed. 'Now, if you want me out of here, I'll need money. I need a thousand quid, and Shirl is going to go out and get it for me, while you, my friend, will stay here with me. Got it?'

Bernie gasped for breath as Gerry eased his grip on his throat. 'A thousand quid?' he squeaked. 'I don't have that much. I can't get that much. The banks are closed, and I?'

The hand was at his throat again. 'But the bank machines never close, do they, Bernie?' Fletcher hissed. 'And I know you've got it; because I did a little recce around the house last night while you were asleep, and I just happened to take a look at your bankbook and that bundle of credit cards you keep in the bottom drawer. I know *exactly* how much you've got, and if you mess me about I'll tell Shirl to double it. I'm being kind to you, Bernie, though you don't bloody well deserve it after shopping me. Now, let's go and talk to Shirl.'

Gerry Fletcher spent all day Sunday watching the street from behind the curtain. He'd hardly slept at all during the night, starting up at every creak and crack in the house, wondering if it was Slater creeping up the stairs. He'd make the stairs creak all right, big man like him. But Luka wouldn't. He'd be up there without a sound, and that thought alone was enough to keep anyone awake.

He'd wedged a chair under the door handle, but he wasn't sure how well the legs would hold against the carpet if someone was determined to come in, so he'd spent much of Saturday night and the early hours of Sunday morning pacing between the door and the window, listening and peering down into the street. But the street lights were old and there were too many shadows for him to see anything clearly. There could be a hundred men out there waiting for him – or none.

Perhaps Slater had decided he was wasting his time and had left after dark. On the other hand, he could have simply moved his car and was waiting somewhere else for Gerry to make a run for it.

He spent the rest of the day either at the window or sitting on the edge of the bed with his head in his hands, waiting for nightfall. He was dead tired, but afraid to lie down in case he fell asleep.

At the window again, he glanced at the sky. A fitful sun had come and gone throughout the afternoon, but now the clouds were heavier and it would be dark in an hour; dark enough to make a run for it if he could summon up the courage.

He heard footsteps on the stairs, then a light tap on the

door as Shirley announced herself. He opened the door. His sister came in, carrying a tray. 'I knew you wouldn't come down, so I've brought you some supper,' she told him as she set the tray on the bed. 'There's some hot tea the way you like it. I know you'll have to be going soon, and I don't want you going off on an empty stomach.'

He reached out and touched his sister's hand. 'You're a good sort, Shirl,' he said. 'Sorry to cause you so much trouble, but you're right, I will be gone soon.'

'You're in real trouble this time, aren't you, Gerry?' she said quietly. 'I'm not going to ask you what you've done or why you did it, but wouldn't it be better if you went to the police? They're not such a bad lot; they'd protect you.'

Gerry shook his head. 'No good, Shirl,' he said. 'They might try, but they couldn't protect me. I'd be dead inside a week if I go to gaol.'

Shirley drew in her breath. 'You didn't . . . It wasn't you who killed that man they were on about yesterday morning at the door, was it, Gerry?'

He shook his head. 'No, Shirl, I swear, that wasn't me. I'll admit I've done some rotten things in my time, but not murder. Trouble is, I know who did; I know what happened, and they don't like that.'

His sister turned away; tears glistened in her eyes and there was a catch in her voice as she said, 'Eat your supper before it goes cold. I'd better get back downstairs and keep an eye on Bernie before he does something stupid. He's been wanting to ring the police all day, and I have to keep reminding him that he'll be in a lot more trouble than he is already if he does. Trouble is, he doesn't know when to leave well enough alone.'

Shirley dug into her apron pocket. 'Here,' she said, shoving a wad of notes at him. 'You'll be needing this. Don't say anything to Bernie. I took another five hundred out after I took out the thousand, and I've only given him the bank slip for the thousand. I'll pop the other one in his book later.'

Gerry picked up the mug of tea. 'Thanks, Shirl,' he said, and meant it. 'You might not be hearing from me for a while, but I'll be in touch when things cool down.'

His sister moved to the door. 'Do you have somewhere to go? Will you be all right?'

'I'll be fine,' he said with more assurance than he felt. 'Don't you worry, Shirl; you know me. I always land on my feet.' He took a swig of tea and set the mug down before turning his attention once again to the window. 'Anyway, I'll be down shortly and be on my way. Oh, yeah, tell Bernie I need to borrow one of his screwdrivers and an adjustable spanner. Well, not exactly borrow, because I'll be taking them with me. Medium sizes should do.'

Shirley looked puzzled. 'What do you want them for?'

'Plates,' he said. 'Plates for the bike. They know the ones I've got, so I'll have to nick someone else's every so often, at least until I'm far enough away that it doesn't matter.'

Gerry waited until it was pitch black outside before slipping out of the house and into the yard next door. He cupped his hand around the small torch his sister had given him, and picked his way through an obstacle course of old wooden forms, a water tank, broken slabs of concrete and bricks half buried in weeds, to where the bike was hidden beneath a tarp and a stack of wooden pallets.

When he'd been forced to leave the cottage in such a hurry, he'd had to leave his regular riding gear behind. But he had his leather jacket, and although he hadn't had time to put it on when he'd roared out of the shed, his helmet was hanging from the handlebars, so at least he had that. Later in the day, a small shop in Bromyard had donated a pair of leather gloves – although the shopkeeper was unaware of the donation until the following day – but he would have to buy some all-weather gear once he was far enough away.

He pulled the wooden pallets away from the bike, stripped away the tarp, and wheeled the bike up to the gate. He eased the gate open and stuck his head out to look up and down the street, but it was impossible to tell if anyone was out there.

Fletcher sucked in his breath. It was now or never, and if he got away quickly, and there was someone out there, he could be gone before they were able to take up the chase. He swung the gate wide and walked back to the bike.

His leg was halfway over it when he thought he saw movement. He started to turn, but suddenly the helmet was ripped from his head and an arm the size of a small tree trunk wrapped itself around his neck and squeezed. He felt himself being lifted clear of the bike before being slammed to the ground. He lay there half stunned, unable to move. A great weight held him down and a large hand covered his mouth. He couldn't breathe, and the rushing noise in his ears made it hard to hear.

But he recognized the voice, and his blood turned to ice as consciousness began to slip away. 'Going somewhere, were you, Gerry?' it said. 'Sorry about this, mate, but this is going to hurt you a lot more than it will me.'

It felt as if his head was being torn off. If he'd had the breath, he would have shrieked in agony, but the arm around his throat held firm, and all that came out was a stifled sob. He felt something warm and wet running down his face. He opened his mouth to scream; to suck in air – and sucked in blood!

His blood! He was choking on his own blood!

His body sagged. A low, gurgling sigh escaped his lips as feeling left him and he slipped away.

Inside the house Shirley Green sat on the edge of her chair staring into space, fists clenched on her knees as she waited for the quiet of the night to be shattered by the sound of Gerry's motorbike. She glanced at the clock. Twelve minutes since she'd whispered goodbye to her brother at the door, and still nothing. Surely he should have been on his way by now?

On the other hand, she told herself, it would take time to uncover the bike and wheel it out to the gate. She'd offered to go out there to see to the gates herself, but he'd said no. Fourteen minutes, and still no sound. Something *must* have gone wrong. Perhaps he'd tripped and fallen over something in the yard. Perhaps he'd banged his head and was lying there, unconscious. But then, she told herself, he had the torch, so he was probably just being extra careful, taking his time, making sure there was nobody out there before making a run for it.

Fifteen minutes.

Shirley got to her feet. 'Something's wrong,' she burst out. 'I know it is, Bernie. You should have gone out there with him. He wouldn't let me go, but you could've gone. There hasn't been a sound!'

Bernie looked up from his paper. 'Oh, for God's sake sit down, woman,' he said irritably. 'What the hell did you expect?

That bike of his would wake the dead. You didn't expect him to start it up in the yard, did you? 'Course he won't. He'll go out the same way he came in. We never heard him come, did we? He cut the engine at the top of the road and wheeled the bike in. First thing I knew was when he knocked on the door, and my big mistake was opening it.'

Bernie went back to his paper. 'He's gone out the same way,' he said. 'Pushed the bike to the end of the road where there's traffic and nobody will pay any attention when he starts it up. He'll be well away by now, so sit down and stop worrying, and just be thankful he's gone. I know I am, so let it be!'

Eighteen

Monday, March 24

S hirley Green couldn't wait for Bernie to be gone. Her husband hadn't been out of the house since Gerry had turned up unannounced on the Friday night, because Gerry had refused to allow him out of his sight. Even so, Bernie didn't seem to be in any hurry to leave this morning.

'No telling what that Dave got up to on that weekend job,' she'd prodded. 'Probably been sitting around chatting instead of getting on with it while you're not there to keep an eye on him. You know what he's like.'

Dave was Bernie's helper. He wasn't a bad worker, at least not while he was being watched, but he was easily distracted, and the offer of a cup of tea could keep him idle for an hour or more.

'I talked to him yesterday,' Bernie told her from behind his paper, 'and he said he'd all but finished in the parlour, and there was just the skirting in the hall left to do, and a bit upstairs.'

'Yes, well, you know what "a bit upstairs" could mean, don't you? You'll probably find he hasn't even started on it.'

Bernie sighed and folded the newspaper. 'Yeah, well, we've been a bit preoccupied with your brother, haven't we?' he said. He glanced at the clock. 'Still, I suppose I'd better be off. Did you do my boots?'

'They're at the back door like always,' Shirley told him, 'so get them on and be off with you. I've got a lot of work to do myself. This place is a proper mess.'

'Looks all right to me.'

'Yes, well, the roof would have to fall in before you'd notice,' she told him tartly.

Bernie shot her a hard glance. 'If you're still worrying about Gerry, you can forget it,' he said. 'He's well on his merry way by now, isn't he? With my thousand quid and all. So if you want something to worry about, start worrying about how we're going to get that back, because I don't see him sending us a cheque in the post.'

He finished lacing up his boots, put on his heavy jacket, then left without another word.

Shirley watched from the front window as her husband backed the car out of the garage. No one had ever accused Bernie of being swift, but he seemed to be even slower than usual this morning, and Shirley could feel the pounding of her heart against her ribs as she silently urged him on.

There. He was gone.

Without even bothering to put on a coat, Shirley dashed out of the front door and into the street. It was quicker than going round the back, and she couldn't see Gerry stopping to lock the gates after him.

She was probably being silly, she told herself. Bernie would have thought so, and she'd had enough of his remarks about her and her brother these past few days to last a lifetime, which was why she'd waited until he was out of the house. He might be right; Gerry could have wheeled the bike up to the main road before starting it, but she had to go and see for herself that he had really gone.

The wooden gates were shut but not locked. At least that was a good sign. She pushed them open.

Her hand flew to her mouth when she saw the bike. It lay on it's side just inside the gate. There was a wet patch on the ground beneath the tank, and she could smell petrol as she moved closer.

Shirley looked around frantically, searching for . . . For what? Gerry? No. She stood there, trying to think. The bike! There must have been something wrong with the bike and he'd had to leave it. He hadn't come back to the house because that would mean he'd be trapped again. He must have made a run for it while he could. Probably gone up to the main road and hitched a lift.

But who would stop and pick someone up late at night like that?

Shirley stood there looking down at the bike, then bent to examine it more closely. There were blotches on the metal, dark brown blotches that looked like . . . dried blood? There was more on the leather seat, on the handlebars – and on the gravel beside the bike.

She stood up and backed away slowly, then turned and ran to the house, where she searched frantically among the clutter for the card she'd seen Bernie drop on the hall table.

Shirley Green was there to meet them when Paget and Tregalles arrived. A uniformed policewoman was with her. 'I tried to get her to come inside the house,' the constable told Paget, 'but she insisted on staying out here until you came.'

'I told Bernie something was wrong,' Shirley Green burst out. 'I knew it last night when I didn't hear the bike start up. I could feel it in my bones, but Bernie wouldn't have it. "Oh, no," he said. "He'll be all right. Always lands on his feet, does Gerry." But Gerry wasn't *his* brother, was he? Wasn't his own flesh and blood, not like he was mine. See? See?' she said, dropping to her knees to point out the dried splotches of blood. 'See where they . . .' she choked on the words as tears streamed down her face.

Paget motioned for the constable to move the sobbing woman back from the scene so they could take a closer look. 'Looks like they got him all right,' Tregalles murmured as he examined the bike and the ground around it. 'From the marks in the gravel I'd say he was dragged through the gate to a car. Forensic should be able to test the blood against his sister's DNA, but I don't know how much help SOCO will be. Doesn't look as if whoever did this left too much in the way of clues.'

'Better give Charlie a shout, anyway,' said Paget. 'And I know Mrs Green is upset, but she seems anxious to talk, so let's get her down to Charter Lane before she changes her mind. And find out where Bernie is and have him brought in as well. I think it's time we had some explanations from both of them.'

Back at Charter Lane, they had to separate the pair. Bernie Green was furious when they finally located him and brought him in. 'You had to do it, didn't you, Shirl?' he grated. 'Couldn't leave well enough alone, could you? I just wish to God I'd never set eyes on that brother of yours.'

'So why were you harbouring him?' asked Paget.

'Not because I wanted to, for Christ's sake!' Bernie burst out. 'He threatened the both of us, and I don't doubt he would have killed us if we?'

'That's a lie!' Shirley broke in savagely. 'Gerry's not a killer. He might have got in with the wrong crowd, but he's not a killer, and you know it, Bernie. If you'd let me go out there last night to see?'

'That's enough from both of you!' Paget snapped 'Get them into separate rooms,' he told Tregalles, 'then let them sit there for a while until they cool down. They've both got a lot to answer for.'

'Any luck with the two songbirds?' Ormside asked when Tregalles appeared later in the day.

'That Bernie's a stubborn little sod,' Tregalles said. 'Had to drag everything out of him, but his wife was more than willing to tell us everything she knew. Not that you'll ever convince her that her brother might have had a hand in killing someone, but she did give us a detailed account of what's been happening these past few days. She says Fletcher knew the house was being watched, and decided to make a run for it last night. But they must have been waiting for him to do just that, possibly Slater if what she's telling us is correct. She said he mentioned an Australian.'

Tregalles sighed heavily. 'I tell you, Len, this case is beginning to get me down. They – whoever *they* are – seem to be one step ahead of us all the time.'

Ormside's phone rang. He scooped it up. 'Yes, what is it?' he demanded.

He listened for a few moments, then looked at Tregalles and shook his head as if he couldn't believe what he was hearing. His expression was grim as he began making notes.

'Right,' he said and hung up. He rubbed his face hard with both hands, then blew out his cheeks. 'Never rains but it bloody pours,' he growled. 'Better get Paget down here. That was a report from Lyddingham. Gerry Fletcher's girlfriend, Rose Ryan didn't show up for work today, and there was no answer when they tried to phone her. So the owner of the shop where she works asked his son to stop by the cottage on his way to town to find out why. The lad found Rose's body in the bathtub. It could be suicide, but the First Response people are treating it as a suspicious death.'

On his way to his car, Paget called Charlie Dobbs on his mobile phone.

'Have any of your people left for the Fletcher cottage on the road to Lyddingham?' he asked when Charlie answered.

'Not yet. I only just heard about it a few minutes ago. Why?'

Paget hesitated. He didn't like to ask favours, but in this case . . .

'Look, Charlie, I'll apologize in advance for what I'm about to ask you, but could you keep Grace away from this one? I'm told it's a drowning in a bathtub, and I'm very much afraid?'

'No need to apologize, Neil. I thought of that myself when I was told about the circumstances, so I won't be sending Grace.'

'Thanks, Charlie. I appreciate it, but please don't tell her I called you.'

Nineteen

'She's still in the bath where we found her,' the uniformed constable told Paget. 'We were told not to touch anything, so we haven't – well, except for the doors. We broke in the back because it was the easiest, and left it open, then opened the front door as well to clear the air a bit. Oh, yes, and we switched the heater off in the bathroom. It was going full blast, and it was pretty ripe in there – still is, for that matter, but not as bad as it was.'

'I understand it was her employer's son who called you. Is he still around?'

'Next door in the other cottage along with the old man who lives there.' The constable consulted his notebook. 'Clyde Nichols is his name, and the old man's name is Hawkins, Tom Hawkins. My colleague is with them.

'Any word from Dr Starkie?'

The constable grinned. 'He called in a few minutes ago. Seems he got himself lost, and he wasn't best pleased. Used a few words I haven't heard in a long while, but I think we got him on the right road. He should be along in a few minutes if he doesn't get lost again.'

'In that case, I'd advise you to tread softly when he does arrive,' Paget warned.

'It's the back room on the right,' the constable directed as the detectives were about to enter the cottage, 'and best take a good deep breath before you go in.'

They paused only long enough to pull on thin latex gloves before going in. The smell had been bad enough at the front door, but the sickly odour was almost overpowering as they approached the tiny bathroom at the back of the house. They stopped at the doorway to take in the scene.

Judging by the fittings and the old-fashioned high-sided tub, the conversion to a bathroom from what was probably a scullery at one time must have taken place a long time ago. The sink and toilet weren't much more up to date, but the electric heater attached to the wall was definitely a recent addition.

A heavy, dark-blue bathrobe lay on the floor. A ragged piece of carpet served as a bath mat, and a large towel was folded neatly on the toilet seat. There was no cabinet or cupboard of any sort – there simply wasn't room – so everything in the way of toiletries sat next to an unopened packet of Pears soap and a spare roll of toilet paper on the window sill above the sink. In fact, apart from the naked body lying on its side with hair matted to the face in a tub devoid of water – and the flies – nothing seemed to be out of place.

'You can forget suicide,' Tregalles said. 'The towel's wrong for a start. I mean, why would she set it there if she'd decided to drown herself?' He touched the inside of the tub. 'Dry as a bone,' he said.

'She may have kicked the plug out before she died,' said Paget. 'Looks like some bruising around the throat and face, but I don't see any other marks on her. Still, we'll see what Starkie has to say when he gets here.'

Tregalles stood looking down at the body. 'Funny,' he said, 'but she looks smaller than I remember. Hair looks lighter, too.' He slipped off one of his gloves and touched it gingerly. 'Like straw,' he said as he put the glove back on.

'You're sure this is the same woman?'

'Oh, yes. No doubt about it. She was the one who was screaming for Fletcher to get out of there.'

'Mind if I play through?' a voice asked. They turned to see one of Charlie's men, loaded down with cameras. 'I'd like to get some pics before the doc shows up. Thought he'd've been here by now, but the bloke outside says he got lost.' He blinked several times, wrinkled his nose and blew out his cheeks. 'Cor! Bit of a pong in there, isn't there? And flies. I hate flies and maggots. Should've brought the gas mask. How long has she been dead? Murder, was it?' He stuck his head inside the door to take a quick look round. 'All right if I open that window?'

'Suspicious death,' said Paget, 'and I think you'd better wait until Dr Starkie and the rest of your lot have had a look at things before you move anything, including the window. Are they here now?'

'Just suiting up,' Haydock said. 'They'll be here in a minute, so I'd better get on.' He wrinkled his nose again. 'But I won't be taking very long, I can tell you.'

Charlie Dobbs was about to enter the cottage as Paget and Tregalles emerged, when he stopped and drew Paget aside.

'I had to tell Grace why she wasn't being sent on this one,' he said quietly, 'and I'm afraid it didn't go down too well. When I told her I didn't think she was ready for it, she got a little hot under the collar, and insisted that it was part of her job and she should be allowed to go. In fact, I'm sure she would be here now if I had let her come, and yet I had the feeling that she was relieved when I insisted that she stay behind. Even so, I don't think I've heard the last of it from her, and I suspect you will be hearing about it when you get home.'

'You didn't tell her I called you, did you?'

Charlie shook his head. 'She won't hear it from me,' he said, 'but she was not a happy gal when I left her, so be warned.'

Clyde Nichols was an affable, if somewhat shaken young man in his early twenties, while Hawkins was almost four times his age, wizened, bent and slow-moving. The constable who had been with them had gone, which was just as well considering the size of the tiny front room, where even four seemed a crowd. Nichols said his father, who owned the shop where Rose Ryan worked, had become concerned when she didn't show up for work, and he hadn't been able to contact her.

'So he asked me to drop in this afternoon to find out if she was all right,' he said.

'How did you know something was wrong?' asked Paget.

'I didn't at first, so I came round here to ask Mr Hawkins if he knew where Rose was, and he said he hadn't seen her since the weekend. But he said he'd heard her shouting late Friday night, but he didn't think too much of it because he said she and her boyfriend were always going on at each other.'

The old man snorted. 'Hardly a day went by they wasn't shouting at each other,' he said. 'So when I heard the car stop outside and then her screaming at the top of her voice a few minutes later, I thought it was him come back, so I . . .' He stopped to catch his breath. He thumped his chest with a gnarled fist. 'Asthma,' he gasped as he reached for an inhaler on the mantelpiece. He used it and sank into his chair beside the fireplace. 'Be all right in a minute,' he gasped when he saw the concern on their faces. 'It can be a right old bugger this time o' year.'

Paget waited for the old man's breathing to return to normal before he said, 'You were about to say, Mr Hawkins . . .?'

The old man looked a bit sheepish. 'Like I said, I thought they was just having another one o' their arguments, so I turned the tele up a bit and let 'em get on with it. Besides,' he continued defensively, 'even if I had known something was up, I couldn't do much about it.' He pointed to two walking sticks beside the chair. 'Whoever it was would be halfway to Lyddingham before I got out the door, and I've got no phone.'

Paget nodded. 'No one's blaming you,' he said. 'Do you recall what time it was when you heard the shouting?'

'Nine or a bit after. I was thinking about going to bed, and I remember wondering if they were going to keep it up much longer and keep me awake, but then it stopped.'

Paget turned his attention back to Nichols. 'So what did you do after speaking to Mr Hawkins?'

'Went out and looked in all the windows, but I couldn't see any sign of life until I got round the back and saw the little window there. I thought it might be a bathroom, and decided I'd better have a look in case Rose had slipped and fallen.'

He paused, frowning for a moment as if trying to work something out. 'To tell you the truth,' he said slowly, 'I don't really know why I did it. It just didn't seem right not to have a look in that last window, so I got a box to stand on from the shed at the back, and got up there to take a look. It was hard to see anything at first, but then I saw her there in the bath. Shook me a bit, I can tell you.'

'You called her Rose. Did you know her well?'

Nichols shrugged. 'No, not really. She's only been with us for a few months, and I've worked with her the odd time, but she kept pretty much to herself. I'm normally in the office,' he explained, 'but I lend a hand in the shop if things get busy or they're short-handed.'

'The shop?'

'The Hide and Seek in Lyddingham. It's quite a large shop.

It's grown a lot in the last few years. We have three full-time shop assistants, and three part-time. We sell hand-crafted leather goods, belts, jackets, handbags, an exclusive line of knitwear, as well as a few selected items from the local glass works.'

'Ever go out with Rose? Chat her up?' Tregalles asked.

Nichols looked surprised. 'Why would you ask that?' he said. 'She's at least ten years older than me.'

'Good-looking woman, all the same. Did you?'

'No.'

'Did she have any particular friend in the shop?'

'I don't think so. In fact she kept pretty much to herself, but she was good with customers, especially the men. She had a sort of way with her.'

'What sort of way?'

Nichols coloured slightly. 'Hard to describe,' he said. 'They just sort of took to her.'

'This way of hers – sexy, was it?'

'I suppose it was a bit. She sold more to men than any of the other girls.'

'Fancy her yourself, then, did you?'

The colour in Nichols' face deepened. 'As I said, she was a lot older than me and she was living with someone.'

'I'll take that as a yes,' Tregalles said. 'Ever been out here to the house before? Take her home in your car, something like that?'

'No. Never. And I don't like what you're implying. Rose worked in the shop, and any dealings I had with her were strictly on a business level.'

'You married, Mr Nichols?'

'No. I'm engaged to be married in June, but I don't see what that has to do with anything. And I'd like to make it clear that the only reason I'm here is because my father asked me to stop in on my way into town to find out why Rose hadn't come in to work today.'

'It may not be relevant at all,' said Paget soothingly, 'but we do have to explore every possibility, Mr Nichols. So what *can* you tell me about Miss Ryan?'

Only somewhat mollified, Nichols shook his head. 'Not much,' he said. 'As I said, she kept pretty much to herself. I knew she was living out here with a boyfriend or whatever, but I only ever saw him once when he came to pick her up at the shop. Can't say I liked the look of him. Scruffy-looking type. Couldn't see him and Rose as a couple at all, but then it takes all sorts, I suppose.'

'You knew we were looking for him?'

Nichols looked confused. 'Looking for the man she was living with? I don't understand.'

'Gerry Fletcher. It's been on the radio and television. You must have seen or heard that we were looking for him.'

Nichols frowned and shook his head. 'I didn't even know his name. I don't have much time to watch television.' He stopped abruptly. 'Fletcher!' he said. 'So he's the one. Yes, I did hear it on the radio several times, but I never connected him with Rose.' His eyes widened. 'Did he . . .?' He flicked his head toward the cottage next door.

'Did he what, Mr Nichols?'

'Well . . . kill her?'

'Why would you say that?' Paget asked. 'I don't recall saying anything about the way she died.'

Nichols reddened. 'I just thought . . . I mean, the questions you've been asking . . .'

'We don't know how Miss Ryan died as yet,' Paget told him. 'Now, you say you saw her in the bath when you looked in the window. What did you do then?'

Nichols drew a deep breath. 'I could see she was dead by the way she was lying there in the tub – and the smell! Even with the window closed . . .' He swallowed hard. 'Which is why I rang the police instead of an ambulance on my mobile phone. I knew they could break in, but I didn't know if ambulance people could do that without some sort of authorization.'

Tregalles said, 'You didn't attempt to break in yourself, then?'

Nichols shook his head. 'I knew I couldn't help her, so there was no point.'

'How long did you have to wait for the police to arrive?'

'Not long. Ten, maybe fifteen minutes. The chap I spoke to on the phone got quite excited when I told him I thought Rose was dead. He took my name and said I wasn't to move until they got here.'

'What happened then?'

'I showed them where I'd climbed up to look in the window,

and as soon as one of the men had a look, they both had a go at the door and broke it open.'

'Did you go inside?'

'No. They told me to stay outside. Not that I wanted to go in anyway. It smelt bad enough outside. God knows what it must be like in there.' He wrinkled his nose at the memory. 'Don't you have *any* idea about what happened to her?' he asked in a small voice.

'We'll have to wait for the doctor's report before we know the cause of death,' Paget told him as he rose to his feet. 'I understand that you have given your address and phone number to the constable, and I should warn you that you will probably be contacted by the coroner's office at the time of the inquest.'

'Will I have to go as well?' Hawkins asked querulously.

'You may,' Paget told him, 'but I wouldn't worry about it if I were you; considering the state of your health they will probably come out here and take your statement.'

Hawkins made a face. 'Rather go to the inquest,' he said. 'I've never been to one of them. Be a bit of a change, wouldn't it?'

'Then don't even mention your health if they send you a notice,' Tregalles advised. 'But how will you get there? The inquest will be in Broadminster.'

'I'll take him,' Nichols volunteered. 'I'll have to go right past here anyway, so it won't be any trouble. All right, Mr Hawkins?'

The old man beamed. 'That it is, lad,' he said. 'That it is!'

Grace stared blankly at the paperwork in front of her. Knowing that Neil would not be home until later in the evening, she had decided to stay on at work and get a head start on her month-end report. But she might as well have gone home for all she'd accomplished, because she was still smouldering over Charlie's decision to pull her from the team.

His words had been going round and round inside her head ever since he and the others had left.

'I'm sorry, Grace, but it's for your own good. I really don't think you're ready for something like this, not so soon after . . .' He'd left the sentence unfinished, but they both knew what he meant.

She'd argued, but to no avail. Charlie had stopped short of making it an order, and she'd had the good sense not to push it to the limit, but the argument had left her feeling frustrated and annoyed, not just with Charlie, but with herself – and guilty, because she felt she'd let Charlie down.

But what was worse, she felt she'd let herself down. She'd been a fool to think that she could carry on as if everything was fine; dodging questions, saying she was 'just tired', when Neil had shown concern. Even before Neil had told Charlie that he was worried about the overtime Grace was working, Charlie had known there was something wrong. He'd told her that the other day. And if Charlie knew, then Neil probably knew as well.

Grace leaned back in her chair and closed her eyes. Probably? Of *course* Neil must know. She'd thought she was being so clever in keeping her secret to herself, but she had seen the questions in his eyes; heard them in his voice . . .

He was waiting for her to tell him what was wrong. He trusted her. She couldn't let him down.

Grace felt the sting of tears behind her eyes. She'd thought she was doing things for the best; thought she could work things out without anyone knowing, but she'd been wrong, and time was running out. There was only one thing she could think of left to try, and the very thought of what might happen if that didn't work was enough to . . .

She thrust the thought away. She had no choice. It simply *had* to work.

They found Starkie sitting at the kitchen table writing up his notes.

'How the hell you expected me to do an examination while this one was still in that monster of a bathtub, I don't know,' he greeted them. 'I may have lost weight, but I'm not a bloody contortionist, and I wasn't going to climb in there with her. So I had one of your constables pull her out. The one with the smirk and smart-arsed questions about my sense of direction. He wasn't smirking quite so much by the time he got her out of the bath, I can tell you. Serve the cheeky young sod right.'

'You would have complained just as much if we'd moved her,' Paget told him. 'So, apart from that, what can you tell us, Reg? How and when did she die?'

'Initial observation, subject to change when I get her on the slab, I'd say she drowned. But the bruising on her knees and elbows, around the shoulders, upper body, throat, nose and mouth, and on her scalp suggests to me that she struggled very hard when someone held her under. All of which, as I said, will have to be confirmed, of course.'

'Any other signs of abuse?' asked Paget.

'Can't tell as yet. As for time of death, it's hard to say. I'm told the electric heater was on and the room was like an oven when they found her, so we may never know exactly. The best I can give you now is two to five days. That high temperature in the room does make it difficult.'

'Which could mean,' Tregalles said softly, 'that what the old man next door said he heard around nine o'clock on Friday night, was Rose Ryan being killed.'

Everyone else was either out in the country with Charlie or had gone to their homes long ago when Grace left the office and went to her car. The sky was clear and the temperature was dropping, which was odd, because they had been forecasting rain. But there was a decided nip in the air, and she wondered if there would be a frost before morning.

She could have walked to where she was going, but now that she'd made up her mind she wanted to be there as quickly as possible; no delays, no second thoughts. If she didn't do it now . . .

She got in the car and fastened her seatbelt. Funny how comforting it felt. It was like someone holding you, keeping you safe.

She thought of Neil, and the temptation was strong to go straight home, to draw strength from his arms and from his love. But that would solve nothing; this was something she had to do on her own.

She drew a deep breath and started the car.

'She'd undressed in the bedroom, her clothes were folded on the chair at the bottom of the bed, and the bathrobe was on the floor beside the tub,' Charlie said. 'So I'd say she was probably in the tub when her attacker arrived, but how he got in, I don't know. There's no apparent tampering with the locks on either door, so either a door was unlocked, or he or she had a key. The back door key is missing, so whoever did this must have locked up when they left and taken the key with them

'She fought hard. There is skin under her nails, so her killer has a few scratches on him – I'm assuming it was a male until I see something that makes me think otherwise – but it would be almost impossible for her to fight back with any degree of success from her position in the tub. Any idea who did this?'

Paget shook his head. 'I wish to God I did,' he said, 'but it looks to me as if once we connected Fletcher to the disappearance of Mark Newman, and he was forced to run, both he and his girlfriend had to be silenced.'

'You didn't have anyone watching the house?'

'Don't have the resources,' Paget told him. 'Best we can do these days is have the local people keep an eye on the place if or when they happen to go by, and then only if it doesn't interfere with their regular duties.'

'So it's wide open?'

'Afraid so, Charlie.' Paget turned to Tregalles. 'But if someone thought it necessary to kill Rose Ryan for fear she might talk, they might do the same to the Greens, so regulations or not, I think we had better make an exception in this case. Fletcher was with them for several days, and these people don't take any chances. So I want someone with them in their house tonight.'

He looked at the time. 'And since there seems to be nothing more to be done here, I suggest we wrap this up and go home and get some sleep.'

Twenty

Charlie Dobbs realized later that he'd seen the car as he drove back to the office, but it didn't register at the time, so preoccupied was he with the night's activities. His men were still out there at the cottage, and they would probably be there for a few more hours, but he would be surprised if they came up with anything worthwhile. He just wished they could find something – *anything* – for Paget to work with, but as things stood now, the chief inspector might as well be treading water for all the progress he was likely to make.

But there was one thing he did know, and that was that they were dealing with an organization of some kind; an organization that didn't like loose ends. First, Mark Newman had disappeared, then Doyle, then Fletcher, and now Fletcher's girlfriend had been killed.

So who was next? Was Paget right? Would they go after Bernie Green and his wife? They should be safe enough tonight with police protection, but that wasn't going to last long by the sound of it.

He pulled up in front of the office. He didn't intend to stay very long, so he parked the car beneath a street light in front of the office rather than going to the bother of operating the coded gate to the underground parking. The car was alarmed, and the engine wouldn't start without the code, so he wasn't too worried about having it nicked. Besides, it was four years old, and not one of the top ten being targeted by thieves this month.

He could manage an hour, he decided as he sat down at the desk and took several papers from his in tray. Reports, and more reports. Whatever happened, he wondered idly, to the paperless society everyone had been talking about when computers came on the scene? If anything, there was even more paper now than ever, and since everyone wanted a copy of everything, there must be millions upon millions of filing cabinets throughout the world just stuffed with useless information.

The thought intrigued him, and he began to wonder if it would be possible to get a government grant to do, say, a five-year study of the filing habits of corporations and businesses. Revenue and Customs, now there would be a good place to start.

Charlie dragged his mind back to the work in front of him, but he'd no more than read the first line when his phone rang. He groaned when he saw the calling number.

'Neil,' he answered wearily. 'I hope you're not calling to say you've got another one.'

'Not exactly, Charlie,' said Paget more lightly than he felt. 'But I do have a missing Grace, and since time is getting on, I wondered if she's still in the office. I tried her mobile phone, but she must have it switched off.'

'I've only just got in myself,' Charlie said cautiously. 'She's not here, but I know she said she was going to stay on here for a while this evening. She's probably on her way . . .'

He stopped. He remembered seeing Grace's car on his way in. Seeing it and yet not registering what he saw, because it was where it had always been in the past, and he'd thought nothing of it. If only he'd been a little more alert he would have stopped, but . . .

'Charlie? Charlie!' Paget's voice rose in alarm. 'What is it? What's the matter?'

Charlie slammed his fist down on the desk beside the phone. 'Damn!' he said. 'Missed the cheeky little sod! Sorry Neil, but would you believe it? A mouse just ran across the desk, bold as brass. I'm going to have to set traps. Now, what was I saying? Oh, yes. I was going to say Grace won't have had any supper, so she may have stopped at that late-night deli she likes on Bridge Street for a bite before coming home. She probably thought that you wouldn't be home until later, so she won't be in any hurry.'

'Yes, that could be it,' Paget agreed. 'Still, I wish she'd leave her mobile on.'

The phone was barely back on its rest before Charlie grabbed his coat and made for the door. Down the stairs and into the car; he was doing fifty by the time he hit the end of the street.

Grace's car was there in front of the flat, and there was a light shining dimly behind the curtains in an upstairs window. Charlie pulled in to the kerb, switched off and left the car. The front door opened to his touch, and suddenly his head was filled with vivid images of the things that had taken place there just three short months ago, and he was filled with apprehension as he looked up the narrow stairs to the light at the top.

It wasn't the landing light – too dim, but he knew exactly where it was coming from. He called out, 'Grace? You up there? It's Charlie.'

No answer.

He took the stairs two at a time, pausing on the landing, facing the bathroom door. It was slightly ajar.

'Grace?' he called softly. No answer. He pushed the door open. It swung back silently. He stepped inside, caught his breath.

'Oh, God!' he whispered. 'Oh, my God!'

Paget couldn't settle. He knew he was being foolish to worry about Grace; she was a very capable woman who could take good care of herself. On the other hand there were a lot of nutters out there on the roads, drunks, dopers, drivers with problems, and you never knew who was coming toward you.

He looked at the clock again. The hands had barely moved since the last time he'd looked. Ten more minutes, he decided. He'd give her ten more minutes . . .

It was as if his whole body had turned to ice. Charlie stood there in the doorway, unable to move, unable to speak as he stared at the old, high-sided bathtub so reminiscent of the one he'd seen earlier that evening. But this one was filled with water, just as it had been on that fateful night three months ago, and Grace lay there, head on one side, one arm hanging over the side, limp and lifeless.

'Grace!' The word choked in his throat as he forced himself to move. 'For God's sake, Grace.' He touched her arm and suddenly a great surge of water slopped over the side of the tub and soaked his sleeve.

Graces eyes flew open. 'Charlie! Where did – what – ? Oh, God, Charlie, you scared the life out of me. I must have fallen asleep.'

'Scared the life out of *you?* For God's sake, Grace, just what the hell do you think you're doing? I thought you were dead!'

Grace struggled to sit up, and only then did she seem to realize she was naked. 'Hand me that towel, please, Charlie,' she said, 'and turn around while I get out.'

He handed her the towel. 'Now,' he said, 'would you like to tell me just what the hell is going on here, Grace?'

'Just give me a minute to get my clothes on and I'll tell you,' she said as she climbed out of the tub, 'but one thing I can tell you is that I feel as if a great weight has been lifted, and I feel wonderful. It worked, Charlie. It really worked!'

'I don't know what worked,' Charlie said, 'but I do know that Neil is worried about you. He phoned me a few minutes ago, and I think the sooner you give him a call and tell him you're all right, the better.'

He heard Grace gasp. 'You won't tell him, will you, Charlie? Please. Let me call him, and then I'll explain everything to you.' Dressed now, she bent and used the towel to mop up the water on the floor, then pulled the plug. 'Thank God it was you who found me here. I hate the idea of keeping anything from Neil, but I don't want him to know anything about this. But let's get out of this bathroom and go down-stairs and put the fire on. The water was so lovely and hot when I got in, and so relaxing that I must have drifted off, but now I'm freezing.'

She found her handbag, took out her phone and clicked on her home number.

'Neil, you're home. I thought perhaps—'

'Grace!' His relief was almost palpable through the phone. He forced himself to keep his voice modulated. 'I was begin-ning to worry about you. Where are you?'

'I'm at the flat. I finally decided it was time to do some-thing with it. Mr Perelli has been after me to turn it back to him, so tonight I decided to come over and sort out a few things. Unfortunately, it took longer than I thought, and I didn't realize how late it was, but I'll be home within the hour.'

She looked across the phone at Charlie. 'Just one more thing I'd like to sort out before I leave. It won't take long.'

'Fine, but be careful on the road.'

'Love you, Neil. I'll be home soon.' She closed the phone and put it away.

'I owe you an apology, Charlie,' she said softly, 'and I owe you my thanks for bearing with me and trusting me when you must have wondered what I was up to, and I can't thank you enough for that.' They were downstairs and Grace was standing with her back to the electric fire.

'But I am going to ask you for one more favour. As I said upstairs, I don't want Neil to know what happened here tonight or what led up to it, so I am asking you not to tell him, and I'll explain why.'

Grace drew a deep breath before going on. 'You see, Charlie, I had a delayed reaction to the incident here at Christmas. I felt fine for about three weeks after the event, and then it hit me. If I so much as closed my eyes it was there in front of me. If I did manage to fall asleep, I would wake up convinced that Mary Carr was in the room. I could feel the razor on my wrists. If I looked down, I would see the blood; see my life slipping away and there was nothing I could do about it. But worst of all, I couldn't sleep for more than a few minutes at a time.

'It kept getting worse. As long as I was awake and busy, I could keep the images at bay, but they were waiting for me the moment I relaxed or went to sleep. I thought I could overcome it, but it kept getting worse. Every night I'd wait until Neil had gone to sleep, and then I'd go downstairs and curl up in a chair. I might manage an hour that way, but suddenly I would be right back here again with Mary Carr, and I would wake up in a cold sweat.

'I really thought I was losing my mind, Charlie. It took me a while, but I finally got up the courage to talk to my doctor. He sent me to see a psychologist, and to make a long story short, he finally gave up on me and sent me to a psychiatrist. That's where I've been going after work these past months.'

'You should have told Neil,' Charlie said. 'He loves you, Grace; he would have helped you.'

Grace moved away from the fire to sink into what had once been her favourite chair. 'I couldn't,' she said. 'Perhaps I wasn't thinking very clearly, but it seemed to me that if I told Neil what was happening, things would never be the same between us. I know he would have tried to help me, but I honestly don't think it would have done any good. I was afraid that I would become something less in his eyes, and even if I did manage to overcome it, he would be forever watching for signs of it happening again.

'The trouble was, no matter what I did, things weren't getting any better. In fact, I think going to the psychiatrist was a mistake, because he kept on about regression, about my child-hood, how my parents treated me, and all that stuff, when I knew that none of it had anything to do with what I was going through.'

Grace fell silent for a moment, then slowly shook her head as if to clear it after coming out of a long sleep.

'I don't know why it took me so long to realize it,' she continued, 'but it finally dawned on me that the only one who could cure me was me!'

Grace spread her arms wide in a gesture encompassing the flat. 'I was afraid to come here,' she said. 'Neil has been trying to persuade me to let the flat go, and he couldn't understand why I wouldn't. But I couldn't tell him why without telling him everything, and that was the last thing I wanted to do.

'To tell you the truth, Charlie, I had just about given up hope when it hit me. I *had* to come here, This was where it happened, and this was where I had to come if I was to ever conquer my fears.'

Her voice dropped to little more than a whisper as she said, 'I didn't know if it would work, but I knew it had to be done. Either it would tip me right over the edge or it would cure me, and I'll be honest, Charlie, I wasn't sure which it would be, and I was terrified.

'Until I got into that bath, and then it was as if everything melted away. I lay back in that tub and I sang. I *sang*, Charlie, at the top of my voice. Every damned song I could think of from hymns to pop to opera. It's a good thing you didn't come in then or you *would* have thought I'd gone mad.' She paused, frowning. 'Come to think of it, how did you know I was here?'

'I saw your car outside when I went back to the office, but it didn't really sink in until Neil phoned and said he was worried about you.' Charlie eyed her critically. 'I must say you *look* better; you even *sound* better, but how do you feel, really, Grace?'

'I feel wonderful,' she told him. 'I really do. The fear is gone and I won't be afraid to go to sleep tonight.'

Charlie rose to his feet. 'In that case, Grace, this never happened. I was never here tonight, and your secret is safe with me. I'm sure you're right, but if you should ever feel the need to talk . . .'

'You're a good friend, Charlie.' Grace stood up and hugged him briefly. 'And thank you for being so understanding.'

'Yes, well, I'm just happy to have you back,' he said gruffly. 'But we'd better get going before Neil starts worrying again and sends out a search party. Come on, I'll see you to your car.'

Twenty-One

Tuesday, March 25

Clouds hung low over the valley and it was trying to rain as Paget drove in to work, but neither clouds nor rain could dampen his spirits this morning, because Grace was back.

It was odd that he should think of it this way, but that was how it felt. It was as if Grace had been away and now she was back. She had even looked different when he'd met her at the door last night. It was as if some dark cloud that had been hovering over her for the past two or three months had been lifted. He couldn't explain it, but she had looked radiant, and she had come into his arms and hugged him as if she never wanted to let him go.

And she was getting rid of the flat! When Grace had called from there last night to say she had decided to let it go, it was as if a great weight had been lifted from his own shoulders. He'd been so afraid that she was keeping it in case things didn't work out between them, but there was no doubt in his mind this morning that Grace was there to stay. No doubt at all after last night.

There was a spring in his step as he entered the building, but the euphoria that had made the drive in to work so pleasant evaporated quickly when he was confronted by the scene of Bernie Green and his wife in the middle of an argument with Tregalles.

'They're saying they want more protection?' Tregalles started to explain, only to be interrupted by Bernie.

'Too bloody right we want more protection,' he fumed. 'They got Gerry right outside our house, didn't they? And they murdered the woman he was living with, so where does that leave us, eh? Are we next? I mean, we hardly slept a wink last night. That young copper you sent over isn't going to be much help if a gang of 'em break in, now is he? I mean he wasn't even bloody armed!'

'Look,' Paget said soothingly, 'I know it must be worrying for both of you, but we simply do not have the resources to give you the sort of protection you're looking for. For your own peace of mind it might be best if you found somewhere else to go for a few days. You will still have to be in court next week to face the charges against you, of course, but as long as we know where you are in the meantime, it might be wise to leave the house. Is there anyone you could stay with?'

Bernie snorted. 'So it's up to us, now, is it?' he said contemptuously. 'Dunno what we pay you lot for. People all round us dying like flies and all you can say is leave the house?' He turned to his wife. 'This is all your fault,' he said bitterly. 'You and that brother of yours. I said we should never have let him in, but oh, no, you wouldn't have it, would you? Well, now, see where it's got us? We're on our bloody own, now, aren't we?'

'You were keen enough to take anything he brought, though, weren't you?' Shirley flared. 'It was all right when you thought you could flog that camera, so don't you go saying it was all my fault. If you'd let me go out to make sure he got off safely, he'd still be alive and we wouldn't be here now, would we?'

She started to cry.

'You should count yourself lucky that you didn't go out there, Mrs Green,' Paget told her, 'because there's a good chance you would have suffered the same fate as your brother.'

Shirley caught her breath, and even Bernie seemed to find the thought sobering. Some of the fire died in his eyes as he said, 'I've got a sister who lives in Hereford, but that's still a bit too close for comfort. Besides, she and Shirl don't get on all that well, so that's no good.' He thought for a moment. 'There's an old mate of mine living in Hull. Retired early a couple of years ago and moved there to be near his daughter and grandkids. He's always said he'd put us up if we ever got round that way. I could give him a ring.'

'Too far away,' Paget told him. 'You're bail conditions won't allow it. I suggest your wife either makes peace with your sister, or you find a hotel in the local area. But don't tell anyone where you're going, and don't phone anyone.'

'And who's going to pay for a hotel, I'd like to know?' Bernie snorted. 'Not you lot, I'll be bound.'

'No, but on the other hand, do you really think the price of a hotel for a few nights is more than your life's worth?'

Rose Ryan was thirty-seven, and she had a record. Petty theft and prostitution for the most part, and she had lived in many of England's major cities at one time or another. Somewhat surprisingly, Rose Ryan was her real name, and even more surprising was the fact that she had kept in regular contact with her parents. They lived in Stockton-on Tees, although as far as Tregalles could tell from cards and letters found in one of the sideboard drawers, she hadn't seen them for a number of years. The job of notifying her parents of her death had been handed off to the Stockton police, and Ormside was now waiting to hear if her parents or a family member would be coming down to formally identify and claim the body.

'I see the last time she was picked up was in London two years ago,' Ormside observed, 'and her address then was in Shoreditch. How long have she and Fletcher been living down here?'

'They moved in four months ago, according to their neighbour, Tom Hawkins.'

'Odd sort of couple,' Ormside mused. 'I wonder how the two of them got together? I can see him living out there close to his job, but not her. Not after spending all those years on the game in the cities.'

'Getting a bit past it, I expect,' Tregalles said, 'so she decided to get herself a boyfriend and settle down. Mind you, she was still in pretty good nick for her age, and she could still pull the men, according to young Nichols; in fact I wouldn't be surprised if he fancied her himself, even if he won't admit it.'

'You're not suggesting that he had anything to do with her death, are you?'

Tregalles dismissed the idea with a shake of the head. 'I think it was the same people who did for Fletcher and Mickey Doyle, and probably Mark Newman as well, but I suppose there's always an outside chance that she was killed for some other reason. I mean for all we know she might have got a bit bored with country life and was playing away from home, but it would be more than a bit of a coincidence if that turned out to be the case. I'm going out to talk to the people she worked with at this Hide and Seek shop in Lyddingham this morning; they might be able to tell me something about her. And I think I'll have another chat with Skinner and the blokes at RGS Removals on my way back to see if they can give me any leads. Fletcher just might have said something to one of his mates that would give us a clue about what he was into.'

'Take Lyons with you,' Ormside suggested. 'He's still stewing over letting Fletcher get away, and he's convinced that's why he's been stuck in here ever since.'

'Right,' Tregalles said as he shrugged into his coat. 'Have we heard anything more on that tip Emma Baker phoned in to Molly the other day? About the bloke she thought she recognized in the bar. Somebody was going to check up on the registration of the car he was driving.'

'It's one of a fleet belonging to a company in Hammersmith,' Ormside told him. 'They sell everything from packing boxes and padded blankets, to full-size containers, so it looks like this bloke is some sort of sales rep. Sinclair's handling it. Check with him when you get back.'

Tregalles and Lyons arrived at the gates of RGS Removals and Storage at the same time as one of the firm's larger vans. Tregalles followed the van in and parked in a space reserved for customers, then sat for a moment to watch and marvel at the skill of the driver backing the long van into one of the narrow loading bays with seeming ease.

As he led the way into the cavernous interior, his thoughts returned to Fletcher and Rose Ryan. He and Lyons had spent a good two hours with Richard Nichols, the owner of Hide and Seek in Lyddingham, as well as members of his staff, yet they'd learned nothing of any consequence about either Rose or Fletcher. Nichols senior had expressed both shock and sorrow at what had happened, but Tregalles got the feeling it had more to do with the possible loss of sales to male customers than any feeling for Rose herself. As for the rest of the staff, all of whom were women, they all said the same thing: Rose Ryan had never talked about the man she was living with, or about her past life.

Tregalles and Lyons found the foreman, Jack McCoy, talking to the driver of a forklift, a towheaded lad of about eighteen. McCoy finished his conversation with the boy, then waved him away and turned his attention to the sergeant.

'Found Fletcher, yet?' he asked. 'Saw his picture on the box the other night, but it didn't say why you wanted to talk to him. So why do you want to talk to him? What's he supposed to have done? You never said.'

'That's right, I didn't,' Tregalles agreed. 'And I still can't give you any details, but I would like to ask you and the rest of the crew a few questions.'

'What sort of questions?' McCoy asked suspiciously. 'Look, I don't know what all this is about, but if Gerry went and got himself in some sort of trouble, I don't know anything about it, and neither does anyone here.'

'I'm not suggesting that you do,' Tregalles assured him, 'but we do need your help. We are asking anyone who knew him if he ever said anything that might help us. He may have said something that didn't mean much at the time, but it might now. Can you think of anything like that?'

McCoy pushed out his lower lip as he thought about it, then slowly shook his head. 'Can't think of anything,' he said at last. 'But then, unless you tell me what sort of thing you're looking for, I can't say for sure, can I?'

'What about his friends? Is there anyone here who was a particular friend of his?'

Again, McCoy shook his head. 'No. Gerry's always been a bit of a loner. Doesn't mix much with the rest of the crew. I'd say your best bet would be the woman he lives with – or has she scarpered as well?'

'Can't do that, I'm afraid,' Tregalles said. 'She's dead.'

'Bloody hell! What happened?'

'Can't say at the moment. Did you know her?'

McCoy shook his head. He appeared to be shaken. 'I knew he was living with someone, but I never met her, and Gerry never talked about her. Some of the lads would bring their wives or girlfriends along to the pub on a Saturday, but Gerry never did.' He eyed Tregalles narrowly. 'Did he have anything to do with her death? Is that why you're looking for him?'

'Now why would you think that?' Tregalles said. 'I didn't say anything about the way she died.'

'Well, no, but first you come here looking for Gerry and you won't say why, and now you tell me his woman is dead, so what am I supposed to think? How did she die?'

Tregalles ignored the question, and nodded in the direction of the loading platform where several men were hard at work. 'I'm afraid we're wasting time,' he said. 'I still need to talk to your men. Some of them must know something about the man.'

McCoy looked doubtful. 'I don't think it will do you much good,' he said.

'I still want to talk to them.'

'Look,' McCoy said, 'they'll only tell you the same as I have. It isn't that I don't want to help, but we've got schedules to meet, and they're all busy as you can see.'

'Pity,' Tregalles said, 'because I would have thought it would be a lot easier if I could get them together for ten or fifteen minutes here and now rather than taking them one by one for the next hour or so, which is my only alternative. Still, you know your own business best.'

McCoy's mouth twisted into a humourless smile as he eyed Tregalles. 'You're a copper,' he said, 'so you should know something about the law. Would you call that blackmail or coercion?'

'Let's call it being practical, shall we? You must have a lunch room or somewhere like that where I can talk to them?'

The two men locked eyes for a long moment before McCoy heaved a sigh and gave in. 'Over there,' he said, nodding in the direction of an open door. 'I'll round them up, but I want them back on the job asap. We've a lot to get done today, and we don't pay overtime for things like this.'

There were eight of them in addition to McCoy. They came in and lined up against the wall and stood waiting silently. McCoy and two of the men took the opportunity to light cigarettes. Their ages varied from the gangly youngster who had been driving the forklift to a short, grey-haired man who must have been pushing sixty.

The fact that Gerry Fletcher was probably dead was not something Tregalles was prepared to reveal to these men at the moment, so he chose his words carefully.

'The reason we are looking for Fletcher,' he said, 'is because we have evidence that links him to certain illegal activities. But what we *don't* know is who his associates are. So what

I would like from you is anything you can tell me about him that might have meant nothing to you at the time, but could have some significance now. I know you might not like the idea of talking to the police about a mate, but believe me, this is serious, very serious indeed, and we need your help.'

The men looked at one another, but no one spoke. 'Come on,' he coaxed. 'You worked alongside the man for months. He must have talked to you about *something*. Did he ever talk about people he knew or things he did off the job? Did he ever say or do anything that struck you as odd?'

The men looked at each other. No one seemed to want to be the first to speak until finally one of the smokers broke the silence.

'Never had much chance, did we?' he said. 'Not with him working over the other side. And he wasn't even *there* half the time.'

'What do you mean by "the other side"?'

'The repair bay,' the man said, flicking his head in the direction of the separate bay at the end of the building. 'And he wasn't a mate.'

Tregalles looked to McCoy for an explanation.

'He did a lot of our repair work,' McCoy said. 'And he used to have to go into town every so often for parts and such. Sort of mechanic-cum-errand boy. We do our own maintenance on our vehicles, apart from major jobs, and Gerry is good at that sort of work.'

'But when I was here earlier,' Tregalles said, 'didn't you tell me that he was a loader and driver, and everyone had to be prepared to do whatever job came along?'

'Yeah, well he was a driver originally, and he did a bit of general work when he first came here,' McCoy told him. 'I didn't realize at the time that you wanted a *specific* job description.' He inclined his head toward the smoker. 'But Stan's right. Gerry did spend a lot of time in the repair shop, and he never really mixed with the rest of the lads.'

'Oh, come on, Mr McCoy,' Tregalles said, making no attempt to conceal his annoyance. 'There's nothing but a breeze block wall between the repair bay and the rest of the bays, and the front is wide open. Hardly a mile away from everyone else, is it?' His eyes swept over the rest of the men. 'So, what's the problem?'

One of the men stirred. 'I can't speak for anyone else,' he said hesitantly, 'but I'm glad he's gone. It wasn't that he *didn't* talk to us. It was the other way round; he never stopped talking. And it was always about him and what he'd done, where he'd been, and the women he'd had in France or Italy or Spain, and God knows how many other places, and I for one was sick of it, so I stayed out of his way.'

Heads were nodding as a murmur rippled through the ranks.

'What about closer to home?' Tregalles asked. 'If, as you say, he was the boastful type, did he ever say anything about his activities or exploits – whatever you want to call them – around here?'

The men looked at each other, then began to shake their heads.

'Mr McCoy?'

The foreman shook his head. 'Not to me, he didn't,' he said.

Tregalles tried again. 'I understand he has done some work for a local farmer. What can you tell me about that?'

McCoy looked mystified. 'Sorry,' he said, 'but I wouldn't know about that. What sort of work?'

'Fixing old farm machinery.'

'Sounds like something Gerry might do,' said McCoy. 'That was the one thing he *was* good at, but he never said anything to me about it.'

The oldest man there suddenly broke his silence. 'Look,' he burst out, 'I've got better things to do than stand around here talking about Gerry Fletcher. If you want the truth, Fletcher is a shifty bastard. I don't know what he's done, but it doesn't surprise me that the police want to talk to him. And as far as I'm concerned he was a lazy sod as well. Always skiving off, supposed to be going to town for one thing or another. He was gone more than he was here.'

He glared at McCoy. 'Tell you the truth, I could never see why you put up with him. Me and the lads had no use for him, nor his—'

'That's quite enough, Sam,' McCoy cut in sharply. 'No need to go on about it.' He turned to Tregalles and shrugged an apology.

'Sorry, Sergeant,' he said, 'but I told you it would be a waste of time. We took Gerry on as a favour to an affiliate

when he quit long-distance driving, but he never did fit in
with the rest of the crew. But he was good on repairs, so that's
where I put him. Now, can I let these men get back to work?'

Tregalles wasn't satisfied, but neither was he getting
anywhere. 'All right,' he said, 'but if you should think of
anything,' he called after the men as they left the room, 'please
let us know.'

McCoy butted his cigarette and was about to leave as well
when Lyons spoke for the first time. 'If Gerry Fletcher was
such a misfit,' he said, 'why would you have him working for
you, at all, Mr McCoy?'

'Because he was bloody good at fixing things on the cheap,'
McCoy said harshly, 'and one of my jobs is to keep costs
down. That man could repair damned near anything on wheels,
so I didn't give a shit about what else he did or what he might
have been up to in his spare time as long as he got the job
done. And that's the truth!'

Tregalles was unusually quiet during dinner. He couldn't get
Sam Udall out of his mind. That was the name of the grey-
haired man who had spoken with such vehemence about
Fletcher. It hadn't been hard to pick Udall's name out of the
list of employees, since he was clearly the oldest one there.
Udall had all but challenged McCoy when he'd said he couldn't
understand why Fletcher had been kept on, and Tregalles had
the feeling that the man might have said more if McCoy hadn't
stopped him.

Tregalles looked at the clock. So why spend the evening
sitting here thinking about it, when it would be just as easy
to go and talk to the man? He didn't live far away. Augustus
Road was just across the river near the station. He could be
there in ten minutes.

In fact, because Augustus Road was lined with cars, and
the only place he could find to park was one street over, it
was closer to half an hour before Tregalles mounted the steps
of number 27 and rang the bell. Faintly, he heard a woman's
voice calling, 'Will you get that, Dad?'

The door was opened by Udall himself. He had a newspaper
in his hand and steel-rimmed glasses shoved up on his head.
His eyes narrowed when he recognized Tregalles, then shifted
to look past the sergeant to take a quick survey of the street.

'What do you want?' he asked suspiciously.

'Sorry to disturb you, Mr Udall,' Tregalles said pleasantly, 'but I'd like to follow up on something I believe you were about to tell us before you were interrupted earlier today. May I come in?' He stepped forward, but Udall moved to block him, and Tregalles was forced to step back.

'No, you can't come in!' Udall told him. 'And I don't know what you're talking about.'

'Oh, I think you do, and I thought you might prefer to talk to me here rather than have to come down to the station with me, but we can do it that way if?'

Udall stepped forward, almost pushing Tregalles off the step. 'Look,' he said, lowering his voice, 'I don't know what you're on about, and I don't know where you got the idea that I do. Like me and the lads told you, we never had anything to do with Gerry Fletcher. He was a blowhard; nobody liked him and he never was one of the crew. And that's *all* I can tell you. If he's done something against the law, it wouldn't surprise me, but I know nothing about it. All right?' He stepped back and was about to close the door, but Tregalles put out his hand and held it open.

'I'm not suggesting that you do know anything other than what you've told me,' he said, 'but I believe you were about to mention someone else, a mate, perhaps, of Fletcher's, when McCoy stopped you. All I want to know is the name of that person. All right?'

'Who is it, Dad?' the woman's voice called.

Udall glared at Tregalles. 'Just someone looking for the Bishops down the road,' he called over his shoulder, then lowered his voice again as he turned back to Tregalles. 'The name's Slater,' he said. 'Nick Slater. Big fellah, Australian. He doesn't work for us, but he comes around a lot, and I think he's something to do with one of the major carriers. Sometimes he's there for a couple of days, then we won't see him for a week, but when he is there he spends a fair bit of time with Gerry – at least he did before Gerry took off. Now, go away and leave me alone!'

'You say Slater spends a lot of time with Fletcher,' Tregalles said. 'Doing what? What are they working on?'

Clearly agitated now, Udall tried to close the door, but Tregalles held it open. 'Nothing!' Udall said in a fierce undertone. 'They don't work on anything – at least not in the shop. They go off in Slater's car together, and I don't know any more than that, so it's no good asking.'

'But McCoy must know,' Tregalles said. 'He *has* to know if he allows Fletcher to take off like that. So what is going on out there?'

'*Nothing* is going on out there,' Udall said desperately. 'It has nothing to do with RGS. Whatever Gerry Fletcher was up to, it didn't involve the company.'

'But it does involve McCoy. Right?'

'I wouldn't know,' said Udall stubbornly. He wiped a hand across his face. 'Look,' he said earnestly, 'I'd like to help, but I can't. I'm sixty-one years old, and all I want is to keep my head down and keep my job for as long as I can, so if there is anything dodgy going on, I don't want to know about it. Understand?'

Udall pushed the door shut without waiting for an answer, and Tregalles heard the solid click of the lock as the key was turned inside.

Slater's name again. Tregalles thought about that as he made his way back to his car. So, what *was* going on out there at RGS, he wondered? Whatever it was, he felt sure that McCoy was in the thick of it.

Twenty-Two

G race answered the phone, then handed it to Paget. 'Alcott,' she mouthed, rolling her eyes and making a face. A call from the superintendent almost certainly meant a disruption to their evening.

'Ah, Paget, glad I caught you in. Sorry if it's not the best time,' Alcott said, not sounding the least bit sorry at all, 'but something's come up and I need you here. And I don't mean the office; I'm at home.'

At home? That was a new one. In all the time he'd worked for Alcott, he'd never been asked to the man's home. 'Has something happened there?' he asked. 'Are you all right, sir?'

'Yes, yes, I'm fine.' He sounded testy. 'But I need you here. Half an hour?'

'Can you tell me—'

'Half an hour,' Alcott said as if Paget hadn't spoken, and hung up.

Paget stood there for a moment, frowning. 'He wants me there in half an hour,' he said in answer to Grace's unspoken question. 'At his house, but he wouldn't say why.'

Her own brow was furrowed as she said, 'That's odd. Did he sound as if he were in some sort of trouble?'

Paget shrugged. 'He *sounded* all right. Abrupt, but that's hardly anything new. I've a good mind to call him back and?'

But Grace was shaking her head. 'You know he wouldn't call unless it was important. Better get going, Neil; the clock's ticking, and he is not a patient man.'

Alcott lived in a semi-detached house on Kensington Drive at the top of Strathe Hill. Built just after the war, there were a dozen like it in the street: small front garden; low brick wall marking the boundary between garden and pavement; a single tree in the middle of the lawn; twin strips of concrete leading to the garage at the side of the house. The superintendent had floated the idea of moving to something a bit more upmarket several times, but his wife, Marion, liked it where they were. As she pointed out, it was paid for, and they certainly didn't need more room now that the girls were gone, and besides, she liked the neighbours, and you never knew who might be next door in a new place.

There was a silver Jag in the short driveway, and Paget wondered about that as he stepped inside the covered porch and rang the bell.

The door was opened by Alcott himself, who hustled him inside and closed the door quickly as if afraid someone might follow the DCI in. 'Just drop your coat on the chair and come through,' he said brusquely. 'There's someone here I want you to meet.'

Paget followed the superintendent into the front room, where a tall, broad-shouldered, grey-haired man with glass in hand, stood ramrod straight in the middle of the room. He smiled and slowly shook his head as he thrust out his hand.

'Country life must agree with you,' he said. 'Last time we met, you were – well, let's just say, not at your best. Good to see you again, Neil.'

Paget grasped the outstretched hand. 'Ben Trowbridge!' he said, shaking his own head in disbelief. 'I didn't expect to see you here. It's good to see you, too. But what brings you here? On holiday, are you? And if that's your Jag in the driveway, things must be looking up. Is Beryl with you?'

'No, but I'll tell her you asked,' Trowbridge said. 'And, no, I'm not on holiday, and the Jag isn't mine, but it is one of the perks of the job.'

Alcott, who had been hovering impatiently, said, 'Superintendent Trowbridge is with NCIS – the National Criminal Intelligence Service,' he added unnecessarily.

'So that's where you went,' said Paget. 'Congratulations, Ben. I'm afraid I've lost touch with what's been going on since I left the Met. How long have you been over there?'

'A couple of years, although I'm actually working with the Europol section and Interpol at the moment, which brings me to why I'm here.' He turned to Alcott. 'And I do appreciate your seeing me on such short notice, and for the use of your house, but I didn't think it would be wise to meet in your office. Shall we sit down?'

Trowbridge settled into a comfortable chair and held up his glass. 'I must say this is a very nice single malt, Superintendent,' he said as Paget sat down facing him. 'I'm sure you will appreciate it, Neil.'

But Paget shook his head. 'Nothing for me,' he said. 'I have to drive home and I have trouble with spirits.' Alcott looked relieved. He'd trotted out the best he had for his visitor, and he didn't want to see any of it go to waste.

'Superintendent Trowbridge has given me a rough outline of why he is here,' he explained as he sat down and lit a cigarette, 'but I suggested that he leave the details until you arrived rather than going over everything twice. Please, go ahead, Superintendent.'

Trowbridge waved a hand. 'Ben,' he said. 'I think we can dispense with the titles while we're here.' He set his glass aside and fixed his eyes on Paget. 'So, let's get down to business, and the first thing I must insist on is that what I'm about to tell you does not leave this room. All right?'

Paget glanced at Alcott, then nodded.

'Good. Now, the reason I am here, Neil, is because I want you to call off the people who have been sniffing round RGS Removals. It's important that you do so, because if you continue, you could jeopardize something we have been working on for a long time.'

'Which is?'

'By definition, trafficking in persons,' said Trowbridge tersely.

Paget frowned. 'And you believe that RGS is involved in moving people?'

'We know they are, but that's only part of it. RGS is merely one link in a very long chain, but they have become a very important one at the end of that chain.' Trowbridge hunched forward, eyes and manner intense as he went on to explain.

'First of all, as I'm sure you know, illegals of every stripe are pouring into this country. They are coming in by every means possible, and they're getting through due to lax immigration rules and cutbacks at Customs They're coming from almost every corner of the earth, including the Middle East, North Africa, Asia and the Orient, but our current target is the organization that is bringing them in from Eastern Europe. Romania, Bulgaria, Albania, the Ukraine, Latvia – in fact you could name just about any of the old Balkan states as well as the old USSR satellite states.

'They deal almost exclusively with those being brought in for exploitation in the sex trade, women and children who are forced into prostitution. Some have been lured by the promise of good jobs when they get here; others have been literally kidnapped in their home country, in fact some of the kids are from orphanages where the people who are supposed to be their guardians have sold them to the gangs, and once they're here, they are bought and sold like cattle to the highest bidder.

'One of the biggest operators is a man by the name of George Kellerman, and he is in the process of setting up a series of auction houses throughout the country, similar to the ones that have been running in Eastern Europe for some time, where the "merchandise", as he calls these hapless people, can be viewed, poked, prodded and "sampled" by potential buyers before they put in their bids. And one of those auction houses has been set up right here on your patch at a farm run by a man called Roper. I'm sure you know the name; one of your men was out there the other day to ask about a man by the name of Fletcher, who had called Roper on his mobile phone. Right?'

Paget nodded. 'Fletcher was involved in getting rid of a van that belonged to a young man by the name of Mark Newman. Newman disappeared about three weeks ago. We wanted to talk to Fletcher, but I think the people he was working for got to him first.'

'Newman is dead,' said Trowbridge flatly. 'He was caught snooping around the farm when they were doing a dry run. His presence there almost blew the entire operation, but once they'd established beyond any doubt that he wasn't a police spy, they killed him. He's buried on the farm.'

Paget settled back in his chair. 'Which tells me that you have someone on the inside,' he said quietly. 'How long has this been going on?'

Ben Trowbridge continued on as if Paget hadn't spoken. 'They came for the Irishman the following morning, and once they'd finished working on him they killed him as well. So you see, we are dealing with some very ruthless and determined people, and they'll simply disappear and set up somewhere else if they suspect that we're on to them, and all our efforts could be wasted.

'Now, they're still pretty jumpy, but they believe they have covered their tracks. Kellerman has a lot invested in this, so he plans to go ahead, and we believe that the first auction in this area will be held toward the end of this week. The actual date won't be set until very close to the time, and even then the buyers won't be told the location. They will be assembled at a staging point, then taken under the cover of darkness to the farm in closed vans. Afterwards, their "selections" will be transported to their new homes in separate vans. There will be major buyers there, primarily from Birmingham, Liverpool and Manchester, but there could be others as well, and Kellerman will be there himself. He has to be there in person or the buyers won't come. It's his guarantee to them that the place is safe.'

Paget and Alcott exchanged glances. 'So you hope to catch the lot once they're there,' Alcott said, 'and you want us to stay out of it until then?'

'Exactly. We'll have everyone we want, and you will be able to close the case on Newman and Doyle.'

Paget said, 'Do you know who did the actual killing?'

Trowbridge nodded. 'A man they call Luka. Luka Bardici, an Albanian. Smallish man, trim, athletic, dark complexion, thirty-something. Quite a pleasant-looking chap, in fact, but deadly. He's responsible for what they like to call "security", and he doesn't mess about if there's a problem. His methods are swift and direct.'

'There must be others involved in the murders,' said Paget. 'Fletcher, for example. We know he was given the responsibility of getting rid of Newman's van, and we know there was someone else with him.'

Trowbridge nodded. 'That's right,' he said, 'but I'm afraid he is dead as well.' He picked up his glass. 'The thing is, do I have your cooperation?'

Alcott was nodding, but Paget had a question. 'You say this man, Luka, actually did the killing, but can you prove it? I don't intend to stand in your way regarding all this other business – God knows I'd like to see these people get what they deserve – but I would also like some assurance that we will be able to get our hands on this man when the operation is over. I want him and anyone else involved in those killings to stand trial.'

Trowbridge pursed his lips as he held Paget's gaze. 'I'm not sure I can give you that assurance,' he said slowly. 'This man has a lot of knowledge about the organization, especially the European end of it, and we believe he can help us.'

'In exchange for what, Ben? We're talking cold-blooded murder, here.'

'And I'm talking about the fate of a great many people whose lives have been destroyed or will be if we don't do this right,' Trowbridge countered. 'For this auction alone, we estimate they'll be bringing in something like seventy-five women and children who will be sold like slabs of meat to men who will quite literally work them to death. If we don't get them now, they could spend the next twenty years in slavery, subjected to every abominable thing you can think of, and a few you never could. They will be forced to do whatever their masters want them to do. Some will commit suicide, some will try to make life bearable through drugs, but they will never have a normal life again, while those who do make it through will be cast aside once they are no longer useful. And this is only one part of the network. Important as it is to smash this ring and put the likes of Kellerman and his ilk behind bars, there are others lined up to take his place, and someone like Luka could prove invaluable to us.'

Paget steepled his fingers and rested his chin on them. The thought of letting the man slip away to negotiate some sort of deal with NCIS or Interpol did not sit well with him. On the other hand, how could he in all good conscience insist on prosecuting the man for murder, heinous as his crimes might be, when leaving him to Trowbridge might prevent many more lives from being destroyed?

'What about when you have finished with him?' he asked.

Trowbridge shook his head again. 'We may never finish with him' he said. 'In any case, I'm afraid it's already been decided. Your chief constable has been apprised of the situation, and he has agreed to cooperate. The only reason I am here today is because I felt you should hear what's at stake first hand, and I wanted you to have the full story. I'm sorry, Neil, but as I say, it's been decided. Luka is ours.'

Twenty-Three

Wednesday, March 26

As Paget drove into work next morning, his thoughts kept returning to some of the things Ben Trowbridge had told him. It wasn't that he hadn't known about the trafficking in women and children – one had only to read the papers – but here in this particular part of rural England it wasn't something they'd had to deal with before. But what had impressed and surprised him most of all were the numbers and the sheer size of what amounted to a worldwide network.

According to Trowbridge, literally thousands of women and children were being smuggled into mainly western countries to be sold into a life of degradation *every year*! And he had the facts and figures to prove it.

Naturally, Grace had been curious to know why he had been summoned to Alcott's house, but although he trusted her completely, he couldn't tell her. 'Is it something to do with your job?' she asked worriedly. 'You looked so serious when you came back. I mean is Alcott ill or something? It seems to me that the only time people go to those lengths to hold secret meetings is when some short of shuffle is about to take place. Are you up for promotion?'

He'd chuckled at that. 'Sorry, love, but it's none of the above,' he said. 'But I can assure you it has nothing to do with my position here or Alcott's, and he's not ill or leaving. Beyond that, all I can say is all will be revealed in due course. Trust me.'

Grace made a face and said, 'Oh, God! You sounded just like Tony Blair then, and you know what I thought of *him* when he was PM! And just how long is "in due course"?'

'I don't know for sure. A few days, perhaps, but honestly, there is nothing to worry about.'

Grace had accepted that, but she would look askance at him from time to time, and he could tell that her natural curiosity would not be satisfied until she found out what it was he was keeping from her.

Asking Grace to trust him was one thing, but he was glad now that he had fought Trowbridge and Alcott to a point where they had finally agreed to his telling Ormside and Tregalles that another investigation was under way.

'They don't have to know the specifics,' he'd assured them, 'but if I simply tell them to drop the Newman case without some sort of reasonable explanation, it could lead to all sorts of speculation and discussion, which is exactly what we *don't* want.

'Ben, I'm asking you to trust me on this,' he said earnestly, 'because I trust these two men, and I know Mr Alcott will agree with me on that.'

Paget smiled to himself at the memory. Alcott hadn't had much choice; if he didn't agree he would be saying in effect that he didn't trust his own men. And when it came right down to it, Trowbridge had seen the sense of the argument.

He arrived a few minutes earlier than usual, but Tregalles and Ormside were there ahead of him, and Tregalles was writing something on one of the whiteboards.

'Something new?' he said, pausing to read what the sergeant had written. 'Who is Udall?' he asked sharply. 'You went to this man's house last night, Tregalles?'

'That's right,' the sergeant told him, 'although I can't say he was pleased to see me. But he did give me Slater's name, saying he was a mate of Fletcher's, and while he didn't actually implicate McCoy in anything, I'm convinced that McCoy knows more than he's telling us, and I think we should have him in for a heart-to-heart.'

But Paget shook his head. This was the last thing he'd expected, and it would have to be dealt with immediately.

'Rub it out,' he told Tregalles, 'then come up to my office, both of you. There's been a development in the case, but I don't want to discuss it here.'

'Rub it out . . .?' Tregalles said. 'But I just said, this could mean that McCoy?'

'I said rub it out!' Paget told him. 'Do it now before anyone else has a chance to see it.' He waited while a clearly unhappy sergeant scrubbed the latest addition off the board, then said, 'Come with me and I'll fill you in.'

The two men exchanged questioning looks as they followed Paget up the stairs. But while Ormside was simply puzzled by the DCI's behaviour, Tregalles was trying to work out what he'd done wrong.

'Close the door and sit down,' Paget said as he took his own seat behind his desk. 'And don't look so hurt, Tregalles. There's a good reason for my telling you to scrub that information off the board just now.'

He settled back in his seat. 'Now, what I'm about to tell you is highly confidential,' he said. 'Unfortunately, I'm not at liberty to give you any details at this time, but we have been ordered to shut down the Newman case temporarily, because there is another investigation involving RGS under way. What I can tell you is that it is a major investigation that has been going on for some time. We've been warned off at the highest level, and I have given my word that we'll stand aside until it's resolved.

'So all activity on this case is to cease immediately. No phone enquiries, no visits to RGS, no talking to anyone out there. Which brings me,' he said, eyes firmly fixed on Tregalles, 'to your visit with Mr Udall last night. Normally, I would applaud the initiative, Tregalles, but this visit of yours could put the whole case in jeopardy, so I want to hear every last detail. I want to know *exactly* what you said, what he said, and what you think he will do – if he hasn't done it already.'

'You can hardly blame me for doing my job,' Tregalles said defensively. 'I mean how was I supposed to know there was something else going on?'

'You couldn't, and I'm *not* blaming you,' Paget said firmly, 'but the fact remains that I need to know every last detail, so let's get on with it and not waste any more time.'

Tregalles had a good memory, so he was able to relate what was said on both sides virtually verbatim, concluding with: 'and I'm almost one hundred percent sure that Udall won't say anything that might jeopardize his position there. As he said, he's too close to retirement. Sorry, boss, but if I'd known . . .'

'I knew nothing of this other investigation myself until last night,' Paget told him, 'so the main thing now is to make sure that no one who has been working on the case, does anything that might cause a problem.'

He cast a speculative eye in Tregalles's direction. 'Have you mentioned this chat with Udall to anyone else?' he asked.

Tregalles shook his head. 'Lyons and I talked about it when we were on our way in from RGS yesterday, but that's all. I haven't seen him this morning, so he doesn't know that I spoke to Udall last night, and I won't tell him.'

Ormside stirred beside him. 'It might be better if you did,' he said. 'But tell Lyons that Udall had nothing to add to whatever he told you yesterday. Otherwise, if he thinks you're dragging your feet, he's the sort who might take it into his head to go off to talk to Udall himself. He's dead keen on getting rid of that black mark on his record.'

Paget nodded slowly in agreement. 'You may be right,' he said. 'As you say, the last thing we need is someone like Lyons sticking his oar in. So find something else for him to do.'

'Just one more thing,' Ormside said. 'Emma Baker called in again this morning to ask what we were doing about tracing the man who was in the Red Lion the other night. We know it's a fleet car belonging to a company in Hammersmith, but we don't have the name of the person who had it out during that time. I think it's a fairly safe bet that he's some sort of sales rep on legitimate business, but after what you've just told us, I think we should drop any further enquiries in case he *is* involved in some way.'

Again, Paget nodded agreement. 'Tell whoever is on it to drop it,' he said. 'I'm sure you can find something more pressing for them to do.'

'No problem there,' Ormside assured him, 'but what do I tell Forsythe – and Emma Baker if she calls again. She can be pretty persistent.'

'Tell them that the man appears to be a legitimate sales rep who passes through the area from time to time, but we're keeping an eye on him.'

As the two men left the office, Paget reached for the phone. Reluctant as he was to call Trowbridge, the man had to be told. If Udall so much as breathed a word to any of his mates about talking to the police, and McCoy got wind of it, the run NCIS was counting on could very well be cancelled, and the operation closed down completely. And all that painstaking work, all the time and energy that had been spent by NCIS and others would go for nought. But worst of all, the women and children, who might have been saved from a life of sexual slavery, would simply disappear, and probably never be heard from again.

Alcott would have to be told as well. Paget began to punch in the internal number, then paused. Better call Trowbridge first; he wouldn't like the news but at least his reaction was predictable. Alcott, on the other hand, was another story altogether.

Lyons was not a happy man. He'd really begun to think that he and Tregalles were becoming a team, and he'd come in this morning full of ideas as to how they should proceed in the Newman case. He'd given it a lot of thought, and it was clear to him that they should be talking to some of the RGS employees on an individual basis away from the work place, and especially away from their boss, McCoy. And, as he and Tregalles had discussed the day before, the one they should talk to first was the old man who had spoken out, only to be silenced by McCoy.

He'd been tempted to tackle the man on his own last night. It would show Tregalles and DCI Paget that he had initiative, and it might help remove that reprimand from his record a little faster. In fact he had taken the trouble to go through the list of employees, and it hadn't been hard to work out that Udall, as the oldest employee on the list, was the name of the man who'd spoken out. And he lived in Broadminster. Lyons had toyed with the idea throughout the evening, but finally decided to observe the rules and try to persuade Tregalles to let him have a go at Udall after work the following day.

But Tregalles had beaten him to it. Not only that, but the sergeant had come up empty.

'It was a wasted trip,' Tregalles told him. 'Udall didn't have any more to say than he said yesterday. He made it plain he had no use for Fletcher, and he said again he wasn't surprised to hear that he was mixed up in something dodgy, but apart from that he couldn't tell me anything else. And if anyone else out there is involved, I believe him when he says he doesn't know anything about it.'

'But McCoy could be involved himself,' Lyons protested, 'or at least he must have known that Fletcher was up to something.

'It's possible,' Tregalles conceded, 'and I'll be following that up, but I'm afraid I'll be doing it without your help, Leo. Sorry, but Ormside is desperately short of people, so you'll be back with him for the time being.'

They came in just before closing time that evening. The man Emma had come to think of as the 'quiet man', accompanied by the Australian – the very man Molly had asked her to watch for and call her if he came in again.

So her memory *hadn't* been playing tricks on her, she thought, trying desperately not to show more than a casual interest as she served them; a Bass for the Australian and an orange juice for his companion. So he must be driving.

Emma glanced at the clock as the two men moved away from the bar and sat down at a table. Even if she could leave the bar without attracting attention and put in a call to Molly, there was no way that she or the police could get there before closing time. People were drifting out already, and Jack would be throwing the towel over the pumps any minute now. She picked up a glass and began polishing it while she watched out of the corner of her eye. The Australian took another drink; there was less than a third left in his glass when he set it down, so it wouldn't be long before they left. Emma tried to think of a way to delay them, but there was nothing she could do . . .

Or was there?

Emma set the glass down and mopped her brow with her forearm. 'Sorry, Jack,' she said wearily, 'but I've got a rotten headache coming on, and I'd really like to go home and get my head down. Would you mind very much if I leave now?'

'Course not,' Tanner told her. 'There's not that much to clean up, so off you go. Be all right, will you? Walking back home on your own?'

'Have been every night so far,' she assured him. 'It's only a couple of hundred yards, so don't worry about it. I'm sure I'll be fine once I've had a good sleep.'

She didn't like deceiving Jack. He was a good boss, but this was something she felt she had to do, and she had to do it now before the men left the pub.

Once outside, she ran all the way to the cottage and around the back to where she kept her car. It was going on fourteen years old; it was rusting out, and everyone called it an old banger, but it had a good engine, and what was more important, it was relatively cheap to run.

She drove back to the Red Lion and parked on the street where she had a clear view of the car park, and she'd only just switched off the lights when the two men came out of the pub. The Australian continued on into the car park, but the quiet man remained on the step, head held high as if sniffing the night air. He remained there until a car pulled up beside him and he got in.

So, he wasn't the driver after all, and neither was that the same car he'd been driving last week. It probably belonged to the Australian, and if she had known that ahead of time she would have taken its number. But here the lighting was poor, and it was impossible for Emma to tell the make or even the true colour of the car, and she certainly couldn't read the number plate.

They came out of the car park and turned right. Emma's heart was beating a little faster as she pulled out to follow them. She had never done anything like it before, but she knew enough not to get too close.

She followed the car out of the village in the direction of Lyddingham. The road didn't go anywhere else, and there was nothing in between, except for a few cottages, one of which, she reminded herself, was where Fletcher and his girlfriend had lived.

The news about Rose Ryan had been all over the local papers. There had been plenty of speculation but very little in the way of facts, and Emma had tried to get Molly to tell her more. Was it an accident or murder? Molly had refused to be drawn, saying only that it was still under investigation.

Deep in her own thoughts, it took Emma a few seconds to realize that the lights ahead of her had vanished. She had travelled this road many times, so she knew it ran straight for at least another quarter mile, so where . . .?

Out of the corner of her eye, she caught the glow of reflected light off to her left. Headlights sweeping the sky as the car she'd been following wound its way into the hills. It was a narrow, winding road, serving a scattering of farms before descending into the valley to join the main road between Broadminster and Ludlow.

Emma slowed as she reached the turning, less certain now

that what she was doing was wise. It was one thing to follow
these men along a well-travelled road, but quite another to
follow them on a back road where farmhouses were as much
as a mile apart.

On the other hand, she would never forgive herself if she
gave up now.

'Right!' she said loudly, more to bolster her own courage
than for any other reason, and made the turn.

It wasn't a bad road, but it was narrow, bordered by high
banks and brambles in some places, deep ditches in others, and
the bends in the road were extremely sharp. It might be all right
in daylight, Emma thought, but not on a moonless night such
as this one. The grades were steep, and there were times when
her headlights were pointed at the sky rather than focussed on
the next turning in the road.

And it was *dark!* Apart from the odd pinprick of light from
a distant farmhouse she could see absolutely nothing of the
countryside around her.

She slowed as she crested the next rise, and suddenly the
hedges were gone and the top of the hill was bare. Emma swore
beneath her breath as she hit the brakes and doused the lights.

'Some tracker you turned out to be!' she muttered angrily.
'Nothing like announcing what you're doing and where you
are to the whole world!'

The darkness closed in around her. She felt as if her face
was being covered with a cloak of black velvet. For all she
could see she might well have been blind.

And she'd lost them.

She peered into the darkness. This had to be the highest
point in the road, because she could see pinpricks of light in
the distance below. But no headlights; no moving glow in the
sky, and that worried her. No matter how far ahead of her
the car might be, she should be able to see some sort of glow
from their lights. She opened the window and listened, but
all she could hear was the ticking of her own engine as it
cooled.

She ran her tongue over her lips and tasted salt; her hands
were slippery on the wheel, and she realized she was sweating
despite the cold that came pouring in through the open window.
She closed it and sat there shivering as she tried to think what
to do next.

It was just possible, she supposed, that they knew the road so well that they had reached the main road to Ludlow, and that was why she couldn't see their lights. If they had, then she'd *really* lost them because they could be anywhere by now.

But just suppose that they *were* on to her and were waiting for her? Sitting there with the lights off, waiting for her to appear. There would be nowhere to go; no way of backing up or turning round.

On the other hand, perhaps they had reached their destination. But that would have to be one of the farms, and that didn't seem too likely; neither one of them had looked like farmers to her, nor did they look like the sort who would be staying at a farm way out here.

But the question remained: if not at a farm, then where? She couldn't go on until she knew, and she couldn't go back, because to try to turn round in the dark would probably mean ending up in a ditch and being stuck out there for the rest of the night.

No one who knew her would ever call Emma Baker fanciful, but alone out there in the middle of nowhere, her imagination was working overtime.

She drew a deep breath, and told herself not to be so silly. Either the two men had turned off long ago, or they were so far ahead of her that she would never catch up to them.

Which meant there was nothing to worry about.

Emma reached for the key in the ignition, then paused. She was anxious to get going, but perhaps it would be best to wait. Just in case, because if they *were* waiting for her, and she didn't appear, they might well think they were mistaken, and go on. Which meant they would have to put their lights on again and she would know where they were.

Emma pulled her coat even closer around her and settled down to wait.

She'd planned to stay longer, but at the end of ten minutes Emma had had enough. She started the car. The sooner she could get down to the main road, the sooner she could go home. It would take her about twenty minutes longer, using the main roads, but that was better by far than travelling this road again. Clearly, sleuthing was not one of her talents. She'd been a fool to try to follow the two men. Next time, leave it to the police, she told herself crossly, and vowed to call Molly

Forsythe first thing in the morning. At least she could tell her
that the Australian was back.

The two men watched from their place of concealment as the
car rounded the corner and carried on down the hill. The waited
until it had passed before turning to walk back up the track to
where they'd left the car.

'I told you it was the woman from the pub,' Luka said.
'I thought I recognized the car when we left the pub. It was
the same one that was parked round the back of the house
when we went in to clear out the kid's room.'

'Yeah, well, I don't know what you're using for night vision,'
the Australian growled, 'but I could barely tell it was a car as
it went by, let alone what make it was and who was driving.
I think you're getting jumpy in your old age, Luka. I mean,
other people do use this road, you know. It could have been
anybody, and I don't intend to worry about it. You can if you
want, but leave me out of it. Anyway, why shouldn't her car
be outside the pub? And why would she follow us? We weren't
in there more than twenty minutes, so unless you said something to her to make her suspicious – I know I didn't – I can't
see why she should take it into her head to follow us. *Did* you
say anything to her, Luka?'

'Of course not!' Luka said swiftly. 'I barely spoke to her.'

'Then, why would she take it on herself to follow us up a
road like this late at night?' the Australian asked as they got
into the car. 'Doesn't make a lot of sense, does it?'

'But she was the one who called the police in when Newman
disappeared.'

'So? They lived in the same house, so why wouldn't she
report the poor bastard missing when he doesn't come home?
What's so strange about that?'

'I still think it could have been her,' Luka said stubbornly.
'And we can't afford to take any chances so close to the time.'

'So stop being so bloody paranoid and rocking the boat,' the
Australian said. 'My guess is it was a local on his way home.
You know what your trouble is, mate? You've been in this job
too long. You see trouble even when it isn't there. You want to
have a go at anyone who so much as looks cross-eyed at you,
so let's not go stirring things up when there's no need. The
boss made it very clear last time he was out here that he wants

everything nice and calm and peaceful before the big day, so let's keep it that way.'

Luka remained silent, but the Australian knew he wouldn't let it rest, and that could mean trouble. The last thing they needed now was another disappearance that would bring the police sniffing round again. So, the question was: should he warn the boss that Luka could jeopardize everything if he wasn't reined in? Or should he say nothing, but keep a close eye on the man himself?

It was a question that was still with him when they pulled in behind the farmhouse.

Twenty-Four

Thursday, March 27

In spite of everything the Australian had said, Luka Bardici couldn't rid himself of the feeling that he'd been right about the car that had followed them. It had been impossible to see who was driving, but the suspicion lingered that it was the woman from the pub – the same woman who had disappeared from behind the bar a few minutes before he and Slater left.

Slater must have said or done something that aroused her suspicions. The man was too brash, too full of himself, and he fancied himself with the 'Sheilas', as he insisted on calling women. Which wasn't to say he didn't do his job, because it was Slater who had tracked down Fletcher and taken care of him, so he did have his uses. Even so, the man talked too much, and that could be why they'd been followed the night before.

Slater might be satisfied that the person who had followed them across the hills was just some local going home, but Luka wasn't one to take chances, which was why he left the farmhouse well before dawn and used his own car to go back down to Whitcott Lacey to check things out for himself. He parked some distance away, then slipped around the side of Wisteria Cottage to examine the car parked behind it.

It was an old car, rusting around the bottom of the doors, and the one that had passed them last night had sounded like an old car. If only he could get inside and start the engine he would know by the sound whether he was right or not, but that was out of the question. Not really sure about what he was looking for, Luka knelt beside the driver's door and shone a light underneath the car. Nothing on that side, but he could see something that looked like thread or torn cloth hanging down on the passenger's side of the car. Bent low, he circled the car. No, it wasn't thread and it wasn't cloth. It was grass caught between the chrome moulding and the rusted panel along the bottom of the door. It was the same sort of grass that he'd found caught in his own car since he'd been staying at the farm. It grew along the high banks bordering the narrow road, and it could be heard whipping against the side of the car on some of the tighter curves.

He felt the grass. It was supple and fresh. It wasn't proof by any means – there were many roads in the area where you could find the same sort of grass – but it was good enough for Luka. As far as he was concerned, his suspicions had been confirmed and Slater was wrong. It *was* the woman from the pub who had followed them. The question was, why? What was it that had made her suspicious?

It couldn't have been anything he'd done; he'd only been in the pub three times in his life, and he'd kept very much to himself each time. So it *had* to be Slater; had to be something the Australian had said or done to make the woman suspicious.

Luka switched the torch off and sat back on his heels The trouble was, she had seen the two of them together and he didn't like that at all. Something would have to be done about her. The question was, what? The boss had made it very clear that he expected everyone to keep a low profile and do nothing that might attract the attention of the police, so even an 'accident' was out of the question at this stage.

But was she *really* a threat, he asked himself? Even if she went to the police, what could she tell them? That she'd lost them? The police couldn't do much with that.

On the other hand, with so much at stake, could he afford to leave anything to chance? Better to silence her and be sure. The question was, how could it be done without arousing suspicion?

The silent vibrator on his phone alerted him to a call. 'Where the bloody hell are you?' Slater demanded when Luka answered. 'And what's all that hissing noise? I can barely hear you.'

'Power lines,' Luka said cryptically.

'You're down there, aren't you?' Slater accused. 'At the house. I remember seeing them on the hill behind the house.'

'It's none of your business where I am,' Luka snapped. 'So what do you want?'

'Not me. It's the boss. He's been trying to get hold of you, and I had to tell him that you were out doing a perimeter check, and phones don't always work out here in the valleys.

I knew you weren't because your car's gone, but you'd better get back to him fast!'

So what was Kellerman panicking about now? Luka wondered wearily. Everything was set; there wasn't anything else they could do, and he would be glad when this thing was over. At least he would be out of this godforsaken backwater, although no doubt there would be others if this one was successful. Kellerman had big plans. Distribution points all over the country, right up as far as Newcastle.

Scotland was something else again. Next to the Russians, they were the meanest bunch of bastards Luka had ever met. They had their own network north of the border, and you didn't even *think* of messing with them if you knew what was good for you.

Still, orders were orders, so the sooner he called Kellerman, the better. He didn't like the idea of leaving the problem of the barmaid unresolved, but you didn't keep Kellerman waiting, and you certainly didn't tell him that there might have been yet another breach of security.

Still, he could give her something to think about; something to keep her from following anyone for a while.

Luka took out a knife and slid the thin blade first into one tyre, and then another. The slits were so small that he could barely hear the air escaping, but two of her tyres would be flat within fifteen minutes.

Emma Baker was trying hard to concentrate on her work – exams would be coming up in another three weeks, and while she knew she would do all right, she wanted to do better than that. But the nightmarish drive into the hills the night before kept intruding into her thoughts.

She couldn't be sure about the role of the quiet man, but according to Molly, the fingerprints of the Australian had been found on Mark's van, so he must be involved in some way. Emma had tried to get hold of Molly, but the detective who had answered her call this morning had told her she wasn't there, and he'd seemed vague about when she would be back.

Emma looked at the clock for perhaps the fiftieth time that morning. Almost twelve. She made up her mind; she would call at lunchtime, and if Molly wasn't there she would ask for Sergeant Tregalles.

*   *   *

DC Lyons sat slumped in his chair, feet up on an open drawer as he munched his sandwich. The office was all but deserted. Ormside had gone upstairs on some errand or other, and the others had all gone to the pub across the street for lunch. Normally, he would have been there as well, but someone had to stay behind, and he was it today.

Seemed like he was 'it' every day, he thought bitterly.

He poked at the load of crime statistics Ormside had dumped on his desk. 'The collator needs a preliminary sort before entering them into the system,' he'd said. 'And keep an eye open for patterns while you're doing it. Might save her some time if you can pick any out ahead of time.'

A mind-numbing task if ever there was one, and certainly not the sort of job that someone with his background and training should be lumbered with.

He popped the last of the sandwich in his mouth, then screwed up the paper it had been wrapped in and lobbed it at the wastepaper basket. An easy shot, but today it bounced off the edge and fell to the floor. Muttering to himself that nothing seemed to be going right these days, he was about to pick it up when the phone rang.

'DC Lyons,' he said, swallowing the remains of his sandwich.

'Emma Baker,' the caller told him. 'I believe you are the detective I spoke to earlier, when I asked to speak to Molly Forsythe. Do you know if she is back yet?'

'That's right, Miss Baker, but Constable Forsythe isn't available at the moment. Can I help you?'

'What about Sergeant Tregalles? Is he there?'

'I'm afraid not, miss. But if it has to do with the Mark Newman case, I've been working very closely with Sergeant Tregalles on that one, so if I can help . . .?'

'It's just that . . . It's just that the Australian was in the Red Lion again last night. You know the man I mean – they found his prints on Mark's van when they pulled it out of the water, and Molly asked me to let her know if I saw him again. Well, I did see him again. He came in last night with another man, and I probably shouldn't have done it, but I followed them when they left.'

Suddenly she had Lyons' full attention. 'We don't advise that, miss,' he said, quoting directly from the manual, 'because

it could be dangerous. But since you did, can you tell me
where they went or what they did?'

'Well . . .' Now that she was actually talking to someone
about it, Emma realized how little she really had to tell. 'You
see,' she said hesitantly, 'I've never done that sort of thing
before, and I'm afraid I lost them when they left the
Lyddingham road to cut across country to the main road to
Ludlow. Do you know the road I mean? It's about a mile-
and-a-half out of Whitcott.'

'Yes, I do, miss,' he said as a memory stirred. Tregalles had
pointed to that very same road when they were on their way
back from Lyddingham, and told him about Fletcher's call to
a farmer by the name of Roper. Could it be that there was
something about the farm that Tregalles had missed? This
could turn out to be just what he was looking for, a chance
– a *proper* chance to show them what he could do. If he could
find out . . .

Emma was speaking again, 'To tell you the truth, I feel a
bit foolish calling about this now, but I thought you should
at least know that the Australian is still in the area, and he
was with the other man – the one who might have been in
the pub the night Mark and Mickey Doyle had their heads
together. So if you would just tell Molly or the sergeant that
I called?'

'No, no, don't hang up,' Lyons broke in. 'Even though you
say you lost them, I would like to hear everything from the
beginning. You may recall something that turns out to be very
important. You say the Australian and another man came into
the pub? Can you describe this other man, Miss Baker?'

It had taken Lyons very little time to pinpoint the location of
a hill farm belonging to a man by the name of Evan Roper. He
studied a contour map of the area, and decided that the best
way to approach the farm without being seen was from the rear.
He would have much preferred a position overlooking the front
of the place, but there was no cover. Approaching from the rear
would mean a cross-country hike of roughly three miles, and
a fairly steep climb, but for someone who had competed in five
marathon events last year alone, from the Fun Run in Knowle
in May, to the Loch Ness Marathon in Inverness in October, a
three-mile walk in the hills was a doddle.

His plan was to conceal himself directly across from the farmhouse on the far side of what appeared on the map to be a gully or shallow ravine, and he found it hard to curb his impatience to finish his shift and be on his way. His mind, that afternoon, was more on planning his approach than on searching for patterns among the crime stats he was supposed to be sorting.

Reluctantly, he decided that he would have to go home to pick up his digital camera and one or two other things before taking off for the farm, but he should still be in position with at least an hour of daylight left for observation.

And if Slater or the other chap that Emma Baker had described should show themselves, he would take pictures. He had quite a decent telephoto lens he'd bought on eBay, so he was confident he could get a reasonable shot of them at that distance.

He looked at the clock again. The time seemed to be crawling by, and he was impatient to be off. He could hardly wait to see the look on Tregalles's face when he plunked the pictures down in front of him tomorrow morning.

It had all seemed so simple and straightforward back there in the office, but nothing was working out as planned. For a start, it had taken him considerably longer to get there than he'd thought it would, and it was almost dusk by the time he'd worked his way into position. And while it had been sunny and warm earlier in the day, the temperature was dropping rapidly, and mist was rising from the valley bottom.

He found cover of a sort in a scrubby patch of trees over-looking the valley, and now, stretched out on a groundsheet, he took his first good look at the farmhouse through binoculars.

His heart sank. What he'd thought would be a good vantage point wasn't anything of the sort. In fact, what had looked like a shallow ravine on the map, turned out to be a broad, steep-sided valley, and one look through the lens of his camera told him that he could never get a decent picture of anything at that range.

Lyons buried his face in his arms and groaned aloud. He'd been so caught up in the idea of proving that he could act on his own initiative, so anxious to 'show them what he could do', that he'd made a balls up of it again.

But there had to be *something* he could salvage from this disaster. Perhaps he could tell them . . .

Tell them what? That he'd deliberately withheld the information he'd received from Emma Baker, so that he could come out here on his own to take a few pictures? And then what? What the hell had he been thinking of? If Paget ever found out . . . Just the thought was enough to make him cringe.

'Idiot!' he breathed. What he *should* have done was report Emma's call to Ormside, and taken whatever small credit there might be for tying it in to Roper's farm. Too bad he hadn't had the sense to think of that earlier.

There was nothing for it now but to leave as quickly as he could and say nothing to anyone about coming out here. He'd give Molly Emma's message in the morning and let her make the connection with the Roper farm. And if she didn't make the connection, he could suddenly recall Tregalles's mention of the farm, and take credit for that at least. It wasn't much, but it was better than nothing.

Somewhat buoyed by the thought, he knelt to roll up the groundsheet and was reaching for his rucksack when he heard a sound, and something cold and hard was pressed against the base of his skull.

'Don't even *think* of moving,' a hoarse voice whispered in his ear. 'Move before I tell you to, and I'll blow your bloody head off!'

Perhaps it was the pent up anger and frustration that made him do it; perhaps it was simply an adrenalin rush that made him lash out without thinking. His forearm smashed with numbing force against the weapon as he jerked his head away. He twisted round, kicking blindly. He felt his boot strike solid bone, and heard a yelp of pain as his assailant went down. Lyons didn't wait. He was up and running for his life, slithering and sliding down the hillside so fast that he couldn't have stopped if he'd wanted to.

His foot went out from under him and suddenly he was flying through the air. He landed hard, tried to stop himself, but the slope was even steeper here, and there was nothing he could do except try to protect his head as he plunged end over end into the mists below.

Twenty-Five

Friday, March 28

A very worried-looking Sergeant Ormside met Paget at the door as he entered the office next morning. 'Alcott's looking for you,' he said baldly, 'and I've never seen him in such a state. Practically blue in the face, he was. Came in like a bloody whirlwind and told me to tell you to get up to his office before you do anything else.'

'Did he say what it was about?'

'Wouldn't say. Just about took my head off when I asked, so I wouldn't hang about if I were you, sir.'

'Nothing that might give us a clue in the night log?'

Ormside shook his head.

'Better get up there and see what it's all about, then,' said Paget as he headed for the door. 'Wish me luck.'

'I think you might need a bloody sight more than luck,' Ormside muttered to himself as the door closed behind the chief inspector.

The superintendent's door was open and Alcott was standing by the window, a cigarette cupped in his hand, eyes fixed on some distant object.

'You wished to see me, sir?' said Paget as he entered.

Alcott turned to face the chief inspector. 'No,' he said deliberately, his voice ominously low, 'I did not *wish* to see you, Chief Inspector. What I *want* is an explanation. I want to know why you, as a senior officer, feel you have the right to jeopardize a major investigation, when you have been given explicit instructions to halt your own investigation? And why you would see fit to send in one of the greenest men you've got to go blundering about like a drunken sailor, is beyond me. This action of yours has almost certainly destroyed years of painstaking work, to say nothing of what will happen to God knows how many young women and children who might have been rescued.' His narrowed eyes bored into Paget's own. 'This is a disciplinary matter,' he continued ominously, 'and I—'

'Which means I should at least be told what I'm accused of,' Paget broke in sharply, 'because I have no idea what you are talking about, and I can't give you an explanation until you tell me what this is about.'

Alcott's eyes narrowed. 'I'm talking about this idiot, Lyons, up at the Roper farm,' he grated. 'Did you really think you could send someone in the back way without him being detected? And what did you hope to accomplish? Good God, man, Lyons has already allowed one man to escape, so what . . .?'

'If Lyons or anyone else was at the Roper farm, he certainly didn't go there with my permission,' Paget broke in. 'Are you sure about this, sir? I mean how—'

'Of course I'm bloody sure!' Alcott exploded. 'I've had the chief constable and a thoroughly pissed off Superintendent Trowbridge chewing my arse off since six o'clock this morning.'

'So, what does Lyons have to say for himself? To the best of my knowledge he's been on desk duties these past few days, and I have no idea how he learned about the farm or what prompted him to go out there on his own. Where is he now?'

Alcott threw up his hands. 'That,' he said thinly, 'is what we would all like to know. One of Trowbridge's men caught him sneaking in the back way to spy on the farm. He tackled him, but somehow or other Lyons broke away, and the last anyone saw of him he was going like the clappers down the hill behind the farm. The mist was rising, and they lost him, so God knows where he is now or how much damage he's done. If he's been caught by the people Trowbridge is after, he's probably dead, and the entire operation will be shut down. The whole thing is an absolute shambles, and I'm being held responsible for it.'

Alcott jammed the half-smoked cigarette into the ashtray with such force that butts and ash flew across his desk.

Paget frowned. 'How did they know it was *Lyons*?' he asked. 'If he got away as quickly as they say . . .?'

'He left his stuff behind. They ran the prints on a camera

and binoculars. They came up with Lyons, and traced him straight back to us.'

'If Trowbridge has someone on the inside, as I suspect he does,' said Paget, 'then he should know if they have Lyons or not. And if his men lost him in the mist, Lyons may have managed to get away undetected.'

'So where is he, then?' Alcott demanded. 'Because if he isn't dead, he's going to wish to hell he was if I get hold of him.'

Paget reached across the desk to pick up the phone. 'Let me check something out,' he said, punching in Ormside's number. He had a short conversation with the sergeant, then waited while Ormside checked Lyons' desk.

'According to the message log,' he said, relaying the information to Alcott as he was getting it on the phone, 'it shows Lyons received a call from Emma Baker at lunchtime yesterday. The message was intended for Forsythe, but she was away, so it would seem that Lyons dealt with it himself. Ormside says Roper's name is on the scratch pad on Lyons' desk, so it looks as if Baker told him something that pointed him in the direction of the farm. I've asked Ormside to check with Emma Baker to find out what she told Lyons, and to see if it will shed any light on what prompted him to go out there on his own.'

Alcott turned from the window to stare at Paget. 'Are you telling me that Lyons held back information and went out there without telling *anyone*?'

'That's the way it looks, I'm afraid,' said Paget. 'And in all fairness, sir, he would have no idea that he was jeopardizing anything, because we kept that information to ourselves.'

'Fairness?' Alcott fairly screeched as he slammed his fist down on the desk. 'I don't give a shit for what this idiot knew or didn't know; he went off on his own without permission or telling anyone, and he is finished as far as I'm concerned, so you can save that little speech for the board at his dismissal if you like, but don't try it out on me!'

'Assuming he's still alive,' said Paget quietly. 'And,' he hurried on before Alcott could say anything, 'if it was Emma Baker's call that prompted him to go out there, I'm wondering how she would know about the Roper farm? If Lyons has been caught, and he tells them who supplied him with the information that sent him out there, Emma could be in grave danger.' He made a move toward the door. 'So, with your permission, sir . . .?'

He waited, but Alcott was in no mood to be hurried. 'She *is* Sir Robert's niece,' he prompted.

Alcott's dark eyes glittered as he shot a warning glance in Paget's direction. But Paget did have a point, and chief constable's niece or not, he couldn't ignore the fact that an innocent person could be in grave danger.

'Oh, get on with it, then,' he growled with a dismissive flick of the hand. 'And for Christ's sake try not to make this into any more of a dog's breakfast than it already is,' he bellowed after him as Paget left the office.

'So what's this flap all about, then?' Tregalles asked Paget as soon as he appeared downstairs. 'Len says Lyons has gone missing, and it has something to do with Emma Baker.'

Before Paget could reply, Ormside said, 'Here's Forsythe now. Did you get hold of Baker?' he asked as she joined the group.

Molly shook her head. 'There's no reply from the cottage, and the people at the college tell me that Emma didn't turn up for class today. And she hasn't called in, which they say is unusual for her, because she always lets them know if she can't make it to class.' She turned to Paget. 'Is Emma in some sort of trouble, sir?'

'To be honest, I don't know,' he confessed, 'but I will be a lot happier when I can talk to her and find out what she told Lyons. You haven't spoken to her since yesterday, I suppose?'

'No, sir. But I can keep trying if you—'

'That can be done by someone else,' Paget told her. 'What I want you to do is go out there yourself and look for her. If she's anywhere in the village, she shouldn't be hard to find. So let us know the moment you do find her, then bring her in.'

'If it's that important, I'll go with her . . .' Tregalles began, but Paget was shaking his head once again.

'Just Forsythe,' he said tersely. 'I want to keep this as low-key as possible.'

'What should I tell her when I do find her, sir?' asked Molly as she prepared to leave.

'Ask her exactly what she told Lyons, yesterday, and let us know immediately, but bring her in anyway.'

Still Molly hesitated. 'It would help a lot if I knew what this was about,' she ventured.

'I'm sure it would,' Paget said, 'but that's all I can tell you at the moment, Constable, so please, just go!'

He watched as Molly made for the door, then turned to face the questioning look on the faces of the two sergeants.

'She's right, you know,' Ormside said. 'This job is no picnic when we know what we're doing, but it's a right bastard when we're kept in the dark, if you know what I mean – sir!'

Tregalles was nodding. 'What *is* this flap all about?' he asked. 'Why is Emma Baker in danger, and what has Lyons done now?'

Paget hesitated, but Ormside was right. Secrecy had its place, but since Lyons had taken matters into his own hands, Trowbridge's operation was already in jeopardy, so the old rules no longer applied. Both Ormside and Tregalles *had* to be told exactly what was at stake. And the sooner he had another talk with Trowbridge, the better.

'If you are calling from Charter Lane, I'm not even going to talk to you,' Trowbridge said when he heard Paget's voice. 'Bloody place probably leaks like a sieve, so if you want to talk to me, do it from an outside line. And no mobiles,' he added sternly before hanging up.

Paget walked down the street to the call box outside the local post office and rang Trowbridge's number again.

The superintendent was barely civil. Paget could almost feel the chill coming down the line as he explained very carefully what had happened, ending with: 'Look, Ben, this man didn't know anything about your operation. As far as he was concerned, he received information that might lead to solving the Newman disappearance. Yes, he was wrong to go off on his own without telling anyone, and we'll deal with that later, but right now I have to know if the people you are after have him, because if they have and he has talked, then someone else could be in grave danger.'

'That, my friend, is your problem,' Trowbridge told him. 'Mine is trying to keep this entire operation from blowing up in our faces due to the stupidity of one of your men.'

'I need an answer, Ben,' Paget persisted. 'I know you must have a line inside. You'd know if they have Lyons.'

'What I might know or not know is none of your business, Neil. I just want you and your crew to stay out of the way.'

'They haven't, have they, Ben?' Paget said.

'Haven't what?' Trowbridge asked irritably.

'Haven't got our man. Because if they had, the auction would be off, and so would your operation, and you would be screaming bloody murder. But I'm not hearing that.'

'You're assuming a hell of a lot,' Trowbridge grated, 'but, all right, yes, you're right – at least so far, though God knows we've got our fingers crossed. To the best of my knowledge, they haven't got him, but it isn't as if I can ring up and ask, is it? I have to wait for information, and contact is sporadic, so all I can do is wait and pray. What concerns me most is that if that idiot policeman has somehow managed to escape detection, he could still be caught. Do you not have any contact with him?'

'Unfortunately, no. But idiot or not, I can't just leave him there. These people are killers.'

'Don't even *think* of going in after him,' Trowbridge warned. 'You'd be putting too many other lives at risk, so stay out of it. We'll do everything we can to make sure we find him before they do, but he's going to have to take his chances for the next couple of . . .' He stopped abruptly.

'Couple of *days*?' said Paget. 'So you know exactly when this is going down, don't you, Ben? And you want me to leave my man out there all that time?'

'I didn't tell you that,' Trowbridge snapped. 'In fact we still don't have confirmation, but what I *can* tell you is if this clown of yours is still at large and hiding, he won't die of starvation or exposure before this whole thing is over.'

'Perhaps not, but he could be injured, and I want some of my people with you when you go in to make sure that our man isn't one of the casualties.'

'No need,' Trowbridge said dismissively. 'We have his picture.'

'Not good enough,' Paget told him. 'We're talking about a man's life, Ben. One of ours, and you know how that resonates in the service. We have a stake in this, and I'm prepared to take this to the top if necessary.'

'Don't try to threaten me, Neil,' Trowbridge growled. He remained silent for a moment, but when he spoke again his tone had softened. 'I can understand your position, Neil, but you have to understand mine as well. Too many things have happened to upset our plans already; I can't afford to take any more risks.'

'I meant what I said, Ben,' Paget warned.

A weary sigh of resignation came down the line. 'All right, then, damn it! *You* can come,' Trowbridge conceded, 'but that's it. Just you; no one else. You will be under my orders, and you'll tell no one about this conversation. Understood?'

'Understood,' Paget told him, 'but I also want it understood that while I'm prepared to let your people try to recover Lyons and get him out of there, I know what can happen in an under-cover investigation as big and complex as yours, and I'm giving you fair warning, Ben: if you do find our man, I want him back alive.'

'You've been watching too much TV,' Trowbridge said deri-sively. 'Do you honestly think we'd *kill* him?'

'No, I don't, but neither do I think you would go out of your way to save him if it meant jeopardizing the operation,' Paget said, and hung up.

'There's no one at the cottage,' Ormside said when Paget returned, 'and Forsythe says she's been in every shop in the village, as well as the pub, but no one has seen or heard from Emma Baker today. She said Baker's car is still there – it has two flat tyres, which she thought a bit odd, because they weren't flat the other day – but apart from that, and the fact that the back door still isn't fixed, she says everything looks normal.

'Tregalles phoned the college and got Tom Foxworthy out of class, but all he could tell him was that Emma was still at home when he left this morning, and he was surprised to learn that she wasn't in class. Tregalles is trying to get hold of Sylvia Tyler in case she knows something, but she's off on some sort of field exercise. So, what do you want me to tell Forsythe? She . . .'

He stopped in mid-sentence. 'What is it, man?' he demanded irritably of a uniformed constable who had entered the room and was now hovering a few feet away. 'Can't you see we're busy?'

'Sorry to interrupt,' the man apologized, 'but I'm looking for DC Forsythe. We've got a woman up front who wants to speak to her. Says she doesn't want to talk to anyone else. Name of Baker. Emma Baker.'

When Emma Baker decided to come into town to find out for herself if anything was being done about the information she had given to the detective she had spoken to yesterday, she'd envisioned a quiet chat, perhaps over a cup of tea or coffee, with Molly Forsythe. She liked Molly; she trusted her, and she wished she had waited to give her the information she had given to the man she had spoken to yesterday. Perhaps she was mistaken, but Emma felt that the man was only half listening to her, especially toward the end – in fact she wondered afterwards if he even believed what she was telling him, because he'd seemed anxious to end the conversation.

But Molly would listen; Molly would understand.

'Miss Baker?'

Emma had been so absorbed in he own thoughts that she hadn't seen Paget and Tregalles approach, and it took her a second or two to gather her wits. 'Chief Inspector Paget . . .' She stopped, not quite knowing what to say to him.

'I'm afraid DC Forsythe isn't available at the moment,' he said, 'but we're very glad you're here because we need to talk to you. Please come with us.'

Emma picked up a large satchel-like bag that had been sitting at her feet, slung the strap over her shoulder and allowed herself to be shepherded down the corridor by the two men. But she was puzzled, and just a little bit alarmed. Why, when all she wanted to do was talk to Molly, would she be greeted by a detective chief inspector and a sergeant, both of whom were looking very serious indeed

She caught her breath and stopped in mid-stride. 'Has something happened to Molly?' she asked anxiously. 'Is that why I haven't been able to get hold of her?'

But Tregalles was shaking his head. 'As a matter of fact, she is out there in Whitcott Lacey looking for you at this very moment,' he told her. 'So it was quite a surprise to all of us when we heard you'd turned up here.' He was about to say more, but was stopped by a warning glance from Paget.

Ushered into a vacant room at the end of the corridor, Emma was invited to sit down. Tregalles closed the door, and both men took their seats facing her. Emma eased the bag from her shoulder and set it at her feet. 'Something *is* wrong, though, isn't it?' she said as she looked at each of them in turn. 'I can see it in your faces. Something . . .' She caught her breath. 'Mark's dead, isn't he?' she said softly. 'That's why you've been looking for me, isn't it, Chief Inspector?'

The question caught him by surprise. Trowbridge had told him that Mark Newman was dead, but Paget had told no one else.

He said, 'No, that's not why we were looking for you, Miss Baker. The reason we want to talk to you is to find out what you told DC Lyons yesterday.'

Emma frowned. 'Didn't he tell you?' she asked. 'He said he was taking it all down.'

'I'm afraid DC Lyons isn't available,' Paget said, 'so it would be very helpful if you would tell us what you told him.'

Emma eyed the grave faces in front of her. 'Something's happened to him, hasn't it?' she said. It was more of a statement than a question. 'Because of something I told him?'

'We'll have a better understanding of that if you will tell us everything you told him, and I would like to record what you have to say. This is not a formal interview, and you have the right to refuse, but it would be of considerable help to us if we have a record we can refer to later if necessary.'

Emma shrugged acceptance. 'If it will help, why not?' she said. 'Do you want me to begin with my seeing the Australian and the other man in the pub on Wednesday night?'

'Everything that prompted you to call us yesterday,' Paget told her as he set the recorder in motion.

'I realize now that it was a very foolish thing to do,' she said, then went on to tell them everything she had told Lyons the day before.

When she came to the part where she described leaving the Whitcott – Lyddingham road to follow the two men into the hills, she saw Tregalles and Paget exchange glances, but they remained silent.

'The trouble was, once I was on that road, there were so many twists and turns, and it was so black out there, that I lost sight of the car, so I have no idea where they went.'

Emma gave an involuntary shiver. 'I wanted to go back, but I didn't dare try turning around, so I waited a bit, then carried on down to the main road and went back home the long way round.

'I'm not usually that impulsive,' she concluded, 'but it's been so long since Mark disappeared, and I thought if there was anything I could do . . .' She shrugged helplessly.

'What prompted you to come in today?' asked Paget.

'To be honest, I wasn't sure that the man I spoke to yesterday had taken me seriously, and I wanted to talk to Molly, because I knew she would.'

'How did you get here?'

'By bus. I would have come by car, but I must have run over some glass or something the other night, because two of my tyres were flat yesterday morning, and I haven't had time to do anything about them. I missed the express bus this morning, so I had to take the one that goes all round the villages, which is why it's taken me so long to get here.'

Emma paused, frowning as she looked from one to the other. 'But you knew that, didn't you? About the car, I mean. Otherwise you wouldn't have asked how I got here.'

'DC Forsythe told us when she went looking for you this morning.'

'Have you told anyone else about following these men?' Tregalles asked. 'Talked to anyone about it at all? Your friends, perhaps?'

Emma was shaking her head. 'No. To tell you the truth, I felt a little foolish about it, so I didn't intend to tell anyone but Molly or you.'

'Even inadvertently? Anyone at the college or the Red Lion, perhaps?'

'No, no one,' Emma said emphatically. 'But why are you asking?'

'Because,' Paget said quietly, 'we have reason to believe that the two men you've described are extremely dangerous, and I think it is possible that they may have become aware that you were following them.' He eyed Emma speculatively for a long moment before going on. 'And if that is the case – and I hope it's not – but if it is, then I think it would be advisable for you to stay somewhere else for at least the next few days. Do you have somewhere else you can go? You mentioned a sister? The one who loaned you the camera. Could you stay with her? Or perhaps with your uncle, the chief constable.'

Emma made a face. 'I don't think so,' she said. 'My sister

has a houseful of children, and Uncle Robert is . . . Well, to tell the truth I'd sooner go home if you think it's *really* necessary. The trouble is, I have exams coming up in three weeks, so I really should be studying.'

'Where's home?' asked Paget.

'Gloucester. But I don't have a car, at least not until I get the tyres repaired.'

'I don't want you going back to Wisteria Cottage for any reason,' Paget said. 'In fact I think it would be best if you go directly to Gloucester from here.'

'But I didn't come prepared for anything like this,' Emma protested. 'Surely I can go back to get some clothes and other things I'll need?'

'You have more clothes in Gloucester?'

'Of course, but . . .'

'And I imagine that's your laptop in the satchel you're carrying?'

'Yes . . .?' she said cautiously

Paget leaned forward to add emphasis to what he was about to say.

'Look, Miss Baker,' he said quietly, 'I can't order you to stay away from Whitcott, and I cannot say for certain that you would be in danger there. But I would feel much happier if you would take my advice and go home for a few days. And you can study for your exams, using your laptop. Isn't that right?'

'Well, yes . . .' Emma looked troubled as she sat back in her chair. 'You are serious, aren't you, Chief Inspector? I mean *really* serious!'

'Yes, I am,' he said.

Emma was silent for a moment. 'What about Tom and Sylvia?' she asked. 'Are they in any danger?'

'No. And as I said, you may not be either, but I don't want to take any chances. Now, about getting you there . . .'

Emma smiled as she shook her head. 'No need to worry about that,' she told him. 'What's the point in having a chief constable for an uncle if you can't call on him for a favour now and then?'

Twenty-Six

Saturday, March 29

B en Trowbridge sat at the table that had served him as a desk for the past few weeks, fingers drumming nervously on the polished surface as he watched through mullioned windows the deepening shadows inch their way across the slopes of gently rolling hills. The sun would drop behind them in less than half an hour, but it couldn't go down fast enough for him.

His temporary headquarters were in what once had been a manor house situated four miles from the Roper farm. Too costly to maintain as a residence, the house had been made over into what was advertised as a 'quiet country retreat removed from the pressures of everyday living'. Seminars ranging from corporate strategy to fitness and meditation had been held there, and as far as the outside world was concerned, its present occupants were members of SSIS, a strategic studies group concerned with internal security. They had taken over the premises for a month, and they had brought their own household and kitchen staff with them.

Trowbridge looked at his watch for perhaps the tenth time in the last half hour: twenty-six hours to go before they could make their first move. After that, there would probably be another two or three hours of waiting for the signal that would tell them that Kellerman was actually there.

If they missed him this time . . .

Trowbridge closed his eyes. He didn't even want to think about that possibility. So many things had gone wrong already, and they still didn't know what had happened to that idiot of Paget's. He must still be down there somewhere, because Paget would have let him know if the man had managed to get out of the valley under his own steam. Trowbridge's men had searched the area as best they could, but even night vision goggles couldn't penetrate the heavy blanket of mist that lay in the valley. And concealed in their camouflaged hides on the brow of the hill during the day, they had scanned the area with high-powered scopes without result, so God knows where the man had got to.

Perhaps he was dead. Perhaps he'd killed himself in a fall down the hillside and had fallen miraculously into a place of concealment. Trowbridge grimaced. An uncharitable thought, perhaps, but he couldn't help taking some small comfort from it. But whatever had happened to the man, Trowbridge hoped he would stay where he was for the next – he glanced at his watch again – twenty-five hours and fifty-three minutes.

The phone rang. He picked it up and said, 'Yes?'

The man at the other end had barely spoken a dozen words before Trowbridge interrupted him with, 'When?' Then: 'Why wasn't I informed before this, for God's sake?' He slammed the phone down without waiting for an explanation.

They'd lost Kellerman in London. They'd followed him as usual to his favourite coffee shop in Horseferry Road for his morning coffee and bagel. He would normally spend half an hour there; one cup of coffee, a refill and a toasted bagel while he read the paper, and then he'd move on. But when he didn't appear after forty-five minutes, one of the watchers had gone in to find that Kellerman had given them the slip.

He supposed it wasn't necessarily *bad* news. It had been clear for some time that Kellerman was aware that he was under surveillance, in fact there had been times when he had turned and given them the finger, so it was hardly surprising that he had made his move early in order to make sure he could leave London without worrying about being followed. And that was encouraging, because it suggested Kellerman did not believe he had any reason to worry once clear of London. The one thing that Trowbridge *had* been afraid of was that Kellerman might call the whole thing off after Newman stumbled into the local operation, and Doyle had to be dealt with. But from what Trowbridge had learned from his source inside Kellerman's organization, Luka had downplayed the breach of security when talking to Kellerman in order to save his own neck.

The one thing that *did* bother Trowbridge, however, was

the ease with which Kellerman had shaken the trackers. Someone should have been inside the coffee shop, but they'd been lulled into believing that the man would follow his daily routine, and Kellerman had counted on that.

He just hoped that no one on his team here would make a mistake like that. If Kellerman was even the least bit suspicious that things were not right, he would stay away. Not only that, but the auction would be scrubbed and his people would melt away. Months of planning would go down the drain, and dozens of women and children would simply disappear.

'All quiet?' asked Mike Bell, Trowbridge's second-in-command, as he entered what was once a library but was now a temporary control centre. 'Any activity at the farm?'

'Nothing out of the ordinary,' the man said, scrolling through the messages. 'A Crawley's van came in at 16.22 to pick up what looked like scrap left over from whatever it was they've been doing in the house to cover their real operation down below. Roper helped the driver carry everything out, then went back in the house when the van left at 17.04. The white van we've seen before came back again at 18.13. Stopped at the farmhouse, then went on down to the barn. Looks like it's still there, and that's about it.'

He fell silent for a moment, watching closely as another message appeared on the screen. 'Seems like RGS is a bit busier than usual, though,' he said. The information in front of him was coming in from the watchers in the field using hand-held units.

'One of those big RangerContinental removal vans came in after most of the staff had gone home at 18.22. But since then, they've had two Ford Transit vans come in, stay about twenty minutes, then leave again.'

'And now,' he said slowly, as his eyes followed the words appearing on the screen, 'Unit Three says he can see another one approaching.'

'Are they loading ? Unloading? What?' Bell demanded. He fidgeted impatiently while the message was being relayed.

'Three says they don't know,' the operator said. 'They drive inside, the door comes down, then some twenty minutes or so later the door goes up again and they're off.'

'In which direction?'

'Toward Lyddingham.'

Bell bent to look at the screen himself. Unit Three was the observation post in a hide on the edge of a small copse on a hillside about a third of a mile away from RGS Removals. But now that it was dark, a two-man team would have moved in much closer to the buildings, and it would be they who were relaying information back to base.

'So the RangerContinental is still there?' he said.

The man frowned. 'Don't think so,' he said slowly as he scrolled back. 'No. It left again at 18.50.'

Bell's eyes narrowed. 'You're telling me a RangerContinental came and *left* again in less than half an hour?'

'That's right, sir. It . . .' The man grimaced guiltily and sucked in his breath. 'Ah! Yes, I see what you mean, sir,' he said.

'Do you?' Bell snapped. 'Pity you didn't before, because—'

'Hold on a minute, sir,' the man interrupted. 'I've got something coming from Unit One. Looks like one of those vans has just been spotted on the road to the Roper farm. Same description.'

Bell stood up. 'Give me voice contact with all units,' he said tersely.

'Right sir. Speaker-phone is on.'

'Unit Four. This is Control. An unmarked Ford Transit is moving in your direction. Watch for it. If it's on its way to the target, you should be seeing it in about ten minutes. Report when you see it.'

Bell stood back, arms folded, eyes on the clock, counting off the minutes. Eight . . . nine . . . ten . . . eleven . . .

'Got it!' said a disembodied voice. 'Unit Four reporting.' There was a pause, then, 'Turning in. Sidelights only on its way to target. Unit Two should be seeing it any minute now.'

'Unit Two . . .?'

'Unit Two. In sight now. Pulling in behind target. Can't see it now for buildings. Hold on a sec. It's going on. Headlights on, going down into the valley.' There was a long pause. 'Disappeared into the trees. Headlights off.'

'Unit One,' a second voice said quietly. 'Another van on its way up.'

'Hear that Four?'

'We'll watch for it.'

The muscles around Bell's jaw tightened. He picked up the phone and punched in an internal number. 'Bell here, sir,' he said when Trowbridge answered. 'I'm in the control room and I think you'd better get down here now! Vans are leaving RGS at regular intervals, and they're going to the Roper farm. We've heard nothing from inside, but I think the cunning bastards have brought everything forward by twenty-four hours, and they're going to hold the auction tonight!'

'We knew they wouldn't bring their cargo in until the last minute,' Trowbridge told Paget, 'so we're guessing that they were brought up here in the RangerContinental, then transferred into the smaller vans at the RGS terminal. There's very little traffic on the road up to the farm, especially after dark, so anything bigger than the vans might have been noticed and remarked upon. And by sending them up there at intervals, they reduce the risk of losing too many if anything should go wrong. There have been five of them so far.'

'You say you're *guessing*, Ben?' said Paget. 'Don't you *know*? What happened to your informant?'

Grim-faced, Trowbridge shook his head. 'We don't know,' he said tightly, 'because we've heard nothing from him since this morning, and there was no indication at that time that plans had changed.'

'Could it be some sort of dress rehearsal?'

'Not a chance. That's exactly what they were doing the night young Newman almost blew the whole operation by snooping around and getting caught.'

'And losing his life,' Paget reminded him.

'Yes, well, these things happen, don't they? None of us could have done anything about that. What we have to concentrate on now is making sure we don't bugger up what is probably the only opportunity we will ever get to break this ring.'

When Paget had answered the phone shortly after nine o'clock that evening, Ben Trowbridge had wasted no time on pleasantries or introduction. 'If you want to be part of this operation, you'd better get over here in the next twenty minutes,' he'd said. 'Kellerman's jumped the gun. We think he's running the auction tonight, and our people are scrambling to get into position now.'

'Where is "here"?' Paget asked.

'Erdistone Cross camp grounds. It's less than half a mile across country from Roper's farm, and it's about two hundred yards up the hill from the crossroads. There's a "Closed for the season" sign at the gate, but we're in a caravan behind the trees. So get your skates on, because we could be on the move at any time.'

In fact there had been no need to hurry, because they had been sitting there now for the best part of an hour and all was quiet.

The inside of the caravan had been stripped of its regular furnishings to make way for the communications equipment, not unlike a smaller version of the mobile incident room Paget had used on a number of occasions. A tall, rather gaunt-looking man, whom Trowbridge introduced as 'my field officer, Mike Bell', sat with an operator equipped with a headset and mike in front of a screen on which short bursts of text messages would appear from time to time.

'We're trying to keep voice traffic down to a minimum,' Trowbridge explained. 'Our spotters were able to get close enough to identify Skinner and McCoy as the two people who stayed behind tonight to meet the RangerContinental, and they're still there, but there's no sign of Kellerman. We don't know how he proposes to get to the farm but he probably won't arrive until the very last minute. What worries me most of all, though, is that we haven't heard anything from our man. We've always known that security would be tight and there might not be an opportunity to call us once things were under way, so we made it as simple as possible for him to send us a "go" or "no go" signal in the event that he isn't in a position to talk to us.

'It's very basic,' he went on. 'All he has to do is press a button once to tell us the auction is a go; twice for Kellerman's arrival, and so on. It's simple and almost impossible to detect; in fact he could be standing talking to Kellerman himself and still send a signal without anyone being aware of it.'

Trowbridge drew a deep breath and let it out again slowly. 'We've monitored that frequency 24/7,' he continued, 'but we've heard nothing since this morning, so I hope to God we've got it right, and this isn't some scheme of Kellerman's to find out if we're on to him.'

The operator spoke without turning round. 'Unit Two

reporting, sir. The vans are leaving. He has two men down there closing in on the barn. There is no light coming from the barn, but their heat sensors are picking up more heat than they would normally expect to see, even assuming the lights are on inside.'

'Which probably means that the entire cargo has been transferred to the barn,' Trowbridge said as he picked up a second mike. 'Unit Four, report,' he said quietly.

'The vans are in sight now,' he was told. There was a pause, then: 'They're going back the way they came, but two cars have taken up positions off-road inside farm gates about a quarter of a mile on either side of the entrance to the target. Flankers. Possibly armed. Over.'

Unit One reported seeing the vans as they passed, and Unit Three reported that RGS appeared to have shut down for the night. Skinner and McCoy had driven off together toward town.

'So now we wait,' Trowbridge said.

'For the buyers?'

'That's right. They should be coming in soon.'

'How do you know they're not already there?' Paget asked. 'They could have come in with the vans.'

Trowbridge shook his head. 'The buyers won't be taken anywhere near RGS,' he said. 'They'll be met by some of Kellerman's men at pick-up points well away from there. They'll be searched to make sure they have no weapons or electronic tracking devices on them, then brought here in vans or SUVs with the windows blacked out so they will have no idea where they are. Once we know everyone is there and the auction is under way, we move in and close the net. Timing is crucial, because we don't know when Kellerman will appear, so unless we regain contact with our man very soon, we are going to have to go in blind and hope for the best.'

'But from what you told me the other day, Kellerman will have to be there personally as a guarantee for the safety of the buyers, and if I were one of them I'd want to see him there when I arrived.'

'I agree. And I'm still hoping for a signal when he does arrive,' Trowbridge said worriedly. 'But it's beginning to look as if we've lost contact with our man. The last time we spoke everything was on schedule, and there was no indication that anything had changed, so I have to assume that Kellerman kept everyone in the dark until the last minute. We don't know if our man has been cut out of the loop and doesn't know what's taking place, or if something has happened to him.'

'A man like Kellerman wouldn't be going ahead if he discovered a spy inside the camp,' Paget pointed out, 'so I don't think you have to worry on that score.'

'That's what I keep telling myself,' Trowbridge said. 'On the other hand, that might be why he's brought the auction forward by a day. There's a huge amount of money at stake, and the last thing he wants is to scare off the buyers, so he may feel he can get away with it.'

He turned to Bell. 'What's happening now?' he asked.

'Not a thing. There is nothing moving on the road at all, so everyone, with the possible exception of Kellerman and the buyers, could be in place.'

'So we wait,' Trowbridge said.

With eyes flicking to the time every few minutes, they waited.

Bell sat beside the operator, eyes steady on the screen, but Trowbridge was restless. If the space had been big enough he would have been on his feet and pacing. Instead, he swung back and forth, back and forth in his chair as he watched the minutes tick by.

'Perhaps he's in a dead spot,' he said suddenly, referring, Paget guessed, to his undercover man. 'Are you sure you're on the right frequency?' he asked the operator.

'Quite sure, sir,' the man replied. He tapped his headset. 'And his signals have been coming through quite clearly up till now, so I don't think that's the problem.'

Trowbridge stood up to lean against the wall, folding his arms in such a way that he could keep his eyes on his watch.

Five more minutes went by. 'Perhaps Kellerman and the buyers *did* come up in one of the vans,' Bell suggested. 'In fact the auction could be under way right now.'

Trowbridge shook his head. 'I doubt that very much,' he said. 'Kellerman will come in separately, as will the buyers.'

'Unless he's there already,' Paget offered.

'We'd know if he was,' Trowbridge said testily.

'What do you know about the actual site itself?' asked Paget. 'It seems such an unlikely place to hold the auction.'

'Which is why Kellerman chose it, I imagine,' Trowbridge

said. 'The man is something of a showman, and as I told you the other day, this is supposed to be the first of several auction houses around the country, so while the place *was* a barn, and looks like a barn on the outside, he had the inside completely gutted. It now contains a changing room, showers, a bar, and a raised runway with overhead and side lighting similar to the sort of thing you'd see at a fashion show, except the buyers won't be looking at clothes.'

A shadow crossed his face. 'It also has several cubicles,' he concluded, 'where customers can "sample the goods", so to speak, if they choose to do so. Something similar has been going on in Eastern Europe for years. Kellerman picked up the idea when he was over there, and decided to improve on it.

'They've been working on this for months,' he continued, 'and as cover to account for the delivery of materials and the comings and goings of the workers, Roper let it be known that he was having renovations done to the farmhouse. Kellerman sent in his own people to do the work, and if it hadn't been for the fact that one of their carpenters had an accident and had to be rushed into hospital, we wouldn't have had the balls-up we did with Newman.'

He shook his head. 'Kellerman is not an easy man to work for,' he went on. 'He doesn't like excuses or delays, and when he wants something done he wants it now! So the people in charge at this end got a bit panicky and decided to take a chance on hiring Mickey Doyle to finish the job. Doyle is known locally to be a bit of a chancer, so they thought they'd be all right. Doyle must have known that there was something dodgy about the job, but they were paying good money, so he wasn't going to ask too many questions. But then one of the electricians, who'd been sent up from London, and didn't realize that Mickey wasn't one of their own, talked about what was *really* going on.

'The trouble was, Doyle just couldn't keep his mouth shut, especially when someone was plying him with drink, and that's where young Newman came in. He was looking for a story that would give him an in with the local paper, and Doyle couldn't resist the opportunity to tell him that he knew something no one else knew.'

'How long have you known all this?' asked Paget.

'Ever since it happened,' Trowbridge said candidly, 'but I'm sure you understand why we couldn't say anything to anyone, not even to you, for fear of jeopardizing the operation.'

Paget eyed Trowbridge narrowly. 'I *think* what you're telling me is that your man was probably present when Newman was being tortured, but kept silent in order to maintain his cover? Was he there when they killed him, Ben? Was he one of the men who picked up Doyle, then killed him, too?'

'That is *not* what I said,' Trowbridge snapped. 'But even if it were true, I'm sure you can see that the future and perhaps the very lives of God knows how many women and children had to be weighed against trying to save the lives of two people who put themselves at risk.'

'But there has to be some—' Paget began, only to be interrupted by Bell.

'Vehicles approaching the farm. Two of them. SUVs. Both capable of seating six or seven people, but impossible to say how many are in there.' Bell fell silent, eyes fixed on the screen. Then: 'They're on their way up to the farm,' he said quietly. 'Unit Two should be able to see them any minute now.'

A single row of words flicked across the screen and Bell spoke again. 'Two says they're continuing on to the barn. Probably the buyers, sir.'

'It *has* to be them,' Trowbridge muttered as he leaned forward to read the words himself.

Diverted momentarily from what he'd been about to say, Paget found himself caught up in the moment. 'How many are you expecting?' he asked quietly.

Trowbridge grimaced. 'That's one piece of information Kellerman kept to himself,' he said, 'but what we do know is that he doesn't deal with anyone but the top men, so our estimate is somewhere between six and ten. They will almost certainly be from Manchester, Liverpool and Birmingham, but there could be others we don't know about.'

He glanced at his watch, then sat down. 'We'll have to give them time to get settled in,' he said quietly, 'so we might as well relax ourselves until it's time to go.'

Twenty-Seven

G eorge Kellerman was there to greet them at the door. He was a short, heavy-set man with a pudgy face and a Cupid's bow for a mouth. A baby face with watchful eyes set deep in folds of skin the colour of dough. But tonight he was all smiles as he greeted his guests and offered them drinks. There were nine in all. Six men and three women, and this was his chance to impress every one of them.

He'd been supplying them for years in one way or another, usually on contract. They would put in an order (minimum advance notice ninety days) for certain ages, certain types, and he in turn would fill the order, usually from illegals already in the pipeline. In the case of special orders, he would put the word out to his contacts in Eastern Europe, and they would make sure that a particular girl or child would be moved up to the head of the line.

Most of the girls who ended up in Kellerman's hands believed they were coming to a better life as waitresses or nannies, earning enough money to send back home to impoverished parents or young children of their own. They were persuaded by glib 'selectors', who painted a glowing picture of jobs awaiting them in the UK. But in some cases – always when young children were involved – a boy or girl who matched the special order profile was simply kidnapped off the streets of Sarajevo, Tirana, Vilnius, or wherever he or she could be found.

As far as the kidnappings were concerned, Kellerman liked to think that what he was doing was no different to the way the press gangs used to operate in the old days. Men and boys were literally kidnapped off the streets to go to sea for king and country, some of them never to be seen or heard from again. Whereas he would argue that his girls and boys would have a roof over their heads and three square meals a day, which was a damned sight better that the king's sailors ever had.

He'd recognized early on that transport was the key. No matter how good the supply; no matter how big the network, transport was always the key. Which was why he now owned or controlled several carrier companies, all of which did a lot of international business.

None of them could be traced back to him – his battery of well-paid legal advisors had seen to that – and much of the business was both legal and profitable. But smuggling in illegals was by far the most profitable.

He'd done well, but he'd always had his eye on the main chance, and when he'd seen the way things were organized in other countries, he decided it was time to expand. Time, in fact, to *control* the market throughout the UK.

This was the first step in that expansion. With more and more merchandise coming in daily, he'd been able to build an inventory of the best of the best. And the ones he was putting up for bids tonight were the pick of the crop, and he intended to make the most of it.

'Jimmy, glad you could come,' he greeted a slight, doleful-looking man. 'And . . .?' He raised an eyebrow in the direction of the blonde, thirtyish woman with him. 'I don't believe we've met,' he said.

'Paula Jones,' said Jimmy Cragg. 'At least that's who she is as far as you're concerned, George. Paula is what you might call my advisor. She's the one you have to impress, because I will be relying heavily on her recommendations tonight.'

Kellerman nodded. 'Happy to meet you, Paula,' he said. 'What would you like to drink?'

The woman eyed him coolly. 'Nothing, thank you, Mr Kellerman,' she said. 'I'd prefer to see what's on offer and get this over with as quickly as possible, if you don't mind.'

Kellerman sucked in his breath. 'Right,' he said, rubbing his hands briskly. 'We'll begin in a few minutes, and I'm sure you'll be more than happy with the merchandise. Please have a seat while I see to my other guests.'

Only two of the others accepted his offer of drinks. In fact there was an air of edginess among the group, and it soon became apparent that no one was in the mood to make this the festive occasion Kellerman had planned.

'This had better be worthwhile, George,' the buyer from Liverpool told him. 'And next time you'd better set up closer to where we are if you want to do business with Alfie and me.' Alfie Morgan was his opposite number in Manchester.

'We will,' Kellerman assured him smoothly. 'As I told you, this is a trial run, and I've already got my eye on a place within thirty miles of where you are.'

He turned to face a woman who had grasped his arm to gain his attention. Grey-haired and heavily made-up, she was at least sixty, and could have passed quite easily for someone's benign-looking grandmother, as in fact she was.

'Bertha,' he said, reaching for her hand. 'Good to see you. I think you'll be pleased with what I've brought you tonight.'

'Then for Christ's sake stop trying to make this look like a cross between a fashion show and the bloody Oscars, George, and let's get on with it,' she said, pulling her hand away.

'But it's an occasion,' Kellerman protested. 'In Kosovo they have all-night parties when they have an auction. I've been there. That's where I got the idea.'

'But we're not in bloody Kosovo, are we, George?' Bertha snapped, 'and I want to get home tonight, so let's get at it. How many do you have, anyway? I hope I haven't come all this way for two or three I could have found at home.'

'Seventy-one,' Kellerman said proudly. 'And they're some of the best you'll ever see. You'll love the little ones, Bertha; we've got some right little beauties, but they'll cost you. And you'll have some competition; Fred Tobin's here, and he'll be bidding against you for them.'

Bertha snorted. 'I'm not bothered by him. But I'll tell you this, George Kellerman: if you try to slip me any HIV positives or any with infections of any kind, you'll be sorry. And I'll be having them checked, so be warned.'

'They're all clean,' Kellerman assured her as he moved away and took up a position beside the runway, 'and they've all been "broken in" as you might say, so you've no worries there.'

He cleared his throat and raised his voice. 'Now, ladies and gentlemen, if I could have your attention, I'd just like to say we'll be starting with a brief parade down this runway and back so you can see everything we have on offer, and then we will bring them out one by one for bids. You know the rules about payment and delivery, so let's begin.'

*　　*　　*

'We have transport standing by to take the illegals away once we've cleared the area,' Trowbridge said, 'and we have a doctor, a nurse and a couple of female interpreters who will come in once the place is secured. We've circulated a picture of your man to everyone,' he continued, anticipating Paget's question, 'so we'll do our best not to shoot him if he's in there – that's assuming he's still alive, of course.'

Small comfort, Paget thought, but he knew it was the best he could hope for. 'How many people do you have out there?'

'Enough.'

'And they're not what I would call regular policemen, are they?'

It was Bell who answered. 'Special Forces,' he said tersely, and Paget realized then why Trowbridge had made no mention of the man's rank when he'd introduced him.

Trowbridge might be nominally in charge, but Bell, or whatever his real name was, would be running the show from this point on.

'We'll take out the flankers down the road first and make sure they don't have a chance to warn the others,' Bell explained to Paget. 'The area around the farmhouse has been swept. Two of their men are in the yard itself, and we know Roper and his wife are still there, but there could be others inside the house as well.

'There are two more outside the barn – they're the drivers who brought the buyers in – but we don't know how many there are inside the barn. Considering the size of the vans, there could be as many as sixty or seventy women and children in there as well as the buyers. Then there is Kellerman himself, and perhaps half a dozen of his men, some of whom may be armed. So we will have to be very careful when we storm the barn. We need to take them completely by surprise, because the last thing we want is to give Kellerman and company a chance to use the illegals as hostages.'

It looked like a soccer team's changing room with open shower stalls at one end, and four rows of wooden benches taking up much of the rest of the room, where fifty-seven shivering young women, and fourteen children sat huddled together.

The water from the showers had been cold, ice-cold, and there weren't enough towels to go round. Their hair, no matter how long or beautiful it had been originally, had been cut short early in their journey across Europe. For hygienic reasons, they were told, and while there was some truth to that, the main reason was a practical one: short hair dried faster on those rare occasions when they were allowed the luxury of a hurried shower before being crammed into yet another suffocating space on the next stage of their perilous journey.

Now they sat huddled together, bodies still damp and numb with cold, refused permission to get dressed again. Some of the smaller children clung shivering to the women who'd become their surrogate mothers, while others stood stoically apart, eyes glazed, staring blankly at nothing.

Luka and Slater, wearing the one-piece coveralls Kellerman had insisted they wear instead of their regular clothes, stood just inside the door, watching as the stoutly-built, grey-haired woman and the two middle-aged men paced up and down between the benches. The two men, also dressed in coveralls, fingered cattle prods hooked to their belts, ready to use them at the first sign of trouble.

But it was the woman who was in control. The men were simply there as back-up, and when a small bell mounted high on the wall rang sharply three times, she ceased her pacing between the rows and went to the door. Hands on hips, she turned to face the room and snapped out an order in Luka's native language, then repeated it in Romanian and English.

'You will go through that door, and you will walk down the ramp to the stage at the end, turn and come back into this room. You will hold yourself erect, keep your hands at your sides, walk properly and make no attempt to cover your body. You will not look at anyone nor say anything unless you are ordered to, and I will be there to keep an eye on you and translate if necessary. The children will go last and each one will be accompanied by one of you. Anyone who fails to observe the rules will be punished. Translate, Irena,' she said, pointing at a tall, dark-haired girl.

The girl repeated the instructions dully in Russian and Polish.

Someone in the third row whispered something to her neighbour.

The grey-haired woman moved quickly down the line to

stop in front of a girl who couldn't have been more than four-teen. 'You said something?' she asked softly.

The girl swallowed hard and shook her head. 'No, I—'

'Don't lie! And stand up when you speak to me!' the woman snapped. One of the men moved forward, prod at the ready, but she waved him back.

The girl rose to her feet, trembling, trying to hold back the tears and failing.

'Now, what did you say?'

'I just said, must we go out there like this?' the girl whis-pered, opening her arms and looking down at her naked body. 'Can't we put something on? Please . . .?'

The older woman smiled and shook her head as she might with a child who had not yet managed to grasp a simple lesson. 'Oh, Trisiana,' she said softly, 'you have so very much to learn. You'll fetch a very good price, my girl; a *very* good price indeed.'

Twenty-Eight

It had seemed like overkill to Paget when he realized how many people were involved in the operation to take Kellerman down, but as Trowbridge explained, traffickers who wouldn't hesitate to throw their human cargo overboard if they were in danger of being caught by a police patrol boat while at sea, would not go down without a fight.

'Some padlock chains around the hands and feet of their victims as a precaution as soon as they board,' he said. 'Most of them make it, of course – the smugglers have very fast boats and the police can't be everywhere – but like the slavers of old, they'll dump their cargo rather than be caught with them. Which is why we have someone like Mike Bell leading the tactical squad,' he continued, 'and why we are stuck here until we get the signal from him that everything is secure.'

If Mike Bell had had his way, and if these were his men, he would have simply killed the flankers and guards. Slit their throats, garrotted them, broken their necks or clubbed them down instead of just putting them out of action temporarily. But his superiors in London had made it very clear to him that this was a police operation, and no one – *no one*, it was emphasized – was to be killed or even seriously maimed unless there was no other choice. The men assigned to him were just as highly trained, but he had to remember that they were policemen, subject to somewhat different rules to the ones he was used to working under.

But they were good and they had done their job well so far. Both ends of the cross-country road had been blocked off; the flankers had been taken out without a sound, and now they were closing in on the farmhouse.

The team on the far side of the valley behind the farm had been ordered to come down and take up positions in the valley bottom, but to keep well away from the barn itself until given the order to move in.

Clad in Kevlar vests, Bell and his team moved like wraiths up the hillside, thankful for the cloud obscuring the moon. They paused, crouching while Bell scanned the ground between them and the house before declaring it clear and moving forward. When they reached the house, two men took up positions beside the front door, and two broke away, one to the left to circle the house from that side, the other circling wide to the right. Bell and one other man moved silently up the narrow lane beside the house, almost exactly as Mark Newman had done almost a month earlier.

They heard voices. Muffled conversation; the scrape of a boot on cobblestones. Bell poked his head around the corner. He could just make out the shapes of two men standing beside Roper's old truck no more than six or seven paces away from the corner. One of them was smoking and moving his feet as if he were cold. His cigarette glowed as he sucked on it, and Bell caught a glimpse of something bulky in the man's left hand. Portable phone? Two-way radio? Impossible to tell, but there was no sign of a weapon.

But that didn't mean there wasn't one within easy reach.

Bell withdrew and signalled his companion to do the same. Safely out of earshot, Bell switched on his headphone mike and whispered instructions to the men circling in from right and left, then moved up to the corner of the house once again.

The two men were still talking in a desultory fashion.

Bell whispered an instruction, then tapped the right hand of the man beside him. The man took a padded glove from his pocket and put it on. Bell did the same, but before putting his glove on, he took a couple of coins from his pocket.

The smoker took one last drag at his cigarette, and as he dropped the butt at his feet to grind it into the cobblestones, Bell tossed the coins, then slipped on the glove.

The coins landed just beyond the two men, a soft clatter on the stones, one of them rolling. 'Mine!' said one of the men swiftly as he switched on a torch and bent to search for the coins.

Bell and his colleague stripped the protective covering from the palm of the glove as they came up behind the two men. Bell snaked his left arm around the man's throat and jerked him upright, then clamped his gloved hand over the man's face. The man arched his back, tried to fill his lungs and found himself sucking raw anaesthetic from the soft, sponge-like pad covering his face. His knees buckled. Bell held him for a couple of seconds longer before lowering him to the ground, while his colleague did the same to the second man. Right on cue, the two men who had circled the house materialized to kneel and slap tape across the unconscious men's mouths and wrap it around their heads. They secured their arms and legs, then dragged them to one of the barns and heaved them inside before taking up positions on either side of the back door. No one spoke. There was no need; they knew what to do next.

One man reached for the old-fashioned latch on the door and pressed down. The door swung inward to his touch, and the two men disappeared inside. Bell spoke quietly into the mike and received an acknowledgement from the man he had posted outside the front door, then followed his men inside.

They went through every room, but the house was empty. And that, thought Bell, was odd. Very odd, because his watchers had not seen Roper and his wife leave. Which meant that either they had managed to slip out unnoticed – and someone would hear about it if they had – or they were down in the barn with the rest of the crew.

But that idea didn't sit well with Bell. He couldn't see Kellerman allowing the farmer and his wife to see what their barn was *really* being used for, so where were they?

The question troubled Bell, but he pushed it to the back of his mind. The good news was that he and his team had managed to get this far without alerting anyone, so the sooner they got themselves down to where the action was, the better.

Back in the makeshift control room in the caravan, the man at the desk took off his headset and logged off his computer. 'All clear at the farmhouse, sir,' he told Trowbridge, 'and they are on their way down to the barn. Mr Bell says he wants the transport and the medics and interpreters up as far as the house as quickly as possible, and they're to stand by for further orders. And you and Chief Inspector Paget can go up there as well if you wish.'

'Can we, now?' Trowbridge growled. 'Big of him, I must

say. Very well, then,' he told the operator, 'pass that message on and get everyone up there on the double.'

He turned to Paget and shook his head. 'Being a super-intendent doesn't seem to have the clout it used to,' he observed with an air of resignation. 'It's a whole new game these days, Neil, and I'm not at all sure I'm cut out for it. There was a time when a superintendent would be right in the thick of it when there was a raid on, but now you find yourself being politely – and sometimes not so politely – pushed off to one side as soon as the action starts. And I must say I resent it.

'On the other hand,' he continued with a self-deprecating grimace, 'I'm not sure I could keep up with some of these youngsters and the way they go about things these days.

'But my blethering on about it isn't helping, is it?' He sighed heavily as he got to his feet. 'So let's go. We can cut across country in the Range Rover, and still keep in contact on the mobile.'

Down now in the valley bottom, Mike Bell sent two men forward to scout the area before attempting to move through the trees to converge on the barn. The night was still, and the slightest sound carried a long way on the cold night air. If they had guards posted, one snapped twig underfoot would be enough to alert them.

A shadow moved in close to Bell. 'The white van is parked at the side of the barn, and the two SUVs are out in front, facing the big double doors,' the man said quietly. 'I reckon they must feel pretty secure down here, because the only people we could find are two blokes nattering away like old women in one of the SUVs. They're sitting in there with the engine running. Probably got a heater in there and they're trying to keep warm. As long as we stay clear of the side mirrors, we can have them out of there before they know what's hit them.

'There's a small door next to the big double doors,' he continued, 'and another small one round the back. The one at the back is being covered by men from Unit Two. They're all down from the top of the hill now.'

'Were you able to see inside?'

Bell felt rather than saw the man shake his head. 'No, sir. The windows have been covered, and the only light I can see is a faint glow coming from under the eaves. But I could hear

voices. Couldn't tell what they were saying, but there is definitely something going on in there.'

'Right, then let's get on with it,' Bell said crisply, and gave
the order to move forward. 'But wait for my orders before
leaving the shelter of the trees,' he cautioned.

'Look, George, we'll be here till bloody Wednesday if we
keep on at this rate,' Jimmy Cragg complained. 'We've had
a bit of a chat, and we want you to bring 'em on in job lots
of five at a time. Except for the kids, of course. We'll have
them in last like you said. All right?'

This wasn't going at all the way Kellerman had planned.
He'd envisioned a festive affair; loosen them up a bit with
drink, get them in an expansive mood, but these northerners
were a hard-nosed bunch, and all they were interested in was
getting down to business.

But if that was the way they wanted it, so be it. Business
was business, but if they thought they were going to get the
merchandise any cheaper by bidding on groups of five, they
had another think coming.

They crouched at the edge of the trees. Bell's eyes were now
so accustomed to the darkness that he could see the silhou-
ette of the SUVs quite clearly on the hard standing in front
of the barn doors.

'The men are in the nearest one,' the man beside him whispered.

'You take the passenger and I'll take the driver,' Bell told
him. 'Stand by,' he said, speaking into the mike, 'and be
prepared to move in on my signal.' He switched off the mike.
'Ready?' he asked the man beside him. 'Then let's go!'

The two men crossed the open space in seconds, crouching
low behind the SUV. Vapour curled from the exhaust pipe,
and Bell choked back the urge to cough. He touched his
companion on the shoulder and whispered, 'Go!'

They slid around opposite sides of the van, grabbed the handles
of the doors and flung them open. The man in the passenger's
seat drew in his breath to shout, but the hand that gripped his
throat made that impossible, and the next thing he knew he was
flat on the ground, and a soft pad was covering his nose and
mouth.

But when Bell attempted to do the same on the driver's side, the man jerked his head back and lashed out. Bell caught his arm and pulled. The man should have come flying out of his seat, but he barely moved – held in place by his seatbelt!

The man opened his mouth to shout, but choked it back when he felt the barrel of a gun jammed beneath his chin.

'Slowly, very slowly,' whispered Bell. 'Undo the belt.'

The man fumbled with the release. The belt across his chest went slack. 'Gently does it,' Bell advised. 'Now, hands on your head and get out slowly.' He backed away, gun levelled at the man's head. The man eased himself around in his seat, slid one foot out, reaching for the ground, then brought his elbow down hard on the centre of the steering wheel, and the quiet of the night was shattered by the blaring horn.

Bell drove a knee into his gut as the man's feet hit the ground, then brought the butt of the gun down hard on his head. The man slumped to the ground as Bell's colleague raced around from the other side of the vehicle to kneel on the man to make sure he was immobilized.

Bell leapt into the driver's seat, flicked on his mike and shouted, 'Ground lights on! Go! Everyone, go now!' He slammed the vehicle into gear and gunned the engine. Portable floodlights lit up the barn. Rubber screamed as tyres bit into the hard standing and the SUV leapt forward to smash into the barn's double doors. The doors sagged but held. Bell slammed the gearshift into reverse, backed away then shot forward to ram the doors again.

The engine stalled and died, but the doors were open and Bell was out and running, yelling, 'Police! Stay where you are!' as the rest of the team poured inside.

A group of naked women in the middle of a stage stood transfixed at the sight of armed and helmeted police charging toward them. One of them screamed, and suddenly they broke and ran, elbowing each other out of the way in a mad scramble to escape through a door at the far end of the room.

A man and a woman ran with them, shoving the girls ahead of them before slamming the door behind them.

A small group of men and women, fully clothed, fell back against the wall and raised their hands as the police rushed toward them.

'Don't shoot!' shouted one of the men. 'For Christ's sake

don't shoot! We're not armed.' He was shaking with fear as he and his friends were surrounded.

Bell, together with half a dozen of his men, raced to the far end of the room. The door was locked. Bell spoke into the mike. 'Lights on the back door,' he ordered. 'And remember, I want Kellerman alive.'

Outside, three small but powerful lights converged on the back door of the barn. It started to open, then slammed shut.

Inside the barn, Bell stood to one side to avoid being shot through the door as he reached out to pound on it with his fist.

'Police!' he roared, then, for the benefit of the women inside, he added, 'No one will be harmed if you come out quietly. Open the door!'

He spoke into the mike again. 'Get the medics and interpreters down here fast,' he ordered.

He banged on the door again, then held up his hand for silence as he pressed an ear to the wall. Someone inside was shouting orders; probably Kellerman, but another sound was rising to drown him out, an eerie, keening wail rising to a screaming howl that sent chills down the spines of those outside the door.

At Bell's signal, one man stood back, automatic pistol at the ready, while Bell and a second man threw their combined weight at the door. The jamb splintered; the door gave way and they stumbled through. Others followed, but stopped dead to stare in amazement at the struggling mass of flesh in the middle of the room. More screaming women had three men backed up against the wall, tearing at them with their bare hands. The biggest of the three suddenly went down to be trampled underfoot. An older man was sinking to his knees. His eyes were closed and blood streamed down his face as he, too, went down.

But the third man, a smaller, dark-skinned man, was crouching low, slashing at the air in front of him with a long, thin-bladed knife, daring the screaming women to come closer.

The noise was deafening, inhuman. Bell roared an order, but he might as well have saved his breath. He fired three shots in rapid succession into the wall above the head of the man wielding the knife.

The noise stopped so abruptly that the silence was almost

deafening by contrast. The women at the side of the room remained frozen in position as if fearing they would be shot if they moved, while the mass of women in the middle of the room began to untangle themselves and struggle to their feet.

'Drop it, Luka!' Bell ordered harshly, 'or the next one will be for you. I won't kill you, but I guarantee you'll never walk again. Your choice.' He raised the gun.

Luka shrugged and dropped the knife. Two men pushed their way through the mob to handcuff him and, on Bell's instruction, bundle him out of the room.

'Away from the wall, please, ladies,' Bell said in as normal a voice as he could muster. 'Those of you who speak English, please translate for the others as best you can. You will not be harmed. I repeat, we are here to help you; you will not be harmed.'

Muttered words in several languages were passed on. Slowly, reluctantly, they moved aside to let him through. He went down on one knee to check the pulse of the big man who lay face down. He shook his head and turned his attention to the older man who was curled up in a foetal position and sobbing quietly.

Bell hauled him to his feet. One of the man's eyes was completely closed, and his nose appeared to be broken. Blood oozed from the scratches on his face, and on his chest where his shirt had been stripped away, but no limbs appeared to be broken and he seemed to be otherwise unhurt. He, too, was handcuffed and led away.

Bell eyed the cluster of women in the middle of the room. There must have been thirty or forty of them huddled together between two of the benches. Most of them avoided his eyes, but a few met his gaze defiantly.

'Please move back,' he said, making a pushing motion with his hands as he walked toward them.

Slowly, grudgingly, they moved back.

'Holy shit!' breathed one of the men behind Bell.

Kellerman, or the thing that had once been Kellerman, lay stretched out on the floor. Part of his face was gone, literally ripped to shreds by clawing hands and nails. His clothes were in tatters and soaked in blood. Beneath him lay a woman, grey hair spattered with blood. He couldn't see her face. Which was, perhaps, just as well, because it had been smashed into the floor so hard that her teeth were spread across the floor in front of her.

And off to one side, half hidden beneath one of the benches, lay another man, battered and bloodied, eyes wide open, staring. A cattle prod lay beside him.

Bell looked around the room, and for the first time saw the children. There must have been a dozen of them; some no more than seven or eight, boys and girls. They were being held tightly by women who glared back at him defiantly as if daring him to touch their young charges.

Women with blood on their hands, on their arms, on their faces. He should have felt revulsion, but all he could feel was pity for these poor souls who had endured unknown horrors since falling into the hands of Kellerman and his cohorts.

'Close the door and make sure no one comes in,' he said quietly to one of the men, then raised his voice to ask, 'How many of you speak English? I repeat, we are not here to harm you but to get you out of here, and I want to speak to someone who understands English and can translate for me.'

A small, dark-haired young woman of about twenty raised a tentative hand. 'A little,' she said almost inaudibly. 'And Italian and Serbian.'

'Excellent! Thank you. Now, please tell them I want everyone into the showers; all of you, children as well, and I want you to make sure you scrub yourselves thoroughly. Hair, hands, face, everything. Do you understand?'

The girl hesitated, eyeing him narrowly as if trying to read his thoughts; looking for some ulterior motive behind his words. Bell pointed to her blood-streaked arms and held her eyes with his own.

'I want everyone to be clean when they leave here,' he said quietly. 'Where are your clothes?'

The girl pointed to small bundles underneath the benches.

'Right,' he said. 'Wash yourselves thoroughly, dry yourselves off and put your clothes on.'

'The towels, they are not dry.'

'Sorry about that,' Bell told her, 'but I'm afraid you'll have to do the best you can until we can get you out of here. Please tell the others. We'll have you in warm blankets soon.'

The girl still looked puzzled, but suddenly her expression changed, and he knew she understood. She turned away and fired off a string of words in a language Bell felt sure was Serbian. She raised her own bloodstained hands and switched to Italian. Suddenly it was as if everyone got the message at the same time, and there was a stampede into the showers.

Bell turned to face his men. 'Head lice,' he said crisply, 'and who knows what else after living in such squalid conditions. They need to be cleaned up before we take them out of here.'

The men exchanged glances. 'Head lice,' one of the men repeated. 'Good idea, sir. Wouldn't want that sort of thing to spread.'

'Right,' said Bell. He pointed at one of the men beside the door. 'Find out if the medics and interpreters have arrived,' he said, 'and tell them I need them in here now.'

As the man left the room, Bell turned to the man beside him. 'Now, let's get these bodies covered and clean up some of this mess.'

Twenty-Nine

When Trowbridge received confirmation that the barn had been secured and the women and children were safe, he issued the order to serve the search warrants that had been issued for Kellerman's home and his offices in each of his nightclubs and so-called massage parlours in London.

'Kellerman must have thought this place was so remote and secluded that he didn't have to worry about an escape route,' Trowbridge observed as the Range Rover descended into the valley behind the house. 'But then, he always did think he was cleverer than anyone else, so I'm sure he thought he'd be quite safe here.'

'And Bell is quite sure he's dead?' said Paget.

'Oh, yes. His face is badly damaged, but Bell says there's no doubt it's Kellerman. And we have his prints and medical history, so verification won't be a problem. Bell didn't say exactly *how* he died; Kellerman was dead by the time he and his men got to him. No doubt it will all be sorted out in due course.'

The man who had been the operator back in the caravan, and was now their driver, said, 'Sounds as if they've found your man, Chief Inspector.' He turned up the volume of the mobile radio.

'. . . hiding underneath a wooden bridge over the stream,' a voice said. 'Claims he's the copper we were told to look for, but he doesn't look much like the picture we have. He's soaked through and suffering from hypothermia, so we've dried him off and wrapped him in a Mylar blanket. He'll survive, but he's buggered up one knee pretty badly, so we'll need a medic. Over.'

'He's damned lucky to be alive at all,' Trowbridge growled. 'He wouldn't be if Kellerman's people had found him.'

On one level, Paget was thankful that Lyons had been found more or less safe and sound, but another part of him could hardly wait to tear a strip off the young idiot, buggered-up knee or not.

The women and children had gone. Those injured in the melee had been treated and taken away by ambulance, while the others were given blankets to wrap themselves in before being shepherded on to waiting buses. From there they would be taken to a facility some twenty miles away, where they would be fed, supplied with fresh clothing and given a place to sleep before any attempt was made to question them.

Paget stood off to one side. There was little he could do but stay out of everybody's way until the ambulance came for Lyons. The police surgeon had examined the injured knee and given the man a shot to kill the pain. 'Keep him warm and he'll be fine,' the surgeon said cheerfully. 'At least he's better off than some I've seen in there tonight.'

Paget hadn't been 'in there'. After having a word with Bell, Trowbridge had come out to tell Paget that Kellerman, Slater, a middle-aged woman and another man were all dead.

'Unfortunately, the crime scene is a complete shambles,' he went on. 'Four people dead, two of them almost torn to pieces by the look of them; seventy or eighty women and children, at least some of whom must have been involved in the killing, but any evidence there might have been has been totally destroyed by all the milling about. And to top it off, Bell said all the women were dirty and scratching at themselves, which suggested lice to him, so he ordered them into the showers to clean up.'

Paget eyed Trowbridge sceptically. 'They may have been dirty, but they probably had blood on their hands and under their nails as well, and Bell should know that you don't get rid of lice simply by showering,' he said. 'In fact it sounds to me as if he deliberately set out to destroy the evidence. Just what the hell did he think he was doing?'

Trowbridge shrugged. 'I'm sure Bell only did what he felt needed to be done at the time,' he said. 'Anyway, it's done now, and the operation was successful.'

'We're also talking about four murders that were committed on my patch,' Paget reminded him. 'I can't just walk away from that, so I need to talk to Bell and the men who were in that room, as well as the women themselves.'

But Trowbridge was shaking his head. 'Trouble is,' he said, 'it's a matter of priorities, and there's a lot to be done before anything like that can take place. These women have a wealth of information regarding how they got here, what happened to them, and who their captors were, and we'll need their cooperation. And that's going to take time, because one thing they've learned along the way is not to trust *anyone,* including the police. And then, of course, Immigration will want to process them, so it could be months before you get a crack at them, and by then I doubt if CPS will even want to touch it.'

He looked off into the distance. 'I'm not suggesting what Bell did was right,' he said, 'but considering who the victims are, and what these women have suffered at their hands, I can't help wondering if that is such a bad thing?'

'Possibly not, but isn't that something for the courts to decide, Ben? And as I said, this is my patch.'

'Duly noted,' Trowbridge said, 'but as I said, you will have to wait your turn. This is my operation, and you are under my orders. So please let me get on with my job.'

'What about the people who killed Newman, Doyle, Fletcher and Ryan?' Paget persisted. 'Are they just going to disappear?'

'One of the suspects is already dead,' Trowbridge pointed out, 'and the other, Luka, will be questioned in due course, as will all the rest of Kellerman's men we've rounded up tonight.' He glanced at his watch and his voice hardened as he said, 'So, if you have any more questions, Neil, I suggest you take it up through your chain of command.'

As Trowbridge strode off, two ambulance men arrived to take Lyons away. They were big men, but surprisingly gentle as they examined Lyons before lifting him on to the trolley. Lyons opened his eyes, said something unintelligible then fell asleep again.

Paget left the barn feeling completely frustrated. 'Lice!' he muttered under his breath. That was just an excuse. Bell had known exactly what he was doing when he'd ordered those women and children into the showers, and Trowbridge was going along with it. It wasn't that Paget wanted to see the women punished for what they'd done – he could hardly blame them after what they'd been through – but as he'd told Trowbridge, that was for the courts to decide, not people like Bell or the superintendent.

He'd been told last week that Luka Bardici was off limits,

but he'd hoped at least to be able to question Slater. If he could make a case against the Australian for at least taking part in the killing of Newman and Doyle and Fletcher – he wasn't so sure about Rose – he just might have been able to force Trowbridge to produce Bardici.

But Slater was dead and Bardici had been whisked away. Chances were that no one would ever stand trial for the killings, and Paget didn't relish the thought of trying to explain *that* to Emma Baker.

His thoughts were interrupted when he was forced to step out of the way while the SUV Bell had used to smash his way into the barn was moved to make way for a long black van. The van swung round and began backing into the barn, travelling its entire length until it came to a halt close to the door of the changing room.

Curious, Paget followed as did several members of Bell's squad. The driver spoke into a mobile phone, then he and his mate got out, opened the rear doors and pulled out four stretchers. The door behind the van was opened by the police surgeon, who motioned the men inside.

Paget leaned against the wall and waited.

He didn't have to wait long before the door opened again and the stretchers bearing body bags were loaded into the van. The doors were closed, the driver and his mate got in and the van drove off.

Trowbridge and Bell emerged from the room. 'Not much point in your hanging about here,' the superintendent told Paget. 'I expect you'll be glad to get back home. Our driver will take you back to your car.'

'Not until I've seen the inside of that room,' said Paget quietly.

'Go ahead,' Trowbridge told him. 'No one's stopping you. Not that there's much to see, and it's not as if you'll need to file a report; we'll be doing that ourselves.'

Do you really think I won't? thought Paget, but he remained silent.

'If I can be of help . . .?' Bell offered. 'Anything in particular you're looking for, Chief Inspector?'

'As a matter of fact there is.'

'And what would that be, sir?'

'Lice,' said Paget caustically. 'I'm looking for evidence of head lice.'

Thirty

It wasn't until he saw the calendar on the office wall that Paget was reminded that the day after tomorrow would be All Fools' Day. Perhaps, he thought cynically, he should wait until then to write his report.

Perhaps he had been the fool for believing that he and Ben Trowbridge could work something out in order to make sure that those who were responsible for the deaths of Newman and Doyle were brought to justice. Trowbridge had made it very clear right from the beginning that he had first claim on Luka Bardici, and Paget had no trouble with that as long as he could get a crack at the man when Trowbridge was finished with him.

But Trowbridge had also made it clear to him last night that it wasn't going to work that way. 'In fact,' he'd said, 'I intend to use the threat of being charged with the murders of Newman and Doyle as a lever to get what I need from him, so I can hardly turn him over to you if he gives us what we want, can I?'

Paget sat back in the chair and rubbed his face with his hands. The trouble was, even if he did get his hands on Bardici, how was he going to prove that the man had anything to do with killing Newman and Doyle? Fletcher, who might have been persuaded to turn Queen's evidence if promised a new identity, was presumably dead, killed by Slater. But Slater was dead, too, so even that avenue was blocked.

Brow furrowed, he stared moodily into space as he tried to decide what to put in his report. Alcott had made it very clear that whatever Trowbridge wanted, Trowbridge would get, which meant that Alcott had had his own orders from higher up, so Paget couldn't expect any help from that direction.

Even the arrest of Skinner and McCoy had been made by members of Trowbridge's team, and the superintendent had made it very clear that it would be his men who would track down Roper and his wife and bring them in.

But his thoughts kept returning to the rage and the sheer desperation that had driven those young women to turn on their captors and kill them with their bare hands. It went against the grain to condone what they had done, but he could understand the pent up fury that had brought them to the point where they felt they had nothing more to lose.

Coaxed from their homes with a promise of a better life, they had found themselves caught up in a hellish nightmare where they were beaten and sexually abused to the point where they no longer had the will to resist. Their captors called it 'pre-conditioning' for their future life in the sex trade from which there would be no escape. Once 'broken', they were transported in almost airless containers buried beneath legitimate cargo on lorries or on ships for hours, sometimes days at a time. They would emerge smelling foul and gasping for air. Many of those who did survive were traumatized for life. Those who didn't were written off and disposed of like so much rubbish. A few losses were acceptable. It was the cost of doing business.

After all that, to be brought to this remote place, stripped and paraded naked to be bought and sold like cattle, must have been the final degradation that had sent them into a killing frenzy. What *did* they have to lose? After what they'd been through, even gaol would almost be a luxury.

Tired as he'd been when he'd finally fallen into bed, Paget hadn't been able to sleep. He'd lain awake, staring into the darkness as the faces of the women and children filing mutely past him on their way to the buses refused to go away. Shivering in their wet clothes, and apprehensive about what might happen to them, some of them were crying quietly, while others stared fixedly at the ground or straight ahead. Those who needed medical treatment for superficial cuts and bruises were patched up and taken to join the others. They had all been told that they were being taken to a safe place, and they'd been assured that they would come to no harm. But why, after what they'd been through, should they trust anyone's word, including that of the police?

'Why should they?' Trowbridge had asked rhetorically during an uneasy truce between the two men. 'Where some of them come from, the police are as bad or even worse than the traffickers. In some cases they *are* the traffickers. God, you should see some of the histories compiled by Europol and the NGOs in Eastern Europe. I tell you, Neil, when I read some of the stuff that crosses my desk, and I hear the stories these women have to tell, there are times when I'd like to take a gun and wipe these bastards out myself.'

Strong words from a man who had seen more than his share of the seamier side of life during his time in the Met.

Yet not surprising, Paget thought, because he, too, had been deeply affected by what he had seen last night.

The plight of the young women was bad enough, but it was the look on the children's faces that had brought a lump to his throat and moved him close to tears. He'd expected them to be scared, even terrified by what they must have seen that night, but when he looked into their eyes he'd felt a chill go through him the likes of which he'd never felt before.

There wasn't a tear. No expression on their faces, nothing in their eyes. They were blank, lifeless and perhaps wilfully blind to what was going on around them. He'd wanted to say something to them; something that would let them know that they were safe, that they would be taken care of, that their lives would be rebuilt, but the words refused to come, and he wondered now whether it would have been a lie if he had been able to find the words.

Now, sitting in his office in the cold light of day, he wasn't quite so certain that what Mike Bell had done last night was wrong. Yes, he'd gone out of his way to make sure that the crime scene was compromised and evidence was destroyed, but perhaps there was an element of justice in what the man had done.

He looked at the clock. Ten past four on a Sunday afternoon. The office was dead quiet, and he'd been there an hour already, yet he hadn't put a single word on paper.

Paget was still struggling with his report when Alcott made an unexpected appearance. He paused in the doorway to light a cigarette, but his dark, bird-like eyes never left the chief inspector's face as he blew smoke toward the ceiling.

'I had a call from Chief Superintendent Brock half an hour ago,' he said as he came into the room and sat down. 'He asked me for details of a raid that took place last night at the Roper farm, and I had to tell him we were still working on the report, and I'd get back to him.

'What I *didn't* tell him,' he continued, 'was that I didn't
even know there had *been* a raid at the Roper farm, *or* that
we had recovered Lyons, because no one had bothered to tell
me. The only thing that may have saved both you and me
from a royal bollocking is that it seems the raid was successful
and Trowbridge was thanking us for our cooperation – but
even *that* was something I had to hear from Brock!'

Alcott flicked his open mackintosh out of the way and sat
down facing Paget. 'So, if it's not too much trouble, Chief
Inspector, would you care to tell me just what the hell has
been going on, and why I have not been kept informed?'

Paget drew a deep breath and let it out again slowly as he
swung his chair around to face the superintendent. Alcott was
right; he should have been informed long before this; he had
every right to be upset, but he had wanted to sort things out
in his own mind before committing anything to paper. What
he hadn't counted on was Trowbridge calling Brock. But
thanking them for their cooperation was just twisting the knife
as far as Paget was concerned.

'You're quite right,' he said apologetically. 'I should have
informed you before this, but I wanted to try to sort things
out in my own mind before I talked to anyone about what
took place last night. And I still can't make up my mind about
what to say in my report.'

Paget wasn't quite sure how Alcott would take what he was
about to say, but he pressed on. 'What I would *like* to do is tell
you what happened off the record – at least for now – because,
while the main thrust of the operation *was* successful, I'm not
at all happy about the way evidence was destroyed, and where
that leaves us regarding murders that took place on our patch.'

Alcott drew deeply on his cigarette, then looked at his watch.
'Go on, then,' he said, 'but be quick about it because I can't
put Brock off much longer.'

'I'll try to be brief,' Paget told him, but it was almost twenty
minutes later when he finally sat back and said, 'And that's
about it. As far as I can see, we've been left with an impossible situation as far as prosecution is concerned.'

Alcott had remained silent throughout Paget's monologue,
but now he sat back in his chair and said, 'You don't look as
if you've slept at all. What time did you get home?'

'Somewhere between three and four this morning, and no,

I didn't get much sleep. Too much to think about, especially the killings and the plight of those women and children.'

'Difficult to see things clearly under those conditions,' Alcott said. 'As for Bardici, I thought Superintendent Trowbridge made it very clear at the beginning that if the fellow could be persuaded to cooperate in breaking up the organization, the benefits would – at least in their estimation – far outweigh putting the man on trial for the killing of Newman and Doyle, even assuming we could find enough evidence to make the charge stick. Fletcher might have told us something if they hadn't got to him first, and now that Slater's dead, I very much doubt if you could get enough evidence to bring Bardici to trial anyway.'

'There were a number of others arrested last night,' Paget pointed out. 'Some of those people must have known what was going on.'

Alcott shook his head impatiently. 'Even if they did,' he said, 'they know they would be dead within a week if they testified against him, and without eyewitness testimony we have nothing. CPS certainly wouldn't touch it.'

'So, apart from anything else, what do I tell Emma Baker?'

Alcott shrugged. 'You can tell her that two people we believe were involved in the death of Newman and Doyle are now dead. In fact, you can tell her if it hadn't been for Newman poking around the Roper farm, we might never have known that it was being used as a staging point for smuggling people into the country. You could even say he played a part in saving many young women and children from a life of slavery. As I recall, Trowbridge told us that Newman was buried somewhere on the farm, so we find out where, then dig him up and give him a decent burial. As for Doyle . . .'

But Paget was shaking his head. 'That's not right,' he protested. 'I think she deserves a better explanation that that!'

'Do you?' Alcott said as he rose to his feet. 'What do you suggest? The truth?' He shook his head. 'Sorry, Paget, but that's not on, and you know it. Apart from that, I suppose you can tell her whatever you like, but if I were in her shoes I think I would prefer to be told that some good has come out of the lad's death, rather than be told that he came very close to buggering up a long and costly investigation, and sealing the fate of all those in captivity.'

Thirty-One

The media didn't get hold of the story until late Monday afternoon, when the Minister for Immigration rose in the House to announce, no doubt with some relief, since he'd been under attack for months on the government's immigration policy, that more than forty people believed to be involved in smuggling women and children into the country for illicit purposes had been arrested. Raids on their homes and business premises, he said, had produced evidence of their involvement with a vast network in Eastern Europe as well as several other countries, and it was anticipated that more arrests would be made in the coming days. He went on to say his ministry was working closely with Europol and other agencies and NGOs throughout those countries, where 'similar raids are taking place even as I am speaking to you now'.

The minister spoke for some twelve minutes on the subject, ending with the hope that this would clearly demonstrate his government's grave concern and commitment to stopping the flow of illegal immigrants into the United Kingdom.

It wasn't often that Paget had a good word to say about Westminster or for the role politics played when it came to common-sense policing, but in this case he was grateful for anything that would shift the spotlight to London.

Despite persistent questions from the media, no details were given regarding the specific number of illegal entrants who were now in protective custody, which led to some creative speculation, especially in the tabloids. Nothing was said about the farm, nor was there so much as a mention that anyone had died. Clearly, Trowbridge and his masters were controlling the information being released, not only to the media, but probably to the minister himself.

The RangerContinental that had brought the women up from the south, had been followed as far as Wrexham, where the driver had stopped to spend the night, and he was arrested Sunday morning when he was about to leave. Roper and his wife were arrested when they returned to the farm on Sunday morning after spending the night in a hotel in Ludlow. When asked how he had managed to leave the farm unobserved, Roper told them that the switch had been made Saturday afternoon, when Kellerman had arrived dressed as a workman in a Crawley's van.

'Paranoid, he was,' he said contemptuously. 'Scared to death that someone might be watching. Had me switch clothes with him so it was me who drove the van away. He even had the wife creep out of the house and into the van behind a sheet of plywood we carried out between us. I mean there's times we don't see anybody out there for days, so who'd be watching us?'

Clearly, the penny hadn't yet dropped for Roper.

'Don't know anything about torture and killings,' he'd protested. 'What they did in that barn was nothing to do with me after I rented it out. All this bloke told me was that they wanted it for meetings every now and again, and I wasn't to go near the place. The money was good, so I did what he wanted.'

Mark Newman's body was found and lifted from a shallow grave behind the barn. Starkie did the autopsy and recorded death by strangulation after being tortured.

The funeral was held the following week in the village church in Whitcott Lacey. Newman's parents were contacted, but only his mother made the journey from Plymouth to identify the body of her son and attend the funeral. She was a small, pale, wisp of a woman, who seemed to be incapable of making a decision about anything, and it was Emma Baker who finally took charge of the funeral arrangements.

'Mark never attended church while he was staying with us,' she told Paget, 'but I think he would have liked a Christian burial.'

Mark's father did not attend.

'The business, you know,' Mrs Newman said vaguely when Paget asked.

Tom Foxworthy was there, as was Sylvia Tyler, together with a handful of villagers for whom Newman had worked at one time or another, but it was a small gathering.

Paget and Tregalles remained in the background during the short service, and were about to slip away when Emma stopped them as they left the church.

'Thank you for coming,' she said, 'and thank you for taking me seriously when I first reported Mark missing. Such a waste of a young life, but at least, as Uncle Bob explained, it was your search for Mark that set off the investigation into whatever it was that was going on at the farm, so in a way he didn't die for nothing.' She frowned as she looked off into the distance. 'He wouldn't tell me exactly what was going on there,' she said slowly. 'He said something rather vague about an ongoing investigation, which I took to mean he wasn't going to tell me anything more.' She shifted her gaze to Paget. 'I don't suppose you . . .?'

He smiled sadly and shook his head. 'I wish I could,' he said gently, 'but like your uncle, I'm not at liberty to discuss it. Sorry, Emma.'

Standing there in the churchyard in the warm sunlight, Emma's voice hardened as she said, 'I'm glad the man who did it is dead. I don't think I could have borne seeing someone like that weasel his way through the courts and probably get off with just a few years behind bars.'

So that was now the official version, Paget thought sadly. And yet, watching Emma's face, perhaps it was for the best after all.

Later that night, with the day's events still on his mind, he and Grace talked about it at length, and it was still on his mind when they went to bed.

'I'm supposed to ignore the fact that people were killed out there at the farm,' he said as they got into bed. 'Murdered in cold blood, and whether the killing was justified or not, it's not up to us to decide. And I'm supposed to ignore the fact that evidence was deliberately destroyed.

'No one will be charged with the killings. Bardici will never stand trial for those murders; in fact he may not even do any time for trafficking or anything else if he cooperates and tells them everything he knows about the network. And that sort of trade-off really concerns me.'

'But they can't just let him go,' said Grace.

'Oh, he'll probably be charged with something and do some time just to make it look good, but I'll lay odds it won't amount to much. I'm sure it's all arranged. I've tried to talk to Ben about it, but it's a done deal and he won't even take my calls.'

'On the other hand,' said Grace gently, 'you told me yourself that the chances of getting a conviction against Bardici are almost nil. You have no witnesses who are prepared to testify, no evidence connecting him to the murders, except, perhaps for the word of Trowbridge's undercover man, and he's not likely to put his hand up, is he? I hate to say this, love, but I don't think the CPS would even look at it, let alone prosecute.'

'Oh, I know you're right,' he conceded. 'In fact that's exactly what Alcott said, but it still rankles. Once you start making deals with the likes of Bardici, where does it stop?' He sighed heavily as he turned out the light and slid down in bed.

'I know how frustrated you must be, Neil,' Grace said softly, 'but you can't expect to win every time.'

'Not with people like Trowbridge and Bell about,' he muttered as he turned to face her. 'And I'd still like to?'

'Enough!' Grace snaked an arm around him and pulled him to her. 'It's over, so let it go and get some sleep! Don't forget you said you wanted to be in court for the case against Bernie Green first thing tomorrow morning.'

'Oh, God! I'd forgotten about that,' he said. He was about to roll over, but the pressure of her body against his own stopped him. 'But if you think I can go off to sleep while you are doing things like that to me,' he said, 'you've got another think coming, Grace Lovett.'

'Thank God for that,' Grace murmured softly, nestling her head against his chest. 'Took you so long to get around to it, I was beginning to think you'd gone off me.'

There were very few people in court. Bernie's hair was neatly combed, and he was dressed in his best suit, white shirt and tie – not that it would have any influence on the outcome, but there was always the faint hope that it might. Paget looked around for Bernie's wife, and almost failed to recognize the smartly dressed woman sitting by herself until she turned her head his way.

'Not a bad looking bird when she's all dressed up, is she?' Tregalles murmured. 'Last time I saw Shirley Green, she had curlers in her hair and she looked a good ten years older than she does now. Amazing what a bit of paint, some high heels and a good bra will do for a woman.'

There were no surprises. Guilty as charged. Six months, which meant he'd be out in four. Bernie and his wife were allowed to have a few brief words before he was led away, but as Shirley turned to leave, she caught sight of Paget, and a slow smile crossed her face as she changed course and came toward him.

She probably wanted to have a go at him for putting her husband away, thought Paget. It had happened to him a number of times during his career, and yet there was something decidedly odd about the way the woman was looking at him. One eyebrow was slightly raised as if she were trying to convey some sort of message to him as she approached.

'I reckon she fancies you,' Tregalles said under his breath, but loud enough for Paget to hear. 'Either that or she's got herself a toy boy while her old man's away, and she's feeling grateful. I'd watch myself if I were you, boss.'

The two men started to move toward the door, but Shirley Green moved swiftly to intercept them before they reached it. Both men watched her closely as she approached. Relatives and even friends had been known to throw acid in the faces of the police when a verdict went against someone close to them, but Shirley's hands were empty.

She moved closer, glancing around as if to make absolutely sure that no one else was within earshot before she spoke, and when she did it was to Tregalles.

'I hope you don't mind, Sergeant,' she said apologetically, 'but I'd like a word with Mr Paget. It's nothing personal against you,' she added hastily, 'it's just . . . it's just a bit private, if you don't mind?'

Tregalles remained where he was until Paget nodded and said, 'It's all right, Sergeant. I don't think Mrs Green intends to harm me.'

Tregalles gave a grudging nod and moved away.

The woman watched him go, but remained silent until she was satisfied that Tregalles was out of earshot. And when she did speak, it was in a voice so low that Paget had to lean closer to hear what she was saying.

'I know we've had our differences in the past,' she said, 'but fair's fair, and I promised myself I'd thank you for what you did if I ever got the chance. And believe me, Mr Paget, you can trust me to keep a secret. I'll never breathe a word to anyone else, and I'll swear to that. You'll never know how happy it made me when I heard. I can still hardly believe it.'

'You're *happy* that Bernie's been convicted?'

The woman stared at him blankly for a second, then grinned in a conspiratorial way as she leaned closer. 'For a minute there I thought you were serious,' she said with a chuckle, 'but you're having me on, aren't you? No, of course I didn't mean Bernie. I meant about Gerry. That's why I got the inspector to go away, because Gerry said it was only the top ones who knew. I know Gerry said I wasn't to say anything, but it's not as if you don't know, is it? And Gerry says he's doing all right where he is, fixed up with a job and all. I'm sure he's learned his lesson this time, so you won't be having any more trouble with him. Bernie doesn't know, and I shan't tell him, and I wouldn't want him to know I'd talked to you. But like I said, I thought it was only fair to say thanks and tell you what a relief it was to find out that my brother is alive and well.'

Epilogue

I t had been a long day, and an even longer week, and Paget was looking forward to a weekend away with Grace. So he was less than pleased when he left the building to see the silver Jag sitting next to his own car in the car park.

Trowbridge was behind the wheel. 'I was beginning to think you slept here,' he said laconically through the open window. 'Get in. We need to talk.'

'Really?' said Paget coldly. 'Perhaps no one in your office thought to tell you I've been trying to do that for the past month. What's so important now?'

'I've been away,' Trowbridge said. 'In Europe. But that's beside the point, so stop being so bloody prickly and get in. This is something you need to hear.'

Paget moved around to the passenger's side of the car and got in. Trowbridge pressed a button and his window closed. 'Bardici is dead,' he said tersely. 'Killed last night in prison where he and the others were awaiting trial on charges of trafficking. Stabbed eleven times, yet no one saw a thing.'

Paget eyed Trowbridge suspiciously. The superintendent sighed as he pulled an envelope from his pocket and slid out half a dozen pictures. 'You saw the man when he was taken into custody,' he said. 'What does that look like to you?'

Paget looked at the pictures. The first three pictures, taken from different angles, showed Bardici sprawled on the floor, head thrown back, arms flung wide, and there was blood all over his clothing. It could have been faked, but the slash across the throat and the expression on Bardici's face had to be real. The next two pictures showed him naked on a slab. The wounds were clearly visible. Paget looked closer. '*Two* weapons?' he hazarded.

Trowbridge nodded. 'One thin, almost a stiletto-type knife, and one with a wider blade. Two people, according to the pathologist, yet a search failed to turn up either weapon.'

Paget handed the pictures back. 'And no one saw a thing? What about the guards?'

Trowbridge shrugged. 'It seems a fight broke out at the other end of the block, and they were all down there when it happened. At least that's their story.'

'So Bardici is dead,' said Paget. 'Fine, I accept that. Now tell me about Fletcher.'

'What about Fletcher? He was killed when—'

'He wasn't killed and you know it!' Paget broke in. 'Gerry Fletcher is alive – or he was when he contacted his sister – which means that his "death" was orchestrated by someone on the inside; someone who was working for you. My guess is the Australian, Slater, because that's who was watching Bernie Green's house, according to Fletcher's sister.'

Trowbridge's grimace was as close to an acknowledgement of guilt as Paget was ever likely to see. 'Stupid of Fletcher to get in touch with his sister,' he said.

He leaned his head back against the leather with a sigh of resignation. 'Fletcher botched the job of getting rid of Newman's van, and when it became known that the police – you – were looking for him, they wanted him dead. Slater was trying to keep him from getting killed, so he staked out his sister's place, because he knew Fletcher had nowhere else to run. He caught Fletcher trying to sneak out that night, but naturally Fletcher thought Slater meant to kill him, so Slater had to put him out of commission. But he needed to leave some of Fletcher's blood at the scene to convince your lot and everybody else that he was dead, so he tore Fletcher's earring out and took half the lobe off with it. Poor sod had to have it sewn up later, but it still looks as if someone chewed it off. Bled like a stuck pig – you know how ears bleed – so there was plenty of blood left at the scene for you to find. He bundled Fletcher into the boot of his car and brought him back to a safe house, then took the earring to show Bardici that he'd done the job.'

Paget eyed Trowbridge thoughtfully. 'Funny,' he said, 'but I don't get any sense of loss in what you're telling me. In fact I might go so far as to suggest that Slater didn't die that night at the farm.'

Trowbridge looked off into the distance. 'You saw for your-self four body bags taken out of the barn, and the official record shows that a man by the name of Slater, who presumably worked for Kellerman, was trampled to death when the people they'd smuggled into the country panicked and stampeded during an attempt by police to free them.'

'Which means that it would be more than a little embar-rassing if he is seen alive,' Paget observed. 'So tell me, Ben. What happened to him? Indulge me.'

Trowbridge pursed his lips and thought about it. Paget had no right to the information, and he had no right to give it, but on the other hand, what harm could it do? Especially consid-ering the fact that he might be needing the chief inspector's cooperation in the not too distant future.

He turned to face Paget. '*Off* the record,' he said.

'Of course.'

Trowbridge, nodded. 'The real Slater is dead,' he said. 'He died in Australia three years ago. The man who worked his way into Kellerman's organization under that name is in fact a member of the Queensland Police. We use some of theirs; they use some of ours. Not just Australia, of course; we have reciprocal arrangements with a number of countries. Beyond that, all I can tell you is that he is no longer in this country.'

'Thank you, Ben,' said Paget, and meant it. 'But since we're talking off the record, there are a couple of things puzzling me. First, why weren't you warned by your man that the auction had been brought forward twenty-four hours? And secondly, how did he manage to get out of that room alive?'

'You might well ask,' Trowbridge said. 'But when Kellerman arrived that afternoon, it was a surprise to everyone, and one of the first things he did was take everyone's phone away from them to make sure that no one could communicate with anyone outside. Kellerman didn't trust anyone, no matter how long they'd worked for him.

'On the second point, our man had the good sense to go down fast and play dead as soon as he saw Bell come in. He took a beating, but he survived. Bell was careful to keep the rest of the crew away while he and one of his men put Slater into the body bag and made sure he didn't suffocate.'

Paget nodded. 'So tell me about Bardici,' he said. 'He must have made a hell of a deal with you if all he was going to be charged with was trafficking. The way the courts are these days, he'd have been out on the street in no time. Was he really worth that much to you?'

Trowbridge shook his head. 'We got nothing from Bardici,' he said flatly. 'He stared us down. He knew we couldn't prove that he killed Newman and the others, and we couldn't bring Fletcher or Slater out in the open to testify against him. Not that Fletcher would have testified against Bardici anyway; he was just as scared of the man as the rest of them were.

'But as it turned out, we didn't need to do that, because we got far more out of Fletcher than we did out of Bardici. I don't know if you were aware of Fletcher's background, but he spent years as a driver bringing in illegals from all over Europe for Kellerman before Customs became suspicious of him. He didn't get caught, but he came close enough to it that Kellerman decided to pull him from the overseas run. Fletcher proved to be a mine of information. He knew the routes, he knew the staging points, he knew which border guards and Custom's officers could be bribed. In fact he knew more about the organization than Bardici did by far, which is why we decided to protect him and let everyone believe he was dead.'

Paget opened the door and prepared to get out of the car, then paused. 'Odd, then, don't you think?' he said. 'I mean about the way Bardici was killed, especially as he'd kept his mouth shut. Not,' he added quickly, 'that I'm sorry he's dead, but still . . .'

'I blame the tabloids,' Trowbridge said blandly. 'It seems that someone got the idea that it was Bardici who supplied us with the information that led to so many arrests in this country and in Europe. It wasn't true, of course, but these things have a life of their own, and we weren't in a position to tell them they were wrong without revealing the true source.'

'I see.' Paget looked off into the distance. 'Any idea who might have started such a dangerous rumour?'

'None at all. My guess is that it came from Europe. The French media picked it up very quickly.'

'And they got it wrong. Fortunate for Fletcher, then, wasn't it?'

Trowbridge made a face. 'Fletcher's an idiot!' he said. 'Not only did he contact his sister, but he left the programme when he had everything going for him. He was fully protected: new name, new place, even a decent paying job, but he just walked away, and we have no idea where he is now. God help him if he ever runs into any of his old mates again, because once they realize he's alive, he won't stay that way for long.'

He glanced at the time and said, 'Sorry I can't stay and chat, but I must be off. I've been in meetings most of the day with your bosses, and I have to get back to London tonight.'

Paget looked surprised. 'Do they know all this?' he asked.

'Good God, no!' Trowbridge sounded horrified. 'I wouldn't trust them with the time of day. And don't you, either,' he warned as he started the car.

Paget watched as Trowbridge drove away. An arm came out in one last wave before the car disappeared. He looked at the time and winced. He'd told Grace he'd be home in half an hour. He hoped she hadn't taken that too literally.